"A gripping epic of sacrifice, revenge, and conquest during the time of Genghis Khan as four very different women struggle to keep his empire from shattering. *The Tiger Queens* kept me riveted from beginning to end!"

—Michelle Moran, bestselling author of *The Second Empress*

"A vivid depiction of warrior women [as] tough as the harsh, windswept steppes [that] nurtured them and who, as the warring Mongol clans battle for supremacy, survive . . . to ensure their men emerge the victors. Gripping stuff!"   —Alex Rutherford, author of the Empire of the Moghul series

"From under the felted *ger* tents of Genghis Khan emerge four powerful women. It is a testament to Thornton's writing prowess that she can so intricately whittle heroines that are both compassionate and ruthless from the bones of our ancestors . . . a stunning achievement!"

—Barbara Wood, *New York Times* bestselling author of *The Serpent and the Staff* and *Rainbows on the Moon*

"A sprawling historical saga centering on the wives and daughters of Genghis Khan. These bold, courageous women make tremendous sacrifices in the face of danger, revenge, and high-stakes survival, all in the name of family love and loyalty. Be prepared to be swept away by Thornton's richly drawn epic of an empire and its generational shifts of power."

—Renée Rosen, author of *Dollface* and *What the Lady Wants*

"They were the Golden Family of Genghis Khan. Yet their lives were anything but golden as they struggled to hold together the very center of the largest empire the world has ever known. An empire that was built in one lifetime, and would have been destroyed in the next had it not been for the wives and daughters of the Great Khan. This is historical fiction at its finest."

—Gary Corby, author of *The Marathon Conspiracy*

continued . . .

"Three generations of strong women live, love, suffer, and triumph in a fresh and gritty setting—Genghis Khan's forging of an empire in thirteenth-century Mongolia. Marginalized in most histories, these Mongol mothers and daughters, empresses and slaves, claim their voices again in Stephanie Thornton's *The Tiger Queens*. Unusual and imaginative!"

—Elizabeth Loupas, author of
The Second Duchess and *The Red Lily Crown*

"Stunning. *The Tiger Queens* sweeps the reader into the ruthless world of Genghis Khan's wives and daughters with a gritty realism as intense as the eternal blue sky and blood-soaked steppes. Vivid characterization and top-notch writing. This story of strong women, their enduring friendships and passions, gives a rare glimpse into a shadowy period of history. A worthy successor to Taylor Caldwell's *The Earth is the Lord's*."

—Judith E. French, author of
The Conqueror, *The Barbarian*, and *The Warrior*

Daughter of the Gods

"Stephanie Thornton's heroines are bold, brave, and powerful."

—Kate Quinn, author of *Lady of the Eternal City*

This is the kind of book that grabs you by the throat and doesn't let go. A remarkable story, remarkably told."

—Kate Furnivall, author of
The Russian Concubine and *Shadows on the Nile*

"An epic saga that brings ancient Egypt to life with vivid imagery and lovely prose. Stephanie Thornton is a rising star!"

—Stephanie Dray, author of *Lily of the Nile* and *Daughters of the Nile*

"Hatshepsut crackles with fascinating complexity."

—Vicky Alvear Shecter, author of
Cleopatra's Moon and *Curses and Smoke: A Novel of Pompeii*

The Secret History

"What a heroine! Stephanie Thornton's Theodora is tough and intelligent, spitting defiance against the cruel world."
                              —Kate Quinn, author of *Lady of the Eternal City*

"Loss, ambition, and lust keep this rich story moving at top speed . . . a remarkable first novel that brings a little-known woman to full, vibrant life again."   —Jeane Westin, author of *The Spymaster's Daughter*

"A fascinating and vivid account. . . . The life of the Empress Theodora leaps from the page."
                              —Michelle Diener, author of *The Emperor's Conspiracy*

"Thornton's well-conceived and engrossing tale exalts a historical figure of 'true grit.' "   —*Library Journal*

"If there is one book you choose to read on ancient times, let it be *The Secret History*. Theodora is a true Byzantine icon, and her story is a timeless inspiration that needs to be heard."   —Historical Novel Society

"You'll feel for Theodora. You'll want to scream, to save her, and to cheer for her bravery all at the same time. . . . Theodora's dramatic tale is exquisitely crafted in this can't-miss summer read. I couldn't put it down for a moment."
                              —*San Francisco Book Review*

THE TIGER QUEENS

THE WOMEN OF GENGHIS KHAN

STEPHANIE THORNTON

NEW AMERICAN LIBRARY

New American Library
Published by the Penguin Group
Penguin Group (USA) LLC, 375 Hudson Street,
New York, New York 10014

USA | Canada | UK | Ireland | Australia | New Zealand | India | South Africa | China
penguin.com
A Penguin Random House Company

First published by New American Library,
a division of Penguin Group (USA) LLC

First Printing, November 2014

LIBRARY OF CONGRESS CATALOGING-IN-PUBLICATION DATA:

Thornton, Stephanie, 1980–
The tiger queens: the women of Genghis Khan / Stephanie Thornton.
pages cm
ISBN 978-0-451-41780-0 (paperback)
1. Genghis Khan, 1162–1227—Fiction.   2. Mongols—Kings and rulers—Fiction.
3. Mongols—History—To 1500—Fiction.   I. Title.
PS3620.H7847T54 2014
813'.6—dc23   2014019843

Printed in the United States of America
1   3   5   7   9   10   8   6   4   2

Set in Simoncini Garamond   •   Designed by Elke Sigal

To Isabella,
for inspiring me to write about the love
between mothers and daughters

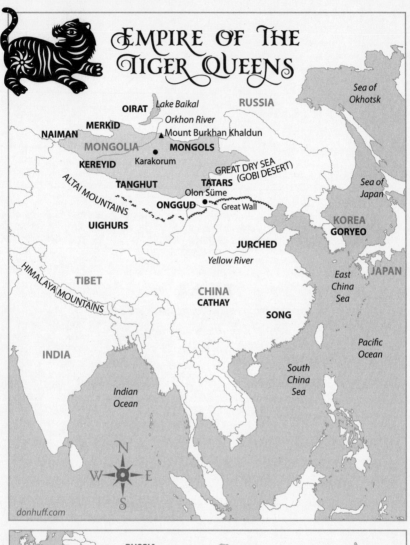

EMPIRE OF THE TIGER QUEENS

Sea of
Okhotsk

OIRAT *Lake Baikal* **RUSSIA**

MERKID *Orkhon River*

NAIMAN ▲*Mount Burkhan Khaldun*

MONGOLIA ● **MONGOLS**

KEREYID *Karakorum*

*GREAT DRY SEA
(GOBI DESERT)*

TANGHUT **TATARS**

Olon Süme Sea of
Japan

ALTAI MOUNTAINS ● **ONGGUD** ●
Great Wall

KOREA

UIGHURS **GORYEO**

JURCHED

Yellow River

HIMALAYA MOUNTAINS

TIBET **CHINA**
CATHAY

East
China
Sea JAPAN

SONG

INDIA

*Indian
Ocean*

South
China
Sea

Pacific
Ocean

N
W ✦ E
S

donhuff.com

RUSSIA

Vienna ● **KAZAKHSTAN**

● Karakorum

● Otrar **MONGOLIA**

**KHWARAZMIAN
EMPIRE**

CHINA

Nishapur ●
IRAN

THE TIGER QUEENS

Prologue

Our names have long been lost to time, scattered like ashes into the wind. No one remembers our ability to read the secrets of the oracle bones or the wars fought in our names. The words we wrote have faded from their parchments; the sacrifices we made are no longer recounted in the glittering courts of those we conquered. The deeds of our husbands, our brothers, and our sons have eclipsed our own as surely as when the moon ate the sun during the first battle of Nishapur.

Yet without us, there would have been no empire for our men to claim, no clan of the Thirteen Hordes left to lead, and no tales of victory to sing to the Eternal Blue Sky.

It was our destiny to love these men, to suffer their burdens and shoulder their sorrows, to bring them into this world, red-faced and squalling, and tuck their bones into the earth when they abandoned us for the sacred mountains, leaving us behind to fight their wars and protect their Spirit Banners.

We gathered our strength from the water of the northern lakes, the fire of the south's Great Dry Sea, the brown earth of the western mountains, and the wild air of the eastern steppes. Born of the four directions, we cleaved together like the seasons for our very survival. In a world lit by fire and ruled by the sword, we depended upon one another for the very breath we drew.

Even as the steppes ran with blood and storm clouds roiled overhead, we loved our husbands, our brothers, and our sons. And we loved one another, the fierce love of mothers and sisters and daughters, born from our shared laughter and tears as our souls were woven together, stronger than the thickest felts.

And yet nothing lasts forever. One by one, our souls were gathered into the Eternal Blue Sky, our tents dismantled, and our herds scattered across the steppes. That is a tale yet to come.

It matters not how we died. Only one thing matters: that we lived.

PART I

The Seer

Chapter 1

1171 CE
YEAR OF THE IRON HARE

He came in the autumn of my tenth year, when the crisp air entices horses to race and the white cranes fly toward the southern hills.

A single man led a line of horses between the two great mountains that straddled our camp. Startled, I set down my milking pail and wiped my hands on my scratchy felt *deel*—the long caftan worn by men, women, and children alike—as my father joined me, grunting and shielding his eyes from the last rays of golden sunlight. Visitors and merchants often found their way to sit against the western wall of our domed *ger*, silently filling their bellies with salted sheep fat until our fermented mare's milk loosened their tongues. I loved to hear their tales of distant steppes and mountain forests, of clans with foreign names and fearsome khans. My father was the leader of our Unigirad clan, but life outside our camp seemed terribly exotic to a girl who had never traveled past the river border of our summer grazing lands.

I finished milking the goats and untied them from the line, watching the shadows grow, eager for the trader's stories that would carry me to sleep that night.

"Borte Ujin." My mother, the famed seer Chotan, called from the carved door of our *ger*, her gray hair tied back and a chipped wooden cooking spoon in her hand. I hated that spoon—my backside had met it more times than I could count on my fingers and toes.

I was a twilight child, planted in my mother's belly like an errant seed long after her monthly bloods had ceased. After being childless for so long, my parents welcomed even a mere girl-child, someone to help my mother churn butter and corral the herds with my father. And so I grew up their only daughter, indulged by my elderly father while my mother harangued me to sit straighter and pay more attention to the calls of geese and the other messages from all the spirits.

My mother was by far the shortest woman in our village, but the look she gave me now would have scattered a pack of starving wolves. "Pull your head from the clouds, Borte," she said. "The marmot won't roast itself."

I lugged the skin bucket of milk inside, ducking into the heavy scents of animal hides, earth, and burning dung. The thick haze of smoke made my throat and eyes burn. The felt ceiling was stained black from years of soot, and the smoke hole was open to the Eternal Blue Sky, the traditional rope that represented the umbilical cord of the universe dangling from the cloud-filled circle. A dead marmot lay by the fire, the size of a small dog, with prickly fur like tiny porcupine quills. Our meat usually came from one of the Five Snouts—horses, goats, sheep, camels, and cattle—but my father's eyes sparkled when he could indulge my mother's taste for wild marmot. The oily meat was a pleasant change.

"There's a visitor on the path." I hacked off the marmot's head with a dull blade and yanked out the purple entrails. My father's mottled dog pushed at my hip with her muzzle, but I swatted her away, daring to toss her the gizzards only when my mother wasn't looking.

Mother sighed and rubbed her temples, squinting as if staring through the felt walls at something far away. "I knew about the visitor before he stepped over the horizon," she said, the beads that dangled from her sleeves chattering with her every movement. Each was a reminder of a successful prophecy breathed to life by her lips, bits of bone and clay gathered from the spine of the Earth Mother to adorn her blue seer's robes.

I glanced at the fire. Two singed sheep scapulae lay on the hearth, cracked with visions of the future. My mother's father had been a holy man amongst our people, but he had passed to the sacred mountains the night I fell from her womb. There were whispers that my grandfather's untethered powers might have found a new home in my soul, and his Spirit Banner still fluttered in the breeze outside our *ger*, strands of black hair from his favorite stallion tied to his old spear, so that his soul might continue to guide us.

My mother stuffed the marmot's empty stomach cavity with steaming rocks. "These strangers will bring great fortune and great tragedy." She spoke as if commenting about the quality of our mares' dung, then pushed a strand of graying hair back from her face and glanced at my palms, slick with blood. "You'd best not greet your fate with foul hands."

My skin prickled with dread. My mother was an *udgan*, a rare female shaman, and had cast my bones only once and then forbade me from speaking of the dark omens to anyone, including my father. Lighter prophecies than mine had driven other parents to fill their children's pockets with stones and drown them. And so I had swallowed the words and promised never to speak of them.

The Eternal Blue Sky was bruised black when I stepped outside, and the scent of roasting horsemeat from a nearby *ger* made my stomach rumble. The water in the horses' trough clung to the warmth of the day and I scrubbed until the flesh of my hands was raw. As on any other night, voices floated from the other far-flung tents. My cheeks grew warm at the grunts of lovemaking from the newly stitched *ger* of a couple freshly wed, the young man and woman who my mother claimed mounted each other like rabbits. The moans were muffled by a new mother crooning to her fussy infant and an old woman berating her grandsons for tracking mud into her tent.

And my father's voice.

I started toward him but retreated into the shadows as a wiry stranger stepped into view. About the same age as my father, the man wore two black braids threaded with gray hanging down his back, topped with a wide-ruffed hat of rabbit fur. Five dun-colored horses grazed in the paddock, laden with packs, their dark manes cropped close. I strained to hear the conversation, but my father only complimented the man on the quality of his animals. The stranger patted the flank of a pretty mare, releasing a puff of dancing dust into the air. Early moonlight gleamed on the curved sword at his hip, an unusual sight amongst my peace-loving clan, but then the light hit his face. I stumbled back, nearly landing on my backside.

His right eye glittered like a black star, but the left socket was empty, a dark slit nestled between folds of wrinkled skin and at the exact center of a long white scar, likely an old battle wound.

"And I thought they called you Dei the Wise." The man grinned at my father, revealing two lines of crooked brown teeth. "You didn't think I'd come without something to trade this time, did you, Dei?"

This time. So my father knew this traveler.

I thought to stay and listen, but the stranger shifted on his feet and his gaze fell on me. I expected a one-eyed scowl, but instead the man's bushy eyebrows lifted in surprise.

I shrank further into the shadows, pulling the darkness around my shoulders. My mother would have my skin if she knew I'd been eavesdropping. Learning more about this stranger would have to wait until he'd filled his belly with our marmot.

I scuttled back to our *ger*, feeding the fire with dried mare dung until it crackled and my cheeks flushed with heat. My mother bustled about, mumbling to herself as she set out five mismatched wooden cups.

"There's only one visitor, Mother."

She ignored me and poured fresh goat milk into two cups, then filled the other three with *airag*. I knew better than to argue what I'd seen with my own eyes.

My mother pulled the rocks from the marmot's belly as the wooden door opened, ushering in a gust of cool air along with my father and his guest. Behind the man skulked a scrawny boy scarcely my height, dressed in the same ragged squirrel pelts as his father and fingering the necklace at his throat, a menacing wolf tooth hung from a leather thong. His black hair was cropped close to his head and his eyes gleamed the same gray as a wolf's pelt. My father's dog gave a happy bark and jumped up, paws on the boy's shoulders as if embracing a lost friend. The boy's hand went to the hilt of his sword, a smaller version of his father's, and for a moment I thought he might stab the dumb beast. I dragged her away by the scruff of her neck and forced her to sit at my feet, prompting a raised eyebrow from the boy.

I turned my nose up at him and looked to the one-eyed visitor as he bowed to my mother. At least the father had manners.

"Chotan," he said to my mother, straightening. "I bear warm words from Hoelun, my first wife and mother of my eldest son."

My mother grasped the wooden cooking spoon so hard I thought it might crack. It took me a moment to recall the story of my mother's childhood friend Hoelun, married to a handsome Merkid warrior who loved her. The story of her shame and dishonor while en route to her new husband's homeland was still whispered around hearth fires, that a desperate Borijin hunter had been tracking a rabbit when he came across a splash of fresh urine in the snow, left by a woman. The man ignored the rabbit and hunted the woman instead, stealing her from her husband and claiming her as his wife.

A one-eyed hunter.

This man wearing a sword curved like a smile was no exotic trader, but instead a kidnapper of women.

The fire suddenly burned too hot, yet a cold sweat broke out on the back of my neck. I stepped toward my mother, well away from the men's side of the tent. "And this must be your daughter," he said, opening his arms toward me. "Her face is filled with the first light of dawn, yet her eyes are full of fire like the sun."

It wasn't my eyes that filled with fire then, but my cheeks.

"Borte's soul is full of fire," my mother snapped. "As was Hoelun's."

"Still is," the stranger said with a laugh. "Fiery women make the best wives." He elbowed the black-haired boy, still standing sullenly at the edge of the *ger*. "They're certainly the best in bed."

At least I wasn't the only one with burning cheeks. The boy looked as if he wished the Earth Mother would open her maw and swallow him.

My father cleared his throat and handed the largest cup of *airag* to his guest. "You must be thirsty after so long a journey, Yesugei. Rest a while and then you can tell us why you've come."

The men stuffed their bellies with so much marmot that my stomach still rumbled when I lay on my pile of furs later, listening to Yesugei's wild tales. His son hadn't yet spoken, only sat on the visitors' west side of the tent as if forgotten by his father and crammed his mouth with marmot as if he might never eat again. His gray eyes darted about, no doubt taking in everything. I burned to know why this one-eyed man dared return to the village of the woman he'd kidnapped, but the heat of the fire pulled me into sleep. The furious whispers of my mother and father entered my dreams, but the rosy fingers of day pushed their way through the cracks of the *ger* when I next opened my eyes.

I wished I hadn't woken when I heard what the men were discussing.

"Temujin would make Borte a good husband," Yesugei said.

Temujin. So that was the boy's name. It meant *to rush headlong*, like a horse racing where it wished, no matter what its rider wanted. He sat cross-legged by the door, sharpening a stick with a wicked-looking knife as his foot twitched. I had a feeling he was ready to bolt at any moment, to saddle a horse and tear across the steppes.

I might beat him to it.

"They're too young." My mother's voice stung like a wasp. I peered through slitted eyes to see my father lay a gentle hand on her arm, the platter of dried horsemeat to break our fasts untouched between them. "I'll not give the only treasure of my womb to a Tayichigud raider," she muttered.

I wondered then if she wished she had told my father our secret instead of keeping it hidden all these years. Now it was too late.

"Since the days of the blue-gray wolf and the fallow deer, the beauty of our daughters has sheltered us from battles and wars. Our daughters are our shields." My father's words were an oft-repeated maxim amongst our Unigirad clan, yet Yesugei's people were well-known as the lowest and meanest of the steppe's families, as sharp clawed and sneaky as battle-scarred weasels. No single man ruled the grasslands, meaning that the belligerent Merkid, wealthy Tatars, fierce Naiman, and even the Christian Kereyids all fought continuous wars for supremacy.

"Borte," my father said in a stern voice, but I kept my eyes closed. "Stop feigning sleep and come here."

I sat up and my mother handed me a cup of goat's milk to wash the bitter taste of sleep from my mouth, but I found it hard to swallow.

"I'd keep my little goat with us as long as possible, forever if I could." My father twirled a strip of dried meat between gnarled fingers, then sighed. "But as much as I might wish it, it is not my daughter's fate to grow old by the door of the tent she was born in."

"My husband," my mother said. "It is not wise—"

My father didn't allow her to finish, only raised his hand for silence.

"I don't wish to be married," I said, praying the Earth Mother would send up roots from the ground to bind me forever to this *ger*. I had no desire to be saddled to the half-wild son of a barbarian raider. Surely my father would not match me to a boy so far below us, and thereby banish me to the farthest and most barren expanse of the steppes.

"One day I'll give you my daughter, to keep the peace between our clans," my father spoke over my head to Yesugei, his hand on my shoulder. I had no doubt that Yesugei might steal what he wanted, as he'd done before with Hoelun, thereby disgracing me forever. I waited for my father to nudge me forward, yet he didn't move. "But that day is not yet born."

I stared up at him, only then noticing the tick of blood fast in the vein on his neck. "Instead," he said, "I invite you to leave Temujin with us for a while, to hunt and herd for me so we can get to know our new son."

Yesugei gave a bark of laughter and clapped the boy on his back, grinning as if he'd just returned victorious from a raid on a neighboring village. "Do you hear that, boy?" he asked. "I just gained you a wife!"

In that moment I wondered if all girls' hearts curled up in their chests and their knees threatened to give way upon hearing the news of their betrothals.

Many cups of *airag* later, Yesugei swung up unsteadily onto his horse's bare back, then dropped the rabbit-fur hat onto Temujin's head. "I leave my son to you," he said to my father, then straightened and glanced at his boy. Temujin bore traces of his father in his bushy brows and the wry twist of his lips, but they differed in the set of their jaws and the slant of their eyes. I wondered if he favored his mother instead, or some ancestor long since passed to the sacred mountains. Yesugei circled his son on horseback, then bowed to my father. "I fear you're not so clever as they say, Dei the Wise, for I have gotten the better end of this deal." He turned his horse to leave, then called over his shoulder, "And you should know, this whelp of mine is frightened by dogs."

Then Yesugei trotted away with his string of horses, heading back to his people, leaving behind a single dun-colored filly as a gift to my father, and a black-haired boy with a scowl like a storm.

My future husband.

Orange clouds streaked the sky that night and the air was so chilled that I jammed my favorite hat—tattered leather with ugly earflaps—over the snarls in my hair before going out to milk the mares. We had quickly learned that the filly left behind by Yesugei was an ill-tempered beast; I'd already been kicked trying to mount her. My father had only shaken his head and sighed. "I should have expected as much from Yesugei the Brave."

I had hoped my father might send Temujin away after such a slight, but instead he made space for Temujin's bed on the men's side of the *ger*. The boy's blanket was still rolled up, as if he was prepared to flee at any moment.

How I wished he would.

I knew in my heart that I should thank the Earth Mother that Temujin wasn't older than my father, fat, and toothless, with a passel of snot-nosed children from other wives, old women who would box my ears and make me gather horse dung until my back broke. At least Temujin's teeth were mostly straight and his skin was smooth—even if he was younger than me and his features seemed permanently etched into a glare. All women married, and I would be Temujin's first wife, the position of honor girls daydreamed about and women fought for.

But I didn't thank the Earth Mother. Instead, I cursed my father for promising me to the son of a one-eyed thief and my mother for not trying harder to stop him. And then it occurred to me—perhaps if Temujin knew what I did about my future, then he would no longer want me. For the first time I considered breaking my oath of silence to my mother.

I looked to the Eternal Blue Sky for a sign, yet the spirits were stubborn that night and the skies remained empty, without even a breeze to hint at the path I should take.

I had just come from telling my friend Gurbesu about my betrothal and my ears still rang with her shrieks of glee. Now I craved the quiet murmur of the river before returning home for the night. I emerged from the forest of tents and gasped at the sight before me. Temujin sat on the back of the dun-colored filly, his fists wrapped tight in the black mane and his ankles digging into the horse's sides as it attempted to throw him. He leaned back just enough that it was impossible to tell where beast ended and boy began. I waited for him to fly into the fence, pondering whether I'd leave him in the dirt or help him up, when the mare slowed and trotted in a circle around the paddock. Temujin grinned then, an expression of such unfettered joy that I knew he thought himself alone.

He saw me when the filly rounded the bend. I took some satisfaction as his eyes widened and he released the horse's mane to run his hands over his closely shaved scalp. The breeze ruffled the hem of my *deel*, carrying a whiff of my scent to the horse.

In less than a breath, she reared up and deposited Temujin on his rump in the dust. The animal snorted and cantered off, flicking her tail and dropping a pile of fresh manure on the packed earth.

Temujin scrambled up and glowered at me. "You startled her."

"So you *do* speak." I'd expected his voice to be that of a boy, but it already bore the deep tone of the man he would soon become.

"Of course I speak," he said, brushing off his trousers. "Did you think I was mute?"

The thought had crossed my mind; after all, he'd done no more than grunt during the betrothal ceremony. I shrugged and folded my arms in front of my chest. "You shouldn't be riding that horse."

"Why not?" He bent his skinny arms to mirror me, then nickered to the filly. "She's mine."

"No, she's not." Then the realization filled my mind. "Your father left us your horse?"

He shrugged. "He would never leave behind anything of value."

Still, he'd left Temujin behind, although his worth had yet to be measured. Yesugei was even slipperier than we'd expected. "She's not even broken."

"My father couldn't break her. That's why he gave her to me." He called to the horse again. The filly's ears flicked as if at a buzzing fly, but then she trotted toward us. "It was either that or eat her."

Temujin vaulted onto her empty back and offered me a hand up. His hands were square and squat, much like the rest of him.

"I prefer not to break my neck," I said.

"She hardly ever throws anyone." He grinned, the expression transforming his young face. "At least not if you hold on tight."

I ignored his hand, knowing I should leave, but instead I grabbed a fist of the horse's mane and mounted behind him. The filly startled and sidestepped for a moment, but Temujin didn't give her a chance to think. Instead, he kicked his heels into her ribs, sending her bolting straight toward the paddock's rickety spruce log wall.

The scream that tore the sky came from my own throat; the paddock was built so tall that no horse could clear it. Yet with Temujin's urging in her ear, the dun-colored filly leapt into the air, arcing over the fence and landing with a jolt so hard my teeth almost cracked.

And then we were tearing out of camp, racing past slack-jawed boys bringing in their goats and old men huddled together trading even older hunting stories. I thought I glimpsed my father, but I blinked as my eyes watered at the speed. I clutched Temujin's bony ribs, feeling my hat fly away and my hair tumble loose behind me.

And then I laughed. Never before had I dashed barebacked over the steppes like this, scattering grasshoppers and racing the cranes overhead.

Temujin's voice joined mine and he urged the horse faster. Only after the filly's pace began to lag did he rein her in. The *gers* of my camp were tiny dots on the horizon, white cotton flowers in the distance.

"So you *can* laugh," he said over his shoulder, mocking my earlier words. The filly ignored our conversation, more interested in the grass at her feet.

"Of course I can laugh," I said, making a face at the back of his head.

Temujin seemed much easier now that his father was gone, as if every step Yesugei took away from our camp lightened his son's heart. I wondered if the same would happen once I left my mother's tent, but the very thought was like a weight pressing against my chest.

"One day I'll be khan of my clan," he said. "I'll have a whole herd of horses like this one. Sheep, goats, and camels, too."

"What, no yaks?"

He laughed. "Maybe a few yaks."

I let my arms hang loose, noting the worn leather of his boot and the countless places where it had been stitched with sinews of various colors and ages. Many boys before him had probably worn the same shoes. I wondered how hard his life had been, how difficult mine would be once we were married. "Your father must be a good herder to be able to spare his eldest son."

I knew even before his spine stiffened that it was the wrong thing to say. "My father is a terrible herder," he said. "But he's an excellent raider."

I searched for something to say. "I suppose that takes skill as well."

Temujin glanced back at me again, then laughed. "Are you always so polite?"

"Are you always so rude?" I scowled, but he didn't seem to mind. "I should return home," I said. "My mother will be wondering where I am."

I feared he would argue, but then he urged the filly into a trot toward camp, forcing my arms around him again. "My father told me before he left that I should be pleased to have such an obedient wife," he said. "I held my tongue."

"You don't care for an obedient wife?"

"I think you're like this filly. You only *act* obedient," he said, "because you don't want anyone to see your true nature."

I let my hands drop completely then, preferring to take my chances on being thrown than to touch him a moment longer. He felt my anger and glanced over his shoulder.

"I meant that as a compliment," he said, his voice quiet. "I think there's more to you than you show the world, Borte Ujin."

"You don't know anything about me."

"I know you don't want to marry me."

I sighed, wishing I was gathering stinging nettles or lancing a boil on my mother's foot. Anywhere but here. "No, I don't want to marry you," I finally said.

"Because I'm coarse, rude, and beneath you in every way that matters." His voice was angry, but his shoulders slumped under the weight of his words.

He spoke the truth, but I didn't care to injure him further. My mother's warning filled my mind, the words that had sworn me to secrecy years ago. There seemed so many reasons to tell him the prophecy, and so few to keep the truth hidden any longer.

I shifted behind him, unable to find comfort. "No, there's something else," I said, each word drawn out. "My mother cast my future when I was born."

"So did mine," Temujin said. "I was born with a blood clot held tight in my fist. My mother claimed the sign meant I was destined for greatness."

I smiled sadly, glad he couldn't see my face. "She may be right."

Temujin seemed to sense my melancholy. "What was your prophecy?"

I hesitated, prompting a low chuckle from deep in his chest. "Consider who my father is, Borte Ujin. Nothing you can say will shock me."

Still the words lodged like stones in my throat. Temujin deserved to know the truth if he thought to marry me one day. Or perhaps he might abandon me now and avert the whole tragedy.

"My mother cast my bones while bits of her womb still clung to me and blood ran down her legs."

"And?" Temujin's hand covered mine and he pulled it to his chest, as if giving me the strength to speak the words.

"I will cleave two men apart and ignite a great Blood War that will rain tears and destruction upon the steppes." The words tasted like ash in my mouth, and my mother's warning echoed in my ears. Suddenly it was difficult to breathe, as if giving voice to the terrible words had cost me more than I knew.

Temujin covered my arms with his, his fingers weaving between mine in the filly's mane. I leaned forward, letting my head rest on his back and daring to breathe deeply of his scent. "I battled a wolf once to get this tooth," he said, his bones vibrating with the sound as he touched my fingers to the necklace at his throat. "You can't scare me away with a warning of blood and war."

My head jerked up. "Then you're a fool."

"No," he said. "I happen to think you may be worth fighting for."

The air around me grew suddenly cold, and I shook my head at his audacity. "You're worse than a fool, then," I said. "You shouldn't taunt the spirits with such jests."

"It's no jest," he said. "I promise I would fight for you, Borte Ujin."

I heard the spirits' shocked whispers in the flutter of birch leaves and the shifting grasses at the filly's feet. I wrapped my arms tighter around Temujin, needing his warmth to ward off the cold that had seeped into my bones.

"Still," I whispered, shivering, "I pray it never comes to that."

Temujin sought me out often over the next few days to ask my opinion about the goats my father set him to herding or to bring me a gift of brown partridges strung by their wings, each shot through the eyes by his arrows. Once he gave me a purple globe thistle he'd found while riding the dun-colored filly, claiming it reminded him of me. I had nothing to say to that, only stuttered as he smiled and sauntered off, pausing to rub the muzzle of each horse he passed.

It startled me to see the people of our camp warm toward this coarse youth from the Borijin clan, the flock of boys who trailed him and the indulgent smiles of old women as he waved to them each evening. Temujin possessed the talent of drawing people to him, a rarer ability even than my mother's gift of sight.

A few nights later, an unfamiliar boy spattered with so much mud that it might have poured from the heavens pounded into our village, his chest heaving like someone dying.

But it was someone else's soul that was about to be called to the sacred mountains.

I was outside our *ger* straining curds of yak milk through a cloth when the boy reined in his horse, a lathered old thing ready to fall over and die. A heavy autumn rain had drenched our village the day before, and the animal's every step squelched with mud. The horse bent its head, lips smacking as it drank from a puddle.

The rider swung to the ground, head snapping back and forth so his thin braids slapped his shoulders like a drum. "Where is Temujin of the Borijin?"

My father set aside his work repairing a strap on my mother's saddle. "Temujin will one day be my son-in-marriage," he said, standing. "What message do you have for him?"

The boy had to tilt his head back to look my father in the eyes. "I've come to return Temujin to his father."

The words felt as if someone had thrown a bucket of creek water on me. I stood rooted where I was as a crowd gathered, their gazes on me.

My father gave a minute shake of his head, as if to clear the visitor's words from his mind. "May I ask why you seek to steal my future son?"

The messenger wiped the sweat from the back of his neck. "On his way home to his wife and younger sons, Yesugei stopped on the Yellow Steppe to join a Tatar feast."

Temujin shifted next to me—I hadn't even noticed his approach until then. He laughed under his breath, but the sound held no joy. "My father never would have feasted with the Tatars," he muttered, his young mouth twisting in a glimpse of what he might look like years from now, a stooped old man with a scowl etched into his skin. "He defeated them in battle too many times."

The messenger continued. "The Tatars bear no love for Yesugei's clan. They recognized him and poisoned him. He is dying."

Temujin swayed on his feet. Without thinking, I reached out and squeezed his hand, cool and dry to the touch. No one should face death alone.

"Where is Temujin?" the messenger repeated. "His father is asking for him."

My father's eyes sought him out. "If my friend thinks so much of his son, I'll let him go." He glanced at our clasped hands. "When he's seen his father again, have him come quickly back."

Temujin pressed his palms together and bent over them, his lips tight. He might not have been the image of a respectful son when his father was here, but then, Yesugei hadn't been the image of a perfect father either. Still, the pull of blood remained.

"I promise to return before the next full moon," he said, the ancient stars flickering overhead. "To you and your daughter."

Temujin looked at me, the question plain in his eyes. The ancestors pushed on me from all sides, whispering conflicting words of duty and sacrifice in my ears. I swallowed hard, meeting his gaze. "I will wait for you," I said. "I promise."

Someone pressed an offering of milk into my hands and I looked up to see Temujin holding a bone cup. Together we poured the white liquid into the earth, sealing our promise to each other.

Temujin didn't bid me good-bye—those sacred words would be spoken only right before death claimed one of us—but instead unclasped his wolf-tooth necklace and tied it around my neck. I touched its edge, feeling the sharpness of its promise as my betrothed mounted his horse. Temujin nodded and then kicked his heels, leaving the messenger scrambling behind him. Mud and tufts of soggy grass flew into the air as the horses took off.

I watched him disappear over the horizon, while the rest of the clan floated back to the warmth of their *gers* until only my father remained.

"He'll return soon, Borte," he said, squeezing my shoulder. "He promised."

Temujin's coming had shaken my world, as surely as a blizzard in summer or the mares dropping their foals on the darkest day of the year, but as his father's eldest son, he might not return if Yesugei died. It would then be Temujin's duty to provide for his mother and siblings, to hunt and herd as he'd promised to do for my father.

If Yesugei died, I might never see Temujin again.

Yet I felt my soul already bound to his. Whether he returned or not, I had only one choice.

I would wait.

Chapter 2

Temujin didn't return.

At seventeen, I was nearly past the age of marriage; all the other girls from my childhood balanced infants at their breasts and at least one more at their hips. I let die the hope that I might be able to overcome the curse I bore and lead a normal life.

I thought myself very wise then, as the young often do, yet I knew very little.

For seven long years I had watched the empty horizon while the birth and death of the seasons forced me to grow into my breasts and hips. I spent the summer days scrying stories from sheep bones with my mother and the winter nights unfolding the messages of my dreams. The swirl of gossip claimed I was a dishonored woman, cast aside by the lowest of the Thirteen Hordes. Worse still, the truth of my curse had spread in all four directions across the steppes, whispered from clan to clan after Temujin left. I shed hot tears and cursed him for spilling my secret to the world, for I could no longer even draw water from the river without the old women of our clan averting their eyes or the young men spitting at my feet.

Still, although my name was stained, it was now Temujin's that was blackened beyond repair.

As the seasons passed, travelers brought us ever-wilder tales, claiming that Temujin had returned to his mother after his father's death, but their clan had abandoned them on the banks of the Onan River. He and his family were reduced to wearing the skins of dogs and voles, to eating roots and even the repulsive fish that ran in the rivers. It wasn't until he took the *anda* blood vows with another young man that he gained an alliance with a second clan, likely saving both him and his family from certain starvation.

Then the stories took a sinister turn. A wizened traveler with a mustache like two silver snakes claimed Temujin had murdered his half brother, a boy who had shared his father's blood, although their souls had unfurled in different wombs. My mind couldn't reconcile the smiling boy in scuffed boots taking aim at his brother's back with a bow and arrow, and the image haunted my dreams. How could I marry a man who had murdered his own brother?

Temujin went on to battle other clans until finally he was captured by the Tayichigud. They strapped a heavy wooden cangue over his neck and shoulders, a terrible form of torture meant to degrade the soul as he was forced to beg from his enemies, unable even to feed himself due to the awkward bulk of the contraption.

I'd be a liar to claim I shed tears for him, for some small part of me believed that Temujin's dead brother and all the other spirits were having their revenge on this boy, whom I now realized I had scarcely known at all. I relished the thought that somewhere under the stars he suffered while I bore the dark stares and muttered curses of my clan. But somehow Temujin managed to escape, and people now whispered that the upstart son of one-eyed Yesugei sought an alliance with Ong Khan, the most powerful leader on the steppe.

All of it mattered, yet at the same time, none of it mattered.

The sheep bones scalded my fingers, but still I held them tight, scowling at their jagged lines, which spread like scars, before thrusting them back into the fire. The angry flames spit at me, the smoke and heat making my eyes water. A tiny grasshopper leapt onto a rock and then disappeared between the blades of green grass. I sucked my fingers, tasting the familiar tang of singed flesh and ash.

It was the taste of a war yet to come, a shadow of dead men and burning steppes. And the bones foretold that I would cause this war as surely as if I myself had wielded the bow and flaming quarrels that started it.

"Borte Ujin, you're quiet as an owl in daylight." Gurbesu hovered over my shoulder like a gaudy dragonfly, long turquoise stones jangling from her ears, as she tried to see the message of my fate. Gurbesu was as bright and bold as a summer day, the lone girl in our clan who paid no heed to the rumors about me, mostly because the gossip that swirled about her was just as plentiful. A herd of her father's shaggy goats grazed nearby, doing their utmost to ignore us. "What do the bones say this time?"

A blind crone could predict the futures of every girl in our camp— they'd all marry men from distant camps and churn out lapfuls of wide-cheeked children who would learn to crawl, ride, and then run across the steppes. The only variation was an early death, heralded by the abrupt end of a fissure on the bone, as the girl struggled on all fours to usher new life into the world.

But the cracks in Gurbesu's oracle bones told the story of a long life that wouldn't end until most of her teeth had fallen out and her breasts sagged to her knees. Her sheep bones remained as white as polished ivory, but the marrow of mine always charred black, flaking away and staining my fingernails with the darkness of war and death.

My mother said it was the strength of my water element that allowed me to withstand the heat of the sacred fire and read the divining bones with such terrible clarity. I often wished I favored the air or earth instead of the most powerful element, for water feeds the Earth Mother, making it stronger even than the mountains. Yet my mother promised that one day I would be grateful for the strength of the rain and river, lakes and streams.

Gurbesu prodded me in the ribs. "What do they say?"

"Nothing about a man like a stallion in my bed. Sorry to disappoint." I mustered a smile and stoked the fire, watching it devour the evidence of my bleak future.

"He doesn't have to be a stallion." Gurbesu giggled. "Maybe a snake, one with a quick tongue."

"Gurbesu!" My ears burned. "The bones said I'll soon have a visitor,"

I said, fingering the wolf-tooth necklace that was always at my throat. It wasn't a full lie; in my dream the night before, a foreign bird with long white feathers had landed on our *ger*, pecking holes in the thick felt until I chased it away. I'd almost mentioned it to my mother to have her make sense of it, but I thought better of it.

"We all have visitors, you silly yak," Gurbesu said. "That's the whole point of the Festival of Games." She gestured with an open palm to the white *gers* that crowded our camp, the tents that covered the steppe like a snow-dotted lake. The men's wrestling—Gurbesu's favorite competition—would begin when the sun reached its crest in the Eternal Blue Sky.

Gurbesu shielded her eyes as she studied the men clustering around the empty horse paddock and ran the tip of her pink tongue over her full lips. Sixteen winters old and with the perfectly round, flushed cheeks so often lauded in love songs, my friend was everything I wasn't—short, plump, and more than willing to let the village boys push open her *deel* and fondle her ample breasts behind the tall pine tree outside our summer camp. Gurbesu's father would be hard-pressed to keep his only daughter from stealing off with one—or likely more than one—of the wrestlers tonight. One day my friend's father would negotiate her bride-price and I'd be alone.

"Speaking of visiting," Gurbesu said, "I noticed you with Degei this morning."

"He needed a poultice. That speckled ewe bit his finger."

"If I were his sheep, I'd bite him, too." She looked at me through lashes as thick as a camel's and we burst out laughing. There were rumors that Degei occasionally used his animals as a man would a woman, an offense typically overlooked in young men, but often prompting parents to find them wives before another season passed. Gurbesu flopped back in the grass, her hair gleaming in the summer sun like a river of ebony. "Degei follows you like a lamb."

"He's about as smart as one, too." I shook my head. "I don't think Degei can be counted as a visitor."

"He might," she said, grinning, "if he visited your bed."

"Gurbesu!" I threw a stick at her, but it only served to make her laugh harder. A shaggy goat lifted its head, sniffed in indignation, and trotted off to the sound of tinkling bells.

Perhaps I should let Degei between my legs. Still, I liked to think I might do better than Degei, with his affinity for sheep and his breath like a rotten mushroom.

I emptied a skin bucket of water on the fire. "We'd best go or we'll miss the festival entirely."

Gurbesu brushed the dust from her felted skirt, the same vivid red as summer poppies. "Let me know if you'd like me to carry a message to Degei," she said.

I rolled my eyes and stooped to gather my leather pouch of divining bones as Gurbesu danced down the path toward the well-trodden horse pasture, where almost all the clans had gathered. She elbowed her way through the crowd surrounding the horse paddock and I followed in her wake. An old man from our clan with an unkempt beard drew a sharp breath and stepped back when I passed. I cursed my uncommon height then, wishing I could disappear as he leaned away to avoid contaminating himself by brushing against me. A whisper traded with the foreigners at his elbow soon cleared our path. Even in a crowd as large as this, I would always stand alone.

I tilted my chin high and looked to the belly of the Eternal Blue Sky, heavy with the promise of rain yet to fall. Gurbesu had reached the paddock's railing and now perched on the top rung, but I dragged her to the bottom after a man with fists like boulders threatened to throw her into a fresh heap of dung if she didn't move. She didn't notice; her gaze remained riveted on the crowd of wrestlers, dressed only in leather vests, breechcloths, and knee-high boots. The majority of the competitors were young, but a few had traces of gray in their beards and more hair on their backs than on their heads. Most wore their vests clasped with bone toggles, but some bare bellies reminded me of autumn hogs, hanging over the red and blue sashes tied around their waists. Of course, it was the men with chests that looked as if they'd been carved from stone that held Gurbesu's attention.

The wrestlers paired off, some evenly matched, but others squared against opponents twice their size and a head taller. They waved their arms in the traditional dance of soaring eagles, then grasped their opponents' waists or shoulders. Gurbesu giggled next to me, but my eyes were on a slender young man not far from us. The red felt of his vest and black leather of his breechcloth were well made, and his cheekbones were exquisitely high but not too narrow.

White boned then, one of the ancient and noble lineages. My family, like most, was born of the common black-bone clans.

He moved with the grace of a dragon as he finished the eagle dance. I watched as he and his opponent locked limbs, wincing as the larger man tried to trip him, and then losing sight of them as the other teams staggered about the field. It didn't matter; the noble would be lucky to leave the field without a clutch of bruises to mar his fair skin.

Gurbesu and I cheered as the number of wrestlers in the paddock began to dwindle, the losers melting into the crowd with their bloodied noses and faces smeared with dirt as the victors faced off against each other until only two remained. To my surprise, the white-boned noble from the first match stood victorious. He'd need the strength of the dragon he so resembled as he faced one of the crowd favorites, a battle-scarred warrior from a distant western clan.

The two performed the eagle dance and clasped hands before using their shoulders to ram each other. They remained locked in what might have been an embrace between old friends for so long that the crowd grew restless, but neither man was able to force the other to his hands or knees to claim victory.

"I hope that smelly ox doesn't drop the young one on his head," Gurbesu whispered. She and I had both seen plenty of matches end that way over the years, leaving men with bruised eyes and broken noses. I forced myself to unfurl my fists, but Gurbesu clutched my damp palm. "It would be a shame to waste such a pretty face."

Still the white-bone and the ox clung to each another. Finally the noble dared to lean back and lunge at his opponent's stomach, locking his arms around the man's thick waist and twirling him around. The surprise attack unbalanced the giant and he tottered, finally crashing to the ground with a puff of dust amidst a mixture of curses and cheers from the crowd.

The winner offered a hand to the giant, who roared with laughter and stumbled to his feet.

"Jamuka of the Jadarin is the winner!" An official in a blue vest bowed before the victor, offering him a wooden cup filled with fresh milk and a pointed blue velvet hat trimmed with sable. The white-bone accepted the headdress and took the cup, pouring the milk into the earth in an offering to his ancestors while the judge tossed traditional cheese curds to the spectators.

The crowd cheered and men rushed forward to clap the winner on the back, likely the ones who had placed bets on his victory. Others grumbled under their breath and stuffed their mouths with cheese, drifting off to watch the horse races or gamble over impromptu games of knucklebones thrown in the dirt. Gurbesu lingered, making camel eyes at several wrestlers still damp with sweat, their knees and hands smeared with dirt. "You go ahead," she said. "I don't want to miss the horse races."

"The races don't start until the sun hits the top of the Black Mountain," I said.

"Then stay," she said, an evil glint in her eye. "I'm sure I could find a visitor to entertain even you."

I rolled my eyes to the dark clouds overhead, feeling the first drops of rain on my cheeks. "I'll find you before the races."

"Meet me at the river," she hollered, fluttering her fingers as she pulled her *deel* tighter around her breasts. A wrestler in snug brown breeches stopped dead in his tracks at the sight of her. I ignored the stab of envy at my friend's easy confidence as Gurbesu laughed and crooked a bold finger at him.

Today our camp had swollen to the size of many villages, filled with the last happy conversations and laughter of reunited friends and family before the first frost killed the grasses and winter's snows cut us off from one another.

And yet I'd never felt so alone.

"It's unfortunate that white-bone didn't join the horse races yesterday." Gurbesu lay on her stomach in the grass along the river, feet kicked up to reveal the skin of her legs while she braided daisies into a chain. I traced the imprint of hoofprints stamped into the earth, mostly dry after today's brilliant sunshine. Gurbesu had met me here after the Festival of Games' final horse races, her normally sleek hair mussed and her *deel* terribly rumpled.

"Why is that?" I asked.

"I'd have liked to see him on a horse—I'll bet Jamuka of the Jadarin can ride more than just a filly."

I threw a twig at her, but she dodged it.

"I wonder if he'll join any of the other wrestling competitions," Gurbesu mused. "I rather liked seeing him in his leather breechcloth."

"I'd have thought his breechcloth was too much for you." I nudged her foot with mine, but she only grinned wider.

"Don't tell me you wouldn't open *your deel* for him," she said. "I'll know you're lying."

I rolled onto my stomach to hide my scarlet cheeks. It didn't matter what I thought; I hadn't seen Jamuka since the wrestling competition and likely wouldn't before he finally left after the Festival of Games.

Gurbesu and I lay in silence long enough that the murmur of the river and the warmth of the sun had almost lulled me to sleep, when a branch suddenly snapped behind us. Jamuka stood there, dressed in black breeches and a red felt caftan open at the neck.

I scrambled to my feet, but Gurbesu only raised herself to an elbow, shifting to show all her curves to their full advantage. "Hello," she said, her voice huskier than normal. She grinned when Jamuka only stared at her. "You're Jamuka of the Jadarin clan, are you not?" she asked, as if questioning a simple herder and not one of the white-bones.

Jamuka blinked and his jaw clenched. "I am."

"We watched you win the wrestling tournament," Gurbesu said, a sensuous smile spreading across her plump lips. "A thousand congratulations on your well-deserved victory."

Jamuka ignored her and his gaze settled on me instead, reminding me of the way heavy snow settles on the branches of a birch tree in winter. I clasped my hands behind my back to avoid picking apart the wool of my sleeve. Even with my height—unnatural for a woman—Jamuka was almost a head taller than me, yet another thing I found disconcerting about this white-bone.

"Are you Borte Ujin?" he asked.

I glanced at Gurbesu, but she only raised her eyebrows. "I am," I answered.

"I've been looking for you," he said. "Daughter of Dei the Wise and the famed seer Chotan."

My heart thudded in my chest. Why in the name of the Eternal Blue Sky had this man sought me out?

Gurbesu stood and crossed her arms over her ample chest. "And I am Gurbesu, daughter of Inancha Bilge," she muttered. But my friend pouted only a brief moment, recovering quickly from the slight. "I just realized," she said, flashing me a wicked grin. "I forgot to milk the goats."

Liar. Gurbesu had so often forgotten to milk the goats that her father paid a girl half our age to care for their herd. My pampered friend could scarcely manage to tell the difference between a sheep and a goat.

My glare was sharper than an arrow, but Gurbesu winked and scampered off, pausing only to call over her shoulder, "Don't forget the archery competition in the morning."

Jamuka watched her go, and for once I wished Gurbesu's hips didn't sway like poppy blossoms in the wind. I thought he might follow her, but he turned back to me, studying my face for so long my cheeks began to burn. "I understand that you're a seer as well?"

It should have come as no surprise that he wanted his future read—few would speak to me if it weren't for my skill with the bones now that my prophecy was known to all.

Still, a spirit whispered to me not to read Jamuka's future. To divine for this white-bone would only court danger.

"I was trained by my mother." I avoided his eyes and brushed off my brown *deel*, a sparrow next to a dragon.

"Chotan is well respected, even amongst my clan."

Far off in the pasture, a goat bleated. I shrugged. "She might still see your future if you ask."

"I'd ask you instead."

I stepped around his shadow, wishing to avoid even that slight contact with him. "You might ask," I said, "but I'd refuse."

He reached out as if to stop me, but his hand fell away at my sharp inhale. "Please," he said. "Chotan is renowned over the steppe, but there are murmurs that her daughter is even more gifted."

I knew I should deny him, yet his words spoke to something within me, dry and withered but not yet dead.

"I'll need a fire."

I produced my knucklebones and a handful of flat sheep scapulae from my pocket, a few old and bleached white, others still soft and the color of mare's milk. Jamuka's eyes widened and I shrugged. "A good seer is never without her bones."

His lip twitched into a smile. "Then I'll make the fire."

The wind shifted as he walked away, and I caught a trace of his soul's scent—horse, pine, and strength. I stiffened at the intimacy and exhaled, unwilling to carry even the slightest fragment of him within me.

I watched Jamuka from the corner of my eye as I gathered grass and dried goat dung while he struck his flints together to start the flame. He seemed a man who would be as comfortable at the elbow of a khan as wrestling with the men of his clan. Yet his interest in seeing his future seemed more than idle curiosity. I wondered what it was this man wished to hear.

It didn't matter what his ears and heart yearned for. I was merely the mouthpiece of the Earth Mother and the Eternal Blue Sky. I would speak the truth.

I waited for the flames to beckon with their heat. Too little warmth and they would hold tight to their secrets; too much and they'd rush to spill their message, irrevocably singeing and ruining the bones, and perhaps even the bearer's future days.

"Choose your messenger." I held out the bones like precious offerings. I expected Jamuka to choose the palest of them all, to match his white-boned lineage, but instead he chose a thick yellowish shoulder bone, one taken recently from an unblemished black ram with great curled horns.

I washed the bone in the river first, then rubbed it with dirt and offered it to the Eternal Blue Sky, so it would carry the remaining three elements into the fire. Balancing the bones over the flames with a greenwood stick, I watched them reveal their secrets, not the soft curves foretelling a life of ease that I expected, but two jagged black fissures intersecting each other. They unfurled like miniature storms to the edge, cleaving the bone almost in half as I yanked it from the heat. Tiny fractures no wider than the hairs of an infant ran toward the two great cracks.

I glanced at Jamuka, but his expression was as smooth as river rock. For the first time I wondered if the Earth Mother might forgive the gift of a lie.

"Perhaps you should choose another bone?" My voice wavered and Jamuka's eyes flicked to mine. Too late, I dropped my gaze.

"You'll never hide the truth with eyes like those, Borte Ujin." His voice was gentle. "I don't shy from the future. Neither should you."

"Only fools rush headlong into that which they cannot see." The bone whistled as it cooled in the summer air, a high squeal akin to the warning cry of a chickadee on her nest.

"Tell me what you see." A note of impatience crept into Jamuka's tone, but there was something more in the way he clenched his jaw. I wondered if he already knew the words I must say.

"Two thick lines stride across the bone without wavering," I said, trying to soften the blow. "Men are drawn to you like sheep to their shepherd."

"I'm ambitious and men will follow me." He smiled, but it didn't reach his eyes. "I've been told this before."

"But you will betray one of those men." I brushed the place where the lines intersected, feeling their sharp grooves with my thumb. A gentle knock cleft the bone in two, a perfect fracture along the lines. I'd seen marrow that black only on the divining bones of one other person. "And one of you shall destroy the other."

"Who?"

His hands covered mine, strong and insistent. I thought to draw away, but instead I hesitated, letting his warmth linger. "I cannot say. The bones show only the skeleton of the future."

Not for the first time, I wondered if divining only half-truths was worse than facing the future blind.

Jamuka's mouth tightened and his expression hardened into a glare aimed at the horizon. "Always the same prediction," he said, his voice rough as he withdrew his touch to rub his cheeks. I folded my fingers over the bones, drawing their heat into my flesh to replace his warmth. "Thank you for the confirmation, Borte Ujin. I trust that you'll not speak of this to anyone?"

Never before had I been asked to keep a vision secret, but I understood all too well the import of keeping quiet such a dark future. I nodded. "You have my word."

"Thank you." He stood and walked toward the forest, picking up a long stick with which to beat the unfortunate bushes on the side of the path.

I watched him go, then threw water on the dying fire, jumping back at its burst of white smoke hissing like an angry spirit. The ashes caught on the breeze and I contemplated the burning flakes for a moment before walking back toward camp, the leather pouch of fresh bones clattering in my pocket like old friends.

Sometimes the spirits offer us a warning of the storm to come.

It's not their fault when we're too blind to recognize it.

Chapter 3

The Festival of Games was almost finished, and soon our village would empty of its visitors, leaving only memories and the trampled grasses to bear testimony to their existence. I'd caught glimpses of Jamuka in the days since I'd read his prophecy, and occasionally I felt someone's eyes on my back, only to find him watching me. Yet we'd not spoken since we stood before the divining fire, and I realized that was how he wished it to remain.

Jamuka had used me for what he needed and now scorned me like everyone else. Although I should have expected as much, I was disappointed to realize that he was no different from all the others.

"I've been looking everywhere for you," Gurbesu said, flopping down onto the pile of wool I was beating into felt. My friend's hair was braided with vibrant red threads, but the fibers of dull brown wool I'd been beating clung to my braids, like nettles of scratchy wool the color of freshly turned earth.

I dropped the beating sticks to stretch my aching back, but Gurbesu snatched them and dangled them out of reach. The other women of our clan typically worked throughout the spring to make felt from the freshly sheared sheep, their songs and gossip binding them together as surely as the fleeces were pounded smooth. Yet I worked alone into the summer.

Once the wool was flattened, my father would help me roll it so it could be pulled behind our horse and turned into felt panels.

I gestured to the low sun and paused to sprinkle water onto the wool. "You must be ill to rise this early."

I expected Gurbesu to pull a sour face, but she only stood and sighed, chewing on her lip. "I haven't slept all night," she said, staring at my stick and then tossing it onto the grass. "Not since Father told me."

"Told you what?" I retrieved the stick, startling a speckled orange butterfly that had landed on a nearby boulder. It fluttered away, its beauty fleeting. "Did he finally manage to sell you to a slave caravan?"

"Not quite." She avoided my eyes. "I'm getting married."

I had to reach out a hand to steady myself. It had been only a matter of time before Gurbesu married some sturdy herder with an eager smile and an even more eager member between his legs, but a part of me still trembled to learn that I would soon be left alone.

"I'm sorry, Borte. I didn't think it would be so soon—"

"Don't be silly." I hugged my friend, trying not to cling to her as if she were already gone. Our clan was surrounded by peoples anxious to fly the black banner of war, shed men's blood, and steal their horses, but we flew the white banner of peace, preferring to marry our daughters amongst the constantly warring tribes and create bonds not easily broken by war. I should have realized that the Festival of Games would provide Gurbesu's father with the perfect opportunity to forge an alliance with a new family.

The Unigirad girls were shields meant to protect the clan. Yet if the bones were to be believed, one day I would become the sword that would spill the clans' blood across the steppes.

"I'm so happy for you," I said. "This is what you've been waiting for."

She moved back, studying my false smile. "You're a terrible liar, Borte Ujin." Her face softened. "But I *am* happy."

My eyes stung when she told me that her bridegroom, Chuluun, was a member of the fearsome Naimans, who lived at least a week's ride west of our nearest camp, farther than either Gurbesu or I had ever traveled. Her marriage would keep the peace between our clans, but I would likely never see her again.

I gathered the courage to ask the question that had been tormenting me. "When will you leave?"

Gurbesu bit her lip again, suddenly entranced with the leather thong that held the end of her thick braid. "In three days."

"Three days?" My screech sent a cloud of grasshoppers flying for safety. "But Chuluun still has to work off your bride-price—"

Gurbesu shook her head. "Chuluun is a widower with a young daughter, so my father agreed to forgo the bride-price in return for my permanent position as senior wife."

"You'll be a wife *and* a mother?" I asked, aghast. Gurbesu was less maternal than a weasel; I pitied the poor girl who would soon call her mother.

She shrugged and flicked her braid over her shoulder, the glossy hair capturing the sun's weak light. "My esteemed father traded me for five of Chuluun's best horses."

We stared at each other, then burst out laughing. Such a trade was more than generous.

Gurbesu touched my hand, suddenly serious. "Perhaps if you talked to your father, he could arrange your marriage into the Naiman clan." She bumped her hip against mine and a grin tugged her lips. "Chuluun has a handsome brother—"

I turned away, making a halfhearted attempt to beat the wool again. "You know I can't do that."

Instead, I would honor a promise I'd made long ago and try to avert the war foretold years before. I would not rain death and destruction upon my people, no matter what the bones said.

Gurbesu pressed her forehead to mine. "Oh, Borte. Who is going to make you smile when I'm gone?"

"Perhaps Degei," I offered weakly, but Gurbesu didn't laugh. "I'm happy for you," I said. "Really, I am."

"If this is what you look like happy," Gurbesu said, cocking her head to the side and folding her arms across her chest, "it's no wonder you frighten away all the men."

I gave her a gruesome grin and she giggled, draping an arm around my shoulders and pulling me down into the cloud of wool. She twirled a downy tuft between her fingers. "I know you think your fate is set—"

"Gurbesu—"

"I'll stuff this wool in your mouth if you don't let me finish," she threatened, shaking the brown clump over my face. "The bones only tell part of the future," she said. "You have to live, Borte Ujin, something you've never been very good at. Search for happiness and I think you'll be surprised by what you find."

The words were pretty, but they rang false. "I'll try," I said to placate her. "Still, I think you'll have enough happiness with your warrior for both of us."

She giggled. "I certainly intend to. Chuluun is built like a stallion, at least where it matters most."

"Gurbesu!" My shock only made her laugh harder. "Please don't say you two are already rutting."

"Just because you won't let me say it doesn't make it less true."

I couldn't help myself; I drew her into a fierce hug where we lay, never wanting to let go. Gurbesu was bold, impetuous, and terrible trouble. Still, she would take a part of my heart with her when she married. If I wasn't careful, soon there would be nothing left.

The days before Gurbesu's marriage blew away like the seeds of a cotton flower in the breeze. Gurbesu and I slept under the stars each night, curling into each other's warmth and talking long into the dark despite our heavy limbs and tired eyes. We both realized these were the final moments of girlhoods about to be set aside forever.

The day of Gurbesu's departure dawned fair and clear with a scattering of black storks in the sky, a good omen for the long future I'd glimpsed so many times in the oracle bones. She wore her mother's red wedding head-dress and laughed at the ribald jokes of married women as they washed her hands and feet and brushed her hair until it shone like a raven's wing. She would leave today with her father and bridegroom, never to return to our clan. I smiled and forced my voice to be light, but Gurbesu pulled me to a corner while the mothers and old women reminisced about their own weddings. "This isn't good-bye," she said, her hands on my shoulders. "We'll meet again."

All the words I might have said lodged in my throat. I pulled her into an embrace and breathed in her soul's scent, the traces of tallow, smoke, and hope. I sniffed and dashed my sleeve across my eyes. "Don't tell me you've decided to become a seer, too."

Gurbesu touched my cheek. "I feel it, deep in my heart. The Earth Mother wouldn't bless me with such a sister only to steal her from me."

And so I watched Gurbesu leave to marry her Naiman warrior. Chuluun was a straight-backed soldier dressed in his finest felts, and he wore at his throat a silver talisman of the foreign god who had died on a wooden cross. I'd touched the wolf necklace I always wore and thought to ask him more about this god of his, but then Gurbesu had laughed at something he said and the words died on my tongue. One by one, the people I cared about left. It was only a matter of time before I was truly alone.

I waited until they disappeared over the horizon, unable to speak from the emptiness that pressed on my chest and made it difficult to breathe. I couldn't force myself to linger a moment longer with our clan's drunken well-wishers. Instead, I ducked my head as if against a winter storm and strode toward the Black Mountain. I climbed until my legs burned, running to and from something at the same time.

At the top of the rocky hill, I curled with my back against a white boulder, its stolen warmth from the day seeping into my flesh. A brown spider skittered across a stone at my toe and tiny white flowers nodded in the breeze.

The tears wouldn't stop once they started, a barrage of sobs and salt water that I was powerless to stop.

I wallowed in my self-pity as the air chilled, letting my sadness consume me until the Earth Mother opened her mouth to swallow the sun.

Wolves howled in the distance and an owl called overhead, searching for a meal of shrews. A branch snapped nearby and pebbles crunched underfoot. I scrambled to my feet, heart thudding in my ears as I waited for a wolf to emerge from the darkness. Instead, a man stepped into view.

Jamuka.

The breeze swirled toward me, bringing the familiar scent of pine needles, horse, and man.

"I was beginning to wonder if you'd decided to pitch your *ger* up here," he said, offering a rare smile.

I rubbed my eyes. "I wanted to be alone."

He ignored the hint. "It seems to me you're always alone," he said, handing me a leather waterskin and a hide blanket, one that smelled of horses and the northern forests of our winter camps.

I opened the skin, expecting the cool scent of water, but instead wrinkled my nose at the familiar tang of fermented mare's milk. "No, thank you," I said, but Jamuka pressed the flask into my hand and wrapped the blanket around my shoulders.

"They'll ward off the cold," he said. "Unless you were thinking of returning to the celebration?"

I winced and opened the waterskin, filling my mouth with the pungent and slightly cheesy tang of *airag*. It burned the back of my throat and I coughed, grimacing as Jamuka chuckled in the dark.

"Not accustomed to *airag*?"

"Today is an exception." I took another sip, feeling its warmth spread through my limbs like a summer breeze. I offered it to Jamuka and he took a long draft.

Jamuka sat and crossed his legs neatly in front of him, every movement precise, a testament to his white-boned ancestors. Next to him I felt like a mangy dog. One with fleas.

We sat in silence for so long that I could hear his even breathing. I prodded a stone with my toe. "You're wondering why I'm up here."

"It's not my place to wonder."

I plucked several blades of grass and began plaiting the strands together. "Sometimes it's difficult to imagine what might have been."

"This life is too short to dwell on what might have been. Focus instead on what still might be."

For one terrible moment, I wished he didn't know of my prophecy, yet it didn't matter. Although word of my curse had spread across the steppes, I'd sworn never to speak of it again.

"Mine is a shadow I won't soon escape." I tried to sound nonchalant but failed.

"Perhaps not." Jamuka shook the flask, still partly full, and handed it back to me, his thumb brushing mine and lingering, and my heart became lodged in my throat. I could feel the heat of him, as if he carried some part of the sun. "Black shadows follow us all. It's our decision whether we allow them to darken our days."

We finished the rest of the *airag* in silence, but I was loath to leave. I smelled his scent again. I breathed deeply this time, wanting to remember this moment, when the mare's milk and the man next to me held the loneliness at bay.

For one night I wanted someone else to be strong for me. Tomorrow I would bear it all again and return to shouldering my past and my future. But tonight I wished to forget, to live as Gurbesu had told me to.

The warmth of the *airag* made me bold, and I dared graze the smooth skin of his cheek with my fingers. He flinched and for a moment I feared he'd turn away, but his eyes grew hot and he drew a shuddering breath. I knew what I wanted, and for once I would reach out and grasp it.

I took his hands and brought them to my breasts under the blanket, trembled at the pressure of his palms through my *deel*, and felt the smoothness of his chest under his felt shirt. I wondered for a moment if it was true what they said, that women were made of the cool surface of the moon, and men the scorching heat of the sun.

I waited for him to push me away. Instead, he pulled me to him, his lips on mine tasting faintly of mare's milk. A warmth I'd never felt before rolled over my body, making me gasp with pleasure. I understood now why Gurbesu had met with boys under the pine tree.

Jamuka's lips caressed my neck and then his fingers traced the leather thong at my neck, lingering on the wolf tooth at my throat. He drew away, leaving me suddenly cold. "We can't do this," he said, heaving a ragged breath. "You don't belong to me, Borte Ujin."

"I belong to no one." I leaned into his hand as he tucked a stray hair behind my ear. "I can do as I wish."

How easily the lie fell from my lips.

Jamuka crouched in the darkness so I couldn't see his face. "That's not true," he said. "And you well know it."

My heart stalled for a moment, then pounded to the rhythm of a galloping horse. "You think highly of yourself," I said, my voice sharp, "to rebuke me as if you were my father."

Jamuka looked at me with an expression of such sadness that I wanted to touch him again, to ease the heaviness in both our hearts. Yet his next words froze my hand at my side.

"I know you can never belong to me because I am Temujin's *anda*." Jamuka's tone was quiet, the same tone a man used when announcing the death of a revered elder.

Temujin. A man I hadn't seen in seven years.

Anda. Blood brothers.

Jamuka and Temujin had swallowed each other's blood, sworn sacred vows before the ancestors so they were closer than brothers of the same womb. The man before me had been Temujin's only ally after his father's death, and it was his support that had ensured the survival of Temujin and his family.

I will cleave two men apart and ignite a great Blood War that will rain tears and destruction upon the steppes.

Such was the curse I bore, the prophecy I refused to fulfill.

I stifled a sob as I clambered to my feet, but the darkness chased me as I stormed down the hill, silently cursing Jamuka while ignoring his pleas at my back. I ran until I could breathe no more and collapsed onto the cold riverbank, pounding my fists and screaming my frustration into the Earth Mother, feeling her silent rebuke.

Still Temujin sought to ruin me, even from afar.

Chapter 4

My mother claimed the steppes had echoed with my laughter as a child, yet as a young woman of seventeen winters, I walked through this life with a heavy spirit, plucking the whispers of the ancestors from the winds and weaving the jagged cracks of bones into warnings and prophecies. The heaviness of the future and the weight of my past stooped my shoulders like an old woman's, despite my soft cheeks and unlined skin.

And then Jamuka had come.

And I, being the fool I was, had allowed that hope to smolder to life again.

There was no trace of Jamuka the morning after our kiss, and I soon learned he had departed camp under the cover of night. I couldn't rail at him for deceiving me but had to content myself with gathering soot from his cold hearth to curse him. And Temujin.

My shouts into the Eternal Blue Sky startled a flock of brown sparrows before I turned the curses on myself. They were black words I could never undo, just as I could never take back my moment of weakness in Jamuka's arms. I swore to the Earth Mother that I would never waver again, that I would bear my necessary solitude like a sturdy oak. I sanctified the promise by adding drops of blood from my palm to the tears already splashing on the ground. It would be far better to water the earth with my own blood than with that of countless men.

The short golden season burned itself out and I spent the long months of winter in dark silence. It was a bleak season full of angry winds that cut through the walls of our *ger* and threatened to crack the skin of our sheep-stomach churn as I pounded our meager supply of winter milk into butter. The wolves grew daring as temperatures plummeted, and men often had to chase the beasts away from our ever-scrawnier herds in a perpetual struggle for life over death. That terrible winter also stole my mother's vision. Her eyes flickered and the light finally went out on the solstice. Since then her tongue had become sharper and her temper flared brighter, but I tried to keep my patience as the darkness of eternal winter surrounded her.

Finally, a false spring warmed the air, teasing the snow into melting so the fields filled with slush and, beneath that, rich, beautiful mud and the first tufts of new grass for our grazing herds. It was a hint and a promise of better days to come.

Yet some promises are easily broken.

The mountains on either side of our camp were still asleep under thick white blankets of snow on the morning I slung a dented iron milk pail over my shoulder, my father snoring beneath a mound of hides. A constant chill had settled in his bones, so deep that the earth below our tent had trembled with his shivering the night before. I dropped a feather-light kiss onto his brow, and another on my mother's forehead, wishing I could smooth away the frown lines etched so deep around her lips that not even sleep could erase them.

I stepped outside into the bracing air, heading toward the paddock. I'd never taken much interest in my father's herd before, yet over the winter I'd studied all the animals, learning which ewes had the thickest wool and what horses had the softest hooves. My father had no sons or brothers to take me in when my parents passed to the sacred mountains, but I was determined not to meet the same fate as Temujin's family, cast out for my worthlessness. I would provide my own milk and meat, and my gift of sight might prove valuable to my clan. Already girls came to me eager for their futures, and one of the old women had sought me out to read the winds on the equinox to determine the best day to move to our spring camp.

I would not be cast aside again, not while I still drew breath in my lungs.

I neared the paddock and set down the pail, blowing onto my hands to warm them and stomping my feet. My father's white mare whinnied and threw back her head, as if to warn me of an encroaching storm or nearby beast. She was too late, for the danger had already come.

Across the field, a straw yellow mare with a hairless tail snorted, steam curling from her nose in the chill morning air. On her back sat a man with broad shoulders and two black braids hanging down his back. I'd have recognized his gray eyes anywhere, stolen from some brooding wolf.

After seven years, Temujin had finally returned.

My blood turned to water and I dropped the milking pail to clutch the rough gate of the paddock, relishing the bite of the splinters as they burrowed deep into my skin. I knew then the feeling of a deer being stalked by a predator and wished that I could flee from what was to come. At the same time I wanted to unleash the pain and fury of the last seven years, to make Temujin suffer as I'd suffered. Instead, I stiffened my spine and hardened my face into stone, hoping he couldn't hear the drumming of my traitorous heart.

And he wasn't alone. Two men flanked him, one with a penetrating stare above his frothy white beard and a ragged squirrel-skin hat framing a weather-beaten face. The other I knew too well, the burning dark eyes set over aristocratic features as he sat stiff-backed in a polished leather saddle decorated with gold coins.

I shuddered and pulled my cloak tighter against Jamuka's gaze, even as my heart thudded in my chest. I'd imagined this scene many times, yet the words I'd rehearsed fled, leaving my tongue empty.

Temujin swung his leg over the horse in one fluid motion, landing with a thud that shook the ground. He was built like a battering ram meant to conquer some far-off city. I stood rooted in place, powerless to stop my future as it strode toward me.

"Borte Ujin." He reached out his hands, but when I didn't move they fell empty at his sides. Temujin was a hairsbreadth shorter than me, so I had to look down my nose to meet him eye to eye. "It took longer than I planned, but I've finally returned to you."

My mind felt frozen in the grip of a winter storm, unable to comprehend this man before me. "When you left you promised my father that you'd return by the next full moon. It seems time got away from you."

"Life sent me some unexpected surprises along the way." He rubbed his wrists, and for a moment I imagined them circled by the rough wood of the cangue. "Still, I promised I'd return." He glanced over his shoulder at Jamuka. "And I always keep my promises."

I didn't answer. A fragment of my soul cried out with joy that I hadn't been forgotten, yet another piece of me wanted to hurl a handful of horse dung in Temujin's face. Instead, I drew myself as tall as I could while I gathered my thoughts, refusing to betray a glimmer of emotion before these men.

The silver-bearded stranger inclined his head toward me, his black felts rustling like the wings of a vulture and rattling the beads sewn with jagged stitches onto his *deel*, bits of ivory earned by a shaman for successful visions. It was only then that I realized he was crippled, his right leg withered and bent at a painful angle.

Temujin caught my recoil at the man's impure energy. "Teb Tengeri has been with me since I left the Tayichigud," Temujin said. "It was he who decreed this was a favorable time to ride to you. Much has happened since we last spoke."

I did my best to ignore Teb Tengeri's probing stare and recalled the children who made a promise under the stars so many years ago, wondering now if anything of that naïve girl still remained.

"I heard of your brother," I told Temujin, watching his expression carefully. "I was sorry to hear of his passage to the sacred mountains."

His passage at Temujin's hands. I stared at those hands now, stained with dark shadows like smears of blood. A flicker of emotion lit his eyes, but it passed too quickly to name.

"Begter was more thief than my half brother," he said. "I could manage his thieving when he stole food from me, but when he stole meat that was meant to feed my family . . ." His voice trailed off and his eyes grew distant; then he blinked and looked at me. "My brother, Khasar, and I killed him to save my mother and younger sister. I became a murderer to save my blood family."

The way Temujin tilted his chin told me he'd do it all again if he had to. My first reaction was revulsion that he had shed his brother's unclean blood and touched death, but when I imagined watching my own mother die of starvation, her eyes growing sunken as her flesh melted away . . .

"I'm sorry," I said, feeling the inadequacy of the words, but Temujin only inclined his head toward Jamuka and the crippled man still inspecting me from atop his silver-white gelding.

"You already know my *anda*, Jamuka," he said. "We've been blood brothers almost since I could ride a horse."

"Yes," I said, not meeting Jamuka's eyes. "I believe you sent him to spy on me."

Temujin had the decency to look flustered. "Not to spy, only to confirm what Teb Tengeri had predicted."

I scowled. There was room for only one seer in each clan, and I would not relinquish my gift, certainly not in exchange for becoming Temujin's wife.

"And what did Teb Tengeri predict?" I asked, folding my arms across my chest. A nod from Temujin, and his seer and Jamuka backed away, out of earshot. There was no doubt who led this band of men, although Temujin seemed an unlikely choice to lead a white-bone and an accomplished shaman.

Temujin turned to me, his eyes warm. "Teb Tengeri traced the sweep of stars on the last new moon and read the blood of a newly slaughtered goat to determine that now was the best time to fulfill my promise to you. I wasn't taking any chances."

The fury at his presumption screamed through my veins, but I turned to stroke the nose of my father's mare, letting the gentle nuzzle of her lips soothe me. "I still carry the curse I once warned you of," I finally said. "Would you bring a storm of death onto the steppes?"

Temujin shrugged. "My strength in battle has already been tested.

With you as my wife I will become a great and powerful khan, and our children will multiply and rule from the Great Lake to the Great Dry Sea."

I snorted. "Did your shaman tell you that?"

"He may have."

I knew not whether his seer was a fraud, only that my curse still clung to me like a branch of thorns. Temujin moved closer, his thumb brushing the sensitive skin on the inside of my wrist. "I want you by my side, Borte Ujin. I had hoped you might still want me, too."

"I don't want anyone," I snapped. "Least of all a man who slanders my name from mountains away."

"What?" Temujin drew away, his eyes narrowing. "That's a heavy charge to lay at my feet."

"Heavy, but just," I countered. "My mother and I were the only ones who knew of my curse until I spoke of it to you. Now it's common knowledge from Lake Balkash to Mount Burkhan Khaldun." I hoped that I'd been mistaken, but my heart fell as the color drained from his face.

"I did speak of your prophecy," he admitted slowly. "But not in the way you think." I gave him the insult of my back, but he caught my hand and moved so I had no choice but to face him. "Please," he said. "Listen before you condemn me as the worst sort of villain."

I gritted my teeth and yanked my arm away, but I didn't leave.

He sighed. "I told my clan your secret after my father's bones had been returned to the earth. I thought little of the prophecy, but the elders believed differently. They argued that I must renounce the bond with you and your people, but I refused. The next morning they broke camp and left us on the riverbank, unwilling to sully themselves with a future war."

My hands trembled so much that I had to clasp them around my elbows. "That's why you were abandoned?"

Temujin closed his eyes, as if to shut out a painful memory. "My mother chased them with my father's Spirit Banner, yelling at them to honor their promise to provide for my father's widow. A few hesitated, but the elders urged them on. We were left desolate, with only our shadows to stand at our sides."

"Your family almost starved that winter," I said, recalling the travelers' stories. Numbness spread up my body, the acrid taste of guilt filling my mouth as I touched the wolf-tooth necklace I still wore at my neck. "Because of me."

Temujin's eyes lit when he saw the necklace, and he touched it, brushing the hollow at my throat. "We became experts at catching fish and digging wild onions." His hand covered mine, square and rough like the rest of him. "But I always hoped it wasn't all in vain."

I struggled then. I'd spent the last seven years watching everyone around me live their lives while my days trickled away like drops of water off melting river ice. I wanted to live, to plunge into the vibrant, ever-changing world I'd always held at bay, but there was still the prophecy, a dark shadow I could never escape.

Temujin seemed to read my thoughts. "Jamuka has pledged that his clan will support me, and our marriage will enable me to seek an alliance with Ong Khan." This was no small thing, for among the chiefs of the scattered steppe tribes, Ong Khan was viewed as the strongest leader. "Not long from now," Temujin continued, "your gift of sight and your father's herds will be prizes many men will seek to steal. Marrying me will not start the war you fear. In fact, it may avert it."

He thought to persuade me, but instead his reminder of my parents made my soul heavy. It was my responsibility to care for my father and mother until they drew their last breaths. But then I recalled my mother's words as I had tucked a blanket around her bone-thin legs only a few days ago.

"You worry about us overmuch," she had said, her voice uncharacteristically soft as she patted my arm. I'd never forget her hands, the wisdom in the brown stains of age and bulging veins gained by years of hard work and sacrifice. "Too much, I think."

"I worry because I love you," I had said, unfastening her braid so I could brush her hair.

She gave an exasperated sigh and pushed away the bone comb, the wattle under her chin swaying. "Your father and I managed to care for ourselves before I carried you in my womb. I can guarantee that we'll continue to do so even after you're gone."

"I'm not going anywhere, Mother. You know that."

She tipped my chin to look at her, her blank eyes still managing to penetrate into my soul. "Your father and I will die warm in our beds, Borte Ujin. You needn't worry about us."

I'd cleared my throat then and blinked to ease the stinging in my eyes. Only now did I realize she'd seen this day and had known the choice I would face. I suddenly yearned to travel to the distant Onan River, to become Temujin's senior wife and rule over his clan, yet to even wish for such a thing felt like a betrayal of everything I knew.

"You already have a seer," I said to Temujin, clinging to my last excuse. "I won't give up my sight."

"Of course you won't," Temujin said. "I have great plans, Borte, large enough for at least two seers."

I had no more arguments left beneath me, as if I'd been standing on lake ice that had melted out from under my feet. Still, I would not answer him now.

"Your plans will have to wait," I said, "until I make my decision."

"I'll wait, then," Temujin said, his voice so full of happiness that I almost smiled. "As long as it takes."

I was tempted to tell him he'd wait seven years as I'd done, but I bit my tongue. I knew not what my answer would be, but he'd have it before the next full moon. Anything longer than that would be a cruelty to both of us.

I spent the next days with my eyes closed, listening for guidance from the spirits in the winds and in the beating of my own heart, but my ears were so full of the chatter and whispers of my clan that I had to put distance between myself and the stifling circle of *gers*, where Temujin's hearty laugh rang out too often for my liking. I left then to sleep under the stars and read the omens of the Eternal Blue Sky, taking with me only an old horse blanket and a felt satchel of dried horsemeat and a waterskin my mother packed for me.

I camped on the banks of a river swollen with spring meltwater, relishing the peace and tranquility of the rushing waters and the occasional jump of a silver trout. One night it rained, soaking through my blanket so I smelled of wet sheep the next morning, shivering and alone.

And I knew then that I didn't wish to face an eternity of lonely days.

I didn't love Temujin, but he intrigued me, and my anger at him had faded since I'd realized the accident of his betrayal of me. He and I had both suffered while we were apart; perhaps together we might be stronger than we were on our own.

And so I packed the remnants of my mother's food in the faded blanket and hiked all morning back to camp. Along the way was a deep lake, one still covered with a thick sheet of ice that wouldn't break until the hillsides were carpeted with fresh green. Two figures glided along the ice's dull surface, and I squinted, recognizing Temujin's solid form and then Jamuka's tall silhouette. They moved over the ice with polished bones strapped to the bottoms of their boots, a common winter pastime for children. The sight of two grown men skating together brought an unbidden smile to my face. A peal of Temujin's laughter rang out, and for a moment I imagined them as boys shortly after Temujin's father died, sensed a bond that went deeper than their taking each other's blood into their mouths during their *anda* ceremony. I pulled my hat tighter over my ears and hurried on my way, not wishing to be seen.

I stopped by my mother's *ger* first, where she proceeded to fill my ears with arguments against my decision. My father was easier to persuade, for Temujin had wordlessly taken my place caring for our herds during my absence. My cheeks flushed at that, for I'd given little thought to who would assist my father while I was at the river. Finally, I retraced my steps and went in search of Temujin. I found him seated by the lake, whittling what appeared to be a fishing pole from a bare birch branch.

"There are no fish this time of year," I said, scowling first at him and then at the ice.

Temujin's hand jerked at my voice, and he almost dropped the pole. "You've returned, Borte Ujin."

"I have," I said, sitting down next to him and stretching my legs before me. The bone skates he'd worn earlier lay discarded by his feet, but there was no sign of Jamuka.

"I hate fish," I said, casting a glance at his pole.

He smiled. "I'd never eaten them until after my father died. They're not so bad, especially cooked with a little sheep fat."

I cringed then, for I'd forgotten that Temujin and his family had barely survived that first winter after Yesugei's death. Without fish from the creeks and roots dug from the riverbeds, Temujin would be only a pile of bones and dust now.

The question was plain on his face, but I refused to answer it. Instead, I closed my eyes, feeling the caress of the breeze and hearing the cry of a hawk far off. I opened my eyes to the softness of Temujin's expression, reminding me of the young boy I'd once made a promise to under the stars, and I drew a deep breath, knowing that this decision could only be my own. "I've decided to keep my promise," I said.

Temujin's eyes sparked, sudden flecks of silver in the gray. "Does that mean you'll become my wife?"

He didn't need my consent, only my father's, but perhaps Temujin was more considerate than I gave him credit for. I could only nod my answer—the words were too heavy to speak again—but Temujin gave a sudden whoop of joy and lifted me to my feet, spinning us around until I was laughing with him.

He kissed me then, a kiss full of impatience for life. My body responded against my will, and I recalled the power this man had possessed even as a child, the ability to draw people to him. I wondered for a moment if perhaps he had managed to cast that net over me, but the heady pleasure at being wanted eclipsed my worry.

Then Temujin broke the kiss and looked at me with a new emotion in his eyes. It took me a moment to recognize the desire there, laid bare for all to see. "Jamuka was right when he said I'd be lucky to win you a second time," he murmured.

I stiffened at the mention of Jamuka, but Temujin didn't notice.

"I am indeed blessed by the Eternal Blue Sky and the Golden Light of the Sun," he said, cupping my face as if I was something precious. "Today I gain not only a wise and beautiful wife, but also an alliance with the greatest khan on the steppes."

Temujin stood to gain all. And yet I wondered if perhaps there was much we might still lose.

. . .

We lingered only until the new moon, an auspicious occasion for new beginnings, but scarcely enough time to prepare for the new life that awaited me. Although the ground under our feet changed as we migrated with the seasons, my mother's *ger* was the only home I'd ever known. Now I was to leave it behind, a thought that made my hands tremble and forced the air from my lungs.

My mother would travel with us, but my father was too ill to manage the entire journey. He would turn back at the river border of our spring camp, returning to our empty *ger* and the colts Temujin had offered as my bride-price. I breathed deeply of the woodsmoke of my father's soul, memorizing each wrinkle of his face and the flecks of copper in his eyes.

"*Bayartai*, Borte Ujin," my father said.

Good-bye.

Those words were uttered only when someone was dying or leaving on a journey from which they would never return. We both knew this was the last time we would be together until we greeted each other on the crest of the sacred mountains. Suddenly it was difficult to swallow.

"You have made me proud every day since you fell from your mother's womb," he continued, pressing his wrinkled forehead to mine. "You'll make me prouder still in the days to come."

He released me then, inclining his head to the man standing a respectful distance behind me. "Take care of her," he said to Temujin, offering him a single feathered arrow, carved by his own hands and symbolic of the fact that Temujin would be head of my family now.

"I will." Temujin clasped the quarrel to his heart and held out his hand for me. I lingered for a moment, longing for nothing more than to remain in the protective circle of my father's arms.

But we all must face our futures. I squeezed my father's hand one final time and turned to the man who would become my husband, lifting my eyes to the east and the new life that awaited me.

Chapter 5

We traveled with Temujin and his men for many days, my mother and I falling exhausted into our bedrolls each night and rising with the sun every morning. This was a stark land, where winter ice still covered the Sengur River, the forests were mere clumps of trees, and the grasses became more sparse the closer we traveled to Temujin's homeland. We arrived to find the *gers* of his clan nestled at the base of the Burgi cliff, close enough to the river to draw water but far enough away to avoid any unseasonable ice floes that might be pushed overland as the river broke apart. I counted only ten people in all as we dismounted our horses, including his mother, Hoelun, and his father's faded second wife, Sochigel, whose only remaining beauty was the exquisite moccasins beaded by her own hands. I would soon discover that Sochigel had fallen silent when her eldest son died, refusing to speak now that the light had gone out of her life.

Hoelun enjoyed a happy reunion with my mother, then circled me and smacked her lips, revealing several missing teeth.

"A plain face, but with fire in her eyes," she said, echoing the words of her husband from long ago.

That wasn't the first time I wished the spirits had gifted me with eyes like mud.

A hunchbacked crone shuffled to my side, bringing a whiff of stale

urine that made me cringe. A childless widow since her only son was killed
in a raid, Mother Khogaghchin had been alone on the steppes when
Hoelun found her and took her into her own tent. The old woman wore a
leather girdle to keep from wetting herself, having long ago lost the power
to control her waters. Her grin revealed gums as pink as a newborn's and a
whiff of the foulest breath I'd ever smelled. "She has good hips, too," she
said. "We'll get plenty of foals from this one."

"My daughter is more valuable than a broodmare." My mother's tone
was biting as she first felt and then cut the ropes of the pack her horse had
carried all this way. Temujin's clan gave a collective gasp as she shook out
a stunning black sable coat, a fur more valuable than a herd of the fastest
horses. She held it up to the Eternal Blue Sky and then held it out in Temujin's direction. "Dei the Wise and his wife, Chotan, wish to offer this sacred
gift to the husband of our daughter, Borte Ujin."

Temujin stared at her for a moment and reached out to touch the fur,
its black hairs quivering in the breeze. He shook his head. "This is too rich
a prize, even for such a woman as Borte Ujin," he said. "I cannot accept
such a gift from those who have already given so much."

My mother pressed the fur closer. "You must take it, to give to Ong
Khan."

Temujin lifted his gaze to mine. This was no gift, then, but the price of
peace. Ong Khan would never refuse such a gift and would pledge to
protect Temujin and his clan, come what may. This exquisite gift might be
enough to keep my prophecy at bay.

"Chotan is right," Jamuka said. "It is a fitting gift, and one that will
bring you renown and a glorious alliance with the khan."

Still Temujin hesitated, but Teb Tengeri finally dismounted his silver-
white horse and hobbled over, inspecting the fur while leaning heavily on
his cane. "This gift shall indeed bring you good fortune," he said.

I scowled at the crippled shaman. Teb Tengeri had separated himself
from us during the journey, riding alone and sharing Jamuka's fire at night.
Only now, surrounded by the familiar curve of the river and the stark
outline of the mountains he knew so well, did the holy man with the
withered leg feel safe enough to assert himself. It was then that I knew Teb

Tengeri for the coward he was and first recognized the hunger for power in his soul.

I recognized it because now that I'd seen the camp I would rule one day, I felt its foreign teeth gnawing at my heart as well.

I shifted, blocking Temujin's view of his shaman, and said, "Good fortune matters naught. This is a fitting gift for the man who has pledged to protect me, despite what storms may wait on the horizon."

Temujin took my meaning and finally accepted the fur. "I am humbled," he said to my mother. "I swear to you that I shall shelter Borte Ujin from any storm, and the steppes shall bask in the warmth of her smiles."

My mother narrowed her eyes at him in such a way that my skin prickled with dread, for despite her blindness, it was as if she was seeing him for the first time. "You shall fail her, Temujin of the Borijin," she said, her voice coming from far away. "Yet without you, she cannot become the woman she was meant to be."

There was a stunned breath of silence before my mother heaved a great sigh, listing dangerously. I caught her arm, frightened by the way she leaned on me. "My mother is weary from the long journey," I said. "Is there somewhere she can rest?"

Temujin nodded, although he didn't meet my eyes. "She can remain in my mother's *ger* until I've built her tent."

"Thank you," I said, pulling my mother in that direction and feeling the angry glares directed like spears at my spine. I pulled her close and hissed in her ear, "Why would you say such a thing?"

Yet my mother didn't answer, and when I glanced back it was to find only one man staring at me.

Teb Tengeri's eyes were narrowed into a murderous stare, aimed right at my heart.

No one spoke of my mother's outburst, and she recovered well enough to duck into my *ger* on the morning of my marriage, ushering in a breath of fresh morning air. The cranes still slept and horses snorted in their slumbers, but my eyes were swollen from a sleepless night spent alone in my new tent. The wedding ceremony would take place in the spring breeze at first light, when the wildflowers open their faces to the sun. A time of new beginnings.

Yet my dreams had been full of late snows and spring hail trampling and killing the happy blossoms.

The day before, the river ice had broken and we women had sweated next to each other to build my *ger* while the men hunted red deer and spotted marmot for the wedding feast. As my mother-in-marriage, Hoelun had pounded the felt panels for my tent with her own hands, and over the years, I would beat in new wool as the panels wore out, slowly making the *ger* mine with my own sweat. I tried not to linger over the embarrassment that my new family couldn't afford proper doors for their tents, settling for a flap of wool to replace the carved wooden door only the bountiful southern valleys could provide.

My mother stoked the fire, adding spruce branches to purify my soul, and worked to ready me for the wedding, her gnarled hands suddenly deft as she worked by feel and memory. She undid the knot of hair I'd worn as a girl, separating and plaiting it into three sections. The braids were stiffened with goat fat and then twisted around a wooden stick and fastened with a leather lace. Her fingers brushed the worn leather thong at my neck, lingering on the white wolf tooth. For a moment I thought she would set it aside, but then she moved on without a word.

Off came my brown skirt with the hole on the hem and my worn leather boots. I stepped into a red felted skirt embroidered to match the flowered belt she cinched around my waist, the same worn by my mother and my mother's mother, generations of nervous women awaiting their future husbands. Next came the leather cone headdress topped with white feathers and horsehair strung with mismatched beads and precious red and pink silk ribbons hanging to my chin. Holding one hand so I could balance the headdress with the other, she helped slip my feet into thin red felt slippers, the toes embroidered with elaborate flowers and upturned in the traditional manner so as not to injure the Earth Mother when I walked.

"Sochigel made them for you," my mother whispered. The gesture made my eyes sting and I struggled to swallow.

My mother clasped my shoulders, her opaque eyes shining as she sniffed both sides of my face in order to carry my scent, and part of my soul, with her. After today, I would no longer be a child, but a woman with a family of my own.

"Hoelun will be your mother now," she said, pressing her cheek to mine in a final good-bye. "But you come from a family of seers. Remember that gift and use it well."

"I will," I said, blinking hard and flinging myself into her arms as the women of Temujin's family burst into the tent. Outside, the air hummed with the deep vibrations of men's *hoomii* singing, and the first blush of dawn lit the sky.

Then my mother and Hoelun took my hands and led me out into the cold air, to whatever the future held for me.

Hoelun sprinkled milk on the ground to begin the ceremony while the men's voices from deep in their throats made the very air quaver. My mother passed the horn cup to Temujin, demonstrating her adoption of him as her son, and then he scattered the remainder of the milk over the earth. My husband stood especially tall in his red headdress, his skin tanned from the sun and his dark hair loose down his back. We faced each other and clasped hands while our mothers wound a single piece of blue yarn around our shoulders, a reminder that we were now bound together. Together, we dropped to our knees nine times to honor the Golden Light of the Sun, the Eternal Blue Sky, the rivers that were the lifeblood of the Earth Mother and the revered mountain Burkhan Khaldun, the khan of all mountains. Temujin shook out a red felt cloak and draped it reverently over my shoulders before allowing me to help him into the black sable jacket. Then we touched foreheads and breathed deeply, inhaling the scent of each other, sharing our very souls.

Temujin was now a part of me, come what may.

The wedding celebration afterward was small, but for the way Temujin's family acted, one might have thought Ong Khan himself had just taken a new wife. A day-old lamb was butchered and Hoelun made the traditional sacrifice to the fire spirits, offering a small piece of purple intestine, a tiny chunk of heart, a strip of meat, and one rib bone to pacify the flames.

Afterward, my new brothers stripped down to their breeches to circle each other in an impromptu wrestling match while taking long gulps of fermented mare's milk. I did my best to avoid looking at the smooth muscles of Jamuka's chest, the bare skin I'd once touched, as he took off his *deel* and shirt to join them. An old horse had been slaughtered earlier in the day, so the meat now cooked in a giant iron cauldron over a roaring fire. I sat between mute Sochigel and my blind mother, glad for once that she couldn't see as Temujin's entire family slurped *airag* straight from the skin jugs and sucked the marrow from their soup bones.

The youngest member of the family approached me then, Temujin's younger sister, Temulun, and thrust a handful of grass and wilted spring poppies at me. "These are for you," she said, her shy smile revealing two missing milk teeth.

"Thank you," I said, making a show of sniffing the blossoms. "Poppies are my favorite flower."

"Mine, too," she said. "But tonight you're even prettier than they are."

She scampered off before I could answer, leaving me smiling into the posy.

Temujin had shrugged off the sable jacket, shedding the black fur to reveal the thick chest and mass of muscle hidden beneath, and joined the wrestlers. He and Jamuka grappled together, laughing good-naturedly as they took turns dropping each other to the ground. I listened with half an ear as Hoelun recounted to my mother the story of when he and Jamuka took each other's blood for the first time, lauding Jamuka's loyalty to Temujin and Temujin's adoration of the *anda* who was closer to him than his own brothers. I tried to close my ears, but then Hoelun shifted to a new topic.

"The Tayichigud attacked us after my husband went to the sacred mountains." Her voice shuddered like a larch in a winter storm. "They tortured Temujin by locking him in a cangue and forcing him to beg for the very air he breathed. I doubt he would have survived had it not been for Jamuka's support. His *anda* saved him when he could no longer save himself."

I didn't care to think of the bond between my husband and his blood brother, of the kiss I'd once shared with Jamuka. I stared at the ground, glad that not even my mother or Teb Tengeri could read my thoughts.

Two scuffed boots entered my vision and I looked up to see my husband, his chest sweat slicked and dusty from wrestling, and bearing a bloody scrape across one shoulder. He held out a hand for me, the fire in his eyes making my stomach buck like a colt.

Somehow, I managed to take his hand and stumble to my feet. I did my best to ignore the heat of Jamuka's eyes on my back, to keep from my nose the scent of pine I remembered from another celebration not long ago.

I would carry the soul of only one man to my marriage bed.

Temujin tied a leather and ivory necklace over my wolf tooth and fastened matching bracelets on my wrists. Two fires to keep evil spirits at bay roared merrily outside my new *ger*, symbolic of the trials we would face together, and we walked between them hand in hand, purifying ourselves with their heat before entering our new home.

This would be the tent where my children would be born, and one day, its walls would be my final sight before I drew my last breath.

Temujin and I ducked inside while everyone else pushed in behind us. A cheerful fire crackled in the center and thick wisps of smoke twisted through the hole in the roof, obscuring the rope that crisscrossed down the far wall in a reminder of the many paths our lives might take. My eyes stung to see new rugs on the floor, ones woven with a familiar pattern of yellow flowers like the fields back home. My mother's final gift.

I dutifully prepared the salt tea that a bride traditionally offered to her guests, then bowed my head as the men and women drained the cups. Someone pressed a jug of *airag* into my hand and toothless Mother Khogaghchin grinned up at me. "One good drink and you won't even feel the pain, my goat."

It would take more than a jug of mare's milk to numb the flutter of panic in my chest, but I took a long swallow, letting it scald my throat. Hoelun bent before me, placing a polished black stone at my feet.

"Our family is strong as this stone," she said, a temporary hush falling over the merriment. "May you be blessed with the strength of the sacred mountains and the fertility of the Earth Mother."

Then Mother Khogaghchin tweaked my nose, laughing so I was made dizzy by the smell of *airag* on her breath.

"Out!" Temujin roared with laughter, ushering everyone to the door as he tossed off his headdress. Most of the men took up singing bawdy songs of encouragement that made my cheeks flame. Yet one man didn't raise his voice in song.

"Jamuka!" Temujin yelled too loud. Jamuka had been almost outside, and he turned slowly now, his face a mask. "No well-wishes from my *anda*?"

"You've been showered with many blessings today," Jamuka said, although his smile didn't reach his eyes. "I pray that you enjoy them."

"You need more *airag*, my friend." Temujin clapped Jamuka on the back. "Rest well and perhaps I'll see you in the morning."

Jamuka's jaw clenched as he glanced at me, as if he couldn't bear to be within sight of me. I wondered at his animosity, whether he believed like so many others that I had doomed his *anda*. I tossed my head in defiance and waited for the tent flap to fall behind him before turning back to my husband.

As I watched Temujin pull off his boots, the tent felt suddenly too hot and too cold at the same time. I craved fresh air but shivered so the beads on my headdress rattled, like the voices of ancestors long since dead. My head pounded in time to my heart so it was all I could do to keep my stomach calm.

I tugged at the bone toggle on my red felt cloak, but the *airag* made my fingers slip. Temujin suddenly stood before me and covered my hands with his.

"Let me help," he said.

But instead of pulling off my cloak, he removed the wedding headdress and tossed it unceremoniously to the ground. I couldn't stop the sigh of relief that escaped my lips, and his mouth curved into a smile. His fingers undid the intricate braids my mother had toiled over and then wove their way through my hair, kneading my scalp and soaking up the tension of the day. The hammers in my skull gradually lessened, but my heart still pounded a steady beat. I knew the tactic, the same used to relax an animal before its slaughter.

But I would grasp this destiny I'd chosen with both hands, uninhibited and undaunted.

I pressed my body against his and caressed the scrape on his shoulder, my fingers coming away with a smear of his blood. The hardness of his desire didn't shock me, but instead made me bold. I kissed him then, relishing his groan as his lips parted under mine. He picked me up and spread me over the black sable coat, covering me with his body. I felt his inhale, the way his soul spread its eager fingers into mine. "I am indeed a lucky man," he said, his voice rough with emotion as his lips brushed my ear.

"The luckiest of men," I murmured, feeling wanton as my skirt bunched up around my hips. Only the thin fabric of our trousers separated us from each other.

He laughed then, and I smiled, my cheeks warming. Outside there was a shout for us to get on with it, then a roar of laughter.

"We'd best do as they say," I murmured.

Temujin pulled me to him. "Do you always do as you're told?"

"Rarely." I worked off his belt and tossed it aside. "You'd best enjoy it while you can."

I awoke the next morning, heavy limbed and sore at the cleft between my legs, but finally free from the worries that had circled over me these past weeks. I noticed for the first time the bristly back of a hedgehog's hide tied over the door for good luck, and wondered at my fortune this far, pondering for a moment whether it would last. I tried to untangle myself from Temujin without waking him, but he reached out and clasped my wrist.

"Stay," he said.

"You don't need me to milk the goats?" I teased. "Or gather dung for the fire?"

"Not today," he said, his fingers moving to caress the underside of my breast. "Perhaps never if I can keep you right here instead."

My body responded to his touch and it didn't take long before my husband was inside me again, both of us gasping at our release. He lay next to me for a moment, then swung his legs over the bed and stretched, every muscle in his body chiseled like the boulders of the sacred hills.

"I leave for Ong Khan's today," he said, shrugging into his leather breeches.

"We won't observe the eight days?" Wedding celebrations traditionally lasted eight full days before the bride's family deserted her. If Temujin left, there would be no reason for my mother to stay any longer. My family was here now, in this tiny tent.

"I must deliver the sable," he said. The stubble of his cheeks scratched my skin as he trailed kisses down my neck. "Don't tell me you'll miss me."

I shrugged, unsure of the answer. "Perhaps I should come with you."

He seemed to consider it as he tied his belt, but then he shook his head. "It's a dangerous journey for any woman, especially you."

I scowled. "I wouldn't slow you down—"

Then I realized what he meant, that he was unwilling to tempt any clans along the way into stealing me and inciting a war. My shoulders slumped, the worries from before settling onto their old perches in my soul.

Temujin kissed my nose. "My brothers and Teb Tengeri will join me to see Ong Khan, but Jamuka will remain here. He'll keep you safe."

I let my husband of one night leave me then, ignoring his brothers' ribald teasing as he kissed me from the door of our *ger*. He walked away with Jamuka, their heads bent in the ever-important discussions of men, while we women remained behind.

I'd done my best to avoid Jamuka since he'd brought Temujin back into my life. Now I'd have to face him whether I cared to or not.

My mother disappeared with Temujin over the horizon that afternoon, for my husband had offered to accompany her cart home to my father before he continued on to Ong Khan. I missed her already, and so it was that Jamuka found me shaking wooden buckets of goat milk and salting the curds with my tears.

"Greetings, Borte Ujin," he said, his voice strangely formal. I recalled the conversation we'd shared on the mountaintop and the way the moon had lit his face, but now I dragged my sleeve across my eyes at his approach.

His easy elegance was out of place in this crude camp, the fine cut of his *deel* and his chiseled features, yet his easy manner now seemed forced, his shoulders squared as if for battle. "I came to see how you fared."

"I'm happy among my new family." I gestured to the bedraggled tents that surrounded us, longing instead to see the bright *gers* and familiar mountains of home. Jamuka studied me and I ducked my head so he wouldn't see my blotchy face.

"You seem as happy as a lost crane," he said. "Just like that night on the mountaintop—"

I held up a hand. "That night never happened."

He stared at me for a moment; then his face hardened. "I see." He straightened and brushed his fine tunic free of imaginary dust. "As you have no need of me here, I'll return to my clan."

"But I thought Temujin asked you to remain—"

"Temujin will return in a few days. Until then you shall have Khasar for protection."

A lone boy to protect me, three old women, and a little girl.

"Does my husband know you would leave his wife and mother to fend for themselves?" I aimed the barb at his retreating back. As much as I preferred Jamuka gone for my own peace of mind, I didn't relish the idea of being left unprotected and surrounded by unknown clans.

He didn't spare me a final glance, as if he couldn't bear to look at me. "My *anda* will understand."

I went back to straining the goat curds and was startled when Hoelun touched me on the elbow, peering through squinted eyes at Jamuka's shrinking silhouette.

"Jamuka leaves our camp in a hurry," she said, both a statement and a question. He took only his horse, leaving the tent he'd shared with Teb Tengeri as the only testament to his existence. "Jamuka has never before gone against his *anda's* wishes."

I shrugged. "He claimed Temujin would understand."

She stared at me overlong, then turned and shuffled toward the *ger*. "I doubt he would," she said, casting a wary glance at me over her shoulder. "At least not yet."

I wiped the sweat from my brow, bent over the fragrant goat-meat-and-onion stew boiling over the cooking stones outside while Hoelun and Mother Khogaghchin worked to stretch the skin of the freshly slaughtered goat. Temujin had returned a week after Jamuka's retreat—puzzled and then annoyed at his *anda*'s disappearance—and we'd fallen into a comfortable routine as I learned that my husband had an insatiable appetite for everything: horses, *airag*, wrestling, hunting. And me.

Ong Khan had received Temujin warmly, exchanging the black sable coat for promises that he would protect Temujin's people. Flush with his victory, Temujin pulled me onto his blankets each night, both of us so eager for each other that we'd often wake throughout the night to rouse the other. I was well loved, and surprised to find I enjoyed my husband's thorough attentions.

"My son uses you well," Hoelun said, straightening to stretch her back. Temulun played at her feet, her fingers tangled in a skein of brown yarn. In the distance Temujin and his younger brother, Khasar, practiced shooting arrows at a bag of feathers strung from a tree. The occasional lucky shot would send a puff of white feathers into the air, like downy leaves twirling to the earth.

"We use each other well," I said, flushing and adding a bit of precious salt to the stew. My arms ached from a morning spent churning butter, turning blocks of fragrant white cheese in the sun, and mixing a cauldron of salt tea with Hoelun's giant iron ladle. Other parts of me ached pleasantly from my night spent in Temujin's arms.

She chuckled. "I pray you will always bring such joy to him. We all hope you will soon gift him with a strong foal."

I'd just buried the bloody rags from my monthly bloods; unclean blood was never burned inside a *ger* because it would offend the spirit of the fire. Hoelun and I both knew there was no child in my womb yet. Hoelun rose then and shuffled past Mother Khogaghchin. "A woman with your gifts would be a prize for any man. A child of Temujin's would mark you as his so other men would be less tempted to lay claim to you."

Mother Khogaghchin raised an eyebrow at me while Hoelun made a great show of sorting through her meager box of dented and mostly broken skinning tools. I ducked my head, recalling the way she'd watched Jamuka ride off only days ago.

I knew then that I'd have to watch myself around my new mother. Hoelun's eyes missed nothing.

Chapter 6

We made plans to break camp and leave the barren cliffs of the Sengur River in search of fresh summer pastures for the animals. The few sheep in Temujin's pitiful herd were sheared, the carts packed, and all the tents save the largest lay dismantled in preparation. We would drink traditional salt tea in the morning before packing everything—including the *ger* poles and the weakest lambs and kids—on the backs of our strongest animals to travel south. I was among the last awake on that fateful night, tormented by the others' snores and the constant pressure of Hoelun's eyes on me.

I drifted toward the world of dreams until a woman's high-pitched scream ripped me back to reality.

At first I thought it was Temulun screaming during a child's nightmare, but then I realized it was Mother Khogaghchin, frantic, her white hair streaming loose behind her like tendrils of the wind.

"Get up," she shrieked. "They're coming to kill us!"

I heard the rumble of approaching horses then, felt the fearful shudder of the Earth Mother. Temujin's enemies had raided his clan countless times during the years we'd been separated, but I'd assumed the alliance with Ong Khan would protect us despite the clans' constant jostling for control of the herds and the spoils of war that would help them survive each winter. My knees trembled as my bowels threatened to turn to water.

"Don't stand there, girl," Khogaghchin yelled, shaking me. "The Tay-ichigud will slaughter us in our beds!"

Hoelun leapt from her blankets, and our meager army of men and boys snapped awake in the face of an assault. The Tayichigud had attacked Temujin before our marriage and weren't likely to forget the insult of his escape from bondage. Temujin slung his bow and arrows over his back, tucked a knife into my boot, and shoved me toward the herds. "Get to the horses!"

I pulled Sochigel toward the wide-eyed animals. The horses pawed nervously at the ground, throwing their manes and snorting as Teb Tengeri pulled himself onto his thick-legged mount without a thought for anyone else. Still running, I realized that Hoelun had fallen behind, dragging Temulun after her. The girl's face was red, and tears streamed down her cheeks.

"Sochigel—"

The old woman nodded, released my arm, and hobbled toward the horses as fast as her old legs could carry her. I ran back to help Temulun, tucking the girl under my arm so Hoelun could clamber onto a dun-colored mare. I passed her daughter up to her.

The first hint of daylight formed a golden backdrop for the growing haze of dust in the east. I turned to find my mount, then gasped at the awful realization.

There weren't enough horses.

"Borte," Temujin hollered, offering his hand. "Let's go!"

"No!" Hoelun yelled, her horse prancing and straining against the reins. "The Tayichigud are after us. They'll steal her if they catch us, just as your father did me!"

"I'd hunt down every last one of them if they did," Temujin shouted.

Cold dread spiraled down into my stomach and filled my mouth with the metallic tang of fear as Temujin echoed the words of my curse. War—and the prophecy of blood and death—would be inevitable if Hoelun spoke the truth.

A silver-white gelding stepped between us, and its rider addressed Temujin, his voice crisp and steady amidst the chaos.

"Your wife will return to you." Teb Tengeri placed one fist over his heart. "I swear it."

"No!" Temujin shouted, shaking his head. His warhorse sidestepped the shaman to stand before me. "My wife comes with us, or we stay and fight."

Nothing in the bones could have prepared me for the decision I now had to make. I couldn't watch Temujin and his family being slaughtered before me, their blood feeding the grasses and their eyes glassy with death.

Bells tinkled behind me and I turned to see Mother Khogaghchin harness a speckled ox to a rickety old cart loaded with wool.

"Borte is safest if she's not with you," she said. "I'll hide her. No one will search an old woman's cart."

"Leave me," I said to Temujin, shocked at the evenness of my voice. I stepped back, lengthening and filling the space between my husband and me with cold air. "I'm safe with Khogaghchin."

The battle in Temujin's heart was written plain on his face. I'd slow his horse if I went with him, and then be forced to witness the inevitable bloodshed. If I stayed behind, at least there was hope for everyone else.

"I won't leave you." He leaned down from his mount, grabbed my hand, and tried to haul me onto his horse's bare back, wasting precious time.

I stood on tiptoes and clasped his forearm. "Everyone here depends on you."

He glanced at his family waiting on their horses, the resolve crumbling on his face. "Wait for me at the Tungelig River," he said, the words hot in my ear as he crushed me to him from atop his horse. "I promise I'll find you again."

My eyes stung, but I took a deep breath of man, earth, and horses. The scent of my husband of only a few days, and the last piece of his soul I might ever possess.

He squeezed my hand, and I felt his deep inhale in my hair. "I love you, Borte Ujin."

"Go!" I choked on the word. "I'll see you soon."

My husband kicked his heels and tore toward the forest with the rest of his family, leaving me alone with an old woman and a speckled ox.

Sochigel already lagged far behind the others, and I offered a quick prayer to the Earth Mother for her protection. Temujin glanced back once and for a moment I both hoped and feared he'd return for me. Instead, he spurred his horse in the ribs and galloped away.

"Hurry, girl!" Mother Khogaghchin waved me toward the cart. "Hide under the wool!"

I dug my way down into the pile of downy wool, as soft and warm as a womb, just as the cart jerked into motion in the direction of Temujin and his family.

"Not that way!" I shoved the wool from my face. "You'll lead the Tay-ichigud straight to everyone. Go toward the raiders!"

Khogaghchin gaped at me as if I'd lost my mind. The dark dust cloud aimed at us grew bigger, hundreds of horses headed toward us as if chased by wolves. "It's their only chance," I said. "Please."

The old woman gnawed her lip with fleshy gums, then flicked the reins. "You're mad as an ibex in mating season," she said. "But you may be right."

The cart turned in an agonizingly slow circle, pointing away from my husband and into the unknown. I ducked under the wool, my heart threatening to break loose from my chest when the thunder of hooves finally surrounded us.

"What's in the cart?"

My throat constricted at the man's accent, the words broken and bent in at least three places. These were not the Tayichigud, but the Merkid, blood enemies of my husband's family and the same people from whom Yesugei had stolen Hoelun. Yet there were three clans of Merkid; I could only hope this wasn't the one Yesugei had wronged.

"Who are you?" the leader shouted. "And where are you going?"

"I'm an old servant of Temujin's mother, with one foot already in my grave," Khogaghchin said. "I helped shear his sheep, and now I'm returning home with my portion of the wool. That is, unless one of you boys would care to remind a dried-up old woman what it's like to have a young man between her legs."

The soldiers laughed and I choked on my shock. "We heard Temujin just filled his bed," the man said. "Is that true?"

"It is, although the girl has the face of a horse."

I scowled at that but bit my tongue.

"We've come to revenge the kidnapping of Hoelun by Yesugei the Brave," the leader said. "Is that Temujin's tent over there?"

I would have snorted had I not been so terrified, but I managed to curse the spirits that these weren't the other two camps of Merkid. Hoelun's kidnapping had likely taken place before these men were born; this was simply a convenient excuse for a raid to steal horses and exert their strength over a weaker clan.

"It is." Khogaghchin smacked her gums and the horses pawed the ground. "I left before the others woke, having helped myself to some extra wool."

The men laughed again and the leader gave the command for them to spread out to find Temujin. Khogaghchin waited until the raiders were behind us to whip the ox. My stomach lurched along with the cart. There were only two remaining outcomes once the Merkid discovered the empty tent: They'd follow Temujin's trail or come back for us. Or both.

I mumbled prayers to the Eternal Blue Sky and the nearby mountain spirits, tasting the wool amidst the smell of my own fear. This was no usual raid. It was revenge.

We heard Temujin just filled his bed.

And I was the target.

There was a delicate balance of power on the steppes that was upset when men from the lesser clans thought to grab power from those with better grazing lands and stronger herds. It was an unfortunate and terrifying truth that women were often stolen along with the horses they'd once herded, and were raped and forced to live as wives to the thieves who had ripped them from their hearths and families. Yesugei had raided the Merkid years ago to steal Hoelun and had set into motion a spiral of revenge and hatred that continued even now that his bones had turned to dust.

These men came to avenge Hoelun, yet it was she who had suggested Temujin abandon me. I wondered for a moment which trickster spirit had a hand in this game, but there was a crack and the cart lurched again. I swallowed my scream, wondering if the Merkid had redoubled to attack. Mother Khogaghchin's blood might be feeding the grasses of the steppe now.

"Horseshit!"

My relief at Khogaghchin's curse was short-lived. I peered through the downy cloud of black wool and moaned in horror at the sight before me.

Dawn was beginning to stretch fully across the sky, illuminating the hopelessness of our situation. Built for strength and not for speed, the rickety old cart had snapped its axle. The crossbar had splintered and one wheel was askew.

Before us lay the open steppe, and behind us, the abandoned tents and the raiders. Beyond that was the security of the forest. We might as well wish for a friendly north wind to swoop down and carry us to safety.

There was only one choice, impossible though it was.

I clambered out of the cart. "We'll have to run for the woods."

Khogaghchin squinted in the direction of the mountains and gave a strangled laugh. "These old legs of mine won't make it halfway there."

"I'll carry you."

It was hopeless and we both knew it, but perhaps some ancestor spirit would send the Tayichigud in the opposite direction if we made a wide enough circle. It was the only option save waiting for their inevitable attack.

The old woman stared at me in disbelief. "The face of a horse and stubborn as a goat. I don't know why Temujin married you."

I crouched and motioned for her to climb onto my back. "We don't have much time."

The storm of hooves and dust changed direction, doubling back toward us.

"Too late," Khogaghchin hissed, throwing wool at me. "Get back in the cart and don't make a sound."

I huddled down into the wool, breathing in the heavy scent of lanolin and my own terror. The rumble of horses surrounded us, and then came the muffled grunts of a struggle.

"I told you—I'm just carrying wool," Khogaghchin said, but panic threaded her voice.

The man from before barked at his men. "Get off your horses, you lazy yaks, and see what—or who—is in there."

Men dismounted and stomped toward me. The cart door creaked and hands pulled off the precious wool, as if digging me out of a cave. But instead of the light of freedom, they pulled me into the darkness of the enslaved.

"She's here." Greedy eyes and two lines of brown teeth leered at me. The soldier yanked me out by my hair, but I gritted my teeth against the pain. I would never let them see my fear.

Another raider held Mother Khogaghchin, her spindly arms pinned behind her back. A third woman was slung over a Merkid horse, her feet hanging down so I could see her beaded moccasins. Silent Sochigel, so proud of her needlework.

"Two old women and a useless slave," I lied, stumbling as the brown-toothed raider pushed me from the cart into the dirt. I scrambled to my feet. "I hope you're proud of yourselves."

Three men looked down at me from their horses, their feathered helmets and tasseled gold belts proclaiming their positions as chiefs. "I am Toghtoga, chief of the Merkid," one said. His nose was big and flat, as if he'd been hit in the face with a heavy pan, and his belt was decorated with the imprint of golden arrows and tied with thick knots of black leather tassels. "Long ago, Yesugei the Brave stole Hoelun from our brother Chiledu. It's taken a generation, but we've finally found revenge on the clan of Yesugei and Temujin."

"I care little for the history of your clan's petty squabbles," I said, crossing my arms over my chest. "Only that you release us."

His grin made me shudder.

"No slave speaks with such fire and surety." The flat-faced chief leaned down to caress my cheek, ignoring my recoil. "You were Temujin's wife, at least until today."

I narrowed my eyes at him. "I'm still Temujin's wife."

"Not anymore, girl," he said. "Now you belong to the Merkid."

· · ·

They gave me to a thick-necked warrior named Chilger the Athlete.

He was the youngest brother of Chiledu—Hoelun's first husband, whom she'd been stolen from—so the Merkid claimed that justice had been done as they bound my wrists and gagged me with a horsehair rag. Chilger plucked me from the ground onto the saddle before him and backhanded me when I struggled, leaving me with white spots in my eyes and a ringing in my ears. "You're a sweet little thing," he said, squinting so his eyes gleamed like black beetles. He twisted my hair around his hand like a guide rope, as the other slipped to my breast and gave it a painful squeeze. "I've a mind to brand you right now."

"Enough, Chilger." The flat-nosed chief glared. "We don't have time for games. You can enjoy your prize later."

Mother Khogaghchin was flung over a horse as well, claimed as a slave like Sochigel, and together we set off in Temujin's direction again, galloping so that my backside rubbed against the hardness of Chilger's desire.

We rode through thickets and swamps toward the khan of all mountains, Mount Burkhan Khaldun, with its forest so dense that a snake could barely slip among the trees. Three times we circled the mountain in pursuit of Temujin, until the sun set and wolves howled in the distance. Mother Khogaghchin slumped against her captor, a grizzled old warrior, her pink mouth open in sleep. Sochigel still hadn't regained consciousness. I sat as stiff as a tent pole, trying to avoid contact with Chilger despite his arm tight around my waist. Although I was bound and helpless, the cold length of Temujin's knife in my boot reassured me, overlooked by the Merkid in their haste to track my husband.

"We have what we came for." The flat-nosed chief spoke to the other two, the wind carrying his words. "There's no point in further pursuit. Revenge is ours."

The three conversed for a moment more, then separated and raised their fists in a salute. Every Merkid warrior lifted his voice in a chilling victory cry that shook the sleeping crows from the trees and made my mouth go dry.

I wondered if Temujin heard the shout, if he would come for me.

Or if I could escape.

As if reading my thoughts, Chilger's arm around me tightened. We turned and galloped away from the mountains, each step taking me farther from my family. The horsehair gag muffled my cry of pain when we finally stopped and Chilger dragged me from the saddle of his brown warhorse. The men hooted and leered, many of them already guzzling *airag* from their leather flasks and gnawing thick strips of dried horsemeat between their teeth. I hadn't eaten since the night before—nestled under Temujin's arm and laughing while his sister tried to juggle balls of felt—and now my stomach roiled with fear and hunger.

But it wasn't to feed me that Chilger dragged me to the shadows near one of the fires. He unbuckled his belt and pulled down his trousers, his member springing stiff and ready from its nest of dark hair.

My hands still bound in front of me, I tried to scramble away, but he yanked me back so hard my neck threatened to snap.

"I like one with a little fight still in her," he said, keeping one hand in my hair and the other shoving up my caftan.

I lashed at his face, aiming for his eyes, but he only laughed at me, at least until I drew Temujin's knife from my boot.

With my wrists still bound, there was never any real chance I'd escape, only the desperate hope of freedom. Before I even straightened, Chilger's boulder of a fist crashed into the side of my head and the knife went flying. The ground slammed into the other side of my face, my cheek skidding across the dirt and pebbles. The heat of the fire licked my forehead.

And then a new fire.

I screamed into the gag as Chilger entered me from behind, his hand digging into my buttocks as he rode me like a horse. The shouts of encouragement and heat of the fire faded until there was nothing but the ground before me and Chilger pounding into me.

When he finished, I lay discarded by the fire, battered and alone. Someone poked my ribs with his boot, then stumbled off with a roar of laughter, splashing my face with *airag*. I became aware of other pains as I slowly returned to my body, tiny pinpricks of agony joining the fire between my legs. My palms were speckled with blood like a bird's egg, tiny pebbles embedded deep in the flesh.

A public rape.

Even if I escaped, Temujin would never want me now. I wished for death then, for my soul to fly free of the violated flesh and sinews that made up my broken body and be reborn in the sacred mountains.

Around me, the men continued to drink and a wrestling match started on the other side of the fire. I curled into myself, unable to stop the tremors that spread from my heart to my fingertips, setting my teeth chattering.

Then came the gentle touch on the back of my head, as soft as a bird's wing as the gag was removed. I flinched and turned away.

"Hush, little goat." Mother Khogaghchin tucked my hair behind my ears and righted my twisted caftan. "Can you stand?"

I shook my head, unable to speak. Now I finally understood Sochigel's silence in the face of such misery. I wanted nothing more in that moment than for death to find me.

"Don't let them see your tears," the old woman said. I bit back the cry of pain as she pulled me to my feet, as unsteady as a newborn colt. "These sort of men are like wolves—they feed off your fear."

"Woman!" The grizzled old warrior who had claimed Khogaghchin as his slave waved his cup in our direction, sloshing *airag* over the side. At her age, and with the smell of urine that always clung to her, surely Khogaghchin was safe from what I'd just endured. "Where do you think you're going?"

Khogaghchin waved him away. Her hands were also bound, but much looser. No doubt she hadn't tried to stab anyone.

"She needs to be cleaned before her husband can ride her again," she said, her face matching their leer. "It will only take a moment."

Husband. My sodden mind couldn't decipher what Khogaghchin meant by that.

"Let them go," Toghtoga said, waving his cup in our direction. "The old woman can barely hobble and the girl will walk so bowlegged we'd be able to catch her no matter how fast she tried to run."

My entire body burned with shame as we stumbled away from the fire and into the black chill of night, skirting the other campfires to find a tiny creek. It was forbidden to defile lakes or rivers with human filth, but my blood and Chilger's seed scorched a trail of contamination down my legs, making me feel like I might never be clean again. I plunged into the black water with a violent splash, wishing it might wash away my soul and leave this desecrated body for the carrion. Hot tears of humiliation poured down my cheeks and I splashed them away until Mother Khogaghchin looped her arms over me, her coarse voice crooning softly in my ear. Only then did I notice that she, too, had washed herself. Perhaps not even age was a protection against these demons that disguised themselves as men.

"That beast is not my husband," I sobbed, finally realizing the full extent of her earlier words. I had lost more than I realized when Chilger claimed me.

"This is how things go for women among the warring clans. You led a peaceful life, sheltered by the clan of your father, but no more." Khogaghchin removed her arms and gave me a sad smile. "You are a Merkid bride now, whether you wish it or not."

I shook my head so hard my teeth rattled. "No. I married Temujin—"

"Chilger has had you," Khogaghchin repeated. "And he's going to want to have you again." She clasped my face between leathery palms, her wrists still bound. "Your old life no longer exists."

I hissed in pain as she used a handful of wet river grass to clean the scrape on my cheek. "Then I'll escape."

"Where will you go?" She scrubbed harder now. "You don't know where Temujin is any more than the Merkid do." She threw the grass in the water and heaved a great sigh. "He let you go, Borte. Temujin won't risk his entire family for a mere woman."

He let you go.

But that wasn't true. I had told Temujin to leave me, but I also knew he wouldn't come for me, not once word of what had just happened spread across the steppes. I belonged to another man now, and Temujin would be a fool to try to rescue me, outnumbered as he was by the Merkid.

I knew now that women were only the playthings of men, to be used when convenient and discarded later. With my body bruised and my soul battered, I even doubted the pleasure I'd once found in Temujin's arms, tainted as it was now by the sharp pebbles still embedded in my palms and the throbbing pain between my legs.

If I hoped to escape, it wouldn't be at my husband's hands, or at those of any other man for that matter. I would rely only on my cunning and my own two feet.

Chapter 7

"Borte!"

I cringed at Chilger's bellow, then grimaced at the newest pain in my face. I'd belonged to the Merkid for two cycles of the moon, and in the first days I'd done nothing but contemplate escape, yet there was no scenario that allowed me to take Khogaghchin and Sochigel with me. Their steady presence at the river each afternoon when we drew water was the only bright spot in these dark days, but the old women's presence also shackled me to this life. Each morning I buried the bloody bandages from the gashes Chilger gifted me on my face, my legs, and my ribs, along with the soiled rags from my monthly bloods. But now my women's bloods were weeks overdue, my breasts sore, and my stomach sour in the morning.

The foul beast had planted a child in me.

Now I had to decide which to sacrifice: the life of a child, or the lives of two elderly women.

We'd traveled to the Kilgho River, where the riverweeds grew as thick as an old man's beard and the stones at the bottom of the creek were polished as bright as camel eyes. The Merkid lashed reeds together to float across to the Bugura Steppe, a barren land full of winds that howled louder than lonely spirits. I'd spent part of the afternoon on the edge of a ravine, allowing the memories of my old life to comfort and strangle me at the same time, contemplating throwing myself from the cliff ledge and putting an end to my troubles. I pictured my body flying, diving like an eagle, and then my spirit soaring to the mountains.

I touched my stomach and tucked away the dream as I picked my way along the path to camp, casting longing glances at the rocky ledge that seemed to beckon me back, the dappled sunlight so delicate and peaceful on this earth.

The night before, Chilger had beaten me after he'd discovered the gashes on my wrists. I'd used Temujin's wolf tooth to cut my flesh, begging the spirits to carry my soul to the sacred mountains. Chilger now wore my husband's necklace around his own thick neck, a reminder that he could take from me anything he pleased. However, he'd left off my shackles, apparently deciding that the cuts on my wrists were proof that I'd been sufficiently broken and would rather die than contemplate escape.

My gift of sight had deserted me in the face of this nightmare, but I was thankful Mother Khogaghchin was still with me to keep my mind tethered. She was constantly accompanied by Toghtoga's future daughter-in-marriage, a hardy girl named Toregene. The child reminded me of Temulun with her downcast eyes and her constant humming that floated like birdsong from her throat.

This life would slowly kill me, but with my chains gone, there was another escape outside of death that made the colors of the leaves and sky bolder, the crunch of pebbles underfoot louder. I touched my belly again, the child that was surely growing there.

It would happen tonight.

The day was like all the others before it, including the blow to the cheek I took after Chilger ate his *kefir*, claiming I hadn't mixed the mare's milk with the grain properly. He rolled away when he finished with me, grunted once, and fell into the sleep of the dead while flies buzzed overhead, trapped by the closed smoke hole. I scrubbed the sacred triangle between my legs with a dirty rag from the leather bucket of lukewarm water by the hearth. My stomach heaved at the stench of sex and sweat, but I pressed my nose into an old horse blanket until I was calm again.

Tucked in Chilger's belt was the knife he'd stolen from me, gleaming dully in the faint glow cast by the embers. I'd never considered harming anyone—much less killing a man—before the Merkid had claimed me, but I desperately wished to stab the blade between his ribs, to watch the shock in his eyes fade to death as I cleaved open his chest.

But I couldn't chance it. The men in other *gers* around us might wake, and then I'd be captured and handed off to the next man, back where I had started, or perhaps even worse.

One day I'd have my revenge on Chilger. I'd sworn that promise to every spirit I could name since that first night by the campfire.

I waited until there were no sounds save Chilger's occasional snort and the low whinny of a horse outside. Then I tiptoed into the cold night air.

Tethered to a lead line stood Chilger's brown warhorse with its stocky legs, a beast as mean as his owner, and one I wouldn't dare touch. But behind him, asleep on her feet, was a yellow mare with a bony knob at her withers. Not a pretty mount, but a strong one.

I stepped around the stallion, opening my palm to the mare as I touched her muzzle. She sniffed my hand, her soft lips closing around the wild chives I'd brought as a bribe.

I undid her ropes, surprised at the ease with which I led her away from the camp. After two months of my docility, it must never have occurred to Chilger that I would try to escape. He knew not of the babe in my womb, or that I would rather die than let any child of mine be claimed and raised by such a beast of a father. I sent a silent prayer for forgiveness as I passed the *gers* where I knew Khogaghchin and Sochigel slept. Once we were far enough away, I swung myself onto the mare's back, clenching her bare sides with my bruised thighs. This promised to be a painful ride, but I gave her ribs a gentle kick and we started into a trot before surging into a gallop. If I could push her until morning, we might have a chance.

If not, I'd soon be left for the wolves, and she'd likely end up in a stewpot.

I don't know how long we'd traveled before the rumble of horses came from behind us. A fearful glance over my shoulder revealed a man melded to his stallion, lit by white moonlight like the shade of some ancestor long since dead, and flanked by an army of men with faces like skulls in the moonlight.

Chilger.

I screamed until my throat was raw and the mare galloped as if flames nipped her hooves. But it wasn't enough.

Slowly, Chilger and the others caught up with us. Hot tears cut swaths down my cheeks when Chilger pulled alongside the mare. One strike of his shoulder sent me flying, and I tumbled from my horse's back, blinded by the white flash of pain as I hit the ground. I gasped for air like I was drowning, but my lungs wouldn't fill. Then the blows began, a thunderstorm of fists.

At first I fought back, but I was no match for the onslaught.

I felt the lightning of shattering bones and the skin of my forehead ripping open. And then a merciful darkness pulled me into its black maw and away from the hell I'd created.

A child hummed in my dream, a somber tune that reminded me of black crows and crisp winter ice. My left eye wouldn't open and every joint and rib cried out in pain. The song stopped when I moaned at the soft hand against my forehead.

"Poor, stupid girl."

I peered through my good eye to see Mother Khogaghchin's scowl, her lips pursed tight. Toghtoga's future daughter-in-marriage, Toregene, hovered at her elbow. I'd seen the child—I guessed she'd seen nine or ten summers—only from afar, but now when her gaze flicked up at me I realized why she kept her eyes hidden. One eye was brown and the other a hazy gold, beautiful but disconcerting. For the first time in ages, my fingers itched for the bones. Hers was a future I would like to cast.

"Chilger beat you within a breath of your life." Khogaghchin dabbed my lip with a red-streaked rag that smelled of metal and milk, then handed it to the girl. "You'll have a scar here to rival any warrior's."

"It feels like a herd of horses trampled me." I tried to shift on my pile of blankets to get more comfortable, but the movement only brought on fresh daggers of pain.

She clucked at me. "You were drenched in your own blood when they dragged you back to camp. Sochigel and I stitched up the worst of your wounds and Toregene has been helping me entice you back to life." Khogaghchin's brows knitted together, then softened. "The colt is still in your belly. Your son is a strong one, not to flee during such an attack."

Despair crashed upon me with the remembrance that I carried Chilger's child. Death beckoned me with its promise of peace, but I would not carry a child to the sacred mountains with me, nor could I bring a babe into this world to be raised by Chilger. It would be better for both of us if the baby never lived to be born. Yet what sort of mother was I to wish for my child's death?

I opened my mouth to speak, but only sobs escaped. Mother Khogaghchin gathered me into her arms. "There, there, little goat. It's not important whose colt grows in your belly. Only the womb that houses him matters."

I tried to rise, but pain lanced through my body and shrill bells rang in my head. Toregene scampered to my side with a cup of restorative cow's blood, still warm—the girl was so quiet I had forgotten she was there. "I've cleaned your wounds with milk from a camel that just gave birth for the first time," she said, ducking her eyes. "To speed the healing."

"Stay and rest," Khogaghchin said to me. "I'll do my best to keep Chilger away."

I drank the blood, taking the animal's strength into my body. I thought to stay awake as Khogaghchin slipped from the *ger*, but my broken body was defenseless against the pull of sleep. Caught between dreams and reality, I felt two small hands on my stomach, accompanied by the hum of a child's lullaby. Toregene looked down on me, her expression terribly solemn for one so young. She shifted and the firelight caught the gleam of silver at her throat, a talisman in the shape of a cross.

"What's that?" I asked, finding the strength to brush my fingers against the warm metal. I'd seen a token like that only once before, on a day when someone dear had left me.

Her face softened. "The symbol of my father's god," she said. "Christ."

"Christ," I repeated. I'd heard the name once or twice on travelers' lips, for the people of the steppes were a practical lot, trading gods as we did horses. Most felt it was best to respect all the gods—including those born in foreign lands—rather than offend any. "He is the god of your father," I said. "And also your own?"

She nodded and caressed the silver talisman. "He died on a cross like this. I try to think of his suffering when I'm sad or lonely."

"Are you often sad?" My bruised heart throbbed for this girl, younger than I'd been when my clan had made me an outcast.

She nodded, and her gaze skittered to the door as if she feared we might be interrupted. "My mother went to the sacred mountains the night I was born. My father left after she died, but he returned last year with a new wife. He couldn't bear to look at me when he came back, to remember how I'd murdered the wife of his heart."

I clasped her hand, although she spoke as if the words were so old that they no longer hurt her. "I'm so sorry."

"I watched my father marry his Unigirad bride before he sent me away. He wore new boots, embroidered by all the Naiman women of our clan, and she wore a dress as red as poppies."

I breathed the name that sprang to my mind, unbidden like a blossom in snow. "Gurbesu."

"Your friend spoke often of you, Borte Ujin." Toregene smiled at me then, the simple gesture transforming her plain face and making her mismatched eyes shine.

It seemed lifetimes since Gurbesu had left me, promising we'd meet again. How I wished we could go back to those summer days, when the spirits were kinder and life was simpler.

"Your father gave you that cross?" I asked. I knew I'd recognized Toregene's cross, on her father's neck before he'd married my friend.

"When he sent me here," Toregene said. "He said it would give me strength, along with Christ's love." She bit her lip, as if perhaps a bit of silver and the love of a foreign god still hadn't fully shielded her heart. "I won't marry Toghtoga's son until I'm older, and there's no one here I can really talk to. I thought perhaps this baby could be like a brother to me, if you'd let him?"

My soul lightened at this child's simple hope, the tentative way her fingers crept toward mine. "I think that would make him the luckiest baby in the world," I whispered. "Although that would make you my daughter as well."

She giggled, her hands splayed over her mouth. "I'd like that."

And that night, instead of searching for sleep amidst Chilger's snores and my body's fresh pains, I recalled Toregene's smile and the happy lilt of her humming, which carried me to my dreams.

Days passed into a week. Or perhaps two.

Khogaghchin and Toregene kept me drugged with poppy juice, but despite their gentle hands, the pain and terror of my beating often followed me into my nightmares. Once I woke to see Chilger hovering over me, felt him moving inside me, and cried out in agony.

I knew not whether that was a nightmare or reality.

I emerged from a restless sleep to the angry screech of a hawk, yet it took my drugged mind a moment to realize that clamor outside was no bird, but the garbled screams of horses and men, terrified mothers and children. Alone in the *ger*, I scrambled from my pile of blankets and crawled to the door, opening it to reveal a scene worse than any nightmare.

The setting sun scalded the horizon and raiders swarmed over the camp like bloodthirsty locusts, hacking with swords and spears at anything in their path—horses, carts, and even human flesh. Blood spattered the earth before me and tents at the edge of camp were already aflame, the air full of angry sparks and horrified screams.

I cried out in fear as someone stumbled toward me, then sagged with relief at Mother Khogaghchin's wrinkled face. She hauled me to my feet with surprising strength for one so ancient. "Do you think I'd nurse you back to health just to see you slaughtered by a band of raiders?" she asked.

"Toregene." I grasped Khogaghchin's wrist. "Where is she?"

"I saw her flee into the woods," she said. "We'll find her."

I ignored my aching bones and we plunged into the maelstrom, but we didn't take more than a few steps before a Merkid woman saw us. She stopped suddenly, her mouth open in a silent scream. A gush of crimson spilled down her chin and over her *deel*, and then she fell forward, revealing a soldier with gnarled black hair and a blade smeared with her blood. His lips split in a maniacal grin at the sight of Mother Khogaghchin and me.

We ran.

Hand in hand, we skirted *gers* aflame like pitiful piles of kindling. Raiders crawled over tents not yet burning, jumping down the smoke holes to slaughter those within before setting torches to the felts. Others beat down tent frames and trampled the scorched wool panels, stomping them into the mud and blood. One soldier carried an armful of Spirit Banners while another hacked down Toghtoga's doorway, the home of his guardian spirit. These men sought the annihilation not only of Toghtoga's earthly clan, but of their ancestors, too.

A man's voice cut through the dark. "Find the women!"

A horse charged out of the crowd and into the darkness, the rider's bloody sword held high. He snarled like a demon wolf dragged from the spirit world, but beneath the mask of bloodlust, I knew that face.

"Temujin!"

I ran to him, the moon and crackle of fire behind me, to seize the reins of his horse. His blade hovered over my head, and I waited for it to come down, to end this terrible ordeal. Then Temujin dropped the sword and in a breath he was down from his horse, clasping me to him so hard I thought my bruised ribs would shatter.

He kissed me, tasting of smoke and death. Despite the destruction around us, I felt safe for the first time in months.

Temujin's hands wove into my hair, as if he feared I might slip away. "The mountain spirits led me here, Borte Ujin." He leaned back then and his expression fractured. "Gods, Borte, what have they done to you?"

I winced as he touched my scarred lip. All the emotions I'd held at bay these past months pummeled me then, but I swallowed the sobs and bile that welled in my throat. Temujin motioned to the crowd of soldiers behind him, and two mounted men stepped forward. The first was Khasar, his younger brother, but the second was a face I knew too well.

Jamuka.

There was a flash of some emotion across his face, and then his expression smoothed into its perpetual mask. "We searched long and hard for you, Borte Ujin," he said, but his voice was as taut as a bowstring pulled too tight.

It took me a long moment to recover from seeing both him and Temujin. "I'd have died many deaths had it not been for Mother Khogaghchin," I finally said, gesturing to the old woman behind me. I knew now that the spirits had sent her to protect and guide me, a precious well of strength disguised by her many years and fragile bones.

Temujin clenched his fist across his heart and bowed to Khogaghchin, giving her an honor I'd never seen bestowed on a childless widow. "Then there shall always be a place for you before my hearth."

"Thank you, Temujin of the Borijin." Khogaghchin stuttered for a moment, then bowed her head. "I've never encountered such kindness in all my years on this earth."

"The Merkid are finished," Jamuka said to my husband, the screams behind us having fallen silent, replaced with the hiss and heat of hungry flames. "Shall we stay or return to the hills?"

"I've found what I came for." Temujin's arm around me tightened, his stiff armor cutting into my skin and reminding me I was still alive. "We'll camp here tonight and then return to the mountains."

"And the rest of the Merkid?" Jamuka gestured to the piles of burned felt that had been the Merkid tents, their wild-eyed horses rearing as they were rounded up as spoils of war, along with a huddle of pitiful women and sobbing children.

"Take them as slaves," Temujin said.

He looked about to say more, but just then a man broke from the shadows, a battle cry erupting from his throat that would have turned the knees of the most hardened warrior to water. He barreled toward us, bare chested and drenched in blood.

Chilger.

I screamed in terror as Jamuka pitched forward, his curved sword flashing with fire and moonlight. His blade caught Chilger's side and the Merkid beast howled in pain. Fury and terror toward this man overwhelmed me, but I found myself rooted where I stood at the same time Jamuka knocked him to the ground, using the wrestling move I'd once witnessed on a crisp autumn day, lifetimes ago. Khasar poised his sword over Chilger's heaving chest. Temujin motioned him to lower the blade, then glowered down at him as if he were some sort of insect.

"We'll shed no more Merkid blood," he said.

But Chilger leered at me, stretching out his thick neck as if to taunt Khasar. "Who is this, Borte?" he asked.

Temujin glanced at me and then stared at Chilger, studying his fat face and the arms as thick as birch trunks. "Borte," he said slowly, keeping his eyes on Chilger. "How does this man know you?"

The words wouldn't come, blown into the wind like seeds on a summer day.

"He is Chilger the Athlete," Mother Khogaghchin finally spoke. "Chiledu's younger brother. They gave Borte to him."

Jamuka uttered a curse under his breath and Temujin's face darkened like a thundercloud passing over the sun. Chilger spat at my feet. "I took Borte into my tent," he said, "and in return, the she-wolf has caused a plague to rain upon my clan. I wish I'd killed her when I had the chance."

And then, before the blade could come down, Chilger jumped to his feet and punched Khasar in the face, doubling him over. Then Chilger took off in the direction of the nearby canyons, where only weeks before I'd almost taken my own life.

Jamuka launched himself onto his horse to pursue, but Temujin's barked order stopped him. My husband's face was etched as hard as a mountain. "Let him go," he said. "The canyons are no place for a man alone. He'll be dead by morning."

Jamuka's hands tightened into fists that mirrored my own. "He has dishonored Borte. For that he deserves to die a most terrible death."

"My wife has not been dishonored." My husband touched my arm and I flinched when he caressed a cut on my brow, still healing. "It seems to me she still bears the scars of a battle well fought."

"Then let me end the battle," Jamuka protested, his hand tightening on the hilt of his sword. "For your honor."

"We brought honor to my clan today," he said to Jamuka, "because you and Ong Khan's soldiers joined me to retrieve the wife of my heart. We've watered the steppes with the blood of the Merkid warriors and emptied their beds of their sons." His arm tightened around me. "And now we'll return home as soon as their women have scattered the ashes of the dead."

I wanted to scream and rail against him then. Chilger should suffer for what he'd done to me; I should have the revenge of watching his lifeblood leak from the demon's body. But as I looked around me at the smoldering ruin of the Merkid camp, I realized with a shudder that too much blood had already been spilled in my name. Despite all my sacrifices, my prophecy had come to pass in a storm of blood and fire.

My hand brushed my belly, the promise of life amidst so much death, and I cringed. It mattered not what happened to Chilger, for I'd never be free of him.

I woke to a darkness as black as the longest winter night, the fire having burned out after I'd finally crawled onto a horse blanket in Temujin's hastily erected tent. Ong Khan's men had returned with word of a Borijin woman wearing embroidered slippers who had fled into the woods rather than return to her family and had yet to be found. Sochigel was too proud to return now that she'd been dishonored by the Merkid, and while I envied her silent conviction, I found that my greed for life was too great to yearn for death any longer.

The ashes of the dead Merkid clung to my skin and nose, filling my mouth with the despair and lost hopes of the dead. I reached out a frantic hand for Temujin, needing his solid warmth to banish the terror that crowded my heart.

But there was no reassuring heat from my husband's side of the pallet, not even an indent from his body. He'd never returned to the *ger*.

I sat on the pallet, legs crossed, my anger at Temujin increasing tenfold with each passing moment. My husband hadn't apologized for abandoning me the night of the raid, hadn't asked toward my treatment by the Merkid, but instead he'd left me again to go gallivanting about in the dark, probably to seize more Merkid treasures for himself. I drew deep, calming breaths and had almost swallowed my craving for the poppy juice when footsteps prowling around the *ger* made my heart skip a beat.

My thoughts flew to Chilger, returned from the canyon to steal me again, and I searched for a weapon, but my fingers found only my discarded leather boots. I held one ready to lob at my intruder as the tent flap lifted, revealing the dull orange glow of a nearby fire.

"Borte?"

I expected an angry Merkid bent on revenge, or Temujin returning from wherever he'd disappeared to. My heart thudded a nervous beat at the unexpected voice.

"You shouldn't be here, Jamuka."

He exhaled and I caught a hint of his smell—pine and man. I didn't know whether to stop breathing or draw the scent deep into my lungs.

"I heard you cry out," he said, ducking to step over the threshold of the tent. He straightened, almost a full head taller than Temujin. "Are you all right?"

"Did you find Toregene?" I asked, ignoring his question. It was only after the men had promised to search for her that I'd agreed to rest. Now I wondered if that had been a mistake, if I should have combed the woods for her myself. Toregene was an intelligent child; she'd know not to come to a strange man calling her name.

"No, but we'll keep looking." His eyes must have adjusted to the darkness, for he laughed then. "What were you going to do with the boot? Throw it at me?"

I hadn't realized I still held it. I set it down with a laugh, small chortles at first that quickly transformed into a torrent of tears that poured down my cheeks. "I'm not right in the head just now," I finally choked out. "I fear I may never be again."

I knew then that Chilger had damaged my spirit as well as my body. Jamuka let my words settle in the dark before he responded. "Life changes us, Borte Ujin. In ways we could never anticipate."

I caught a glimpse of his face, the glow of firelight making sharp the angles and hollows of his cheekbones. But it was his eyes that stole my breath, the naked yearning exposed there.

"Where is my husband?" My voice was too loud, threatened as I was by this fresh danger.

"He'll return soon," he said, his eyes as mournful as they'd been the night of my marriage.

"Thank you for helping Temujin," I said, for there was nothing else to say. Still, my words seemed pitifully inadequate.

"I didn't do it for Temujin," he said. "I did it for you."

My mind was a flurry of emotions, none of which made any sense. "Jamuka—"

"I left after your marriage to avoid disgracing myself with my feelings for my *anda*'s wife," he said. "And I'll never forgive myself for not being there to protect you when the Merkid came."

All the right words, all from the wrong man.

"I've tried so hard to fight this." Jamuka's voice rasped and I caught the faint scent of *airag* on his breath. Suddenly the grace of Jamuka's white-boned heritage fled and he stood in front of me, just a man before a woman.

The anguish on Jamuka's face was raw, more powerful than his words. He shuddered when I touched his cheek and he clasped his hand over mine, our fingers twining tight as if they belonged together.

"I love you, Borte Ujin," he said. "From the moment I laid eyes on you."

I drew away. "You can't say such things—"

"No," he said. "I *must* say them. I swore if we found you that I'd tell you how I felt, come what may. I might be a fool, but I'm not a coward." He held both of my hands, the touch of our palms so insignificant and yet so intimate. "What do you want, Borte? To stay here with Temujin?"

It was an unfair question, come too soon after this second raid, yet I could see that it cost him dearly when I didn't answer.

"You'll stay with him, won't you?" he asked. His shoulders slumped and the fire in his eyes banked. "Because it's the honorable thing to do."

I laid my hand on the thick leather armor over his chest. "I'm far from honorable," I said, tasting the bitter tang of the words before I spoke them. "I'm pregnant."

He stepped back as if I'd scalded him. "You carry Temujin's son?" He gave a strangled cry. "He gains all and I lose everything."

I didn't have a chance to correct him. Men murmured outside and Jamuka widened the distance between us as the tent flap opened. Temujin's unmistakable scent of smoke and horseflesh filled the *ger*.

"There you are," I said, quashing my flutter of nerves at being caught alone with Jamuka, but if Temujin thought it odd that his *anda* was in his tent, he gave no indication. "Where have you been all night?" I asked.

He grunted. "Dealing with the rest of the Merkid."

"So you left me alone and unprotected?" My voice turned frigid. "Again?"

I couldn't see my husband well in the dark, but his head jerked toward Jamuka as he kicked his boots off. "I didn't leave you alone. Jamuka returned from the woods to stand guard."

If only he knew the danger Jamuka posed. "Did you accomplish all you intended?" Jamuka asked, once again the white-boned noble.

Temujin grunted. "I did."

"Good." Jamuka glanced at me in such a way that I knew they were hiding something. "Then I'll leave you now to assist with directing the distribution of the Merkid spoils."

"My share must be divided evenly," Temujin said. "Make sure every man who fought receives his portion."

Jamuka bowed over his fist. "As you wish."

"Jamuka was the first to answer my call to arms to search for you," Temujin said after the tent flap fell behind him. "He's the best man I've ever met."

"Better than you," I muttered.

"What?"

"You let the Merkid take me," I said, despising the note of hysteria that crept into my voice. "I thought you'd come back for me, and now you've let Chilger escape—"

I pressed my fist against my lips to stop myself from saying more. I expected him to hit me then, but he only offered his hands in surrender.

"I don't deserve anything from you," Temujin said, "but I beg one favor from you, wife of my heart."

I glared at him. "And what is that?"

"Hit me. Or kick me. As hard as you can. And as many times as you want."

My jaw fell to my chest. "You've gone mad."

He shrugged, but the effort seemed to cost him. "You're angry. When a man is angry, he hits things. Or kills someone. As you're stronger than most men I know, I suspect that the same could be said for you. I've no wish to die, but it can't hurt to let you beat me."

I scoffed, but after a moment's hesitation I let my fists fly and kicked him as hard as I could manage, releasing all the pent-up rage of the past months, growing ever angrier when I realized my full force wasn't affecting my husband. At first he stood as still as a boulder, but he changed tactics once my nails came away with skin. "I made a terrible mistake, Borte Ujin, one I'll never make again," he murmured into my ear even as I jerked away and he struggled to subdue me. "I'll protect you to my dying breath, but you have to let me."

I finally allowed the warmth of his body and the rhythm of his breath to calm me. Only then did I realize his chest was damp.

I drew back, half-blind in the dark. His shirt smelled not of the salt of sweat, but of a familiar metallic tang, there above the smoke and horse-flesh.

Blood. Not the cold blood of the dead Merkid where they fell with the night, but something fresher.

"What is this?" I drew back, holding out my hands and feeling the film of death upon them. "Whose blood have you spilled?"

As if another death mattered after so much slaughter. Yet something—perhaps my sight or a persistent spirit—whispered that it did.

The silence held so long that I feared he wouldn't answer, but he finally touched my outstretched hands, mingling life and death. He sighed then, and I knew what his answer would be even before he held out the wolf-tooth necklace.

"Chilger will never hurt you again."

My heart soared as if broken free of invisible chains, knowing I would never again have to fear Chilger's intrusion in the night. My fingers curled around the familiar token, now blackened with the blood of the man who had sought to break me. Temujin had carried out my revenge on Chilger, had taken the stain of cold-blooded murder on his soul for the second time since his brother's death. But then I remembered the child I carried and knew that neither Temujin nor I would ever be free from Chilger even as I recalled Mother Khogaghchin's words.

It's not important whose colt grows in your belly. Only the womb that houses him matters.

Yet it did matter. My fingers wove between Temujin's—just as they'd done moments ago with Jamuka's—as if I might weave his soul into mine so easily. "I'm glad he's dead."

"I killed him with my bare hands," he said. "And I was glad to do it."

"Good." I closed my mind against the image of Temujin's fists pounding into Chilger. "But I'll never be free of him."

"As time goes on—"

"No." I shook my head. "I'm pregnant."

The tent grew cold, as if a north wind had blown open the tent flap. "I see," Temujin said, his voice thick with emotion. "And the child is his?"

I knew the answer, but Khogaghchin's warning bound my tongue. Alan the Fair, mother of all the Mongols, had once been pressed to name the father of her sons despite her lack of husband. She'd claimed that the light of the sun had planted the seeds of life in her womb, but I had no such excuse. Still, I'd been through too much to be turned away by my husband, or merely tolerated out of obligation. So instead I cloaked the truth in a lie.

"I don't know."

I strained to see Temujin's face, waiting for the words that would cast me out to die a miserable death alone on the steppe. Instead, he peeled off his bloodstained shirt to reveal the thick bands of muscles on his chest and arms. "Then I shall greet the babe as my own."

I stared in shock at this man I'd married. "You wouldn't cast me out?"

"Would I throw out the mother of my child?" He laughed, but the sound was flat. "I see I must work harder to earn your higher opinion."

I had no answer for that, so he sighed and patted the blanket beside him. "Come lie beside me, wife, and keep me warm. Killing and raiding are hard work."

I did as he asked, feeling the hardness of his legs through his felt breeches and my filthy *deel*. I was glad when he didn't ask for more, for I knew it would be a long time before I could respond to my husband's touch. He fell immediately into an exhausted sleep so that I greeted the new dawn alone, Temujin's promise and Jamuka's declaration of love echoing in my ears.

I was a fool then to believe we might enjoy peace after all that had happened, and an even bigger fool to think we'd witnessed the fulfillment of my prophecy.

For what we would soon face would make all we'd survived pale in comparison.

Chapter 8

Ong Khan's troops returned to their leader, but Temujin and Jamuka rejoined their clans at the outskirts of the Black Forest, near the holy site dedicated to the Earth Mother. Every spindly birch was looped with blue felt sashes—each representing a prayer to the sacred spirit—and the ground was pale from the profusion of milk offerings poured into the earth. I was loath to leave the Bugura Steppe and the woods I believed still hid Toregene and Sochigel. The girl with the mismatched eyes had disappeared as if she'd never existed, and although I'd ordered the piles of dead Merkid to be searched, we'd found no trace of her body or her faintest footprint within the forest. It would be a miracle for so young a girl to survive on the steppes alone, but I poured an offering of milk from a mare who'd just delivered her first colt into the earth each morning in the hopes that the Eternal Blue Sky might protect her.

It wasn't only Toregene's safety I worried for, but our own as we approached our new home. The position of our camp troubled me, situated as it was on the borderlands of the fearsome Tatars, a mountain clan renowned for their skill in battle. My dreams were still plagued with the scent of scorched wool and blood. Always blood.

Bone weary after many days in the saddle, I had scarcely let the tent flap fall behind me when Hoelun entered unannounced, bearing a pile of heavy blue felts and a familiar polished birch-bark pole knotted with horsehair.

"No." I sank to my knees, the single word drawn into a moan. I wondered then how many burdens my shoulders would be forced to bear.

"Your father journeyed to the sacred mountains first," Hoelun said, reverently placing the package with its lifetime of memories on the ground before me. The black strands of hair from my father's Spirit Banner fanned over the felts of my mother's tent. "Your mother followed him shortly after. The messenger said that death claimed them while they slept, that your entire clan sang them to the sacred mountains."

Just as my mother had foretold. I wished now for her wisdom but realized I'd already broken my promise to her by forsaking my own gift of sight.

"Did they know—" I took a deep breath as Temujin entered our *ger*, his expression telling me he'd just received the news. "About me?"

Hoelun shook her head. "There wasn't time to inform them of the Merkid raid."

My mother had once prophesied that Temujin would fail me, but she and my father had died believing I was safe. I was grateful for that.

I blinked hard, willing Hoelun to leave. I cared little for my mother-by-marriage after her willingness to sacrifice me during the raid. Blood meant everything to the Borijin clan, even excusing Temujin's murder of his half brother, Begter, yet my blood would always belong to the Unigirad, a certain deficit in Hoelun's eyes. I turned instead to Temujin. "I'll raise my mother's tent today," I said, my voice breaking.

Mongol men were bred to be warriors, as restless as the wild horses they so loved, but we women ruled the hearths. It was tradition to raise the *ger* of a Mongol woman, the home of her heart, so that her soul might live on after her death. My husband nodded and clasped my shoulders, his presence as strong as the mountains he so loved. "Of course you will."

And so it was that instead of feasting on the day of my homecoming, I smudged my forehead with cold ashes and walked alone onto the steppes to raise the tent poles of my mother's *ger*. Behind me, our tents were white specks on the horizon, guarded by a man on horseback. I recognized

Temujin atop his new yellow horse, taken as spoils during the Merkid raid, but it took me a moment to realize that my husband wasn't guarding the camp.

He was guarding me.

I watched as another rider joined him, tall and slender atop his saddle. Jamuka.

I turned my back on the men as I erected my mother's tent and unrolled her felts, breathing in the scent of her cook fires and herbs, trapped over the years in the precious wool. My father's spirit would reside in the horsehair banner outside our *ger*, and I would visit my mother's spirit within these thick felt walls.

I could only pray they would both watch over me.

The days piled up on one another, their weight turning the season to that of falling leaves, and the days grew shorter even while the whispers over my belly grew louder. My claiming by Chilger had become common knowledge—the mischief of the Merkid slaves we'd claimed—and although my skin had grown thick after the seven years of gossip when Temujin first abandoned me, sometimes it was near impossible to remain indifferent to the smothered giggles and blatant stares.

The tents of Jamuka's clan remained pitched alongside ours in the green expanse of the Khorkonagh Valley, both groups flush with their victory over the Merkid. One morning as I dressed, I learned the real reason why Jamuka's clan lingered.

"Jamuka and I will take our final vows today," Temujin said. My back was to him as I slipped my favorite brown wool caftan over my head, gladly reclaimed after my ordeal with the Merkid. The material was worn to the softness of wild columbine petals and already snug around my middle. It was difficult to imagine that I'd soon be a mother, that I'd face the ordeal of childbirth and then greet a child whose face might always remind me of everything I so desperately wished to forget.

I exhaled slowly, letting my fears fly loose into the air. I smoothed the wool over the gentle swell of my belly. "What vows?" I asked.

"The *anda* vows." Temujin sat cross-legged near the fire, rubbing sheep fat into his bowstrings.

I fumbled with my belt, my fingers suddenly loose. "Haven't you already taken vows?"

"Years ago." Temujin chuckled. "The first time we exchanged children's toys with our blood. Jamuka gave me a knucklebone carved from a roebuck and I gave him one of brass." He set down the bow. "But we're no longer children. Today we exchange much weightier gifts, and one day Jamuka will help me become a khan."

"Did Teb Tengeri tell you that?"

"You don't care for my shaman." Temujin smiled indulgently despite the venom in my voice. "Why?"

"He's no true seer." The words were as hollow as my heart. My husband was flanked by one false shaman and another who'd forsworn her sight. I'd begun to dream again when my feet had touched this holy ground, often visions of Toregene dancing with three young girls, yet the bones and divination flames repulsed me, reminding me of the scent of death and burning flesh after the Merkid raid.

"Teb Tengeri predicted your return to me."

"A lucky guess."

"Perhaps your visions will return in time. As you heal." He picked up the bow again and balanced it on the open palm of one hand, then set it aside. "I don't deserve you, Borte Ujin, but someday you'll be greater than a seer. One day I'll be a khan—maybe even the Great Khan—and then I'll make you khatun."

Khatun. Queen.

I pushed away the idea, as likely as birds in the sky turning into stars.

"Khatun of a clan of outcasts and misfits?" I scoffed. "That's hardly a title."

"We all start somewhere." Temujin stretched out his legs in front of him. "And Jamuka is hardly an outcast."

I stiffened, then forced myself to relax. "Jamuka is not part of your clan."

"No." Temujin stood and cleared his throat. "As my *anda*, he's closer than the family of my birth. And he's here to lend my clan some semblance of dignity."

As was I.

And I carried none of Temujin's blood, and the child of another man in my womb. I wondered then whom Temujin would favor if pressed: his blood family, his *anda*, or his only wife.

"So Jamuka comes when you call him?" I asked. The white-bones were not faithful dogs. If Jamuka lingered, it was because he wished to.

"He answered my call to rescue you."

I turned my face and struggled to keep my voice light. "What will you trade with your pledges now that you're grown men?"

"This."

A shimmer of summer sunshine flowed over his hands. A belt of pounded gold with a design of intertwined arrows and a fringe of black leather tassels.

"Toghtoga's belt," I said.

Temujin nodded. "And his warhorse, the yellow mare with black mane and tail."

They were rich treasures indeed, yet Jamuka was well accustomed to such luxuries.

"Can you afford to give so much?" I asked.

Temujin smiled. "I have more than enough riches now that we've vanquished the Merkid. A horse and a belt are mere tokens of my brotherhood with Jamuka. Our shared wealth proclaims our alliance to the world and our plans for ruling the steppes one day."

I knew Jamuka's motivation for fighting the Merkid—uncomfortable as it made me—yet I was stunned to realize that my kidnapping had provided the perfect excuse for my husband to attack the wealthy clan. Temujin was richer than he or his father had ever been. The fact that my dignity and honor had been traded for gold and horses made me feel more degraded than I had before the fire with Chilger.

Temujin hesitated to speak, as if he sensed the change in my mood. "You've overcome so much, Borte, yet I have one more thing to ask of you."

My husband had no right to ask favors from me, so my voice was laced with frost when I answered. "And what might that be?"

"Will you officiate the *anda* ceremony?"

I shook my head. "I can't, not without my gift of sight."

His eyes shuttered, as if I'd denied him something precious, and he shrugged. "As you wish. Yet it would mean much to both Jamuka and me if you'd reconsider."

It was precisely because it meant much that I would never reconsider.

Both camps joined together that afternoon, a sea of brown faces as plentiful as the steppe grasses. The sky was smudged as gray as charcoal, but we women sweated through the day, butchering a horse and two goats and lugging leather buckets of fermented mare's milk to the open expanse of green chosen for the feast. A single ancient pine tree grew on the plain filled with stunted birch, its massive trunk gnarled like the hand of a lonely old woman.

This was the Great Branching Tree of the Mongol, the most sacred of the Earth Mother's holy sites.

When the time came for the bloodletting, Temujin and Jamuka faced each other at the base of the tree, their clans forming a circle of flesh and blood to further bind our people together. Temujin wrapped Toghtoga's golden belt around Jamuka's waist, then raised his arms as Jamuka wound another stolen Merkid belt around my husband's middle. These were no small gifts, but precious treasures that would proclaim the great alliance of these conquerors to every clan on the steppes and persuade the assorted khans to seek further alliances with my husband and his *anda*. And yet a tiny voice in the back of my mind wondered if perhaps the other leaders might view Temujin and Jamuka together as a formidable threat now.

And whether the blood brothers might someday see each other as threats to their own power.

A raindrop spattered on my nose, but the sun broke through the dark clouds then, illuminating identical swirls of wind embossed on the belts, as if the very spirits blessed this moment.

The men exchanged horses, the yellow mare for a tan warhorse with a diamond on its forehead. The blood brothers mounted their new prizes and ambled around the tree, pausing at each direction to honor the water of the north and air of the east, the earth of the west and fire of the south. Once finished, Temujin grinned at his *anda*, but Jamuka's taciturn expression remained unchanged, as if his thoughts had flown from this holy ground.

Then the men dismounted and their knives flashed with the Golden Light of the Sun. They slashed the soft flesh of their wrists and ribbons of blood unfurled toward the ground. Temujin tipped his arm so Jamuka could take some on his tongue; then Jamuka did the same.

"I pledge my eternal friendship to my *anda*, Jamuka," my husband said, his teeth tinged with scarlet. "I shall love this man forever, as if we had shared the same womb."

"And I pledge my eternal friendship to my *anda*, Temujin," Jamuka said. "I swear to keep no secrets from my blood brother until the day the last of us draws our final breaths."

I bristled when Teb Tengeri stepped between the men, wrapping a white sash around their wrists, a responsibility that might have been mine. Blood dripped down unheeded now, staining the sash with crimson. "When two men become *andas* they become one," he said. "They will never desert each other and will always defend the tents of their brother. Thus shall it always be between Jamuka and Temujin."

The two clans erupted into cheers and everyone flocked to the blood brothers, one short and wiry like an underfed wolf and the other as long and graceful as a dragon. I studied Jamuka's features from under my lashes, yet his faraway expression from earlier had fled and he embraced Temujin now, clapping my husband on the back as if they were brothers born of the same womb. The people quickly took to dancing around the Great Branching Tree, men and women holding hands and laughing while the men's deep singing rose into the Eternal Blue Sky. Our people danced until they'd beaten down a ditch as deep as their ankles and raised the dust to their knees.

"Borte!" Temujin motioned me to where he sat with Jamuka. "Join your husband and his brother."

To me, Jamuka raised his cup of mare's milk, still full. There was no denying his beauty, as if his face had been chiseled by the hands of spirits. My husband turned to answer some question, and I escaped toward the rough-hewn table laid out with platters of boiled horsemeat, the grease already congealing on top.

I almost dropped a plate of salted sheep fat when Jamuka touched my elbow. "You are unhappy," he said. "I can see it in your face."

I expected everyone to be staring at us, but the clans continued with their revelry, oblivious to the truth Jamuka spoke. Hoelun's gaze lingered on us for a moment but flicked away when my eyes caught hers.

"You shouldn't speak of such things," I hissed under my breath, making a great show of rearranging the plates.

Jamuka gave me a sidelong glance that made my knees tremble like a newborn foal's. "I'd fight as many men as there are stars in the sky if it meant I might see you smile at me with true happiness." He drew a tortured breath. "I've tried to fight my feelings for you, Borte Ujin, but it would be simpler to forever darken the Golden Light of the Sun. With Temujin serving under me, I'll be Great Khan one day, but that vision is complete only with you as my Great Khatun."

His words were so similar to Temujin's earlier that day that I almost choked.

"That can never happen," I whispered.

"I know." His voice quivered with emotion. "Yet honor and loyalty seem poor replacements for what might have been."

I'd thought much about how my life would have been different had I refused to marry Temujin, if I'd somehow become Jamuka's bride instead. Yet this life would be wasted with worries of what could never be.

"Temujin has his own ambitions about becoming the Great Khan," I said.

"Temujin is a strong warrior, but he'll never be more than a minor khan, not with his black bones and Yesugei's blood in his veins." Jamuka spoke without spite, the tension apparent around his eyes.

"I, too, am black boned," I said, clutching the dented iron plate in my hands.

"Yes," he said sadly. "Yet you're not positioning yourself to become the Great Khan, are you?"

I set down the plate and stared at him then, seeing a man grown thinner since the night of the raid, the circles under his eyes darker than I remembered. Love and ambition had taken their toll on him; I wondered if one might destroy him in the end.

I wanted to touch him then, but Mother Khogaghchin was at my elbow, grinning her toothless grin. "I need you, Borte Ujin. One of the goats has gone missing—"

I scowled, but her knobby hand tightened on my arm and she pulled me away from Jamuka.

"Which goat is lost?" I asked as the crush of people thinned and I could almost breathe again. "The sickly white one?"

Khogaghchin dropped my arm. "The only thing that's lost here is your good sense."

"I don't know what you mean." Yet I did, all too well.

"Hoelun is watching you, and Temujin, too." Khogaghchin smacked her gums. "It's not difficult to guess what they all see."

"And what might that be?"

Khogaghchin stared at me like I was a small child. "My poor girl," she finally said. "After all you've suffered, don't throw away your chance at happiness."

I wasn't throwing it away. I was clinging to it like a drowning woman.

"I won't. I promise." I touched her cheek to mine, reminded of the last embrace I'd shared with my mother. Khogaghchin tweaked my nose and shuffled off into the night, several shaggy goats trailing close behind her.

Temujin kissed my palm as I took my place beside him again, and my heart lurched as Jamuka emerged from the crowd and sat alone. Hoelun and Teb Tengeri whispered together, a pairing I didn't care for, and their eyes darted to me far too often.

We were no longer at war, yet danger surrounded me on all sides.

Ong Khan may have offered to make my husband leader of his warriors, but I wondered again whether he would someday fear the power my charismatic young husband wielded in the name of the aging leader. Yet the khan wasn't my immediate concern, for as autumn turned to winter, and winter to spring, I felt the danger in staying so close to Jamuka. I was blind without the bones and I worried for my impending delivery, the hours when I would labor supported by only Mother Khogaghchin and scowling Hoelun. Even more, I was terrified that the child might arrive bearing the black eyes and thick lips of his blood father. Temujin filled his days with hunting and fishing, withdrawing from me so some days we spoke rarely or not at all, as if he needed this time to harden his heart against what the future might bring.

One afternoon I walked toward the river despite the cramp in my side and my swollen ankles, needing the chatter of the water to soothe me. Once there, I threw off my boots and stepped into the calmest bend, gasping at the snowmelt of the creek as I curled my toes around the polished rocks. The spotted trout fry darting between my feet and the river and racing clouds overhead made me feel alive, and the baby's visible movement under my caftan reminded me that soon I would be responsible for bringing another life into this world. I wished I could ask my mother if she'd felt the same terror before I was born, if she'd worried that she'd forget to feed me or that death might claim her before she could gift me with my name.

Barefoot and with my boots in hand, I was glad for the sun peeking out of the clouds when I decided to return home. I didn't get very far, for halfway along the river path two men on horseback stopped me in my tracks. Mounted on a white stallion was a Tatar chief, his red cone headdress in brilliant contrast against the gray sky and gold coins sparkling on his horse's bridle. I forgot to breathe for a moment, and then I retreated, stepping on silent feet so the enemy chief wouldn't hear me, but I swallowed a curse as the second man turned to reveal his profile.

The gurgle of the river carried Jamuka's words downstream as he calmly conversed with the Tatar chief. It was the Tatars who had poisoned Temujin's father, and they continued to despise his son's clan. There was no good reason Jamuka should be speaking to our sworn enemy instead of slitting the man's throat while he had the chance.

I huddled behind the skirt of a towering pine while they spoke; neither man smiled, but nor did they argue. The Tatar handed Jamuka two small brown pouches before bowing his head and galloping away. Jamuka turned his horse about, and with the blood roaring in my ears, I crouched low to avoid him seeing me. Hooves pounded in my direction and he tore past like the wind, taking with him my chance at confrontation. Something small and brown tumbled unnoticed from his pack.

The Tatar chief's gift was lumpy in my hand when I retrieved it from the grasses. A mound of gold coins lay nestled inside the burlap sack, clinking like wind chimes and smelling of the countless hands that had touched them over the years.

Tatar coins.

Surely they meant nothing, perhaps a payment in exchange for trading horses. But I knew of no horses that would fetch so much gold.

I tucked the bag into the pocket that once held my divining bones, my mind roiling with the question of how to confront Jamuka when I returned to camp.

I was saved from making that decision by a more immediate issue.

The birth pangs started slowly at first, as if my morning meal of dried goat meat and wild pasqueflower roots disagreed with me. I pushed the belt of pain across my belly with the heel of my palm, focused on putting one foot in front of the other.

Somehow I made it back to camp, although I had to stop with each pain. Temujin was the first to see me, and he jogged along the path. "What's wrong?" he asked, looping his strong arm under mine. "Is it time?"

I only moaned, sinking to my knees as a fresh pain ripped along my abdomen. My insides threatened to turn to water and I clenched fistfuls of grass to keep from crying out. Temujin knelt behind me, rubbing my back and the nape of my neck.

"My mother," I panted as the pain ebbed. "To my mother's tent."

Never before had I so craved my mother's vinegary tongue and gentle touch, but I could only hope her spirit would guide the other women's hands to massage my belly and catch my son.

And usher me to the sacred mountains if I should die tonight.

Temujin scooped me up and I clung to him, drawing upon his warmth and strength for the battle yet to come. When I next opened my eyes I was in my mother's *ger*, as if I were a little girl again, awakening from an unpleasant dream. Temujin set me on the dead brown grasses and breathed deeply, filling his soul with my scent.

Perhaps I wasn't the only one who feared I might die tonight.

"I'll fetch the mothers for you." His hands were light when he pulled me to him, as if he feared he might further injure me. "I love you, Borte Ujin. Never doubt that."

The fresh pain that snaked around my abdomen stole my ability to speak. I sank into darkness as Temujin left, focused on the burden of each inhale and exhale. Too late did I realize I'd let him leave without a response.

If only I knew what I would have said.

The next day was a blur of pain, a solitary war all women must fight. Sometimes fragments of memory return to me, treasures from a world suspended somewhere between life and death.

Soft hands on my brow.

Pain ripping across my abdomen.

Gentle murmurs and the tang of sheep fat rubbed into the tender skin between my legs.

Straining naked on all fours, mesmerized by the fire's hypnotic dance and tasting the salt of my sweat and tears.

A final scream, ripped from my own throat.

A baby's wail and cries of joy.

Light.

Red-faced and with one ear smashed into his head like he'd laid on it the entire time he'd been in my belly, my son was perfect.

He lay curled on my bare stomach, tiny clots of black blood embedded in the creases of his arms and legs while he squinted at me with solemn eyes. He bore no trace of his true father, a precious blessing from the Earth Mother and the Eternal Blue Sky.

My womb was strangely empty, but my heart was overfull.

Mother Khogaghchin forced me to drink fresh colt's blood from a special bone cup carved to resemble a pregnant woman's belly, clucking at my tiny sips of the fortifying brew and then rubbing more of the blood on my son's pink gums. His tongue darted between crimson-stained lips, but he didn't cry as I expected. Hoelun's face crinkled as she massaged my stomach to ease the afterbirth. I would bury it tomorrow, my first duty as I emerged from my childhood *ger* no longer merely a woman, but a mother.

"He's a fine boy." Hoelun gently packed clean felt and moss between my legs and covered me with an oxhide blanket. The rags would be burned tomorrow, for the first blood of a mother must be offered to the Eternal Blue Sky. "Strong with bright eyes, although no blood clots in his hands."

I smiled, for the story of Temujin's birth and the blood clots in his fists was famous within his clan, so that even the smallest children could recite it around the main fire. I wondered who had decreed that such a sign meant future greatness for so small a child, if perhaps it had been a story created by Hoelun to reassure herself after Yesugei kidnapped her. I kissed my son's head, the thick black hair still tangled with traces of my womb, as Temujin burst into the tent.

"Leave the way you came, you feebleminded goat!" Hoelun screeched at her son. "Men are forbidden in birthing tents!"

The air inside the *ger* was still fresh with the salty tang of blood, but my husband rarely followed any rule that didn't suit him. He was bloodied, too—his palms stained red from the required sacrifice. A brown-and-white colt lay tucked on the threshold as if merely asleep, the same animal that had offered its blood to sustain both my son and me after the birth. Hoelun continued to curse at her son, but Temujin paid no attention to his mother. Instead, my husband's gaze flicked to the child I held; then he stared at me as if he'd never seen me before.

Sitting with my breasts bare, my son nursing greedily and the battle behind me, I was stronger than the fiercest warrior. Now I understood how soldiers felt when they returned triumphant from the battlefield.

"I'm already here, Mother," Temujin said slowly. "And not even your foulest insults could chase me away."

"Borte delivered a boy," Hoelun said grudgingly, and Temujin stared at me awestruck. "They need to rest," she added. Mother Khogaghchin stoked the fire a final time, but Hoelun laid a hand on Temujin's arm and whispered something in his ear. There was no hiding the shadow that passed over his eyes.

Not even childbed shielded me from the whispers and secrets. My teeth clenched and my arms tightened around my son.

Temujin crouched beside me, his eyes dark as the hide flap fell behind his mother. "My son," he said, his huge hand with its battle scars cradling the baby's delicate head. He breathed deeply, drawing in his first breath of my son's soul.

"What will you name him?" I had borne the child, but tradition dictated that his father should name him.

My husband's gaze flicked to mine, then dropped to the child at my breast. "He shall be called Jochi."

Jochi. *Guest.*

My throat was too tight to swallow, much less breathe. I knew then what Hoelun had whispered: of my bloods before the Merkid raid, that this child couldn't belong to Temujin. I waited for my husband's fury at my deception, for the words that would cast us both out to a drawn-out death as winter and starvation stalked us.

Instead, Temujin's face filled with light stolen from the sun as he watched Jochi drift to sleep. Perhaps my husband would accept my son, my firstborn, the boy who should one day inherit Temujin's position as leader. Jamuka had once claimed the clans would never accept a black-bone as their leader, and I knew with a painful certainty that no one would accept a khan believed to be sired by our sworn enemy.

I looked down at the boy I'd woven of sinew and bone, overwhelmed by the need to protect him. My son would have to fight for his place in this world from this day forward.

And I would teach him to survive.

Chapter 9

We shared the same camp with Jamuka for nine more months, until the summer's first moon, the Red Circle Day. Our cluster of tents swelled as more clans came to join the peaceful circles of *gers* ruled by the famous blood brothers, so that it was soon impossible to hear one's thoughts above the din of voices and animal sounds. All knew that Ong Khan was an old man and either Jamuka or Temujin would one day replace him. So renowned were my husband and his *anda* that even the Tayichigud returned with their famous yellow bridles, the clan of my husband's birth and the same sour-faced elders who'd cast out Hoelun and her children after Temujin's father had died. Hoelun raged against their return, but Temujin ignored her protests and, despite my objections, directed them to set up their tents near Jamuka's.

A traitorous clan camped near a possible traitor. I'd doubted what I'd seen with my own eyes, yet Jamuka had become distant and occasionally even cruel in the months since Jochi's birth, whipping his horses until their flanks ran with blood and once picking a fight with Temujin over the spoils of a recent raid. The argument would have come to blows had Temujin not acquiesced and gifted the entire cart to Jamuka.

Our camp grew, and so, too, did my son. Many believed Merkid blood flowed in Jochi's veins; others knew not what to think, only that Temujin treated him as his firstborn, despite his name.

My husband would dandle Jochi on his knee, tickle his ribs, and throw back his head with untamed laughter at the little boy's bubbles of spit. I'd seen Temujin roar in anger at his men and I often winced at his crass jokes when he thought I wasn't listening, but around us my husband was nothing but tender and kind. And although I felt a pang to hear it, my heart fluttered with relief when my son spoke his first word as he and Temujin rode together.

"Da."

At night my son nestled into my chest, his mouth warm on my nipple as he nursed in his sleep, Temujin's comforting heat on my back. And, many months after my son's birth, I finally allowed Temujin to become my husband again, opening my robe one night and letting his body cover mine. Tears slipped from my eyes when he entered me, but then he kissed my eyelids.

"I'll stop," he said. "We don't have to do this."

I drew a shuddering breath and wound my arms around his neck. His familiar scent comforted me. "Yes, we do," I said. "I want this."

It wasn't like before, leaving me breathless and trembling for more, but feeling Temujin inside me reminded me that things were as they should be. I wanted nothing more than to mend the ragged edges of my soul, rent apart by Chilger and the Merkid. The scars on my spirit and face would always remain, but I'd learned that I could survive much on my own, and I knew that Temujin was a different sort of man entirely than Chilger had been. I also realized that although my husband wasn't perfect, I might one day learn to love him.

Yet we continued to live under Jamuka's shadow, making it impossible for me to truly open my heart to Temujin, even as I gave him my body. Jamuka seemed to have withdrawn his pursuit of me after Jochi's birth, yet I'd seen him watching us once with an anguished expression worthy of a mortal wound. I learned to avoid him, and therefore avoid the confusion of my heart.

Still, Jamuka's words from the night of the raid would come to me unbidden as I drifted to sleep or repaired the stitching on Temujin's leather quiver.

He gains all and I lose everything.

Perhaps Jamuka sought to gain against his *anda* in the alliance with the Tatars, but I refused to face the hell and destruction of another raid.

It was then, when I finally felt secure in my husband's affections, that I dared speak of what I'd seen on the morning before Jochi was born. We were alone in our tent, our bellies full after a meal of mutton stew, when I broached the question.

"How well do you trust Jamuka?" I asked, although I already knew the answer.

"With my life," Temujin answered. He tucked a camelhair blanket around our sleeping son, Jochi's cheeks still flushed from the games they'd played while I'd scraped our soup bowls clean.

"Would you trust him with all of our lives?" I stacked the iron bowls on our low table, next to a silver platter Temujin had kept from the Merkid raid. "Not just my life and Jochi's, but your mother, Khasar, and Temulun's? Mother Khogaghchin and all the other allied clans as well?"

Temujin's brows furrowed and for a moment I saw anger flicker over his features. I had yet to bear the brunt of his fury, but I was willing to take that chance now.

"You know not what you speak of," he said. "If it wasn't for Jamuka, I'd have died long ago—"

"I saw him meeting with the Tatar chief on the day that Jochi was born. The Tatar gave him this." I pulled the burlap sack from where I'd hidden it under my mattress these past months, still filled with the filthy Tatar coins.

Temujin gave the bag a puzzled look as he thumbed through its contents. "I'm sure Jamuka has an explanation for this. Perhaps he was trading . . ."

"Or perhaps he's planning something with the Tatars. We'll pass by their border when we leave this camp, won't we?"

Temujin nodded slowly.

I took the bag from his hands, dropping it on the silver platter with an unsettling jangle of gold. "So I ask you again, do you trust him with our lives?"

"Jamuka would never betray me," Temujin said, but there was a brittleness to his words and I knew he was thinking of Jamuka's recent coolness. "And I will protect you and my family to my dying breath, Borte Ujin. You know that."

I did know that, but I feared it might not be enough. Somehow, I would find a way to cleave my husband from his dangerous *anda*.

Finally we had to move to find fresh pastures, yet Temujin planned to share our winter camp with Jamuka, despite my urging to join Ong Khan's camp instead.

"I'm no more than a slave in Ong Khan's camp," my husband said, helping me remove the last of our *ger*'s felt panels. "Here with Jamuka, I'm an equal." His smile showed off straight teeth, except for the back molar he'd lost in a recent boxing match with his brother, Khasar. "Jamuka stood by me when no one else would," Temujin said. "My *anda* has asked us to remain with him and so we shall."

"This camp is too small for two leaders, especially when you're one of them," I said, grunting to pull down a stubborn framing pole. It wouldn't budge, so finally I kicked it until it collapsed. Sometimes I wished I could kick sense into my husband as easily.

"Promise me you'll speak to him," I said, glowering at the tent, my husband, and the steppes beyond.

"If it will make you happy," he answered, yet I could see that the thought of such a confrontation was far from pleasing to my husband.

"It will make me happier than if we all wound up dead," I muttered.

My husband would never believe a word against Jamuka until he looked down and saw the shaft of his *anda*'s spear buried in his stomach. Yet I was determined that would never happen.

The lines of white *gers* melted like piles of snow until only the pressed grasses and worn trails attested to the time we'd spent camped on the Tuul River. The first days of our journey would be perilous as we remained on the periphery of Tatar territory, the same place where they'd once poisoned

Yesugei when he'd returned from arranging Temujin's betrothal. Jamuka and Temujin rode their *anda* horses, the leaders of two lines of people and animals like brown snakes creeping over the spine of the giant steppe. I hadn't pressed the issue of the Tatars with Temujin again, but the palpable tension between the two blood brothers made me guess that Temujin had broached the subject, perhaps unsuccessfully. Behind Jamuka rode his favored warriors, surly and silent after a celebratory bout of *airag* and wrestling the night before. I rode behind Temujin on a mare the color of wet earth, Jochi in his sling on my back, where he liked to chew on my braid as his new teeth came in. Hoelun drove her cart behind us, pulled by two of the most stubborn camels I'd ever met.

We traveled by day and slept under the dark blanket of sky those first nights. People laughed and sang, happy to be on the move again, their songs joining the braying of cattle and yaks, the bleating of sheep and goats. Finally, only two nights after our departure, Jamuka reined in at the base of the mountains, the most treacherous part of our journey. Dusk stretched pink fingers across the Eternal Blue Sky. Hoelun and I had fallen behind but lifted our heads to see Temujin riding toward us with his wretched shaman trailing.

"Jamuka wishes to stop," he said, reining in beside his mother. Teb Tengeri halted as well, giving his mare free rein to search for some shred of grass not yet trampled back into the earth. "He believes we should camp at the base of the mountains, his clans to the east and ours to the west."

That would put us nearest to the Tatar tribes. If Jamuka was our enemy, now would be the time to strike.

Hoelun pursed her lips. "This isn't even half as far as we'd planned to travel."

Further up the line, the carts continued their steady procession, but Jamuka gazed at us from his horse, as rigid as a boulder on the horizon. In later years, I would wonder if I should have held my tongue that night. But I had not cast the bones in too long and thus stumbled blind into the chasm of the future. I knew only one thing: I would not allow Jamuka to betray my family or my people.

"This is the perfect place for the Tatars to attack us," I told my husband. "Did you speak to Jamuka?"

Temujin's scowl was black. "I did. He claimed the coins were payment for several of the Tatars' best horses."

Not even a child would believe that story, yet I could see in Temujin's expression how he struggled to reconcile the idea of his beloved *anda* as a liar and possible traitor. I nudged my horse closer to his. "How do you know Jamuka isn't hoping we'll be ambushed?"

Temujin's bushy brows drew tighter. "Why would he want that?"

"Jamuka would do anything to be the Great Khan one day," I said. "To be greater even than his *anda*."

Temujin gave a bark of laughter, but it rang hollow. "Jamuka would never betray me."

I recalled the promise I'd once made to Jamuka to keep his future secret, but I couldn't allow words so carelessly given to now endanger my family. "I cast Jamuka's future when you sent him to the Festival of Games. He will betray you, and one of you will destroy the other," I said. "I saw it in the bones."

"Bah." Temujin waved that away. "We took a sacred vow that we would never harm each other, that we would keep no secrets from each other. I will not believe such evil of my *anda*."

"I, too, have seen it in the bones," Teb Tengeri said. I found it convenient that the shaman had waited until now to speak his opinion, but as he agreed with me for once, I held my tongue. Yet Temujin still refused to leave his blood brother.

I clasped the pommel of my saddle. "Do you see now? Jamuka is only loyal when it serves him."

"He told me he wants to be Great Khan one day, after Ong Khan dies," Temujin said, staring into the distance. And in the meantime, Ong Khan would support whichever *anda* he believed would prolong his own reign, never wishing to see himself toppled from power by either young leader.

"There can only be one khan over our clan," I said. "Jamuka sees you as competition."

Competition for our khan's helmet, me, and so much more.

"Jamuka will forever carry your blood," Hoelun said. "But he is a false *anda* if what Borte Ujin says is true. You must do as she says, or put your clan in danger. We cannot risk a battle against Jamuka and the Tatars."

Everything Hoelun did was to protect her children, an impulse I could now understand. I knew something had shifted if Hoelun now supported me, but I was glad for the backing.

"We'll be safer away from these mountains," I said. "We can pass him in the night, use the river to cover our sounds. Surely some of the clans will choose to join us over Jamuka."

Temujin's grip on his reins tightened, his lips almost white. "I'll inform Jamuka we've agreed to camp here." I opened my mouth to protest, but he cut me off with a sharp glare. "Then we'll ride through the night." He kicked his horse then—the same one Jamuka had given him at their final *anda* ceremony—and rode off, spewing angry clouds of dust.

I scarcely breathed as we tiptoed past Jamuka's distant camps that night, as silent as winter hares despite the river's helpful noise. Mothers kept their infants at their breasts and even the wagon wheels ceased to creak, so all I could hear was the steady beat of my heart in my ears.

I waited for Jamuka to emerge from his tent and order us to stop, but his clans slumbered in the distance, their cook fires glowing like red eyes in the night. Sometime before dawn, we became aware that we were being followed. We urged our horses faster, fearing Jamuka's clan and the Tatars. Yet this was not the fast-moving attack of soldiers bent on slaughter and revenge, but the plodding dust cloud of women and children, old men and their herds. We halted at dawn to count all those who had chosen Temujin over Jamuka. Rings of camping circles spread behind us, smoke from fires and the scent of roasting meat filling the cool morning air.

They would grow like weeds as the days slipped into weeks.

I began to doubt myself, to believe that I'd accused Jamuka of conspiracy when there was none, but the others seemed to sense the battle to come. I knew not the colors of the clans' bridles, but Temujin pointed to them from the top of a hill shaped like a camel's back.

"Geniges, Boroghul, Manghud. The Besud, Suldus, Khongkhotan, and the Sukeken. The Ol Khunug, Ohorolas, Duberi, Saghayid, Jurkin, and the Barulas."

Assembled like herds on a grassy knoll, spread before us were more clans than I had ever seen in one place, all here to show their support for my husband. Some were tribes already close to Temujin, but others were so close to Jamuka they might have shared the waters of the same womb. My husband gestured to the final group, their yellow bridles so bright none could miss them. "And the Tayichigud."

I leaned my head against his shoulder. "The clan of your birth has come full circle, then."

"Indeed they have." He preened like a hawk but then sobered. "The Tatars have announced their alliance with Jamuka. They claim to honor an agreement made with him from long ago."

"I'm sorry," I said, and I was. Temujin only nodded.

"This was his doing," he said, his voice edged with iron. "I gave him my blood, but it wasn't enough."

"This new Jamuka isn't the same man you swore vows to," I said. "His lust for power has overcome his love for you, for everything."

Even his love for me. Or perhaps his love for both Temujin and me had withered away, leaving behind only his black jealousy and naked ambition.

We had hoped to separate peacefully, but that night a Tatar rider came from Jamuka bearing an official declaration of war, returning a bag of brass knucklebones, the golden Merkid belt, and the yellow-and-black warhorse: everything Temujin had ever given him save the blood in his veins. I feared that one day Jamuka might demand that, too.

In return, the leaders of the largest clans, some of them Temujin's distant uncles and cousins, asked to meet with my husband. Teb Tengeri also joined them and stared vacantly into the fire, his arms tucked into his wide sleeves and his snowy beard brushing his lap. I sat cross-legged on the women's side of the tent while the rest of the men drank cups of fresh goat milk—no *airag* tonight to muddle their minds—and faced Temujin with somber faces.

"We wish you to be our khan," the head of the Jurkin said. He was twice Temujin's age, but he bowed to my husband. "Lead us, Temujin, son of Yesugei the Brave, and we'll gather the finest spoils of war: the greatest tents, finest women, and strongest geldings. If we forsake you, may you take away our children, wives, and tents."

Temujin's face belied none of the shock I felt; instead, he gave a wry chuckle. "My friends, I have my own tent, wife, and child." He hesitated, drumming his fingers on his knee for a moment before answering. "Yet I'll gladly accept your alliance."

The Jurkin raised his head. "Then you shall lead us to victory over the white-boned imposter Jamuka!"

The men pounded the ground with their fists, but Teb Tengeri's voice broke through the drumming of earth and flesh. "You have done a great deed in uniting these great clans," the false shaman claimed, "and although there is more work to be done, the whispers of the spirits swirl in my ears tonight."

I snorted in derision. Several of the men glanced at me with startled expressions, so well had I hidden myself in the shadows. Yet my husband was spellbound, leaning forward as if riding into battle. "And what do the spirits say?" he asked his seer.

"They no longer recognize the boy Temujin, replaced as he has been with a great leader. From this night forward, they wish to call you by a new name, one befitting the future Great Khan and leader of the People of the Felt." Teb Tengeri stared eerily at my husband, his eyes unblinking. "They wish you to be called Genghis Khan."

Genghis. The name meant *all-powerful.*

This was a gift my husband could not refuse, though it came from the mouth of an imposter. There were few things we could carry with us to the sacred mountains, yet our names traveled with us even after death, and to change them was no small decision. My husband's gaze caught mine. I recognized the raw hunger there, the desire to prove himself that I, too, had felt since leaving my mother's tent and the same I'd often recognized in Jamuka's eyes.

But Jamuka had already declared war; there was no going back now.

I gave an almost imperceptible nod, and my husband grinned.

"I accept the name the spirits have chosen for me," he said. "Just as I accept these new alliances!"

The men leapt to their feet and roared their approval, splashing the grass with milk and clapping one another on the back as if celebrating a simple wrestling match. I slipped outside, into the bracing night air and the realization that my husband was no longer a common man dreaming the simple dreams of driving his animals to fresh pastures and ruling his blood kin.

And as the wife of a khan, that meant I was now a khatun.

That night the men sacrificed a black stallion and a white mare to sanctify their new alliance. Then Temujin—Genghis now—replaced the white banner outside our *ger* with one made of black horsehair.

Black, the color of death and war.

My words in the dark had done more than separate Temujin and Jamuka. They had started a war.

Chapter 10

1190 CE
YEAR OF THE IRON DOG

I stood next to the fast-rushing creek, alternating between pounding my boys' shirts on a sun-soaked boulder and dunking them in an iron basin of water, listening to the other wives and mothers speculate about the battle being fought at this moment. I might be khatun, but here at the river, I was just another woman caring for her family. Six years had passed since we'd broken from Jamuka, and in that time more clans had flocked to join us. Three days ago Genghis—the name still sometimes felt foreign to me—had ridden out with thirty thousand men to challenge Jamuka in the Field of Seventy Marshes. Battle scars riddled my husband's body, and he was both loved and feared now, an able leader who drew men like bees to a fragrant summer globeflower. Genghis was proclaimed a *bataar*—a hero—for conquering the unconquerable more times than anyone could remember, and the People of the Felt sang songs to him each night around the fires. Teb Tengeri had predicted a victory at this coming battle, but to me that promise was worth less than the time he used to speak it. I worried for my husband as I always did, picking at the skin on my thumb until it bled. I was uneasy for Jamuka, too, though I'd never admit it to anyone. I was unable to reconcile the elegant noble I'd once kissed with the brutal warrior he'd become.

Even amidst the death and destruction of war, life went on. Genghis and I now had three sons—Jochi, Chaghatai, and Ogodei. Several leaders had proposed to marry their sisters or daughters to Genghis as lesser wives, but each time he refused them, claiming he needed no wife other than me, and preferring instead to negotiate betrothals for our boys despite their youth. Ong Khan had once denied Genghis' request to marry into his family—the old fox would never commit to a permanent alliance with either Genghis or Jamuka—so my husband sent an emissary to discuss bonding Chaghatai or Ogodei with the daughter of Ong Khan's brother. Due to the cloudiness of the blood in Jochi's veins, no mention was ever made of marrying the lovely Sorkhokhtani to him. I wasn't sure whether to be angry or relieved that my eldest son was often ignored when it came to the intrigues of power and alliances.

Ogodei lifted his caftan and let loose a stream of yellow waters into the creek, but my barked reprimand sent him scuttling toward the bushes so he didn't further defile the river. He finished and gave me a mischievous grin, then yawned into his pudgy hands. This youngest son of mine preferred to sleep and drink both his days and nights away, growing quite fat in the process. I dearly loved to nibble the rolls on the backs of his knees. I stretched my back and rubbed my belly, weighted like a stone with the new child I'd recently discovered I carried inside. This one felt different already, bringing a strange craving for river trout and the return of my dreams of Toregene, dancing in a field with three other faceless girls.

Toregene. I pushed away the memory and let the sunshine warm my cheeks. We'd never found Sochigel, but I'd heard whispers of a girl with mismatched eyes sighted amidst Jamuka's clan. I dared to hope, but I doubted whether I'd ever see the child again. Instead, I prayed that her god with the silver cross would keep her safe from harm.

Ogodei settled down to stacking rocks, and I shielded my eyes from the sun to see a disturbance on the horizon. The lazy dust cloud clung to a smaller contingent of heavy-footed men and horses than had departed three days ago, devoid of victory songs and trudging, as if they'd grown weary of life in the time they'd been away. My heart lodged in my throat until I found Genghis at the front of his men, dust streaked and weather-beaten, but alive. My sons ran up behind me, clutching my *deel* as the army approached, but Jochi took one look at his father's face, then herded his younger brothers away.

Teb Tengeri had been wrong. The Field of Seventy Marshes had been a decisive victory for Jamuka, and many of our men still lay where they'd fallen, their bones stripped bare by black vultures and left to dry in the sun. More had been taken prisoner.

Silence fell over the camp and the air refused to stir, so no one dared even to whisper as frantic wives and mothers searched the sea of filthy faces for the men they loved. I gathered the reins of my husband's warhorse as he dismounted, the weight of all he'd seen slumping his proud shoulders. Our warriors clustered around him, their eyes red with exhaustion and visions of death.

"When will we fight again?" they asked.

"Soon," Genghis answered. "So long as we have blood in our veins, we'll fight."

The men mustered a cheer, but a riderless white warhorse distracted me. It raced toward camp as if being whipped, and the faces at the back of the crowd began to swivel away from my husband. I knew something was wrong before the animal slowed and a woman's scream ripped the air. The crowd parted, more shrieks joining the cacophony until even the winds seemed to join the cry, the sound forever searing my mind. Genghis lurched toward the horse and grabbed its flapping reins. The beast wheeled about and I moaned into my fist, seeing the nightmare that had made even the winds screech with horror.

A man's head dangled from the matted tail, black blood crusted at the jagged flaps of skin where it had been hacked off. The eyes crawled with flies, the jaw hanging limp and the tongue pale and dry. I recognized the man from the gold ring still attached to his ear. He was Chaghagan Uua, one of the archers who had ridden out so proudly behind my husband only three short days ago.

The woman screamed again.

Uua's wife. Now his widow.

Tying Uua's head, the most sacred part of his body, to the unclean hind end of the warhorse had defiled the soldier's eternal soul, leaving his body lost and his family shamed. His spirit would never be whole again, would never fly to the sacred mountains to greet his ancestors.

My voice rose with those of the rest of our camp's women, keening for the unjust loss of such a warrior instead of singing the song that would have ushered his soul to the sacred mountains. This was the work of a monster, yet the Jamuka I knew was no such demon.

Genghis' sword flashed silver, and the white warhorse bowed to its knees with a spurt of scarlet. Blood spattered my husband's boots and the desecrated beast collapsed to the ground with a gurgled exhale.

"Gather fresh horses and provisions." Genghis raised his fist in the air. "We ride to seek revenge for Chaghagan Uua!"

Despite the men's exhaustion, his words were met with a lusty cheer this time. Saddles were transferred to new warhorses, raw meat and milk paste packed in their bags, and waterskins refilled in a flurry of dust. The soldiers mounted their horses in a thunder of hooves, leaving the women to deal with Uua's decomposing remains. As khatun, it was my duty to help Uua's widow prepare his body, but I could do more for our clans elsewhere.

I whistled to my mare and was already in the saddle when a surly voice stopped me.

"Where do you think you're going?"

Hoelun glowered at me, arms crossed under her sagging breasts and the white hairs on her chin quivering like bristles on a boar's snout. "There's a body to clean and a horse to butcher," she said, almost shouting to be heard over the sounds of keening.

"Uua is past saving," I said, "but I might be able to stop Jamuka from killing more of our people."

"You've seen this in the flames?"

I thought to lie, but instead I shook my head. Nothing I'd seen had been able to stop this war, so I still saw no reason to read the messages of bone and marrow.

Hoelun grabbed the bridle. "Jamuka won't stop this war for you, Borte Ujin. Not anymore."

"You knew?"

"About Jamuka's feelings for you?" she scoffed. "I'm almost as old as the hills, but I'm not blind. My only concern was whether you reciprocated his feelings."

"Is that why you told Genghis about Jochi's father?" Even now I refused to speak Chilger's name; I still sometimes woke from nightmares of him hovering over me, leering at me with twisted teeth and foul breath.

Hoelun shrugged. "It wasn't until the night that you urged my son to leave Jamuka that you proved where your loyalties lay. Too much has happened since then for Jamuka to end this war."

I jerked the leather from her hands. "We won't know unless I try." Jamuka had overstepped the bounds of warfare today; perhaps I'd return only as a head tied to my mare's saddle.

"What about your children?" Hoelun asked. "And the babe in your belly?"

My hand brushed my stomach, the solidness of new life there. "The Earth Mother and Eternal Blue Sky will watch over us." I patted the wide sleeve of my *deel*, revealing the sheathed dagger I always kept there. "And I don't go unarmed."

Hoelun sighed. "You're fiercer than a tiger guarding her cubs, Borte Ujin. I'm afraid I misjudged you when you first came to us."

"We do what we must to keep safe those we love." I understood her protectiveness over her son now, her willingness to hurt others—even me—in order to shield him. I gestured to the thirteen circles of white *gers* over her shoulder. "I now have many to protect."

Hoelun gave my knee a resigned squeeze. "Then may the Earth Mother watch over you."

I kicked my heels, heart in my throat as I followed my husband and his men, letting the caterwauling of the women fade into the distance. A blind man could have followed the army's path, the clods of broken dirt and crushed petals of white and purple wildflowers that would never nod their heads to the sun again.

I trailed their dust cloud until my legs grew numb in my saddle and darkness started to fall. The soldiers traveled with reserve horses, so they rarely had to stop to rest the animals, but I had only the mare beneath me, and a layer of white lather covered her flanks. I was saved from having to make the decision whether to stop as a terrible sound reached my ears over the pounding of her hooves. The low keening of hundreds of men rumbled into the Eternal Blue Sky, and for a moment the wind shifted so I thought I heard the wails of grief from the women in our camp mingled with the howls of our men. Trapped in the middle, I almost turned back, but I was drawn inexplicably forward, as if the hands of the dead nudged the small of my back and tugged my horse's reins.

I came upon them, and the men parted to let me pass, recognizing their khatun despite their glistening eyes. I wished later they'd cursed me and stopped my horse from taking another step. The air danced with the smells of an abandoned feast, full of cooking meat and campfires.

Inside the vast circle of men were the charred remains of campfires hastily doused, some with wisps of white smoke like departing souls swirling in the air. The barren field was pocked with almost a hundred priceless iron cauldrons, too expensive to leave behind, as tall as a man's chest and wide enough to boil half a horse.

I edged my mare closer to one of the giant pots and peered over just as Genghis saw me.

"Borte, don't!"

But it was too late.

A man stared at me from under brackish water, the flesh of his cheeks boiled away and his eyes gaping sockets. Strands of hair floated on the surface like black weeds in a pond, and his lips curled back in a silent scream.

It was the face of a man boiled alive.

I tumbled off my mare and retched, clutching handfuls of earth as the stench of boiling meat seeped into my nose and there was only air in my stomach.

Jamuka had done this. There had been bloody battles, raids, and skirmishes between our peoples these past six years, but the man I had once known no longer existed. Hatred closed around my heart like a fist but loosened as guilt pummeled me. I had urged my husband to break from Jamuka, so my hands, too, were stained with these men's blood.

And for that I could never forgive myself.

"Remember this, People of the Felt." Genghis' voice broke above me, then gained strength to pulse with barely restrained fury. "That devil Jamuka has destroyed our brothers' souls. Let no man's ears be empty of this travesty. The Golden Light of the Sun and the Eternal Blue Sky will not suffer such a crime to go unpunished."

There was silence, then gentle hands on my waist as Genghis helped me back onto my horse.

"Stop him," I hissed, trying to find somewhere to look that didn't scream of death. I settled on my husband's eyes, slate gray with sadness and flecked with molten anger.

"I will," Genghis said. "I swear it."

I shuddered to pass the watery graves, letting my mare find her way through the maze of death. It was then, while passing the last of the cauldrons, that I felt the first emphatic kick of the babe in my womb. I hadn't sought the future in a long time, but many believed a child's destiny could be foretold in part by the spirits that first urged it to life while in the womb. My mother had been caught in a spring rainstorm when she felt me jump like a fish in water, and Hoelun claimed the wild air of summer had breathed life into Genghis while she galloped across the steppes.

The babe in my womb had been urged to life by the vengeful spirits of the departed. And thus, this child I carried would forever be touched by death.

We received more news from Jamuka's camp as winter settled around us, freezing the ground solid and stalling the war as we all struggled to keep our herds alive.

Genghis had laid waste to the Naiman clan before the Field of Seventy Marshes, ordering his outnumbered men to light five campfires each so the petrified enemy would believe our soldiers to be as numerous as the stars in the sky. Their clan was destroyed, but there was a rumor that five women had escaped and sought refuge with Jamuka. Now we learned that Jamuka had claimed the beautiful young widow of the warrior Chuluun and made her his wife, and that she declared that Genghis and his people never bathed, that we smelled like fresh camel dung, and that our clothes were filthier than the underside of a yak's belly.

Gurbesu.

Again the specter of my girlhood friend taunted me from afar, first from Toregene's lips and now this. Jamuka cast his web wide, increasing the number of ties that bound us while also placing my friends and family in harm's way.

I wondered if perhaps that was his intent.

I was brought to the birthing tent past my time and labored while the sun twice rose and set, alternating between fighting for life and wishing for death to claim me. Finally, my daughter fell into this world, howling like a wild dog gnawing its own afterbirth, dark eyes glaring and fists clenched. She almost killed me in the process, ripping me so Hoelun was scarcely able to sew together my ravaged skin. "This girl tried to send you to the sacred mountains," she muttered, a sinew string between her lips as she threaded a bone needle. It was difficult to hear her over the squalling child. "This should be the last foal you give my son."

To move required more effort than I could manage as she began stitching so I stared at the soot-stained ceiling, gripping handfuls of damp bedcovers. "I'm Genghis' wife," I murmured weakly, between clenched teeth. "It's my duty to fill our *ger* with children."

Yet all I wanted to do now was sleep, despite the shadow of death that still lurked at the entrance of the tent.

"You are also khatun," Hoelun said from between my legs. "Which you can't very well be from the sacred mountains."

Mother Khogaghchin, now beyond ancient, crooned and washed my crying daughter's naked pink body with a damp rag. Her gnarled hand smoothed the baby's shock of black hair into lying smooth against her forehead, but it sprang back up. My child's hair looked like a porcupine had made its den atop her head.

Quiet finally fell as Mother Khogaghchin laid her on my chest and the babe found my nipple. Already I had the breasts and stomach of an old woman, but the Earth Mother and Eternal Blue Sky had blessed me with four strong children. For that I was grateful.

I drifted toward sleep as my daughter nursed, scarcely noticing as Hoelun left to summon Genghis while Khogaghchin finished wiping my daughter with a rag. The old woman's shocked exclamation startled me, pulling my nipple from the baby's mouth so the tent erupted in so savage a howl that my ears rang.

"What is it?" I rearranged myself so my daughter could continue nursing, her glare fiercer than ever as she sucked greedily.

"Her hand." Mother Khogaghchin stared as if the child might be missing a thumb, but all ten of her fingers curved like talons. Khogaghchin pried open a little fist—earning a sharper glare—to reveal a shiny blood clot like a black pearl. "Just like her father," she whispered, removing the clot gently, reverently, as if it were a precious gem. I took it, watching it stain the creases of my palm as Genghis pushed into the tent, looking as haggard as I felt. It was only as he entered that the shadow of death was finally banished from the birthing tent, as if the familiar foes had greeted each other too often on the battlefield.

Genghis crouched at my bedside, shadows under his eyes as if he hadn't slept in days. "My mother claims it was a difficult birth." He took my hand in his, mingling the blood of my womb with that of the birth sacrifice. "She says I might lose you if you go again to the birthing tent."

"We'll worry about that when the time comes." I tried to pull my daughter off the nipple, but she gave me a scowl that so reminded me of her father that I chuckled, although the movement cost me dear. "Right now you should meet your very greedy little girl."

Genghis touched one of her tiny fists. After a moment's hesitation, the child's fingers opened like the petals of a mountain daisy, still streaked with blood and tipped with ragged nails. My husband filled his lungs with her soul and exhaled.

Only then did I see the tears in his eyes.

"I'd call her Alaqai," I said, smoothing her furrowed brow. Genghis might name our sons, but I would name our daughters. The child stared at her father, as if memorizing his every feature. Her lashless eyes blinked, then finally fluttered closed. "This was in her hand," I said, revealing the black clot of blood. Genghis drew a sharp breath and looked at the child with new eyes.

Alaqai. *Palm of the Hand.*

I protected Jochi like a mother wolf, but my sons needed little of me after they tired of my milk. This girl would be my own, the daughter I would teach to pound felt and carry the stories of our clan. For the first time in so many years, I felt the urge to scry again, my fingertips itching to hold the bones, to teach her how to read the cracks and shadows in the marrow.

"Alaqai," Genghis said, letting the name linger on his tongue. "A fitting name for a warrior born with a clot of blood in her fist."

"A warrior?"

"Of course." Genghis pressed his lips to my forehead so I felt his smile. "She'll be the fiercest marmot on the steppes."

"Marmot?" I arched an eyebrow and sniffed the air. "Have you been too deep into the *airag* already?"

"Not yet, although there's a jug or two waiting for me outside." He chuckled and ruffled our daughter's damp hair, earning a gentle slap from me lest he wake her. "Alaqai has another meaning outside Palm of the Hand, at least among the clan of my birth."

"And what is that?"

He laughed, a low rumble that started deep in his chest. "Siberian marmot."

I laughed then, and Alaqai's eyes fluttered open. This time it was Genghis who shushed me with a mock frown.

"I'll teach this little scrap of fur how to ride," he said when she'd settled back to sleep. "To throw a spear and launch an arrow."

I knew he worried for my safety while war raged around us, and now we had a daughter to protect. I patted the blanket next to me so we might rest together. "And if she'd rather spend her days felting and cooking your stew?"

"She can learn it all," he answered. I let my husband curl around me, his warmth seeping into my battered bones and flesh as he stroked Alaqai's forehead. I wanted that moment to last forever, yet his next words stole the breath from my lungs. "I'd die before I let anyone touch you, or the children," he said. "And that day may yet come."

I couldn't imagine a life without Genghis now, or our family. They had filled my heart and made me whole again, but also left me vulnerable. "Train her, then, but know that nothing is going to happen to you."

I'd endured much already, but I doubted I'd survive if tragedy ever befell my children.

After the Field of Cauldrons, it seemed we played a child's game of find-and-catch with Jamuka. We would charge and he would feint; then we would switch places, neither side gaining any discernible advantage.

One night while the boys were with their father—Alaqai was a fussy baby and her screams often drove them to sleep with the horses—Mother Khogaghchin shuffled into my tent, closing my new birchwood door behind her. My husband's raids had yet to end the war, but they occasionally brought a wealth of trade goods from the south and the east, precious salts and iron weapons and finally even a proper door, emblazoned with painted images of the Five Snouts that never failed to entrance Alaqai.

I was already abed that night, bone weary from a long day of tending to my daughter and beating felt with the other women. Khogaghchin's white hair framed her leathery face like the glow of the moon, and for a moment I glimpsed what she might have been as a young woman, strong and determined. Then I blinked and the image was gone, replaced with an old and feeble crone.

She sat at my bedside, her hands cool and dry over mine. "I've come to sit by you, Borte Ujin," she said.

I moved to rise, but she clucked her tongue at me. "Rest, daughter of my heart. You've earned it, spending your days caring for us all with little thought to your own spirit." She paused for breath, bracing her hands against her knees for support. "I realized tonight when I couldn't sleep that I am now an old woman, and you are my family. I thought I might sleep better closer to you."

"Then rest," I said, although I knew her snores—louder than an ill camel's—would keep me from my own sleep all night. I'd manage so long as she didn't wake Alaqai.

Khogaghchin lay next to me, but I drifted to sleep first. I woke not to the rumble of her snores but to utter silence, not even the gentle crackle of the fire, which had burned out in the night. My hand brushed hers, but this time it was cold.

"Mother Khogaghchin?" I leaned closer to feel her cheek, but it, too, was cold. Only the smile on her lips was still warm, reminding me of the day I'd first met her as a new bride.

I was mother to a nation and I would never let my people see me cry, but I raised my voice to guide her spirit to the sacred mountains, then broke down and sobbed in the darkness of my own tent, pulling Alaqai to my chest and crying for the second mother I'd lost.

We bleached Mother Khogaghchin's bones in the sun and buried them with the honor of a woman who had birthed fifteen children. I erected her *ger* near my mother's, one stark white and the other dulled by the sun, both providing me solace. It was there that Alaqai took her first steps, and for a moment I imagined both my mother and Khogaghchin smiling down on us. Time raced ahead without us, whether we wished it to or not.

Alaqai grew out of her fussiness and weaned herself, giving us a glimpse of the independent streak that none of my sons possessed. My only daughter was a terror, racing about camp on her pony and flashing the most adorable smile while stealing cups of salted milk. I trembled to think of the havoc she would wreak once she was older.

With no child at my breast, I quickly fell pregnant again, much to my husband's horror. The clans watched my stomach swell, scheming amongst themselves as to which woman might replace me as khatun if I died in the birthing tent, and each night Genghis and Hoelun prayed to the Eternal Blue Sky for my safe delivery.

I was determined to enjoy these months of what I knew would be my final pregnancy, even going so far as to dry extra goat meat until the rafters creaked from the added weight, all in preparation for what might be the last months I would spend with my family. It was a difficult pregnancy, with my swollen ankles and growing inability to sleep, and I grew more terrified of entering the birthing tent with each passing day, although I tried to put on a brave face before Genghis and the children.

When my time came, I struggled even more than I had with Alaqai, for my body had not yet fully healed. After the first full day, I begged Hoelun to cut me open and remove the child, but instead she pressed on my stomach so hard I screamed, turning the child lodged there.

My last child was born amidst my cries, tearing me apart inside as Alaqai had done outside.

A son.

"There will be no more children," Hoelun commanded me as the after-birth emerged. This time I could only nod. We named our son Tolui, after the three stones that make up the hearth at the center of our *gers*. Tolui would be our Prince of the Hearth, who would care for us in our final years.

I hadn't the strength to feed my son, so a Merkid slave whose babe had died was brought to give him suck. At the time, I envied the girl her youth and round breasts as my milk dried up in a final punishment of excruciating pain, but I wondered later if she had made him weak, if perhaps my milk would have made him as strong as his brothers. Still, Genghis treated me as a precious bride, feeding me bits of sheep fat with his own fingers as I struggled to recover.

"You've given me four sons and one demon of a daughter," Genghis said, wiping away my tears as I focused my eyes on the dried horse and goat meat hanging above my head. It was two weeks since the birth and still the world spun underfoot when I tried to rise. I'd scarcely managed to bathe my son today and, exhausted, had left the fouled water in its iron basin, where a spotted goat now lapped it up. "I order you to rest and recover," Genghis said. "For I need my khatun."

Yet what kind of khatun could no longer welcome her husband into her bed, to join with him and create new life? I struggled to find a new role for myself, and finally it was Hoelun who gave me the words I needed.

"You are mother of the People of the Felt," she said. "You told me that once, before the Field of Cauldrons, and now you must act the part. Eat and rest to regain your strength."

"But Genghis—"

Hoelun waved away my concern. "Surely you are not so dull a wife that you cannot think of ways to please my son without opening your legs to him."

My face burned the same fire as the flames in my hearth then. "I'll think of something," I mumbled, not wanting the conversation to continue.

Hoelun cackled and patted my leg. "That's my girl," she said. "Now, drink your calf's blood and I'll bring you more sheep fat. I'll get some color back in your face if it's the last thing I do."

Slowly, I regained my strength, but Tolui had already been fitted for a saddle by the time I felt well enough to resume all my duties, and I still grew short of breath and required frequent rests to keep my head from spinning.

As the willow buds unfurled their fuzzy heads and sent out yellow sprigs of pollen, we finally garnered enough support from the clans to declare war against the Tatars, the mountain clan that Jamuka had allied himself with before Jochi's birth. Our soldiers mounted their horses with the men of Ong Khan, the great leader who still wore the black sable furs I'd brought to my marriage. Together, the men attacked the Tatar fortress in the Ulja River valley, nestled amongst the birch and larch.

The men were gone for days while we women performed our chores and tended the children. We should have been used to the long waits and constant doubts, but we scarcely slept by night, and by day, our tempers frayed as eyes darted constantly to the horizon.

Finally, the thunder of hooves and cloud of dust heralded their return. Tasting the familiar tang of fear and excitement as we waited to hear what the battle had brought, I untethered Tolui from the rope that kept him from the hearth fire and herded the children like goats to meet their father. Ogodei yawned into his hand—there was little in this world that could interest that son of mine outside food and wrestling—but Jochi held Alaqai on his shoulders. My sweet boy was now a gangly youth who had begun to braid his hair like a man, and my heart stalled to realize he would soon ride out with the men.

We heard the men's songs and whoops of joy before we could make out their expressions, and the sound of sweet victory rolled across the camp, the women and children calling to the men like summer cranes.

Flanked by his younger brother, Khasar, and his general Belgutei, my husband rode his warhorse at the front of the men, his cheeks ruddy and his smile like a beacon of sunshine. Before I could stop her, Alaqai squirmed down from Jochi's shoulders and darted forward, her little legs pumping and black hair streaming out behind her. I thought she might be trampled and lunged after her, but she dodged between the horses, chortling with golden laughter that made me want to nuzzle her close and never let go. The daughter I thought would be only mine grew more like her father with each passing day, making me proud and lonely at the same time.

Genghis joined her laughter and scooped her into the saddle before him. He galloped close, then dismounted and pulled me into a hug so tight I could scarcely breathe.

"By the Earth and Sky, I missed you," he whispered into my ear.

I peered at the river of wagons making itself seen behind the men, creaking loudly with the weight of the spoils of war. "You were too busy raiding to have time to think of me."

"This is the first time I've known you to be wrong," he said. "For I always think of you, Borte Ujin." He kissed me then, a kiss that broke every rule about propriety and made the men around us whoop and holler, bringing fire all the way to the tips of my ears. Still, I kissed him back, glad to have my sweat-stained, dusty wolf of a husband home.

Genghis finally released me and bowed to his mother, then swept her off her feet with a roar of laughter. Hoelun laughed with him, her white braids tied with blue string flying behind her. All around us, mothers and wives were pulled into similar embraces, and triumphant fathers tossed squealing children into the air.

Genghis climbed onto a boulder and silence fell like a hammer as every face turned to him. "People of the Felt," he cried. "The Tatars have been routed and their dust scattered into the wind. Never again shall they raid our horses, steal our women, or murder our children."

I hugged Tolui tight and squeezed Alaqai's shoulder, but she stared at Genghis with the rapt attention she reserved only for him.

"Today your men bring you the spoils of war," my husband continued, "but tonight we feast!"

The people let out a deafening cheer so loud the mountains might have trembled, and Genghis sprang from the boulder and wrapped his arm around my waist, as giddy as if he were wooing me. "Come see the treasures I've brought home."

He led us to the carts, lifting Alaqai onto his shoulders. A brown wool blanket covered the first wagon like a mound of earth.

"This is it?" I asked, a smile dancing on my face. "You fight the Tatars and all you have to show is an old horse blanket and a cart?"

"I let the men divide the spoils." As leader, Genghis was entitled to all the booty, but giving it to his soldiers was his common practice, making his men love him even more. He grinned, then whisked off the blanket in a cloud of dust. "But I kept a little something for us."

I coughed, then gasped. Gleaming in the sunshine was a giant silver cradle carved with flowing willow branches and intricate flowers, more delicate than a spider's web. Genghis reached inside and retrieved a silk blanket, as pale as the morning sky and covered with tiny seed pearls gleaming like tears. "They belonged to the Tatar chief," Genghis said. "To his son, actually."

I didn't ask what had happened to the child.

The second gift was a Tatar boy-child, tied in the corner of the cart and cowering like a lamb about to be slaughtered. Gold rings glinted in his nose and ears, and a band of yellow silk lined with sable still shone proudly around his waist. Hoelun joined us then, and reached out her hand to touch the child's shoulder. The boy flinched. "A nobleman's son," she said. "Does he have a name?"

Genghis shook his head. "None that we know. He spent most of his nights in camp writing in the dirt in the Tatar script, but he doesn't speak, or if he did, he has forgotten how. I thought you might care for him, seeing as you excel at raising wild boys."

"He shall be called Shigi," she said, waving my children over. They poked the gold ring in his nose and admired his belt. "Give him a few days and he'll be tearing about like the rest of your herd."

Our children giggled and ran off with the Tatar boy, more interested in his people's stolen horses than in a cradle of silver gleaming in the sunshine or the fact that he could write. That was a skill none of my children possessed, and already I saw this child and his talent as more valuable than any cart of gold or silk.

"There's still one more treasure," Genghis said, chuckling as Hoelun shuffled after them, hollering.

"You have another Tatar child hidden in the sleeve of your *deel*?"

"No." A smile teased his lips. "A new title. Ja'ud Khuri. Ong Khan finally decided to ally with us, and he promised to award me the title Jautau as well once this war is over."

The Pacifier. And perhaps one day, the Peacemaker.

I looked askance at my husband and saw the pride in his face, the happiness reflected in his eyes.

Peace and happiness.

But I knew my husband. Genghis had surpassed his father and almost every other man in living memory, no mean feat for the abandoned son of what had once been the weakest clan on the steppes. This war had shown him his talent for commanding men and directing battles, had whetted his appetite for conquest and power.

For the first time, I realized that conquering Jamuka might not be enough for him.

"There's something else," Genghis said, but the smile had faded from his face.

I traced the intricate flowers on the cradle with my fingertip, marveling at the workmanship. "Is this something as grand as a silver cradle or a new title?"

"Not exactly." My husband heaved a great sigh. "We captured two Tatar noblewomen—Yesui and Yesugen—the daughters of the Tatar chief. Yesui was recently married—her husband tried to return for her, but I ordered his head cut off after my men captured him."

I waited for him to continue, cocking my head when he didn't speak. "I take it these women are slaves now?"

"Not precisely." Genghis clasped his elbows over the leather armor he still wore. "I married them."

I stared at him, aghast. "You married them?" I wanted to sputter or rage at him, but my mind reeled and I forced myself not to scream, not here where people might overhear. "Without even consulting me?"

"They've requested to share a single tent, far removed from camp." My husband reached out as if to touch my hands, but one look at my face and his arms dropped at his sides. "I encourage my men to intermarry with those we've conquered," he said. "There is no better way to bind the Tatars to me—"

"Than to take their women as wives." I recoiled in disgust at the image that rose in my mind, my husband entwined with two beautiful sisters while I boiled mutton over a hot fire to feed his sons and daughter. "And just how many other women do you plan to take to your bed?"

"They're my wives in name only, Borte," he said. "I made a promise to you, but I could no longer ignore my generals' urgings."

"They told you to do this?"

He nodded. "My Four Dogs of War have never understood why I have only one wife, but I was able to put them off until . . ."

"Until I could no longer be your wife." My anguish was so thick it almost choked me. My ruined body had brought this upon me, proclaiming my uselessness to the world. Painful moments passed and I touched my scarred lip, thinking of all I'd endured for this man.

I'd endured much, but I'd also been given much. I squared my shoulders, ignoring the roar of blood in my ears. "Then I release you from your promise."

"I don't wish to be released from my promise. You are the only wife of my heart," Genghis said, bringing my hand to his chest so I could feel his heartbeat. "You and no one else, Borte Ujin. I'll set the women aside if you ask it."

How I longed to demand it at that very moment, yet I knew I could never speak the words. I was khatun, not the wife of a petty herder, and I'd known there were sacrifices I'd have to make.

If only I'd realized how painful those sacrifices would be.

"Keep your wives," I finally said. "But you'll swear now, and again before your Four Dogs, that only the children of my womb shall be your heirs. I am your khatun, not some old crone to be pushed aside by these Tatar princesses."

"I'll gladly swear it," Genghis said. The silver fire in his eyes was banked now, as if something between us had been irrevocably destroyed. We would always be man and wife, but our relationship now would be forever changed. "I could never have asked for a better wife, or mother of my people."

And then my husband bowed to me, a gesture of such reverence and respect that tears sprang to my eyes. "Go," I said. "Bring your women to me tomorrow before your generals and I will welcome them as a khatun should."

And I would clutch that title and my dignity with my last shred of strength, so that they could never be wrested from me as my husband had been.

Chapter 11

Yesui and Yesugen were fair skinned, with gleaming black hair and waists unthickened by the future children my husband would surely get on them. It was petty, but I contented myself with the fact that Yesui's nose resembled a hawk's beak and Yesugen squinted as if she were an old woman losing her vision. I wore my *boqta*, the towering khatun's headdress made of willow branches and covered with green felt, bedecked with a male mallard's feathers and strings of polished jade beads. With a false smile, I welcomed my husband's wives to the clan with a ceremony of salt tea and hearth smoke, although the fires were built with dung, as I refused to sacrifice precious pinewood for the women. Genghis kept his word, so I rarely saw the Tatar sisters, allowing me to almost forget their presence in the face of more pressing matters. We gained strength and numbers after decimating the Tatars, but shortly after the New Year, Jamuka summoned a *khurlatai*, a conference to decide the new khan. Men voted with their presence, and Jamuka's followers cleaved to him in droves. We woke one morning to discover that the Tayichigud, the clan of Genghis' birth, had deserted us, just as they had after Yesugei had been poisoned by the Tatars. They and Jamuka's other clans sacrificed a mare and a stallion, then bestowed upon him the title Gur-Khan.

Khan of Khans.

It was the ultimate risk and it played out precisely as I knew Jamuka had hoped. Furious at his newly declared rival, Ong Khan sent a messenger to Genghis. The man's horse was drenched with streaks of white lather and was half-dead by the time he reached us.

"We attack Jamuka's forces on the day of the full moon," the messenger exclaimed, panting. His face was stained with soot in preparation for battle and his braids threaded with black string.

Black, the color of vultures and rotting flesh.

Jamuka had grown too powerful, so once again, Ong Khan sought to balance the power between the two *anda*. My husband consulted with his Four Valiant Warriors—the four most daring and courageous of his many generals—and agreed to join Ong Khan in this final battle against Jamuka. If Genghis and Ong Khan won this battle, they would likely win the war and my husband would one day wear the headdress of the Great Khan.

If they failed, I would soon stand among the People of the Felt as a widow.

Tolui whimpered in his sleep the night before the full moon, but Alaqai crooned a lullaby to her little brother before I could get up. I lifted to one elbow to see my children in the silver cradle, my daughter's arm wrapped around her brother as she made up new verses more to her liking. A two-stringed horsehair fiddle often accompanied the common milking song, but her sweet voice needed no instruments.

> *"The mare's milk flows like*
> *The green grasses of the steppes*
> *And the cow lows for her calf.*
> *The rivers ripple with sunlight,*
> *Goats cluster like woolly clouds,*
> *Leaving their dung all around."*

I stifled a chuckle at the last line, for at least we knew my daughter wouldn't end up a singer or plucking a *shant*. Ogodei and Chaghatai snored through the song on the boys' side of the *ger*, but Jochi slept under the stars with the soldiers. My solemn son had just taken his first wife and was eager to prove himself, to rid himself of the stain of his birth, and thus he'd asked to be allowed to join his father on the field. I'd protested until my voice was hoarse, but Genghis had remained steadfast, convinced this was something my son needed to do.

"You can't protect Jochi forever," Genghis had said. "He's a man now. It's time the clans viewed him as such."

Yet never before had both my husband and my son ridden to battle at the same time.

Realizing I wouldn't win the argument, I spent the day beseeching the Earth Mother and doubling my offerings of milk to the spirits. At dawn, the two armies would charge at each other, riding up and down the sides of the mountain, reforming and charging like waves. My firstborn would be among them, leaving me wondering whether all mothers felt so terrified and powerless as their children ignored their admonitions to stay small and instead grew into adults with minds of their own.

Genghis tossed in his sleep next to me and finally woke, his lips moving in a silent prayer so his first words of the day would be dedicated to the khan of the mountains and the Golden Light of the Sun. I waited for him to finish, then traced the line of his jaw, and he stared at me with such intensity that I almost blushed. Then he kissed me.

My husband never left for battle without first kissing me, but we both sensed this time was different. He rolled atop me and I threw caution to the winds, opening my legs to receive him and seeking to hold him for as long as I could, even as the sunlight stole precious time. I hadn't allowed Genghis into my bed since he'd returned with his new wives, so our coupling was silent but fierce, an urgency in our grappling flesh and swallowed cries. He withdrew before his seed spilled into me, protecting me even now, and afterward, as the children stirred, he caressed my cheek.

"You are the light in my sky, Borte Ujin," he said, breathing deeply. "I love you."

I touched the pale scar on his chin, and another on his shoulder. "And I love you, even though there are times when I'd rather strangle you."

I helped him dress in his leather armor, tying his leather greaves and handing him his domed helmet. He gave me a lingering look, as if he would say something more, but then stepped into the dawn, leaving me to ready the children. I swore to the ancestors I'd remain dry-eyed when we bid him good-bye before all the clans. There would be time for tears later.

The children dressed hurriedly, all except for Ogodei, who dawdled as he always did. I snapped at him and finally tied the sash on his *deel* too tightly. Together we stepped outside to the acrid tang of storm clouds and rain on the horizon. A great storm arose from the wooded mountains across the steppe, angry clouds racing across the sky and blotting out the sun.

Jochi waited with Shigi on the other side of the camp, where Genghis spoke to Khasar, his younger brother. Shigi, the young Tatar captive raised by Hoelun these past years, now filled out the shoulders of his boiled leather jerkin. He would accompany the men today not as a soldier, but as a scribe, recording the exploits of my husband and his warriors in the new Mongolian script my husband had commissioned him to create.

"It bears little difference to the Uighur script," I'd heard him murmur to Alaqai during one of their infrequent lessons.

"But I don't understand Uighur either," Alaqai had said, wrinkling her little nose. "The marks all look like the scratchings of a drunken chickadee to me."

Genghis had commanded Shigi to write for a nation, but I bade the Tatar scribe to instruct my unruly brood in reading and writing, a skill I myself lacked. I wasn't sure whose was the more difficult commission.

The sable edge of Genghis' helmet rustled now in the wind and he stared at the nearest mountain—one with a crooked back like a camel's—where Jamuka and his soldiers were camped. The storm clouds cracked and growled overhead with an unnatural ferocity, the lightning tearing the sky in two and making the children shriek and clutch my legs. I'd heard stories of this from my mother, ancient battles in which powerful seers called on the spirits of the winds to destroy their enemies. My throat tightened at the idea of both my husband and my son riding into a battle fought in part by spirits.

"It's their shamans," I said, sinking to my knees and spreading my fingers into the earth. The reverberations of enemy drums pulsed up through my knees and palms. The ground in my vision swayed then and I gasped, eyes screwed shut against the vertigo.

Genghis lay sprawled in the jade green grass, his dried lifeblood staining a path from his neck to where it had watered the earth. His white warhorse had been skewered through the spine, the shaft of the arrow buried in his hide, and a lifeless hand lay open on a slate-colored rock, palm up to the Eternal Blue Sky. The early morning light warmed the spine of a camel-backed mountain on the horizon.

My eyes snapped open to the flesh-and-blood version of my husband, hale and solid as he mounted his white warhorse, the same animal I'd just seen dead on the steppes. The beast snorted and stamped its front hooves while the winds ripped around us. The mountain behind them was the same as in the vision and the grass an identical shade of brilliant green, damp with dew.

I had forsworn my gift of sight, yet it sought me anyway.

I rose slowly, glad for the solid earth below me. "Jochi," I said, my knees threatening to buckle. "Fetch a cup of milk to offer to the ancestors before you and your father ride out."

"But—"

"Fetch a cup of milk." My voice brooked no argument. Jochi looked about to protest, but Shigi cleared his throat.

"Perhaps we should make an offering as well," Shigi said, smiling. "Asking that I don't drop my brushes and ink during the battle."

My son kicked a rock and stalked off with an exaggerated sigh. "Don't go," I said to Genghis, waiting until my son was just out of earshot. Our relationship had been strained since the Tatar raid, but I couldn't imagine my world without my husband, empty of his constant grin, his deep rumble of a laugh, his warmth against my back at night. "I saw the outcome of this battle. You will be wounded." I couldn't bring myself to say the rest.

I saw you dead.

Genghis chuckled. "You've seen my scars, wife of my heart. I'm often wounded."

I dragged my gaze to his, the wind whipping hair into my eyes. "This time you'll be more than wounded."

I watched the understanding dawn in his eyes. "You saw my death?" he asked, and I could only nod. A vein in his neck throbbed and I longed to kiss it, to feel the life pumping through it. "When?"

"A moment ago. The vision came to me unbidden."

He dismounted so we stood almost eye to eye, and I knew he believed me. "It will happen today?"

"Today, tomorrow . . . I couldn't see, only that it was here, in this battle," I said, remembering the slant of sunlight on the crooked mountain. My husband would die here, unless I could keep him from battle. "You were wounded in the neck."

A man cleared his throat behind us. Teb Tengeri stood in my shadow, leaning on his cane, his features as smooth as river ice. He was dressed in the full regalia of a seer today, swathed in a *deel* sewn with colorful silk tassels and gold discs to reflect the spirit world, and crowned by an iron helmet mounted with yellowing antlers. "The Great Khan will indeed fall in this battle," he said to Genghis, looking past me. "But he shall not die."

My hands curled into fists and I wanted nothing so much as to sink my nails into the shaman's face. I had seen it—my husband would bleed his lifeblood into the steppes today. "I saw his wound, the death mask on his face," I growled.

Teb Tengeri shrugged, an elegant movement for a half man with a beard that looked as if it might harbor a den of shrews. "Perhaps your vision is faulty."

I hissed with rage, but the shaman paid less attention to me than to the buzzing of an errant fly.

"What about the storm?" Genghis asked, stepping between us. "I cannot risk losing men to the winds."

Teb Tengeri glanced at the approaching clouds, his braids whipped by gusts that cut through my *deel* like knives. He crouched to the earth and tasted the film of dirt on his thumb, then lifted his shoulders in an unconcerned shrug. "The storm is hollow as a bone. I could chase it away."

"Do it," Genghis snapped. "Send it back where it came from; make it hail and sleet upon their heads."

Teb Tengeri clasped his hands before him, fingers as twisted as the Great Branching Tree. "As you wish."

"He lies," I muttered as he walked away. "None of us can stop this storm."

And no one could stop the spirits if they decided to call my husband to the sacred mountains today.

"Perhaps not." Genghis touched my cheek with the same hands that knew precisely how to touch me in the dark of our *ger*, the same hands that held our children when they were first presented to the Eternal Blue Sky. "What will be, will be. It is not my place to fight it."

"Please don't go." My throat felt as if someone had cinched a harness around it so I could scarcely swallow. "I can't bear to watch you leave, knowing what I'll see the next time I look upon you."

"Then you'll have to close your eyes." Genghis pulled me into an embrace, and his chest expanded in a deep inhale, drawing my scent—my soul—inside his lungs, a piece of me to carry into his final battle. Greatness did not come without risks, and today my husband was prepared to make the greatest gamble of them all.

"You're a miserable piece of horse dung," I said, stepping back and swiping at my eyes as Jochi reappeared. "I'll never forgive you if you die now."

Genghis threw his head back and roared with laughter, making me smile through my tears. How could the Earth and Sky be so greedy as to claim such a man?

My son handed me the cup of milk I'd ordered and I chanted a prayer, letting the earth and its spirits drink the offering as I poured the liquid into the ground. Genghis kissed our children, then paused to unwind a red string from his braid and tie it around Alaqai's wrist. "Be good for your mother while I'm gone, little marmot," he said, tweaking her nose.

"I'll try," Alaqai said, fingering her new bracelet with a sigh. "But it's so hard to be good."

Jochi touched my shoulder then and produced a lopsided grin. "Don't worry, Mother," he said, giving me a jaunty wink. "I'll keep an eye on Father."

Shigi offered a smile as well, although his eyes lacked any spark of mirth. "And I'll keep an eye on your son, Borte Ujin," he murmured.

Winter gripped my heart in its icy embrace. My husband and son stood before me, strong boned, the blood still pumping through their hearts, and yet I'd seen other men race into battle only to have their broken bodies sprawled in the grasses later that day.

"Thank you, Shigi," I whispered.

Genghis kissed me then, his lips lingering a long while before he strode to his warhorse. He hadn't said *bayartai*, but I touched my lips, knowing that this kiss was different from all the others that had come before it.

It was the kiss of good-bye.

The storm conjured by Jamuka's shamans rose and swooped down on us, fiercer than a black hawk, shrieking in our ears and blinding our men. Then, just as suddenly, it climbed into the sky and retreated back the way it had come, trapping Jamuka and his men under its wings. Later we would find Tayichigud bodies in the ravines on the mountainside, lying where they'd fallen, some trapped beneath their horses after they'd stumbled in the dark.

As the sky cleared, our men turned wide eyes to a low rumble at the far end of our camp. It was Teb Tengeri, pounding his skin drum and beating the earth with his bare fists, his deep voice ululating into the spirit world. The silk tassels on his robe flashed and swirled as he danced, the gold discs sewn onto his chest catching the daylight and throwing it back to the sky in blinding flashes.

Genghis would never give up his shaman now that the winds seemed to obey his commands, no matter how I wished him to.

For the rest of that day and much of the next, I kept the women's hands busy with butchering several old horses for either a victory celebration or a funeral feast, but my mind returned time and again to where my husband might be at this moment. I trembled to think that a Tayichigud warrior—or perhaps even Jamuka—was even now striking the deathblow that would end Genghis' life. Finally, as the sun grew heavy on the second day, the cries of the watching children heralded the return of our soldiers. Alaqai took my hand in her little one with its nails bitten to the quick and Hoelun squeezed my other palm—a flesh-and-bone chain of three generations of our family's women, and for that I was grateful.

No happy song flew to us on the too-still air. Instead, there was only silence, the horses walking as if pulling heavy loads. Alaqai wriggled like a fish on a hook and gasped at the tightness of my grip, so I hefted her onto my hip instead and searched for her father's weathered face and Jochi's toothy smile. Instead, Khasar rode at the front on his yellow warhorse, his face as gray as a dead man's. At his side rode Shigi, his jaw clenched tight and his fingers stained with ink.

I couldn't bring myself to ask the question burning in my throat, for I already knew where my husband lay right now, his flesh likely feeding the wolves and vultures. "The Tayichigud lost many men and have pitched their tents until morning," Khasar said. "We have many wounded soldiers, but our clans won the day."

I looked past him, desperate for the sight of the skin sledges dragging the wounded home. My voice cracked. "And Genghis?"

Khasar dropped his eyes and bent his head. "Shot in the neck with an arrow."

My knees threatened to buckle, and I clasped Alaqai and Hoelun for support as a mourning cry rent the air. I would not collapse before my people. "Where is my son?"

Shigi glanced up then, his eyes pools of despair. It struck me then how poorly men deal with grief, how it is women who must bravely face the sorrows that men create. "Missing," he said. "I watched them ride off together, chasing after Jamuka's own horse. I'd have stopped Jochi if I could . . ."

I wasn't aware I'd closed my eyes until I felt a gentle touch at my elbow. "All is as it will be," Hoelun said sadly, looking suddenly the old woman she had become. She addressed Khasar. "Go, and bring our sons back."

The bodies of soldiers fallen in battle were typically left on the steppes to feed the carrion and the Earth Mother, but it wouldn't be Khasar or anyone else who laid out the corpses of my husband and son. It would be my hands that retrieved them and readied their bodies for the mountains. At least the vision had prepared me for what I would find.

"No," I said. "I'll go."

"Absolutely not," Hoelun said. "You'll be taken by the Tayichigud." She spat onto the dirt at the mention of the clan that had once betrayed her.

"Only I can claim Genghis and Jochi." I lingered on their names, struggling to make sense of this new world where my husband and son no longer breathed the same air I did or felt the Golden Light of the Sun. "Khasar will see to my safety."

"I'd go as well," Shigi said. "If you don't mind, Borte Khatun."

"So long as you bring a sword along with your paper and pens," I said. "It seems only fitting that you be there to record the end of Genghis' story."

I choked on the words, but Hoelun stepped aside. Khasar and Shigi followed behind as I walked to the horses, concentrating only on putting one foot in front of the other. The People of the Felt parted as I passed, their mournful keening like an invisible mist in the air. Wives reached out to touch me and a young girl hugged my knees. I looked down to see Alaqai staring up at me with her father's eyes, the red string he'd given her still tied to her wrist.

"I want to come with you," she said.

I touched the top of her head, the glossy hair always matted with tangles no matter how often I tried to comb them. "Your place is here, little marmot," I managed to say. "In case your grandmother needs help protecting your brothers."

Alaqai cocked her head as if contemplating my request. She likely realized she was being tricked, but I could almost hear her father's last instructions in her mind. "All right, Mother," she finally said, crossing her arms over her chest. "I'll get my bow and quarrels."

"Good girl," I said, choking as I thought of the quiver of arrows Genghis had given her on her last naming day, every point sharpened and each feather fletched by his own hands. Although he'd never admitted it aloud, I knew Alaqai was his favorite child, the one cast in his own shadow. Now her memories of him would fade until she could scarcely recall the way he pushed her to ride harder than her brothers, or to nock an arrow for a perfect shot at a waiting doe. "Your father would be proud," I whispered after her, my eyes stinging.

I mounted my mare and rode toward the mountains with Khasar and Shigi beside me, knowing that when the sun rose again I would confront the crooked mountain and my vision.

The trampled grasses were like a rabbit warren, trails left by deserting men and fleeing horses leading in every direction across the steppes. By the time we reached the foothills, my legs felt as if they were full of needles and all the warmth had drained from my hands. The silver sickle of the moon emerged with dusk, and the men and I dismounted as we approached the ravines. I led my mare by her bridle to keep her from tripping, but I stumbled over something the size of a rotten log. It was more giving than the cold earth and smelled worse than any forest decay. My horse reared and I scrambled back from the dead man, gagging on the stink of his spilled entrails and feeling the icy fingers of death reach inside me to wrap around my heart. His face was frozen in a rictus of terror and my hands shook as I scrambled back, trying not to breathe, but still smelling the taint of death.

How many souls could I carry with me? Already I carried fragments of my mother and father. Genghis. My sons and daughter. And I'd once breathed in part of Jamuka's soul, snaring my future with his and urging us all closer to this war we now fought. Now this nameless man stained my soul with his impure blood on my skin and his death in my lungs. The weight of all their spirits pulled me down as if their hands reached from the earth, knowing that my own soul would wish to fly away once the sun rose.

Silent tears streamed down my cheeks as I thought of Genghis' and Jochi's bodies sprawled like this, possibly already crawling with ants. I swallowed a sob at the thought of my firstborn nestled in the high grasses as he'd once been cradled in my womb. I'd sworn to protect him, and I'd failed.

"We can't go farther until daybreak," Khasar said, clearing his throat. Clouds obscured the full moon, making it dangerous to continue.

"Fine." I dashed my sleeve across my eyes. "We'll find them when the sun hits the ridge of the camel-backed mountain."

Shigi gave me a strange look in the dark. I realized that he hadn't heard my prophecy, but I didn't elaborate. It didn't matter if we searched through the night—nothing would change what I would soon discover.

Occasional groans came from the rocks throughout the night, uttered from the throats of men more dead than alive. I slept not at all, curled in my *deel* against a boulder and shivering as the air chilled. The early dawn filled the ravine and revealed a battlefield in the shadow of the crooked mountain. Corpses and dead horses lay scattered among the boulders, their eyes staring endlessly at the images of the sky and earth that they carried with them to the sacred mountains. Khasar, Shigi, and I stumbled from body to body, and I dreaded the moment when I would stare into my husband's sightless eyes.

And then I saw it and time stood still: a hand splayed over a gray rock, the green grasses rustling in the breeze, and the sun crowning the camel-backed mountain above us.

I willed the moment to disappear, yet nothing had changed when I forced open my eyes.

It was his face among the broken grasses and the crushed blue flowers. His one long braid was like a black snake on the earth, his shins still covered by the leather greaves I'd help tie. The lips that had kissed me only yesterday were still now, pale and stiff.

"Get away from him!" bellowed a man's voice behind me.

I whirled around with the dagger from my sleeve poised to strike. I was no warrior, but I would kill whoever had done this. Khasar raced toward me, an arrow already notched in his bow.

But it was no warrior who'd crept behind me, sword raised.

"Jochi?" I said.

"Mother?" He gave a cry of relief, no longer the brave soldier who had ridden into battle yesterday, but only a frightened young man who needed his mother.

"Thank the spirits you're alive," I said, crushing him to me, reveling in his warmth and heaving chest. "I'll never let you out of my sight again."

We stayed that way for a long while, Khasar and Shigi standing a ways off and pretending not to see a warrior weep with his mother. Finally, I peered through bleary eyes at the hand still in the grass. "And your father?" I asked, my voice trembling. "Was it a clean death?"

Jochi shook his head, and for a moment I imagined all manner of atrocities Jamuka might have committed against Genghis. "He's alive," Jochi said. "He took an arrow to the neck, but it wasn't deep." He pulled an elegant quarrel from the back of his belt, its tip stained with blood. "I couldn't bear to leave it as it was."

The words penetrated my brain slowly, like sunshine after a dense fog. "Alive?" I sank to my knees and felt at his neck, first with my fingers and then kissing the faint tremor of life there. The other side of Genghis' neck was packed with a crimson rag; a thin leather thong held the bandage in place. Only then did I notice the dried blood staining Jochi's lips. It was an invitation to the black spirits of death to spill one's blood into the ground, and so my son had taken my husband's blood into his body, had bound their souls as closely as if Genghis' seed had sired him.

"I swallowed as much of the blood as I could," Jochi said, "but there was so much that I had to spit the rest onto the ground once my belly was full." To touch death or another's blood made one unclean. My son cringed as if fearing a reprimand for defiling himself with his father's blood, but he continued when the rebuke never came. "He called for something to drink so loudly that I had to sneak into the Tayichigud camp to steal milk." He gestured to a worn leather bucket on the ground, then pulled back the stained cloth to reveal shiny white lumps floating in hazy water. "I couldn't find milk, but I fed him the water from these yak curds all night."

I stared at him, then burst into laughter, becoming so hysterical that Jochi and Khasar both stepped back and the crows that feasted on the dead fluttered into the air, casting their beady eyes at me while Shigi's pen scraped over his paper. My husband was alive, and all because of my son's quick thinking and a pail of yak curds. Jamuka had once claimed that life changes us, and he was right. This life was full of surprises, and I was thrilled and humbled that my sight had shown me only the worst of this day, that I'd been bested by Teb Tengeri.

I continued laughing until a clammy hand clasped my wrist. Then I screamed and scrambled to my feet.

"I scarcely think that's the appropriate response to welcome your husband back from the dead." Genghis stared at me from the ground, his speech slow, as if he'd drunk too much *airag* the night before. I fell to my knees and took his face in my hands, covering him with kisses.

"If you ever pull a foolish stunt like this again," I said, "I swear I'll kill you myself."

"I feel like you already tried." He recoiled from the pool of dark blood on the ground before looking to Jochi. "I heard what you said, son of my body, and I'm happy to owe you my life," he said, making my heart soar as Khasar tore grasses to cover the defiled earth and spare our eyes. "But I have one question."

"Yes, Father?"

Genghis winced. "Couldn't you have spit the blood farther away?"

Chapter 12

1204 CE
YEAR OF THE WOODEN RAT

We gathered the spoils from the Tayichigud camp and left their bodies to feed the grasses. In all our years of fighting, none of Genghis' Dogs of War or his Valiant Warriors had ever deserted, yet we heard reports that Jamuka's clans—even the Jadarin of his birth—were abandoning him for his cowardice in fleeing when the storm and battle turned against him at the crooked mountain. Genghis' generals advised pursuit, but my husband was in no condition to traipse over the steppes in search of his *anda*, nor would he allow anyone else to confront his blood brother. I offered a prayer of thanks to the Earth Mother when the first frost hardened the grasses and hoped that the winter snows would bring peace and much-needed recovery for my weakened husband.

It wasn't only his clans that left Jamuka, but his wife, too. The first snows came early that year, bringing a lone woman to our lines of *gers* as thick white flakes fell overhead. It had been years since I'd seen Gurbesu, yet I recognized my childhood friend at once when Khasar shoved her into our tent. Jealousy fluttered in my chest as I touched my chapped lips and crossed my arms under my tired breasts, which had suckled my children, for Gurbesu's lips were still plump and her *deel* remained tight across her ample chest.

"A Jadarin spy," Khasar said, pointing his spear at Gurbesu as she stumbled onto the beaten brown grass inside my *ger*, smelling of the cold. My husband stood before her, legs planted wide and his hands hidden inside the wide sleeves of his *deel*, where he kept at least one dagger, usually more.

"I'm no Jadarin," Gurbesu said, still on all fours on the ground, the snow on her hair melting to water before the heat of the fire. "Although I'll admit I was Jamuka's wife before he cast me out."

Genghis let her linger on the ground. "I believe you once claimed that my people smelled like fresh camel dung and our clothes were filthier than the underside of a yak's belly. You must be here on important business to brave such barbarians as stand before you now."

She dared to look up then, first at Genghis and then at me. Her eyes widened and her mouth fell open, revealing a jaw of still-perfect teeth. "Borte Ujin," she breathed, her gaze falling on the wolf-tooth necklace I still often wore. "Is that you?"

"Borte Khatun now," I said, trying to keep a serene expression, but she squealed as if we were children tossing the air-filled bladder of a goat.

"It *is* you," she said, scrambling to her feet. "I told you we'd meet again, but you didn't believe me—"

"Don't take another step," Genghis snarled. Khasar reached for his sword and Genghis glowered first at Gurbesu and then at me. "You know this woman?"

"We were children together," I answered. "Gurbesu married Chuluun of the Naiman after the Festival of Games, before you sought me out the second time."

Of course, that was also the first time Gurbesu had laid eyes on Jamuka. I remembered her lying by the river, annoyed when he rebuffed her advances so that I might scry for him. So much had changed since then, it seemed as if I were viewing the memory through someone else's eyes.

Gurbesu sobered at the mention of her first husband. "Chuluun was killed in battle, but I was too young to be widowed. Jamuka recalled me from the Festival of Games and claimed me for his wife." She threw back her shoulders as if riding into battle. "Jamuka and I argued when I said he wouldn't win this war. He knows he will lose, but he refuses to beg his *anda*'s forgiveness for the good of his people." She snorted. "What few there are left of them, anyway."

"So he cast you out?" I didn't wish to probe, but neither did I want a spy endangering my people and my family.

She nodded, her lips twisted tight. "Over a week ago."

Genghis scoffed. "I cannot believe that Jamuka would so dishonor the wife of his heart."

Gurbesu snorted. "Jamuka's heart had been claimed long before he took me." She gave me a pointed look so I felt as if we were seventeen winters old once again, and discussing which man I should take first to my bed. "I had to travel across the steppes as the frost hardened the ground," she continued. "I thought I would die amongst the grasses when the first snow began to fall tonight, but then I saw the smoke from your fires."

"And your children?"

Again, the battle stance, chin tilted and shoulders squared as if defying the world. "I lost my only babe—a son—after Chuluun was killed. Born too early," she said. "Jamuka's seed never took root in my womb." Her hands fluttered; then she clasped them in front of her. "Chuluun arranged the betrothal of his only daughter after we married. I never knew her."

"Toregene."

Gurbesu stared at me then, her expression clear that she thought I'd seen this in the bones. "I met her," I said. "When she was with the Merkid."

"You did?" Gurbesu's eyes clouded with confusion, then cleared as she likely recalled the story of my capture. "Is she here now?"

My heart grew heavy as it always did when I thought of Toregene. "She ran into the forest when the Merkid were raided. That was many years ago, and I never saw her again."

Gurbesu's face fell. "So she's dead, like so many others."

I was surprised to see tears shine in her eyes. "Many died that night," I said. "But I've always hoped to one day find Toregene."

And yet the years had passed, still with no trace of her. Hope was a difficult thing to keep alive after so long.

Only the pop and hiss of the fire interrupted the silence before Genghis finally cleared his throat. "Borte Khatun," he said, catching both our attentions with my formal title. "Will you vouch for Gurbesu of the Uni-girad?"

His was no simple question; I knew not the woman Gurbesu had become in the years since we'd been girls or whether her word could be trusted. Still, I craved her company and this link to my childhood.

"I will."

Gurbesu's face lit in a smile, but it didn't reach her eyes. She linked her arm in mine. "It'll be like old times between us, Borte Uj—" She caught herself. "Borte Khatun."

Even then, I knew that to be untrue. Too much had changed since I'd last hugged Gurbesu and watched her step over the horizon with her first bridegroom for things to ever be the same.

Still, it would be pleasant to have Gurbesu around again, to listen to her chatter like birdsong and to laugh at the gossip that always followed in her wake. Yet, as I watched Khasar and the other men's greedy eyes follow her swaying hips from the tent, I wondered whether allowing Gurbesu into our camp might be more trouble than it was worth.

Unable to sit idle even as his wound mended, my husband negotiated with the clans while the snows drifted deeper, casting a wide net for the betrothals and alliances that would bind all the People of the Felt closer together. Yesui and Yesugen both became pregnant—neither wife seemed strong enough to do anything without her sister doing it as well—and birthed my husband two more daughters. A girl from the west was found for Chaghatai to marry in the spring, and Ong Khan's brother offered to marry his only daughter into our family.

I had sniffed at that. As I'd often worried, our alliance with Ong Khan had recently disintegrated. The treacherous old chief recognized my husband's growing power and denounced us as he'd done to Jamuka before the Battle of Seventy Marshes, claiming that Genghis sought to topple him from his throne once Jamuka was finally defeated. Ong Khan's duplicity had cost him dearly this time; he encountered a guard at the old Naiman border who refused to believe that the old man was the Khan of Khans, and it took one bloody slice to promptly relieve old Ong Khan of his head.

It was rumored that the befouled head had been placed on a sacred cloth of felt in the back of a Naiman *ger* and danced to amidst the music of a horse-head fiddle before finally being kicked outside once maggots hatched from its eyes. Such outrageous sacrilege could scarcely be tolerated, even against our enemy, but secretly I thought the punishment just for the old khan's betrayal.

"Sorkhokhtani is a Kereyid princess," Genghis said one night shortly after we'd received the marriage offer from Ong Khan's brother. Our remaining children slept huddled near the hearth, just Ogodei, Alaqai, and Tolui, now that our elder sons were grown. "Jamba Gamu seeks to right the wrong done against us by his brother. Her blood will bind us to the old order."

Genghis rubbed the new lines seared into his cheeks. "If we kept Sorkhokhtani close she could care for us in our old age."

"You would marry her to Tolui, then?" I whispered, gingerly lifting the quiver of arrows from the crook of Alaqai's arm as she lay among her bedclothes. Despite my protests, my daughter slept with her weapons, and I feared that one night she'd gouge her eyes out with the tip of a quarrel. I'd come to accept that this daughter of mine was a shadow of her father—who also slept with an assortment of weapons—especially after I'd made several mangled attempts to teach her the skills she'd one day need as a wife and mother. She excelled at driving the horses that rolled the heavy bundles of rolled wool for felting, but she'd almost burned down our tent while making horsemeat stew. I took no pride in realizing that my daughter's future husband would likely starve to death.

Alaqai *would* marry one day and leave us for her husband's clan, as our sons would leave our circle of *gers* to forge their own camps. All save one. As our last son, Tolui would remain with us always, our Prince of the Hearth.

Genghis and I smothered smiles as Tolui snored openmouthed. "I hope Sorkhokhtani doesn't need much sleep," I muttered, wincing as Tolui's snores turned to outrageous gurgles. "Your son snores louder than a herd of yaks."

"He gets that from his mother," Genghis said, looking entirely serious.

I chucked Alaqai's muddy boot at him, but he dodged it. "Keeping Sorkhokhtani near us will renew our alliance with Ong Khan's clan."

That, more than anything, would determine our children's matches. As my marriage to Genghis had been made to keep the peace, so, too, would our sons and daughter find their mates. I wished to stall time, to keep my remaining children under my *ger*, but I thanked the Earth Mother for each day the sun shone on my happy family. Still, the puckered scar on my lip and the fresh pink flesh on my husband's neck were reminders that such joy was tenuous at best.

Sorkhokhtani's caravan of silk and horses arrived on one of the brightest days of spring, accompanied by her father to share the milk of the betrothal agreement. I would not bid farewell to my sons so they might complete their bride-price, but instead gathered daughters as the clans sought the privilege of marrying into the family of the future Great Khan. The People of the Felt sprawled before us in a sea of brown faces, including Gurbesu standing up front in a stunning red *deel* and Shigi in his black scribe's cap, already taking down notes with the pen and ink he carried in his sleeves. Alaqai and our elder sons stood behind us, but Tolui squirmed at my side, uncomfortable in the stiff new *deel* and blue headdress I'd made him wear. Almost twelve summers old, he had cheeks that were still round, and every so often he suppressed a cough, one he'd picked up as winter had ebbed.

Jamba Gamu stood to the side of his daughter's horse and Genghis helped her dismount, a symbolic acceptance of our future daughter even as he threw his head back with a triumphant roar of laughter. Tolui grinned back at his brothers. "My wife is prettier than any you'll ever have," Tolui whispered, but Ogodei only winked at Alaqai and then yawned.

"Too bad you can't marry her for another four years, little pup," Ogodei drawled.

Tolui opened his mouth to argue, but I silenced him with a glare that threatened to turn him to ash. Together we stepped forward to greet Sorkhokhtani. She'd seen perhaps seventeen summers and immediately bowed to us, the brass bells at the ends of her tall red headdress tinkling. I would soon learn that this new daughter of mine was a creature of music, filling her days with the sounds of bells and her horsehair fiddle rather than with idle chatter as girls were often wont to do.

"I bring Genghis Khan and Borte Khatun greetings from the Kereyid," she said, her voice reminding me of a stream slipping over the smooth stones of an ancient creek bed. Her features were as delicate as the rest of her, save a brown mole high on her left cheek. "I am honored to one day marry your Prince of the Hearth."

I laid my palms lightly on the girl's shoulders, as fragile as birds' wings, and I pressed my forehead to hers. I was accustomed to my sturdy Alaqai, who was always ready to rough-and-tumble with her brothers, and wondered whether Tolui's intended wife was as delicate as my youngest son. I wondered then at her thoughts, whether she was as terrified as I had been to meet my new family, or if she viewed this as an opportunity to continue her family's prestige. Her skin glowed like a ripe moon and I offered her a warm smile, but her expression remained placid.

I linked her arm through mine to introduce her to her new home, and vowed then that I would not spy on Sorkhokhtani as Hoelun had done when I'd arrived to share her hearthstones. Still, I wondered at this girl's secrets, at the hidden desires of her heart. From the hooded expression she wore, I had a feeling that she'd not soon share them with us.

Only months later and despite my many protests, my husband rode into battle against the remaining Merkid clan—the last of Jamuka's followers. Genghis routed their bedraggled soldiers and returned with a meager caravan of spoils, having allotted most of the treasure to his deserving men. He gifted Sorkhokhtani a priceless two-stringed *tobshuur* carved from a single ancient birch tree, and Hoelun a black cart drawn by a sleek white camel as befitted the mother of the future Great Khan. Shigi's eyes bulged at a gift of a stack of pristine paper with a set of gilded pens and a silver inkpot. Each of our children received new swords. Alaqai's was thinner than the boys', but the hilt was inlaid with jade and decorated with golden tigers.

Yet Genghis' gift to me was the most precious.

I stood with Alaqai and Sorkhokhtani when my husband lifted a finger in the air, the grin on his face infectious. "I found something amongst the Merkid which would be common to most, but priceless to you, wife of my heart. I've scoured the steppes for this these many years as our children grew and the circles of our *gers* swelled." He paused for dramatic effect. "I searched not for some*thing*, but for some*one*."

I knew before he beckoned to the huddle of Merkid women standing behind a tall cart that it would be Toregene. The girl with the mismatched eyes was now a woman grown almost to my height, with the first whispers of lines at her brow and an angular body composed entirely of the straight lines of a towering pine tree. Shigi and the others behind me gasped when they saw her eyes, but I ran to her, enveloping her in a hug that almost knocked her over. "You wonderful, terrible girl," I breathed. "Where have you been all these years?"

She swallowed but didn't speak, the silver cross at her throat somewhat tarnished now, but still reflecting the sun's light. It was Genghis who finally answered for her. "She was married to one of the last Merkid princes," he said, his tone low and lacking any triumph. "I saw her eyes and ordered the men to spare her."

To spare her a public rape, but not the death of her husband and her people.

Those eyes that had saved her no longer sparked with life but were now clouded with pain. There was more than simply a dead husband and the shock of a midnight raid. I hugged her again, puzzled at her hiss of pain as I pressed her to me. Only then did I catch the familiar and unpleasant scent on her, stronger than the pain and suffering that roiled from her.

Sour milk.

I realized then that the front of her *deel* was stained with many days of rancid breast milk, the last testament of an infant who had been ripped from his mother's arms and was now no more than dust. Genghis was brutal when dealing with other men but forbade the killing of any child shorter than the linchpin of a camel cart. Yet sometimes not even my husband could control everything that happened in the heat of battle.

Toregene's eyes welled with tears as understanding dawned across my face, and she bit her lower lip to keep it from trembling.

This courageous woman before me had survived a second raid and the murder of her husband and child—perhaps even children—and then endured the agony of many days' journey being jostled in a cart while her breasts hardened and her milk dried away. I recalled with a shudder my own terrible ordeal with Chilger and how Toregene had opened my heart to hope again. I had so little to offer her, but I would heal this girl as best I could, although part of her was surely shattered beyond repair.

"You brave girl," I whispered. "I don't know how you survived all you did, but I'm glad that your god protected you."

"Sochigel found me in the woods after the first raid," Toregene said, her voice as low as the flutter of a dove's wings. "She helped me find roots and berries to eat, until we came to the other Merkid camp. They took me in, knowing I'd been betrothed to Toghtoga's son, but Sochigel chose to remain in the woods. I never saw her again."

I sent a silent prayer of thanks to Sochigel and clutched Toregene to me, pressing my cheek to her hair. "I'll care for you now," I said. "As you once cared for me. All right?"

She nodded and her eyes filled again with tears, but she blinked them away. "Thank you, Borte Khatun," she whispered.

I wondered then if I should tell her that her stepmother, Gurbesu, was here, too, but there would be an opportunity for that later, as there would be time enough to discuss Toregene's position in our clan. This girl would be no slave, nor would I allow anyone to claim her as a wife until she was ready.

"I've waited for you a long time, Toregene." I pressed my forehead to hers and inhaled, claiming her as mine. "Welcome home, daughter."

Chapter 13

In the end, it was Jamuka's own supporters who finally betrayed him and delivered him to our hands.

Deserted by all his clans, Jamuka huddled with five men, the last of his followers, and together they roasted a great mountain sheep with curved horns. But when Jamuka fell asleep, the men seized him and dragged him bound and gagged to our camp, thinking to claim a reward for his capture.

The five men spat on Jamuka and kicked him after they'd thrown him to the dust at Genghis' feet. Khasar and the Four Valiant Warriors flanked my husband, hands on the hilts of their swords, while Shigi remained in his usual place, hidden in the shadows while he recorded every word and gesture on paper. This was a public spectacle under the dark sweep of night, and even the children had joined the crowd, boys and girls who knew nothing of a life free of war. Our clans believed they were here to witness Jamuka's fate, but from the way Genghis glowered at the other men, I feared more than one man's blood would be shed tonight.

"Here's the brown vulture you sought for so long," one man said, landing a blow to Jamuka's cheek. The face that had once been so beautiful was now swollen, scarcely recognizable save the almost black eyes that peered at us.

"Stop," I said, feeling the weight of my *boqta*, the green khatun's headdress. "Only the khan can pass judgment on this man."

Yet from the myriad emotions passing over Genghis' face, I knew not what that judgment would be. Jamuka had caused us much pain and grief over the years, but now I saw him for what he truly was: a lonely shell of a man whose dreams had deserted him entirely. The white-boned dragon I'd met at the Festival of Games had been honest and loyal, a good man, but this man before me was broken, having allowed the darkness of greed and jealousy to overtake all the light in his soul. He had no wife and no clan, no brothers or children to sing his songs after he traveled to the sacred mountains. He was a man not to be hated, but to be pitied.

The shortest of the men pretended not to hear me, then landed a kick to Jamuka's ribs so hard there was a crack like snapping twigs. Jamuka moaned and his pupils rolled back to reveal the bloodshot whites of his eyes. "We knew the great Genghis Khan would be happy to see this traitor again." The short captor leered at my husband. "And, of course, we'd be happy to accept any reward you might feel we've earned for our work."

A vein in my husband's neck pulsed angrily, but he calmly stroked the end of his long mustache. His eyes never once strayed from the man. "And what sort of reward," he asked, "do you feel you've earned?"

The man glanced at his comrades and one of them nodded. They'd discussed this in advance. "Horses and silver," the short one said. "And positions in your army."

"I see." Genghis turned to me, yet beckoned to Khasar and the other guards with a crook of his finger. "Yet how could I trust you, men who lie in wait to turn upon their leader?"

The captors protested but fell silent as Khasar's and the soldiers' cold swords touched their necks.

"The only reward you've earned is a merciful death," Genghis said.

Jamuka's former followers moved to draw their swords, but with a swift movement my husband sliced off the head of the short man. It fell to the ground with a spray of crimson as the body collapsed forward with a thud. Khasar and the Four Valiant Warriors made short work of the other traitors, slitting their throats. Genghis blocked my view, but I sidestepped him and nudged the head with my boot, careful not to sully the leather with the unclean blood. "It's unfortunate their deaths were so quick," I said.

Genghis stared at me for a moment, then chuckled as slaves dragged the bodies away. "You never cease to amaze me, wife of my heart."

I knelt before Jamuka then, waiting for the reassuring wave of hatred, but the emotion wouldn't come. Instead, I was filled with revulsion and pity for this man who had been stained with a prophecy as dark as mine, yet had squandered all his opportunities—and the lives of many men—in his quest for greatness and power. I loosened the horsehair gag and the ties at his wrists and ankles, which were crusted with filth and blood, the leather thongs tied so tightly they had sliced deep into his flesh. He watched with dead eyes, then struggled to stand, and when that proved impossible, he pulled himself to sit. I was shocked at how thin he'd become, his sharp shoulders and skeletal hands better suited to a corpse long dead.

I glimpsed the future then, and shuddered at what awaited.

Seeing that his former *anda* could no longer stand, Genghis crouched to speak to him eye to eye. It might have been a gathering from long ago, at least if one could ignore the slaves scurrying to cover the puddles of fresh blood with dried grasses.

"We are old men now," Genghis said to Jamuka. "It is time to re-member what we had once forgotten."

Jamuka's voice was as faint as the rustle of a crane's wing flying overhead. Gone was the proud dragon with the golden future, replaced by a frail man with a corrupt soul who shivered despite the dung fire burning brightly at his back. "Long ago, I declared myself to be your *anda*. We spoke promises which were never to be forgotten." He looked up with eyes shining with tears and remorse. "I should have kept my promise, but my face was blackened with jealousy." He bowed his head. "I shall be forever sorry for that."

I glanced at Genghis to see his eyes bright with tears and softened my expression, silently pleading with him. I waited an eternity, then exhaled with relief as he gave a tight nod.

"*Anda* Jamuka," he said, "I do not live in the past. Join my clan and let us be allies now that we are together again."

The crowd rumbled at that, unsure of Genghis' motives. If Jamuka rejoined us, my husband's conquest would be complete, but war might break out again at any time. Jamuka's unfocused eyes moved first from Genghis and then to me. I searched for a flicker of hope there, the faintest trace of a dream fulfilled with Genghis' offer. Instead, Jamuka shook his head. "There can be only one sun in the sky, and my sun has set. I shall be forever known as a traitor."

Genghis stood, protesting and full of bluster, citing all the times Jamuka had been loyal to him in their early years and how he'd rescued him from certain death many times over, how he'd even rescued me.

Jamuka held up his battered hands to stop Genghis' rant. "Please," he said. "I ask only one thing."

My husband ceased pacing then. "You have merely to say it and it will be yours."

"I am ready to journey to the sacred mountains," Jamuka said. "I ask that you do not shed my blood when you kill me. I would greet the ancestors a whole man, so my soul might protect your children and your children's children."

I thought of Chaghagan Uua, with his bloodied head tied to his horse, and all the men boiled alive in the Field of Cauldrons. I wondered if Jamuka's request was born from cowardice or if perhaps he really did seek to right the wrongs of this life from the sacred mountains. He would surely forfeit his life, but despite his blackened soul, perhaps some small shred of his former honor still remained. That was what I chose to believe, for otherwise, the long struggle Jamuka had fought against avarice and despair had been lost entirely.

Genghis cursed under his breath and the crowd roared, thirsty for blood, but my husband raised his hands. A hush fell then, Genghis wielding the silence as skillfully as he did his sword.

"I could refuse you," he finally said. "If I wished, I could make you live the rest of your days by my side."

Jamuka hung his head. "That is your choice. Still, although I deserve to die a horrific death, I ask only for a clean one."

Genghis stood stone-faced, then gestured for Khasar and the other warriors. Their *deels* were still stained with blood. "We will honor the last wish of my *anda*. Execute this man by breaking his neck, but do not shed his blood. His bones will be buried with all due honor."

Then he clasped Jamuka's hands with his own and drew a deep breath. I imagined for a moment the faint wisp of Jamuka's dying soul entering my husband, felt its traces from long ago flare deep within my own soul.

The warriors took up their positions behind Jamuka, but they hesitated when I knelt and lifted Jamuka's head to look into his eyes.

"You should not touch me," he said, recoiling. "I would not taint you with the stain of my dishonor."

"I will touch you," I said. "For who else will sing the song to guide you to the sacred mountains?"

He blinked then, and a single tear fell down his swollen cheek. "I will watch you from their highest peaks, Borte Ujin. My spirit shall always guard your family, as I should have done in life."

My hand lingered on his cheek, but I gave a terse nod to Khasar before my vision blurred entirely. I held Jamuka's hand as he was hauled to his feet. There was a long moment of silence, and then, with a deft movement, Khasar twisted Jamuka's neck. There was a snap, and the crowd cheered as the last trace of light finally left the eyes of the man I'd once loved and hated.

We buried Jamuka's bones in the cliffs of a snowcapped mountain so high it grazed the underbelly of the clouds. The wind whipped my hair, worn loose these past weeks in mourning, and generations of ancestors, young and old, wailed in my ears. The ground was rocky here, slick with last night's rain, and a lone magpie preened in the dead birch before me.

And at the base of its white trunk . . .

My voice rose in the song I had sung weeks ago as Jamuka's spirit had fled his broken body, flying into the Eternal Blue Sky toward his new home in the sacred mountains. Wild dogs and hawks had circled me the day my daughters and I brought him here, but today I had slipped from camp at first light before Alaqai, Toregene, or Sorkhokhtani could follow me. This time there was only the wind at my back.

Cups of fresh camel milk and leather sacks of dried horsemeat joined the platters I'd left forty-nine days ago, their offerings long since eaten by the spirits or scavenging animals. I'd waited until the last possible day to return to the open burial, praying that I would find only bones when I returned, a sure sign that the guardians of the sacred mountains had accepted his spirit. I built two fires, striking flint over dried goat dung and feeding the flames until they shuddered in the wind, as if unwilling to burn in so harsh a place. I passed between the two sentries to burn away any lurking evil spirits, just as I'd done on the night of my wedding.

The white silk shroud I'd used to cover Jamuka's face the day he died flapped in the wind, revealing a yellowish skull with two lines of white teeth protruding from the open jaw. A trace of his dark hair still clung to the scalp, and here and there was a patch of dried tendon or skin, but the winds and the sun had done their work as I'd hoped. Tenderly, as if touching the cheek of one of my children, I gathered Jamuka's bones into a birch basket Toregene had woven for me.

"Remember your promise," I murmured to his spirit. I closed my eyes and leaned into the warmth on my shoulder, the same as when his hand had lingered there the night we'd stood together on a similar mountaintop. The heat spread to envelop me like a blanket on a stormy winter night, but when I opened my eyes it was to find that the clouds had broken and the sun shone down on me.

It was not for myself that I prayed, but for my children, my sons and daughters, both those of my womb and all the others I'd spread my wings over, and my children's children, yet unborn. As I'd worried years ago, my husband wasn't content to merely unite the clans of the steppes. Only the day before, Genghis had declared war against the Jurched Empire in the east, further unifying the People of the Felt in preparation to attack the foreign walled cities, to plunder their riches and seize their trade routes.

"Protect us," I prayed to Jamuka's spirit, feeling it hover nearby as I often felt Mother Khogaghchin's and my parents'. "For we shall need your protection now more than ever."

PART II

The Khan's Daughter

Chapter 14

1206 CE
YEAR OF THE FIRE TIGER

My mother named me Alaqai, Palm of the Hand, thinking that the clot of blood in my fist when I fell from her womb meant that I would follow in my father's footsteps to become a great leader. Yet to my father I would always be *tarvag takal*, his Siberian marmot. But our people's word for *marmot* has another meaning, one that brings to mind black boils erupting on a man's skin, the fevered flush of a child's forehead, the last rattle of air in a woman's dying lungs.

Tarvag takal means *marmot*, but it is also the name of the plague our people fear.

The spirits of countless dead soldiers had breathed life into me while I was still in my mother's womb, surrounded by the scourge of war on a battlefield.

And so my name is one of power. And also of death.

The eagle soared silently through the air, a stark outline of brown and gold against the Eternal Blue Sky, and a screech that would have curdled the blood in any warrior's veins accompanied its dive to earth. My pulse thrummed in my ears and I clutched my gelding's reins, standing in my stirrups for a better view. The sun-drenched grasses waved wildly and a hidden fox screamed as the raptor made contact. I sat down hard in my saddle, a triumphant grin on my face. I'd witnessed plenty of horse races and wrestling matches in my fifteen years, but never the fabled Kazakh eagle hunt.

"It's no wonder my father recruited you and your riders into his army," I marveled to the young Kazakh soldier next to me, his hat the same shade as freshly spilled blood. I'd met him only that morning and had persuaded him to let me accompany him with his eagle instead of watching the races. "I'd almost trade my horse for that eagle of yours!"

"He's a fine animal, Alaqai Beki," the Kazakh said, giving my black gelding an appraising stare. His gaze continued its way along my legs and farther upward. This man knew my title and my position as Genghis Khan's only daughter, yet I hadn't troubled myself to even ask his name. It didn't seem like it mattered.

"I said I'd *almost* trade," I said, tossing my long braid over my shoulders. "I'll ride Neer-Gui until the day he dies."

"Neer-Gui?" The Kazakh's furrowed brow deepened the lines in his face. "You named your horse?"

Mongol horses were meant to work and then fill a stewpot. Neer-Gui meant *No-Name*, so I hadn't broken the unspoken rule against naming him, and I'd skewer anyone who tried to butcher him. Unfortunately, the yearly winter slaughter of geldings fast approached, and it would be difficult to persuade my mother that he wouldn't be more useful as sausage. "The only person I like more than Neer-Gui is my father," I said with a shrug. "It only seemed fitting that he have a name."

The Kazakh stared at me as if I'd spoken Turkic to him, so I kicked my horse and galloped across the plain, trailing my long shadow and hearing him holler to his warhorse. I reached the kill site first and reined in hard. The eagle perched atop a pile of shimmering orange fur, blinking her brown eyes when the Kazakh collected her onto his thick leather glove.

"Can I hold her?" I asked. I ached to touch this stunning creature before the opportunity passed forever.

He hesitated and the eagle cauled hungrily, revealing her silver-white tongue. "The Khan would have me disemboweled if she hurt you," he said, raising his hand to stall my protest. "But you may feed her."

I unsheathed my knife with a grin and made quick work of the fox, cutting a slit down its belly, careful to avoid puncturing the stomach and spilling its putrid contents, and peeling the thick fur away from the glistening pink sinews. I sliced a long strip of flesh from its hind leg and dangled it above the eagle's hooked beak. Kazakhs withheld food from their eagles before a hunt, so the famished raptor snapped up my offering.

"You are a beautiful bird," I said to her, resisting the urge to touch her gleaming wing. "And a mighty warrior."

"The eagle hunt is only for the eyes of men," the Kazakh said, repeating the excuse he'd first used to put me off. He maneuvered the bird onto the carcass, letting her tear into the warm muscles as a reward as he carelessly tossed the fox pelt onto his saddle. "If any of my soldiers discovered that I'd shown its secrets to a woman, even the daughter of the Great Khan—"

I glanced about the empty sweep of green, unable to hear the sounds from my father's *khurlatai*, even swollen as it was with clans come from as far as the Altai Mountains to install him as Great Khan. "I appreciate the risk you took," I said, stepping closer and trailing a finger up his chest. The fox pelt shimmered in his saddle, its sunlit hairs trembling in the breeze. The fur would make a decadent trim on my new hat for the coming winter. "And I believe I still owe you."

I'd promised the Kazakh only a kiss in exchange for showing me his eagle in action, but the heat of the sun and the width of his shoulders made me want more, and he was happy to oblige. His caresses were coarse and hurried, but as the saying goes, even foul water will quench a fire. I shed my *deel* and pushed him back into the grass, loosening his trousers and grinning at his slack-jawed expression. He recovered quickly from his shock, his fingers digging into the backs of my thighs, and I concentrated on the rhythm of his body under mine. I was dimly aware of the sun beating down on my back and the grasshoppers chirping in the sedges as a thin wave of pleasure made me shudder. The Kazakh finished with a grunt and I rolled away, shrugging back into my light summer *deel*. He was still lying in the grass with his trousers around his knees when I took the fox pelt from his saddle and buried my face in it, breathing in the animal's musk amidst the sunshine.

"You're a generous man," I said, batting my eyelashes shamelessly and ignoring the smear of fox blood on my fingers. "Would you mind terribly if I kept this?"

He sat up and rubbed his jaw, his pupils still dilated. "I don't know—"

"I'm sure your eagle can catch another one." I threw the fur over my shoulder and vaulted onto my horse's back. The sun hung brightly over the distant mountains—if I didn't hurry I'd miss the wrestling competition. I kicked my gelding's ribs and glanced back through my tangled hair to see the Kazakh standing by his warhorse, fumbling with his rope belt and wearing a bewildered expression. The eagle let out a shrill cry like laughter and Neer-Gui snorted in derision as he ran.

I laughed with them, rubbing my cheek against the fox pelt. Like most men, the eagle hunter had underestimated me simply because I was a girl.

After all, no man expected to be bested by a Siberian marmot.

The shadows were short and I scrambled to keep my footing, feeling sweat trickle down my temples as my burly opponent and I danced around the ring. Only men and boys were allowed to compete in the wrestling competition, but I'd had enough time after the eagle hunt to bind my breasts under a blue vest and smudge my face with mud and a bit of manure so no one would recognize me.

I attempted to maneuver my arms around the man's shoulders, but he blocked the move and lunged to grab my braid.

"This will be the end of you, boy." Boroghul's snarl revealed bits of horsemeat stuck between his crooked teeth. My father's favorite cook, Boroghul had taken time out from distributing food and guarding the precious gift of wine brought by the Onggud in order to compete in the wrestling tournament today. He had teats like an old sow and his bare belly glistened in the summer sunshine, thick black hairs curling over the waistband of a breechcloth stained with horse blood and charcoal.

"Get him, Alaqai!" Tolui jumped up and down from the edge of the ring where he stood next to Ogodei and Toregene. My brothers Jochi and Chaghatai were much older than me, and too busy trying to impress my father to spend time with their younger sister, so I spent most of my days wrestling and racing with Ogodei and Tolui, although I'd seen less of Ogodei recently. Toregene had agreed to marry him a few months before the *khurlatai*, becoming his second wife although she was several years older than him. Ogodei's first wife had been barren for three years, but Toregene's stomach already swelled with their first child, which my favorite brother crowed about so often I'd threatened to sew his lips shut more than once.

Of course, I could barely wield a needle; I'd have better luck shooting him in the mouth with an arrow.

Boroghul's eyes widened in surprise and he lurched back. "Alaqai? As in Alaqai *Beki*?"

Toregene yanked Tolui to her and whispered something in his ear. Wearing an official blue judge's cap, Shigi stared at me from the middle of the ring before shaking his head; he certainly wouldn't appreciate my bending the rules. Having recently been appointed both judge and scribe for the People of the Felt, Shigi wore dark smudges under his eyes from all the late nights he'd spent working on the Jasagh, my father's new code of law. Tolui jabbed the air with his fists, sloshing *airag* over the jug he held, which Ogodei quickly requisitioned as he hollered a brother's helpful advice in my direction. "Uppercut!"

I took the momentary advantage of the distraction and let fly a scream like the Kazakh's golden eagle before launching myself to his right. Boroghul turned just as I'd hoped, and I leapt to his front and slammed my elbow into his soft belly. For a moment it was like a pebble thrown upon a mountain, but then he gasped and crouched over, suddenly weak in the legs. I slammed into him one last time and used the toe of my turned-up boot to hook his ankle, and he crashed to the earth with a dull thud.

There was a moment of hushed silence, and then Shigi stepped forward. The sun caught the gold ring he wore in his nose, and for a moment I feared he'd declare the match invalid. Instead, his eyes sparkled and the corners of his mouth twitched. He took my hand and lifted it in the air, pressing the traditional victor's bowl of cheese curds into my free hand. "The small one wins!" Toregene let out a whoop of victory as Shigi leaned down to whisper in my ear. "I only wish you'd told me you were competing."

"So you could forbid it?" I asked, waiting for a tirade as I tossed the curds to the waiting crowd. Men dove for the treats, likely made from my mother's own churn before the sun rose this morning.

"No," Shigi answered. "So I could have bet on you."

I grinned like a fool as Tolui collected bets from men twice his size. Ogodei tossed me a rag and my share of the earnings, then draped his thick arm around my shoulders while I scrubbed most of the manure from my face. "Next time try to finish a little sooner, eh, little sister?" he said, ignoring the trail of people that seemed to always crowd his shadow. Of all my brothers, Ogodei had inherited my father's ability to draw people to him, both men and women alike. "I drained a full jug of wine waiting for you to finish off that lout."

I sniffed the dark dregs of his container, wrinkling my nose at the sour smell of the alcohol that the Onggud delegation had brought as a gift to my father. They claimed the drink was made from fermented grapes, and they had brought dried versions of the fruit, which my brothers and I had tasted and spit into our hands. Eating dung would have been preferable to these Onggud foods, although all my brothers except Jochi had warmed immediately to the wine.

I glanced across the corral at Boroghul, wincing as another of the cooks cuffed his head with a harsh fist. "That boy was half your size," the second cook yelled. "What in the name of the Eternal Blue Sky happened?"

Boroghul yelled something about drinking too much and his head hurting, although I hadn't smelled any alcohol on his breath. My brothers were another matter entirely; I felt half-drunk just breathing near them.

"I did throw him, didn't I?" I chuckled to Ogodei as he ruffled my hair and handed me my tiger sword, which he'd been holding for me. I slipped the blade into my belt as Tolui rejoined us, my fingers lingering to trace the striped beasts in what had become my ritual after a win.

"A beginner's move." Tolui grinned, his voice too loud and his words slightly slurred. "You can do better, sister."

I glared at him and cringed as a few of the other wrestlers nearby gave me strange looks.

"Didn't he say your name was Alaqai?" one of them asked. "Doesn't the Great Khan have a daughter by that name?"

"He does," Tolui answered, his grin showing off a gap where he'd lost a tooth in a drunken brawl. "And she just beat all of you!"

Boroghul turned to stare at me with a black expression. "You'd best shut your mouths," I said, grabbing my brothers by their arms. "Unless you want to fight that whole crowd. Alone." I glanced at the pitch of the sun and winced. "We're late. Father's going to be furious."

"I wouldn't worry about your father," Toregene said, grabbing Ogodei's free arm and pulling him along as we broke into a run. "It's your mother who will wring our necks."

I cringed, my ears already ringing with the inevitable tongue-lashing we'd soon receive. There wasn't even time for me to change out of my wrestler's vest. "She's going to kill us," I groaned.

Together we ran through the endless rows of white tents, darting around herds of dirt-streaked children and the veritable city of cauldrons stewing hundreds of butchered goats and horses. In the center of camp stood the tallest *ger* of all, like a colossal snowcapped mountain surrounded by petty foothills. My mother had pounded new felts for months for the occasion, and her new tent was now at least fifty paces across instead of fifteen. For the first time in my life, a white Spirit Banner flew outside, the hairs from my grandfather's favorite horse fluttering in the wind along with the nine strips of white felt. My mother had packed away the black banner only the day before, uttering a prayer for everlasting peace as she closed the trunk lid over the symbol of war.

Inside our tent were gathered the leaders of all the great tribes, and sitting in the middle on a black felt rug would be my father, surrounded by his family.

Most of it, anyway.

Wishing I could crawl under the back side of the *ger* and magically reappear behind my mother, I instead stepped inside. My eyes alighted on my mother's tall green *boqta* headdress, which made her even more imposing than she already was. My grandmother Hoelun flanked her, and

Tolui's soon-to-be-wife, Sorkhokhtani, sat at their feet, playing her *morin khuur*. The horse-head fiddle was supposedly created when a jealous wife discovered her husband riding a winged horse to meet his beloved in the sky. The wife cut off the horse's wings so it fell from the air and died, but the shepherd used its skin and tail to create the first fiddle. Somehow Sorkhokhtani's instrument managed to combine the sound of the steppe's breeze and the neighing of wild horses, but now it stopped midnote.

Despite her wide eyes, Sorkhokhtani was as pristine as we were disheveled, although for her to be otherwise would mean the spirits had turned the world upside down. Everything came easy to Sorkhokhtani, for she'd been raised and educated as a Kereyid princess, meaning she could pour salt tea without splashing her voluminous silk sleeves and also debate religious texts—never raising her voice, of course—with Shigi instead of enduring his interminable lessons on the simple letters that swam before my eyes. Sometimes I worried that my mother loved her best, for dutiful Sorkhokhtani was most like my mother, whereas my soul's fire was constantly at odds with my mother's water.

And yet again, I'd disappointed her.

The clan leaders and their wives swiveled to face us, and their gasps accompanied my mother's withering glare and my father's laughing eyes. I touched my hair and came away with bits of dried grass, remnants of my romp with the Kazakh. A rare heat flared in my cheeks, but I shrugged and offered a contrite smile. "We got lost among all the tents," I said, prompting an eager nod from Ogodei. Toregene lifted her eyes heavenward.

That comment deepened my mother's glare, but my father only chuckled. "I notice you found your way well after the wrestling competition," he said.

Tolui belched then, releasing sour *airag* fumes and earning my father's scowl. I'd watched our father drink countless men to the ground, but he wouldn't take kindly to Tolui's blatant disrespect for this momentous occasion. I thought to make an excuse for him, too, but I'd said enough already.

I cast my eyes to the rug and took my place behind my mother. "I'll deal with you later," she snarled as I passed. Sorkhokhtani gave me a sympathetic frown and began playing again, picking up in the middle of an epic tale about the hero Jangar, a song that often required several days to complete the entire story.

I could look forward to my mother ordering me to gather dung every day for the next year. And she'd probably force me to cook again, until I succeeded in poisoning our entire family. Yet there were new lines between her brows, and I wondered what fresh worries had imprinted themselves there.

I straightened my shoulders, determined not to earn her additional wrath for slouching, when my eyes fell on Gurbesu. My mother's childhood friend was no longer young but was still striking in her customary red *deel*, and she looked far younger when she gave me a playful wink. I returned the gesture as my father addressed his followers. "People of the Felt," he announced, pitching his voice so each man had to lean forward to hear him, as if this were an intimate conversation with one man instead of almost a hundred. "You have come here to pledge support for me as your Great Khan. I shall reward those who fought with me to create this nation, and make each of you the ruler of one thousand households."

The clans who supported my father had swelled since the Blood Wars had ended, and as such, each required a leader loyal to my family, as opposed to a chief chosen only for the blood in his veins. The positions were largely ceremonial, yet I'd heard my mother and father discuss this plan as a way to further tighten my father's net around all the clans and avert a future war. The households of the lesser clans would provide soldiers for my father's supporters, and I supposed the positions offered were a great reward for my father's generals. He called up each leader to bestow additional war spoils upon him and confirm him as chief of a clan. In return, the men bent their knees nine times before Father, sealing their promises to each other. Teb Tengeri started the procession, and Sorkhokhtani informed me later that there were exactly ninety-five men honored that day, but I yawned into my hand and thought of the feast we'd soon have instead of listening to their accolades. I finally perked up as our family received their shares: ten thousand households for my grandmother Hoelun, nine thousand for Jochi, five thousand for each of my other brothers, and four thousand for my uncle Khasar.

Finally it was time to move the ceremony outside. The men of the newly proclaimed Nine Paladins, including Shigi, grabbed a fistful of the black felt cloth upon which my father sat and lifted him into the air with a collective exhale. I followed behind my mother and gasped at the thousands of people who had gathered in the sunshine, their expectant faces turned toward their new Khan.

Every child grows up in awe of her father, but it was at that moment that I realized the power my father held. At his command, all the men gathered here would ride against our enemies and decimate their cities. The children still on their mother's backs would grow to serve his desires and obey his commands. My father had always ruled our family, but now he ruled an empire.

The chiefs carried him toward a wooden platform erected especially for this ceremony, graced only by a wooden bench carved with galloping horses and inlaid with flecks of white bone. Reverently, the men laid the black felt carpet upon the green grass, then stepped back and allowed my father to mount the steps.

Teb Tengeri came forward then, leaning heavily on his twisted cane. I spared a glance for my mother, noting the sour expression she always wore when she was forced to accommodate the seer. A hush fell as he addressed the crowd, although it would take the winds and mouths of men to carry it to those farthest away.

"People of the Felt," he said, his voice strong for one so thin. "You have traveled from far-flung mountains and deserts to lend your weight to this proclamation. Today you have chosen Genghis, son of Yesugei, to be your Gur-Khan. From this day forward, the Eternal Blue Sky and the Golden Light of the Sun shall grant him his authority, in order that he might rule his peoples justly. Should he fail to do so, may his face be blackened with shame and his empire shatter to a million pieces."

I jumped as soldiers behind us beat their skin drums together, thudding a steady heartbeat while Teb Tengeri poured an entire jug of frothy mare's milk into the earth. In perfect unison the thousands of brown faces bowed over their hands, then lifted one palm to my father.

"Hurree, hurree, hurree." They breathed the ancient prayer of acceptance.

My father nodded once, securing the heavy responsibility they'd placed upon his broad shoulders, and took his place upon the Horse Throne. My mother sat on a leather stool at his side, the epitome of the wise and dutiful wife, almost entirely obscuring Yesui and Yesugen as they sat cross-legged on the ground behind the throne.

My father flung his arms open then, and the hordes before him stomped and roared their approval, a sound so deafening that the city walls beyond the Dead Lands must have quaked in terror. I caught his eye then, and he grinned, then threw his head back and roared with pleasure.

My father, the man who'd taught me to ride a horse and string a bow, was now the undisputed Great Khan of all the Mongols.

And as his eldest and favorite daughter, I wondered what that meant for me.

I ducked my head to hide from my mother and the inevitable tirade I'd receive for the wrestling escapade, disappearing into the celebratory crowd after my father took his throne. People around me discussed the new laws he planned to pass forbidding the kidnapping of women and decreeing total religious freedom for the smattering of Christians, Saracens who accepted the teachings of Muhammad, and Saugata followers of Buddha who had found their way into our empire. The Jasagh—my father's new code of law—also outlined the new divisions in the military, forbade urinating into water or ashes, and ordered the execution of a horse thief who could not repay his crime with horses or his own children. As *airag* jugs were emptied and my father left his throne—my heart fell when I saw Boroghul approach him—words slurred and talk turned to bawdy songs. Fights broke out amongst men who wouldn't remember the insults that left them with black eyes, and more than one couple slipped down to the river for celebratory trysts. I amused myself by kissing a second Kazakh behind a tree—his clumsy fumbles made me swear to steer clear of Kazakhs in the future—and ignored his protests when I slipped away after gauging the time it would take my mother to fall asleep. I slunk on silent feet to her *ger* but halted when I heard voices within.

"You must do this, Temujin." The tightness in my mother's muffled voice and the use of my father's old name made me hesitate on the other side of the felt walls.

"I've already taken two other wives," he said, using the same tone as when I'd pressed him too far for something. "I promised you my only heirs would be your children."

"I'm asking you to break that promise." There was a pause and I could imagine my mother covering his hand with hers. Like all Mongols, my parents rarely touched in public, but in the privacy of their tent, she often laid her head against my father's shoulder or let him wrap a hand around her waist. "This isn't a decision I've come by lightly," she said, her voice breaking.

"Surely one of the boys, or even Alaqai—"

I pressed my ear closer to the felt at the mention of my name, but my mother scoffed. "Our sons are drunkards," she said. "And as much as I love her, Alaqai's soul is full of fire. She's wilder than the desert winds."

My cheeks flared at her accusation. The words might be true, but they cut deep all the same.

She continued. "Only Jochi has the abilities to succeed you."

"The clans will never accept Jochi." My father's voice grew rough with some unnamed emotion, and I wished I could see his face to put a name to it. Jochi was the acknowledged firstborn son of Genghis Khan, but his unfortunate name spoke louder than any enemy he might vanquish or all territories he might one day claim for our people. I'd heard him discuss plans with our father to travel north after the coming winter, to conquer the forest peoples of Rus, and wondered if he hoped for an opportunity to prove himself. Or perhaps to separate himself from us.

"I know they won't support Jochi," my mother said. "Genghis, I would give you more children if I could—"

"You'd never survive another battle like the one you fought for Tolui. I'd never forgive myself if I sent you to die in the birthing tent."

"Then you must do this. Your generals have pressed you to take another wife for years, and Yesui and Yesugen have only given you a passel of girls—"

Yesui and Yesugen rarely strayed into our camp, but my mother grew tight-lipped and short-tempered whenever my father visited them. Between them they'd birthed a stillborn girl and three living daughters: Khochen, Tumelun, and Checheyigen. All three were silly things with runny noses whom I did my best to avoid. "Who would you propose I take as a fourth wife?" My father's voice was taut. "To marry the daughter of any of my chiefs would be to set one atop the others. I cannot do that."

"It must be Gurbesu."

Even I blanched at my mother's recommendation. Gurbesu had been the only wife of our worst enemy, a shamed woman without any children to care for her. Then I saw the brilliance of my mother's plan, even before she spoke it aloud.

"Marrying Jamuka's widow will be the final end to the great war," she said. "No other man will think to marry her then, to carry Jamuka's banner against you. She's proven her ability to conceive. She may yet give you sons."

"There is the question of whether Gurbesu would have me," my father said, resignation in his voice. "I will not take her against her will."

"Gurbesu will have you," my mother said, her voice heavy.

I knew she was right, for without a husband or sons, Gurbesu scarcely eked out her survival, relying upon my mother's generosity and the abundance of wool and milk from our herds. She would be a fool to refuse such an offer, to go from taking milk from our mares to becoming wife to the Great Khan.

My parents' voices fell to murmurs, and I knew then that my father embraced my mother. I turned to go, to seek my bed under a tree or perhaps find alternate entertainment with one of the many soldiers available, although my heart wasn't into a tumble in the grasses right now. Instead, I had taken only a few steps when I was startled to see Toregene and Shigi standing behind me. Her broad cheeks were flushed in the moonlight and her braids had come loose from their ties. I ducked my head and continued on, knowing they would follow me.

"How much did you hear?" I asked.

"Most of it," Toregene said.

I wondered if that included my mother's rebuke against me, but I could guess from the weight of Toregene's scrutiny that it did.

"Your mother is a strong woman," Shigi said, his voice reverent. "Her sacrifices make her a worthy khatun."

"She spoke against me," I said, my cheeks still warm.

Toregene linked her arm through mine. "The truth isn't an insult," she said, echoing my earlier thought. I made a sound of outrage in my throat, but she only chuckled. "I wouldn't change you even if I could, sister of my heart." She leaned in so that only I could hear her next words. "The only question is, would you?"

We'd come to the campfire where my brothers passed wine jugs amongst their friends while Ogodei boasted of my escapade in the wrestling competition, drawing awed looks in my direction and making the tips of my ears burn. I learned then that the cook Boroghul had been so angry after I'd beaten him that he'd cornered my father after the ceremony and demanded that girls be forever banned from the wrestling competition. In order to placate one of his favorite cooks, my father had decreed that all future wrestlers wear only breeches and open vests over their bare chests, barring any chance of a woman being able to sneak into the matches. I didn't doubt that Boroghul had spit in my mutton after that, but my father had told me later that he was so proud of me that he'd give me the next foal his stallion sired *and* he'd ensure that Neer-Gui was safe during the Slaughter of the First Snows.

That meant my horse wouldn't end up in Boroghul's stewpot, so I supposed it was a fair trade. But my wrestling days were over, and that made my mood blacker than usual.

Tolui leaned against Sorkhokhtani, asleep with his mouth open and an empty jug tucked into the crook of his thin arm. Even now, she managed to look as delicate as a red-crowned crane, the firelight accenting the sheen of her complicated hair knot. She shrugged and offered me a wan smile as Toregene took her place beside Ogodei, Shigi sitting opposite them with an inscrutable expression. I knew I should join my brothers and sisters, but Toregene's question rattled in my mind, begging for an answer. Did I want to remain the same and enjoy the carefree and privileged life I'd always lived? Or did I wish to change?

Only a day before I'd have answered without hesitation. Now I no longer knew.

Gurbesu accepted my father's proposal, as we'd all known she would. I wondered if she relished the idea of her new position or saw this as her only route to survival.

There was little extravagance to the marriage ceremony, rushed as it was to occur before the clans left the *khurlatai*. Gurbesu had no family tent for her husband to collect her from, so my mother had offered her own. I'd seen my proud mother leave at dawn, hiking in the direction of the empty *gers* near the forest, the ones belonging to her own mothers. I thought to follow her but guessed she'd scold me and send me back. Instead, I joined Toregene and Sorkhokhtani to help ready Gurbesu, as she had no female kin to braid her hair and tie her sash. Sorkhokhtani played her horse-head fiddle, ostensibly so she was spared having to speak to our new mother, and Gurbesu chattered louder than a magpie as she stained her lips with berry juice until they gleamed as red as blood. We all bowed our heads when my father appeared at the entrance of my mother's *ger*, my scowling brothers trailing him like a cape. Yesui and Yesugen remained in their tents outside camp, but my mother now stood with the men, her very presence sanctioning this marriage. Her grass-green *deel* matched her headdress, yet her lips were tight and her eyes remained flat even when Gurbesu gave her an impetuous hug.

"Thank you, Borte Ujin," I heard her whisper. "We are truly sisters now."

My mother's lips grew thinner, but she still bent down and placed the traditional polished rock at the bride's feet. This was typically done in the wedding tent, but I doubted my mother wished to see the tent my father would now share, or worse, the marriage bed.

"Our family is like this rock," she said, her voice carrying and silencing the crowd of nobles that had packed themselves between the *gers*. "Sturdy and powerful, building mountains and empires. May you, too, be powerful as stone, and make our family ever stronger."

She murmured something in Gurbesu's ear, then pressed her forehead to her friend's. My mother was the most important woman on the steppes, and possibly beyond, but she sacrificed her happiness now to secure my family's power. I wondered if she thought it a fair trade.

My father clasped Gurbesu's hand and led her the short distance through the two purification fires to the small *ger* across the way. He lingered outside to cast a glance at my mother, then slipped inside after his fourth wife. The crowd of his handpicked ministers and generals jostled forward, all eager for salt tea and the opportunity to rib my father with their coarse jokes. In the shuffle, I lost my place near my family and found myself next to Teb Tengeri.

My mother despised the shaman, but I was apathetic toward the crippled old man in his blue *deel* that smelled as if it had gone unwashed since before I was born. Still, despite the press of warm bodies all around us, I felt cornered by my father's seer when his penetrating brown eyes snared me. My heart lurched when his hand brushed against mine with a rattle from the beads on his robe, ivory and glass trinkets earned from each of his supposed visions. His might have been an accidental touch had it not been for the way his thumb pressed against the pulse in my wrist. Just as quickly, he recoiled from my touch.

"You carry death in your heart, just like the vermin you're named for," he hissed, tucking his hand into his wide sleeves as if scalded. His expression contorted as he eyed the sword in my belt. "Death's own foot soldier."

I touched the tiger sword—my mother insisted I wear it while foreign clans surrounded us for the *khurlatai*—but Teb Tengeri ducked his head and pressed forward then, leaving me to puzzle over his words. Moments later, Shigi filled the empty space left by the shaman, flanked by Tolui and Sorkhokhtani. My youngest brother would soon marry his betrothed, yet I'd noticed Tolui seek out Sorkhokhtani several times during the *khurlatai*. Once they were married, I'd be the only one of my mother's children left unwed, a thought that made me lonely and exultant at the same time.

Shigi scowled at the seer's retreating back. "What did Teb Tengeri want?"

"I don't know," I answered. "He mumbled something about me being vermin." I squinted at the shaman as Gurbesu's *ger* finally swallowed him. Teb Tengeri would bless her marriage bed tonight, nothing my family or I cared to see. "I think his horse bucked him onto his head one too many times."

"Or that's what he wants you to think," Sorkhokhtani said. I mulled over her words—Sorkhokhtani rarely offered her opinion, but she was typically correct when she did.

I caught sight of my mother then, retreating into the privacy of her tent. As first wife, her white *ger* maintained the camp's easternmost position, with its the first glimpse of the sun, and now Gurbesu's smaller tent stood to the west behind it, like the tail of a bearded star. Sorkhokhtani whispered something in Tolui's ear and parted from him, motioning for me to follow. Toregene waved to us from the crowd and together we followed my mother inside. She had already removed the tall headdress with its feathers and beads, and her green *deel* lay in an uncharacteristic pile on the ground. She stood with her back to us, dressed only in her undertunic, bereft of all the other armor of the khatun. Then she turned and, for the first time in my memory, I saw tears running unchecked down her cheeks.

"I've never let them see me cry, not even when he married Yesui and Yesugen," she said to us, her voice trembling as she touched the scar on her lip and lifted her shoulders in a gesture of helplessness. "Remember that when you rule over your own camps: Your people must never see your weakness."

I stood rooted to the spot, rendered immobile. My mother possessed the power of a khatun and the wisdom of a mother, but also the frailty of a simple woman who loved a man. My mother's love for my father—and even for us, her irresponsible brood—gave her strength but also left her vulnerable.

It was Toregene who moved first, followed by Sorkhokhtani, both of them gathering my mother into their arms. I stepped forward hesitantly, unsure how to act toward this mother who was suddenly so human.

She pulled me to her and enveloped me in her crisp smell, like the earth after a spring rain. "One day you'll all be wives, and your husbands will break your hearts," she told all of us, drawing a shaky breath. "But you must remember that love is the only thing that makes this life worth living. And I love all of you." She squeezed us tighter. "So very deeply."

She released us and wiped her eyes with the backs of her hands. "Let's have some yogurt and go to sleep," she said, and I marveled at her ability to pack away her momentary frailty, to act as if nothing unusual was happening while her husband bedded another woman in the next tent over. My father had married Yesui and Yesugen, but they'd always been removed from our lives. Gurbesu would be impossible to ignore.

We drank our yogurt, filling the air with idle gossip to keep my mother's mind from wandering to what lay beyond the threshold. Finally, after the camp had grown silent and the light of the moon filtered through the top of the tent, we pulled the grass-stuffed mattresses from their wooden frames and shoved them together, lying side by side like sisters.

It was only after Toregene and Sorkhokhtani had settled into sleep that I felt my mother's lips brush my forehead, as delicate as the flutter of a moth's wings. "I love you, Alaqai," she murmured. "You are the only daughter of my womb, and nothing can ever change that."

My eyes burned then, and I shifted closer to her, wondering if she knew I'd overheard her comment about my wildness. But then, my mother knew everything. I found the place on her shoulder where my head had always fit so perfectly, and tucked my feet under her legs as I always had when my father was gone and dreams of rearing horses and lightning had woken me as a child.

"I love you, too," I whispered.

Chapter 15

The last of the clans finally left the *khurlatai*, taking with them the warm weather and leaving in their place the persistent morning dew that heralded an early frost. Over the following weeks, my father sent men to drive the herds to the southern river, hoping for extra time to fatten the animals before the Slaughter of the First Snows. Winter was a long siege against death for us; the slaughter would claim the geldings—my father still promised Neer-Gui's safety—and the old animals when they were at their fattest to keep us from having to feed them during the long months of snow and ice. The butcherings of that lone day would keep us in sausage and dried meat until spring's thaw.

Our entire family gathered inside my mother's tent to eat together for the first time since the *khurlatai*; the smoke hole was open wide to the twinkling stars and a healthy fire crackled on the hearth. The fresh air and skins of *airag* going around flushed our cheeks and loosened our tongues.

My father sat between my mother and Gurbesu, a strange juxtaposition of two women who could not have been more different. My mother looked aged beyond her years, but her childhood friend might have passed for my older sister, especially in the firelight. Where my mother was tall and lean, Gurbesu was short and didn't own a straight line on her body, made even more curvaceous because my father's seed had taken root in her belly. We'd learned of this only a few days ago, and now she looked wan, and often excused herself, presumably to heave into the bushes. Perhaps a difficult pregnancy would be the payment for her easy life and the disruptions she'd caused our family.

Gurbesu still managed to smile and defer to my mother, who had outdone even herself with the spread of boiled mutton, salted cheeses, and fresh yogurt before us. All my mother had done since the announcement of Gurbesu's pregnancy was pound butter and hold court over her stewpot. We could all plan on becoming very fat over the coming years if Gurbesu's womb proved as fertile as it appeared.

My father left his place by the fire to sit by me, laying his bow across his lap and the empty pot from our recent meal of horsemeat stew at his elbow. I stood practicing my aim with a spear, shifting my balance while attempting to skewer a nearby sheep skull through the eye with varying amounts of success. I should have smelled the snare being set when my mother didn't scold me for putting several holes through her rugs, but I realized too late that the tent had fallen silent, everyone's backs to us so the only sounds were those of the crackling fire.

"I've had a message," my father finally said, working the leftover stew grease into his bowstring. "From Ala-Qush of the Onggud."

"The Onggud?" I asked when no one else spoke, retrieving the spear I'd just thrown. "Were they threatening to kill you?"

The Onggud had lent their support to my father at his *khurlatai*, but only because they realized that, as our neighbors to the southeast, my father would soon cast his gaze to their lands. In truth, they despised us, ruled as they were by Ala-Qush's ancient lineage, and they often referred to us as wandering, bloodthirsty heathens. The city-dwelling Onggud, also known as the People of the Stone Walls, were our opposites in every way, living behind high walls in crowded cities that smelled of human waste, and growing their food so their bodies were eternally weak from the lack of meat and white foods. The journey to the Onggud territory took at least six weeks over the inhospitable Great Dry Sea, and many who undertook the trip never returned. Still, they were luckier than those who were forced to reside in such miserable conditions.

"Nothing so dramatic as plotting my assassination." My father smiled then, but he avoided my gaze. "The Onggud are pragmatic. They realize I've targeted their Tanghut neighbors for a winter conquest."

My mother gave a loud exhale then. "All because your father sent them a message after his *khurlatai* telling them so," she added, her back still to us as she patched a hole in an old *deel*. There was no such thing as a private discussion in a *ger*, but I could have done with fewer ears listening to this conversation. "The Tanghut of the Great High White State have the iron, silk, and silver your father craves for his growing empire."

"Won't the Tanghut hide behind their stone walls?" I asked.

"The strength of a wall depends on the courage of those who defend it." My father gave an evil grin. "The Tanghut will quake with fear before they even see my army."

All else I knew of the opulent Tanghut was that they mainly worshipped the seated Buddha, and, as the main manufacturer of all manner of manuscripts and texts, Shigi often extolled their academic virtues. They sounded like a people in need of conquering.

"I've scarcely unified the Thirteen Nations; without a common enemy they might turn upon themselves again. The Onggud don't wish to fight us," my father continued. "Ala-Qush seeks an alliance so we will bypass his people on our way to the Tanghut."

"That's convenient for Ala-Qush," I said, throwing the spear again. It knocked against the arch of the sheep's eye bone, but no thrill of victory ran up my spine as it had before. Instead I felt a shiver of foreboding.

"The alliance is also convenient for us," my father said, setting aside his bow and standing beside me. "I need the Onggud if I'm to conquer the Tanghut. If the two allied against us—"

"It would mean another great war." I retrieved the spear. "Congratulations on your alliance, then."

"Alliances are not simply agreements," my father said brusquely, adding his hands to mine along the shaft of the spear. "They must be sealed with more than words."

And I knew then what he would say, what he had offered Ala-Qush. The realization must have dawned on my face, for my father nodded.

"Ala-Qush has agreed that you may take the place of precedence on the north side of his Great House, facing the door."

The place of the senior wife. My mother's place in our tent.

"But he's already married." I wanted to add, *and he's twice my age*, but held my tongue for once.

My father tucked a stray lock of hair behind my ear. "I won't force you into this marriage, *tarvag takal*," he said.

"But you need the alliance," I said, seeing the map in my mind, even as I set down my spear. Shigi had often tried to teach me to read, but the foreign symbols cluttered my thoughts until I could hardly think straight. However, I'd grown up watching my father scratch battle plans into the ashes of our hearth, and now I could envision the entirety of his empire and those that lay beyond his reach. "And you need someone to supply your arrow messengers when you campaign against the Tanghut."

"It is an important mission," my father said. "One I cannot trust to anyone else."

My chest felt empty, as if my heart and my very breath had been stolen from me. I had no wish to stay forever under my mother's *ger*, but my marriage was no simple matter. When I wed, I would gain a new husband and family as any woman did, but also a new people to rule. If not Ala-Qush and the Onggud, then some other ruler and his petty kingdom. Yet this was what my father asked of me.

I stared past him then, to the southeast where my fate waited, like a panther ready to spring. "I'd like some time to think about it," I said.

"I knew you would," my father said. "But Ala-Qush must have an answer before the snows make the journey to Olon Süme impossible."

My mother finally stood then, setting aside the *deel* she been pretending to mend and placing her palms on my shoulders. "No one can take your place here, Alaqai, but you would make a good *beki* for Ala-Qush." The Onggud had forever been a vassal state and now they would bow a knee to my father, but I might be their princess, their *beki*. My mother pressed her forehead to mine, her quivering voice dropping to a whisper. "You would make us so proud."

It was suddenly difficult to swallow as I looked around through bleary eyes, realizing that everyone was watching me. All the treasures in my life were in this *ger*, and I might soon leave them far behind, carrying only memories and the weighty expectations of my family on my back.

"We need your help," my mother said one morning only a few days later. From my bedding, I peered through one eye to see her dressed in a stained *deel*, frayed along the sleeves, and her hair pulled back in a simple braid. The way the meager fire cast her in shadows, she might have been a girl again. "It snowed while you slept and the men have arrived with the geldings."

The Slaughter of the First Snows.

Panic tightened my throat; already the time for my decision was trickling away. I covered my eyes with my arm, but my mother flung off the blankets. The new chill in the air would remain until the spring thaw, icing over our water buckets at night and finally freezing the meat we'd need to survive the long winter that yawned before us.

"Get up, Alaqai." Her tone was the same as when she'd ordered me to gather dung as a girl. But I wasn't a child anymore.

I didn't answer.

"If you want to eat this winter," she said, "you'll help us with the slaughter. Either you walk into the blood tent yourself or I can drag you there myself for everyone to see."

I rolled over to gauge if she was serious. She was, of course.

"I don't want to work in the blood tent. I'll lasso the geldings instead."

But my mother shook her head. "I told your grandmother Hoelun and the other widows that you'd help them. They need a girl with a strong back."

"More like they need a girl who hasn't gone deaf yet to listen to them complain about their aches and pains."

"You might one day be *beki* of a great nation, Alaqai. You must start acting like it."

"When I'm *beki* of a great nation, I'll have someone else stuff the sausage for me."

She waved away my words. "You cannot climb a mountain without taking the first step."

I rolled my eyes at the oft-quoted proverb, used for everything from urging me to milk the goats to shearing uncooperative sheep. Still, the slaughter meant plenty of tidbits of meat to nibble on all day, a thought that made my stomach rumble in anticipation. With any luck, I might nab a fire-seared goat tongue.

"Fine," I said. "I'll help, but only for a little while."

I was slow to dress, despite my mother's urgings, so by the time we stepped outside, geldings screamed and goats brayed as they ran from the boys who chased them with knives.

Men wielded axes over the carcasses of animals already dead, hacking off heads, hooves, and legs to the sound of cracking bones. Women and children scuttled about to spread skins over the snow to dry, the steam from the fresh hides rising into the chilled air while blood seeped into snowy footsteps.

And the smell: everywhere the stench of meat and death.

And life.

I offered up the traditional prayer to the spirits for this great gift, without which we'd all die during the winter. And tonight we would feast on the oily meat, stuffing our stomachs until we could no longer move.

I gripped my mother's hand, suddenly remembering. "Neer-Gui?"

"Your horse is safe," she said. "Your father ordered Sorkhokhtani to pen him with his warhorse."

I sagged with relief, but it was short-lived.

From the outside, the blood tent looked like any other *ger*, but inside the humid cloud of tainted air and scarlet-stained earth assaulted my senses. Fresh horse heads lay piled in the center, their dull eyes open and severed necks covered in clumps of black blood. A girl-child stood with a leather swatter, ready to crush any flies that threatened to land and lay their eggs. Wooden troughs were piled high with hindquarters and chunks of meat, and trays of red muscle and white ribs hung from the ceiling beams like ladders to the sky, adding the occasional drip of blood to the mess of death already underfoot.

"Send the girl for Toregene if you get too tired," my mother said, indicating that I should join a cluster of squinty old women squatting over bowls of entrails and wielding sharp knives. At my grandmother's feet were ropes of yellow intestines, like piles of oversized snakes.

I turned to tell my mother I'd changed my mind, but she'd already disappeared, perhaps anticipating my sudden weakness. I remembered her words in our *ger*, but this was no great obstacle I had to overcome, only a mountain of intestines and chopped meat. With a long-suffering sigh, I shuffled to the wooden seat.

It was my job to rinse and stuff the intestines, to fill them with the tiny chunks of meat and brains that the old mothers' deft fingers had already minced. Once I had shoved enough meat inside, the intestine was tied off with a bit of sinew and thrown over a tall pole. I was soon covered in blood and stained with offal while a veritable forest of sausages grew around us.

I lost myself in the monotony of the work, my thighs burning from squatting while I concentrated on the movement of my fingers and listened to my grandmother complain about her latest bout of indigestion and the other crones commiserate about their stingy daughters-in-marriage, who didn't offer them enough butter from the household churns. Several of the women filched raw meat, grinning at me while mashing the tidbits between pink gums.

Finally the tent was too full to hold another horse head or string of sausages. My shoulders ached and my mind was numb by the time I stumbled out into the early dark of a winter night.

Toregene and Sorkhokhtani met me then, as if they'd been lurking outside the blood tent waiting for me to appear. Toregene raised her brows and plugged her nose, coughing dramatically. "Alaqai Beki," she said, "you smell terrible. And you look like you've been stuffing sausages all day."

"You don't look so fresh yourself," I said, nodding at the animal blood that stained her *deel*. "And I don't smell any worse than you usually do with all your potions." In truth, I enjoyed the earthy scent that clung to Toregene from the herbs she gathered and brewed into poultices: the yellow pasqueflower for upset stomachs, burnet roots to suppress bleeding, and globeflower for chest pains. I'd asked once where she'd learned so much about medicine, but my mother had sent Toregene out for freshwater before she could answer. As soon as the door shut behind her, my mother had reminded me that Toregene had lived a life before she'd come to us.

I'd scowled at that. "But I only asked—"

"I know what you asked," my mother said. "But that doesn't mean that Toregene wishes to answer questions about her past to an impertinent girl."

I waited until her back was turned before I stuck my tongue out at her.

"And if you must know," my mother had continued, her narrowed eyes making me wonder whether she'd seen my insolence, "Mother Khogaghchin taught Toregene some of what she knows. In fact, I believe I was Toregene's first invalid."

I didn't know what to say to that, suspecting my mother referred to the murky part of her life after she first married my father. I only knew that she'd been kidnapped by the Merkid, that Jochi had been born shortly after, and that I'd get snapped at if I asked further questions.

I swiped my thumb now across Toregene's nose, leaving a smear of blood and who knew what else. She gave a mock howl and jumped back, making both Sorkhokhtani and me laugh as tiny snowflakes drifted around us and tangled in our hair.

"Your mother saved you a goat tongue," Sorkhokhtani said. "It's waiting in her tent."

"Along with enough sausage to feed an army," Toregene said.

"No sausage," I groaned, straining to put one foot in front of the other. "I never want to see another intestine as long as I live."

"What?" Toregene teased. "Did you discover today that you're not made for crone's work?"

I realized then the simple trap my mother and sisters had sprung on me. They'd known the Great Slaughter would show me the ordinary life that yawned before me here. Still, I wasn't ready to make a decision yet. Instead, I threw my arms open, hugging both of them to me and sharing with them the slick of blood and offal on the front of my *deel*.

Amidst their shrieks, I laughed, realizing how hard it would be to leave my sisters behind, and also how difficult it would be to stay.

That night I went to my father and told him I would marry Ala-Qush.

My father grunted his approval while my mother beamed at me, although she seemed to blink from the cook smoke more often than usual. "You're the fiercest marmot on the steppes, Alaqai Beki," my grizzled father said, pressing his forehead to mine. "You'd make any father proud."

Still, tears stung my eyes. I had only the winter left with this family before I forged a new one, and I knew the days would pass too soon.

That winter was the worst anyone remembered, a *tsagaan zud*, or white famine, with towering drifts of snow too deep for the Five Snouts to reach the frozen grass underneath and storms that buried our starving herds. We took the smallest sheep and goats into our *gers*, but each morning outside we'd find the carcasses of ice-crusted animals, their eyes frozen open in the frigid temperatures. The unlucky meat was destined to be burned, but my mother ordered Ogodei and Tolui to bury a few animals in the forest snows under marked trees. "Better to eat impure meat than to starve days before the spring thaws," she said, ignoring their scowls to hand them metal shovels.

And it wasn't only our animals that perished that season. On the darkest day of the year, Teb Tengeri made the ominous prediction that my uncle Khasar sought to topple my father from his place as Gur-Khan, a rumor that opened a deep rift between my father and uncle. Fearing there might be truth in his shaman's words, my father had Khasar locked in a cangue, and it took my grandmother Hoelun to put the family to rights again. Roused from the warm *ger* she rarely left in her old age, she pushed through the crowd and unlocked Khasar from the cangue before turning on my father.

But instead of railing at him or striking him, she crossed her ancient limbs beneath her in the snow. Seated like a child awaiting a story, she wordlessly undid the ivory toggles on her *deel* and tugged the robe open, revealing leathery brown breasts that sagged to her midriff. Dark like distended bruises, the nipples touched her navel, and her ancient skin was riddled with white birth scars from the children she'd once carried. There was a collective gasp and people hurried to avert their eyes at this terrible indecency. My father moved, presumably to cover his mother, but she raised a gnarled hand and screeched at him.

"Do you recognize these breasts that nourished you and your brother?" she howled, holding the wrinkled flesh in both hands. "As an infant, you could drain one of these breasts, but Khasar could empty both. You and your brother came from the same womb, are built from the same bones, and drank from the same breasts." She sneered at my father then, her voice reaching a fevered pitch. "What sort of leader are you to claim you've killed all your enemies, yet you can't stand the sight of your brother?"

Her anger spent, she suddenly transformed from an angry she-wolf into a haggard old woman, and all eyes turned to my father.

His jaw clenched, and his voice pulsed with anger when he spoke. "We have heard our mother," he said, his words clipped and formal. "And we're ashamed of what we've done."

With that, he turned and stalked toward the horses, leaving angry footsteps in the snow. My jaw dropped, for I'd never before heard my father admit to any wrongdoing. He was invincible to me, as indomitable as the blue-gray wolf from which we all sprang. My mother ignored him and stepped forward to support my grandmother.

The next day, meddlesome Teb Tengeri was gone, having fled under the cover of night and later found to be agitating nearby clans to support him in a bid for power against my father. It didn't take long for him to be dragged back to camp and his neck broken in response to his treachery, his body discarded in a far-off snowdrift.

Shortly after, my grandmother Hoelun passed in her sleep, discovered frozen in her bed after she failed to emerge from her *ger* in several days. Our entire family mourned as my grandmother was carried to the icy cliff that would hold her bones for eternity. We fell silent for three nights to show respect for the mother who had given us life and protected us.

But the winter wasn't only death. It brought life, too, and the promise of a future yet to come.

Babies are rarely born at convenient times, and Toregene's child chose to begin the long process while we were all abed. The river had groaned and threatened to break only days ago, lightening our hearts to think that we'd soon be able to draw water without boring through an unforgiving plank of ice, but now a late blizzard raged outside. None of us would have known of Toregene's coming battle had it not been for Sorkhokhtani, for Ogodei snored next to his wife, sleeping off a bout of hard drinking from the night before.

Sorkhokhtani had gone to check on Toregene and now ran to my mother's *ger*, her hair snarled with ice and eyelashes crusted with snow as she struggled to close the tent door behind her. "Her waters broke," she said, but my mother was already up, shoving her feet into heavy leather boots. And then, bowing to my father—"With the help of the Earth Mother you'll soon have a grandson, Khan of Khans."

My nose dripped despite the smoldering fire and my cheeks felt too frozen to smile. I shoved my fox-fur hat—I'd had plenty of time this winter to sew the Kazakh's prize fur into a winter hat complete with floppy earflaps—to cover my face, but someone shook my foot.

"Get out of bed, Alaqai Beki," my mother said. "It's not every day that you get to witness a mother and child battle for life."

"I'm not married," I mumbled. "It would offend the spirits for me to be in the birthing tent."

"You and Sorkhokhtani will be married women soon enough," my mother said. "I'd not send you to your own birthing tents without knowing what you face."

For a moment I wondered if that was kindness or cruelty on her part.

"You struggled for days to birth Tolui," I said. "Can't Toregene wait until the sun rises?"

"Remember those words when you're struggling alone on all fours, wishing for some woman—any woman—to rub your back or massage your feet."

I cursed under my foul breath and rose, pulling the hat I'd slept in farther over my ears. "I'm coming," I said. "But I'm not rubbing her feet."

"Fine." My mother's face disappeared behind a brown wool scarf. "You can massage sheep fat between her legs to ease the babe out instead."

I blanched and looked to my father for escape, but he only grimaced and wrapped a thick bearskin blanket around his shoulders. "I don't understand you women," he said. "I'd spend a lifetime in the Great Dry Sea before I'd push another human out of my arse."

My mother ignored him and beckoned me with an impatient hand. I drew a resigned breath and followed. We formed a human chain against the blinding snow, but thankfully, Toregene's tent was within stumbling distance. We passed Ogodei on his way out, his head bent against the storm.

"I'd rather stay out here all day than in there," he yelled over the wind. "Care to join me, Alaqai?"

"Don't you dare," my mother said, pulling on my arm.

I cast a longing glance at Ogodei's back as my mother pushed inside Toregene's tent with a furious gust of wind and snow.

A wall of welcome heat hit me first, followed by the sour smell of something utterly primal. Toregene crouched naked near the fire, her only adornment the silver cross talisman at her throat. She panted and her body swayed as if she was listening to faraway music. She hadn't noticed our entrance, her eyes closed as her hands pressed against her stomach, obscuring the dark line that cleft her belly at the navel. My mother shed her coat and scarf to kneel by her adopted daughter, murmuring in her ear and wiping hanks of sweaty hair from her face.

"It's not yet time," Toregene managed to say between gasps.

"It certainly looks like it's time," I muttered, resisting the urge to cover my nose and close my eyes.

"I think Toregene is the expert here and not you, Alaqai," Sorkhokhtani whispered. "She's done this before. More than once, actually."

"What?"

"She had children with her Merkid husband," Sorkhokhtani answered, shedding her extra layers of winter wool. "You might know these things if you took time from your games to listen to other people."

I stood openmouthed by the door as Sorkhokhtani stirred the potent brew of boiling herbs Toregene had gathered this autumn in preparation for the birth: the heart-shaped seed pods of shepherd's purse, dried purple cranesbill petals, and fragrant valerian root. I'd listened with half an ear while she told me about each on the last sunny day before the snows fell, the leaves and petals already brittle from the night frosts. Yet Sorkhokhtani was right; I'd been too consumed with thoughts of Ala-Qush's proposal and had never thought to ask how Toregene knew which herbs would stop her bleeding and which would dull the worst of the birth pains.

I knew that my father had brought Toregene to us after the final Merkid raid, but a black pit opened in my stomach to think of what had happened to her children.

"Boil water," my mother finally ordered me, peeling off her hat. "And warm the sheep fat over the fire."

I cringed at the idea of what the fat would be used for but did as she instructed, glad to keep my hands busy as my mother laid Toregene on the bed and checked between her legs. "Toregene's right," my mother announced. "It will be a little longer yet."

We settled in, my mind still churning while Sorkhokhtani raided Toregene's rafters for strips of dried goat meat. We passed around the salty meat and took turns holding Toregene's hand with each fresh surge of pain. I'd expected a dour environment, having heard stories of my mother's struggle to drop my brother, so I was surprised at the easy gossip and jokes that filled the time between Toregene's pangs.

"It's too bad we can't arrange for one of us to always be in the birthing tent," Sorkhokhtani said once, after we'd all laughed at one of Toregene's jokes that compared men's members to sheep tongues. I'd avoided looking at my mother then, hoping she'd never learned of my experience with certain male parts.

"So we could always stink of blood and one of us would always be in agony?" Toregene asked, taking little sips of melted snow from the bowl my mother offered her. "That sounds worse than any demon's punishment."

"It would teach the men to gather dung and cook their own stews," Sorkhokhtani said.

"They'd never survive," my mother proclaimed from behind me, prompting nods and girlish giggles. She hovered over me, then squeezed my shoulders and pressed her lips to my temple in an uncommon display of tenderness.

I'd always felt most comfortable around men with their brash camaraderie and simple talk, but I realized then that the struggles and burdens we women bore bound us closer together, forging us ever stronger.

Finally, the real work began. Toregene's body seemed to rebel, and she lost control of her stomach and bowels.

"This is normal." My mother arched an eyebrow at my look of disgust after Toregene finished retching, then thrust the putrid bowl at me. "They don't call birth a battle for nothing," she said. "We women must triumph even over our own bodies."

I didn't dare inhale, and stepped outside only long enough to fling the foul mess into the howling winds. Perhaps I wasn't quite ready to join women in everything.

Toregene began pushing then, screaming and clutching her blankets as she begged her god of the cross to steal her spirit and end her misery. I stood terrified, watching the surges tighten across the bulk of her naked belly. Sorkhokhtani alternated between pressing warm towels and rubbing sheep fat into the patch of livid flesh between Toregene's legs, thankfully relieving me from having to fulfill my mother's threat. I almost plugged my ears when Toregene's next scream rent the air, then caught a glimpse of that new pink flesh that began to emerge from the yawning thatch of black hair.

Transfixed, I scarcely heard my mother when she ordered me to take one of Toregene's legs, and stumbled to follow the instructions when she yelled them a second time. Amidst our urgings to push, Toregene let fly a final animal scream. A pale, blood-streaked mass slipped into my mother's waiting hands. She ran a practiced finger inside its mouth and was greeted with a forlorn wail.

"You have a healthy son, Toregene," she said with a rare smile, placing the child on his mother's flattened belly.

Toregene marveled at the child for a moment—I refrained from mentioning that his face was mashed flat and his legs bent like a frog's—then she looked at all of us with glistening eyes. "A son for Ogodei," she said to my mother, offering her the baby. "Although he has my chin and nose."

"What will you name him?" my mother asked, wrapping the child in a waiting blanket. I recognized it as one my mother had felted just after Toregene's announcement that she was pregnant.

"Güyük," Toregene answered.

"A fine name," my mother said, giving the howling bundle back to Toregene.

We took turns then, breathing Güyük's new scent as he drifted off to sleep while my mother poured a bowl of calf's blood for Toregene—unfortunately not fresh—and my mother delivered the afterbirth. I wondered then what part this tiny child would play in our family's lives, what roles we women would play.

Only time would tell.

Chapter 16

1207 CE

YEAR OF THE RED HARE

Time can be an ally or an enemy, its precious moments rushing by or dragging on forever. In the months before my marriage I often wished I could cling to the rare days of spring and summer, yet sometimes I ached to race ahead and greet my future as Beki of the Onggud.

Winter's brutal punishments had weakened our surviving horses; the animals needed spring's fresh shoots of grass to smooth their knobby backbones and pad the hollows between their ribs before they could undertake crossing the southern desert of the Great Dry Sea. Summer's heat rendered the Dead Lands impassable, and only once the days shortened again could we attempt the six-week trek across the barren swaths of heat and emptiness. Each day seemed to stretch for an eternity, but bundled together they passed in a blur, like drops of water in a fast-moving river.

All too soon I was called to a second birthing tent as Gurbesu dropped another girl for my father: Al-Altun. The name meant *Subordinate One*, Gurbesu's acknowledgment of her position as my father's last wife and her children's inferior rank.

That the child was a girl meant my mother's sacrifice had been in vain, yet now I would make my own sacrifice for our family.

The birch leaves were tinged with yellow, fireweed cotton choked the air, and the bar-headed geese flew overhead to their winter feeding grounds. It had been almost a year since my father told me of Ala-Qush's marriage proposal, and now it was time for me to leave.

On the evening before I would depart for the Onggud capital of Olon Süme, I stared slack-jawed at the waiting carts. The line was as long as a water dragon, its belly full of weapons and provisions, silk and silver taken from our vanquished enemies. All this, along with my father's soldiers, would accompany me to awe Ala-Qush and my new people.

Not wishing to look at the carts any longer, I busied myself with brushing Neer-Gui and inspecting his smooth hooves for the coming journey. I'd chosen not to shear his mane or tail like my father's warhorse, but instead secured the hair from my gelding's eyes with a tall leather thong between his ears. I thought he looked rather dashing, but Ogodei had commented that my gelding would end up fighting off the stallions now that he looked like a broodmare.

So it was that Toregene found me that night, water buckets in both her hands and little Güyük drooling in his sleep on her back.

"Where have you been?" she hissed, her eyes darting about nervously as she blew a puff of air at a stray hair dangling in front of her nose. Water sloshed at her feet. "I've been looking everywhere for you."

I jumped back to avoid the water and followed her gaze, but saw only a herding boy returned late for the night. "What's going on?" I asked.

"I'd rather not have your mother chop out my tongue for this," Toregene whispered, beckoning me with a jerk of her head. "Follow me."

The allure of something forbidden called to me. I had yet to pack the felts for my new tent—my mother doubted whether Ala-Qush's family even knew how to felt, much less whether they'd share their daughter panels with me. Who knew whether I would ever sleep in a *ger* after tonight, anyway; the Onggud built their tents of wood and stone, as solid as the walls that surrounded their cities. The felts could wait.

Toregene's tent smelled of the late-blooming fireweed stuffed into a jug on her lone table, and it was difficult to remember the scene of bloody struggle that had taken place when Güyük was born. A log popped and the shadows on the walls jumped, illuminating Sorkhokhtani's dark form sitting on the ground, where she tended the hearth fire with an assortment of pots and baskets spread behind her.

"Hello, Alaqai," she said. She shrugged at the question in my eyes and picked at the wool pilling on her sleeve. Perhaps she'd been dragged here, too.

"What's this about?" I asked, hands on my hips. My frayed temper after a long day threatened to finally unravel.

"I wanted to speak to both of you before you meet your husbands for the first time," Toregene said, gingerly sliding Güyük from her back. She tied the sling with its sleeping child to the bed. Satisfied that it was secure, she sat on a bright red pillow, stretching her legs in front of her with a ragged sigh. I remained standing.

"I've already met my husband," Sorkhokhtani said. "Tolui and I have known each other for years now."

"I mean before you greet your men in bed," Toregene said, as if speaking of the clouds in the sky, or the amount of horse dung she needed for her fire.

"I don't need that sort of advice," I said, with a wave of my hand. After all, I was no blushing virgin who'd never taken a man between her legs. "And I have much to do—"

"Alaqai Beki, do you know the way to rule a man?" Toregene asked. She nudged one mud-caked boot off, then the other. "Because it takes more than just pulling up your *deel* for him."

I'd had plenty of lovers and envisioned my marriage as something akin to taking on a new horse, not an act that warranted deep contemplation. Toregene seemed to read my mind. "Men are simple creatures," she said. "Not unlike a goat or a yak. But you wouldn't ride a goat, and you wouldn't take a yak across the Great Dry Sea. Just the same, each man is different. Take your brother Ogodei, for example."

I really didn't care to hear about my brother's prowess—or lack thereof—as a lover, but Toregene didn't even give me a chance to cover my ears.

"Ogodei isn't interested in the finer points of tumbling," she said, sighing so I wondered if perhaps her Merkid husband had been a more generous lover than my brother. Again, I pushed the thought from my mind. Toregene had something in her palms—sheep fat from the smell of it—that she proceeded to massage into my hands. Normally I'd have groaned with pleasure, but this discussion made me feel like I was sitting inside a tiger's mouth. One wrong move—

"Any woman who can brew *airag* and stew a goat will capture your brother's heart," she said, flipping her braid over her shoulder. "Fortunately, I happen to be skilled at both, whereas his first wife can scarcely manage to salt horsemeat."

I wanted to say that there was nothing wrong with almost poisoning your entire family each time you attempted to feed them—after all, I'd done it several times myself—but decided against it.

"You and Sorkhokhtani must discover what your men want," Toregene continued, "thus assuring your place as their main wives."

"But we'll already be first wives," I said. "My father guaranteed that."

"But a second wife can easily supplant the first." Toregene's gaze dropped out of modesty, but a devious smile curled the corners of her lips as she released my hands to pour us bowls of *airag*. "I did."

"Yet none of my father's wives ever supplanted my mother," I said.

"Your mother and father share a rare bond," Toregene admitted, sipping her *airag* from an ivory bowl carved with depictions of the Five Snouts. I'd have bet my tiger sword that it was her famous brew, although I couldn't fathom how she'd managed to hide a jug from Ogodei. "Your parents' love would stand regardless of how many wives your father took or how many women he has on his raids."

I'd never thought of my father claiming women after his battles, and I didn't care to begin now.

"I won't meet Ala-Qush until almost the day we marry," I said, feeling irritated. "I can't anticipate what he'll want from me."

"You'll have to work fast, then," Toregene said. "Because he'll want you in his bed that same night." She turned her attention to Sorkhokhtani. "Now, as for Tolui . . ."

"Tolui likes to drink and to rut," Sorkhokhtani said, shifting from one hip to the other. "Preferably at the same time."

My jaw fell open, but Toregene laughed. "Well done, Sorkhokhtani."

Our future Princess of the Hearth shrugged. "Don't look at me like that, Alaqai. It's not as if you haven't tumbled in the grasses yourself."

I turned the conversation back on her. "No wonder my brother clings to your shadow."

Her delicate fingers fluttered in her lap. "I've taught him a thing or two, mostly because sinking his spear into me is the only thing that keeps him from crying into his bowls of *airag*."

I frowned then, thinking of all the times this winter that Tolui had become so sloppy with *airag* and Onggud wine that my mother had ordered him out into the frigid cold to sober him.

"There's no greater feeling than your blood boiling with lust. Don't you miss that?" I asked them both.

Sorkhokhtani shrugged. "I haven't had any man except for Tolui. Our coupling is nothing to make my blood boil"—she raised an eyebrow at me—"but I can tolerate it."

Toregene only stared into the bowl of *airag* cupped in her hands. "We're not all so fortunate to feel passion with our husbands; sometimes we find love instead where we least expect it." Her sharp glance killed the question on my lips. "You may be lucky and come to love Ala-Qush, but if not, don't think for a moment that I'm sanctioning you tumbling another man once you're married. You don't want your children to end up like Jochi."

My unfortunate brother with his murky blood. Toregene's message was clear: I might find love with another man, but I was never to act on it.

Sorkhokhtani shot me a mischievous grin. "Although I'm sure you can make Ala-Qush's blood boil if you can ride him all night long."

I laughed at that. I knew not which spirit goaded Sorkhokhtani on, but I would miss this new girl when I left for Olon Süme.

"And you'll have to deal with Ala-Qush's other wife, the one he's been forced to set aside for you," Toregene said to me. "That will be no small task."

Her unsaid words hung heavy in the air. That woman would view an untried girl as an easy target. I'd have six weeks in the Great Dry Sea to ignore the inevitable, but now seemed as good a time as any to start heeding other people's advice.

I heaved a great sigh and finally sat down, folding my legs under me. "I suppose I can sleep in my saddle."

Toregene's smile lit her already lined face and she raised her bowl to me. "There's a good girl. Perhaps we should start with a discussion of which herbs can harden the softest of male flesh?"

I found myself wishing that night would never end as I joined in the laughter in Toregene's tent, drinking enough *airag* to set my head throbbing, and sneaking back to my mother's *ger* with Sorkhokhtani only when the chickadees heralded the coming dawn. In my absence, my mother had rolled and bound my waiting felts, and they stood like dutiful sentinels outside her door. Folded in a pile between them was a new *deel* and trousers dyed with the juice of red goji berries. Tears stung my eyes at the precious gift and the realization that daylight meant the end of this life and the beginning of a new one. It meant leaving my sisters and brothers.

And my mother.

One of Tolui's snores exploded from inside the tent, like the snort of two great rams poised to smash their heads together. Sorkhokhtani groaned and I clapped my hands over my mouth to stifle my sleep-deprived laughter.

"Between all the sex and the snoring, I'm never going to sleep once we're married," Sorkhokhtani muttered.

"Dose him with *airag* and stuff your ears with wool." I gasped for breath, then pulled her into a heartfelt hug. "I'm going to miss you."

"And we'll miss you," Sorkhokhtani said, her hands fluttering awkwardly against my back. "You'd best go and ready yourself now if you want any peace and quiet," she said, her gaze straying to the spreading light on the horizon.

"I'll be back before the sky surrounds the sun," I promised, giving her another quick hug and grabbing the scarlet bundle my mother had left for me.

The early song of a dun-colored jay accompanied me to the river, its surface shimmering like wet trout scales. I flung off my clothes and dove in as I'd done as a child, when I'd swum naked with Ogodei and Tolui. The river was bitingly cold and I gasped as my nipples puckered and gooseflesh rolled down my skin. To keep from defiling the river, I shivered my way back to the bank and scrubbed myself dry with my old caftan. The new *deel* and trousers were soft against my skin, evidence of the extra beatings my mother had given them, and I took care plaiting my braid down my back. I would bid my mother farewell with a clean body, if not a clean soul.

It seemed the entire sprawling camp had woken while I bathed, and it took me longer to retrace my steps as I bid farewell to childhood friends and women I recognized from drawing water at the river. They patted my cheeks and bid me a long life filled with easy winters and many children. When I finally neared my mother's tent, my entire family stood ready to see me off. My brothers were closest in line, quaffing from a skin of wine. They bowed their heads to me—the only time I'd ever see them do so—and Ogodei offered me the wine.

I arched my eyebrow and took a sip, feeling it scorch the back of my throat and spread its warmth into my belly. "Feeling generous this morning?"

He tweaked my nose as he had when I was little, offering me his most jovial grin. "Don't say I never gave you anything, sister."

Dwarfed beside Ogodei, Tolui sniffed. His eyes glistened so I knew he was already drunk before I hit the wall of alcohol on his breath. Tears and drunkenness were common partners for my youngest brother, although it seemed early even for him to be red-faced with drink. I wanted to shake him by the front of his *deel*, to tell him to start acting like a man, but his lower lip quivered.

"I'll miss you, sister," he managed to choke out.

I pulled him to me then, not wanting his last memory of me to be a rebuke. I was sure my mother would fill his ears with reprimands later. "I'll miss you, too," I said, shooting Ogodei a meaningful look over my brother's shoulder. "Listen to Sorkhokhtani," I said as Ogodei sighed and led him off, hopefully to drop him in a horse trough. "You're lucky to have her."

I worried about my youngest brother, for although he wasn't

mean-spirited, he lacked Ogodei's good humor and ability to hold his liquor. I had to trust that Sorkhokhtani would protect him, as it was no longer my job to do so.

Next in line was Gurbesu, her daughter, Al-Altun, crying fitfully in a sling on her back. "Go with your head high to your first husband," Gurbesu said, then leaned closer to whisper in my ear. "And if you don't find happiness with him, remember that he may not be your only husband."

I shot her a look of feigned shock, but Gurbesu's words didn't last long in my mind, coming as they did from a woman who'd walked between the purification fires with not one or two, but *three* men. I didn't plan to be widowed once, much less twice. And if I did lose my husband, I wouldn't need to remarry, since I'd have already borne many strong sons. Then I'd have earned my title as Beki of the Onggud, and my independence.

Standing next to Gurbesu were my brothers' women, Toregene and Sorkhokhtani at the forefront, both wearing dark smudges under their eyes from our sleepless night. Sorkhokhtani pressed a *buree*, a small flute carved from a ram's horn, into my hands.

"So you never lack music," she said. "Think of me when you play and you'll never be alone."

I wondered then how often she'd felt lonely when she'd first come to us, if she sometimes felt that way still. It was one more thing I'd never thought to ask.

"I don't know how to play," I said, forcing the words over the growing lump in my throat.

"True, but what else are you going to do for six weeks in the desert?" She kept a straight face, but her eyes sparked with mischief. "And it's a child's flute, the easiest to learn."

I chuckled and squeezed her hand. I'd never thought to try my hand at music, but now I would, if only to be reminded of long winter nights in my mother's tent, warm by the fire with Sorkhokhtani's music filling the air.

Toregene was next, with Güyük sleeping peacefully on her back. I hadn't expected gifts, but she looped a thin strip of leather around my neck, a worn silver amulet tucked in the middle. Her cross.

"I can't take this," I said, covering her hands. "It's your god's emblem."

She smiled, a serene expression compared to the raucous laughter I'd witnessed in her tent. "Christ has kept me safe all these years, and now I hope he may protect you. The Khan has ordered Shigi to join him on campaign, so he'll watch over you as well." Her mismatched eyes shone at that, and I squeezed her hand. Toregene and Shigi had always been close, more concerned with their books and scrolls on herbs and religion than with riding and wrestling. "I'll pray for you both," she continued, "for Ogodei has promised me a tent for worship when we set up our own camp this summer."

"You're leaving?" Somehow I'd expected that everything would remain the same after I left, my family's lives frozen like winter ice since I'd no longer be here to witness them.

She pressed her forehead to mine, her hands clasped loosely around my wrists. "Everything changes, sister of my heart, whether we wish it or not."

I filled my eyes with the last images of my sisters and brothers, knowing that time would distort their faces and smiles in my mind. Then they parted before me, clearing a path to my waiting parents.

My mother stood beside my father, dressed in a crisp new green *deel* with my father's wolf-tooth necklace at her throat, her black-and-gray hair perfectly coiled under her tall green *boqta*. In her hands she held a second headdress I'd never seen before, two curving horns of black leather on a cap of crimson felt, twisted with gold and dangling waterfalls of white and red beads.

A *beki*'s headdress.

I sank to my knees before her, feeling the weight of everyone watching as she placed the headdress atop my hair, heavier than any helmet.

"Don't you dare cry," she whispered, raising me. "Or I might start, too."

My mother's eyes were bright with unshed tears as she laid her hands on my shoulders. I offered her my right cheek, then my left, and she breathed two deep inhales, one near each of my cheeks, filling her memory with the scent of me.

Suddenly my knees felt as wobbly as a newborn colt's. This might be the last time I saw my mother.

She tilted my chin and gave a minute shake of her head. "We will meet again, Alaqai. Two queens—one grown stooped and the other like a child—shall part once more with tears in their eyes."

With her words came the smell of divining smoke and burned bone. Since Teb Tengeri's death, my mother had become our people's official seer, wary of the messages of the bones but unwilling to allow another fortune seeker to take advantage of so powerful a position. I brushed away the thought of future tears. All that mattered was her promise that we'd see each other again.

"I love you, Mother," I said.

She smiled, crinkling the scar on her lip and revealing a rotten tooth in the back of her mouth. She cupped my face in her rough hands. "And I love you, Alaqai Beki. Don't look back, and never forget that you are the daughter of Genghis Khan."

"And the daughter of Borte Khatun," my father said, his long mustache twitching as he smiled at my mother. "That counts for far more than being the daughter of a leathery-faced, bowlegged conqueror."

"Go, Alaqai Beki," my mother said. "Go, and make us proud."

My father took my hand and led me away from the *ger*. I resisted the urge to look back at my mother and clenched my teeth to keep my chin from wobbling. Neer-Gui stood at the head of a contingent of sixteen hundred of my father's men. A brilliant blue cloth had been tied around the pommel of my saddle, a gift from my mother and a prayer to the Eternal Blue Sky to keep me safe. I could make out a familiar face amongst the crowd of men; Shigi sat tall in his wooden saddle decorated with silver medallions, but he stared beyond me with a solemn expression, as if he, too, was leaving something precious behind. I didn't have time to ponder that, for the Four Dogs of War bowed their heads to me, a sign of respect I'd never received from the generals, even as the favored daughter of Genghis Khan. After my father saw me safely delivered to Ala-Qush and instated as the Onggud's new *beki*, he would march with these men against the Tanghut in what promised to be a quick campaign.

I stood as tall as I could, keeping my back to my mother as tradition demanded. We were as different as a mother and daughter could be, but I felt the love radiating from her like warm sunshine on a new spring day.

She would not cry and I would not look back, at least not until we were too far from each other for anyone to see.

Instead, my mother would use a *tsatsal*, an ancient wooden paddle, to fling drops of mare's milk into the air, pouring a path of white that would guide me even under the darkest sky. She would do this every day until I returned to her.

And one day I would perform the same ritual for my daughter.

I mounted Neer-Gui, keeping my eyes on the rump of my father's massive black warhorse. Tonight I could pour my tears into the Earth Mother, but for now they stayed buried inside me.

I would soon learn tears weren't the only things I would need to keep buried.

Shigi and my father let me travel that morning in peace and it was only after the sun reached its highest point in the sky that we stopped to rest the horses and eat the bundles of roasted mutton my mother had packed in our saddlebags.

My father sat next to me and unwrapped the meat from its brown-and-white-spotted goatskin while the soldiers tucked into their meal of dried curds, singing of horses and women between bites. Each of the men in the heavy cavalry wore an iron helmet and coat of mail and carried two bows, a lasso, and a battle-ax, yet despite their load each seemed invigorated at the thought of the coming conquest. Shigi settled next to us, as easy next to my father as he was with his scrolls. I knew my father had set his adopted Tatar brother to recording this campaign as well as finishing codifying the Jasagh so the final legal code might be shared with the rest of the clans, including the new edict that decreed that all members of the Golden Family were above the law. Even now, Shigi retrieved his perpetual stack of papers while he ate, so I wondered if he might leave greasy thumbprints on his fine descriptions of my father's cavalry or the latest law forbidding the washing of clothes until they were worn out.

"No friend is better than your own heart." My father recited the ancient saying while he chewed. "Yet your heart seems troubled, *tarvag takal*."

I offered him a wan smile and removed the headdress, twisting my neck with relief. "I fear I'll fail at the task you've set before me. The Onggud are learned people, and I am not."

It was only one of the many reasons that I dreaded meeting the strange foreigners I would rule, but the safest to discuss.

Shigi set down his pen, balancing his portion of meat on one leg and a waterskin between both knees along with the thick stack of paper. "It's true that the Onggud are blessed with much wisdom: shamans learned in the ways of spirits from faraway lands, scribes to record their histories, and great sculptors living in the shadow of the Great Long Wall."

I scowled when he didn't continue. "Thank you," I said. "I feel much better now."

He gave an elegant shrug. "It's not my fault you refused to sit still long enough to learn anything during my lessons."

I rolled my eyes. "Because if I had, then I'd be as wise as their scribes? Or at least as wise as you?"

Shigi gave me a slow smile. "That, my dear Alaqai, you could never be."

My father chuckled and clapped a heavy hand on my knee. "Even with all that wisdom, the Onggud cities would fall if I directed my armies against them," he said, his voice roughened from years of inhaling smoke inside dark *gers*. "There are many kinds of knowledge, Alaqai Beki, and of all my children, you are the wisest. You have your mother to thank for that."

My scowl deepened. "My mother is no longer here to guide me."

"No, but she has stretched you to the height of men."

I nudged his toe with mine. "That's only when I wear that infernally heavy headdress. Take it off and—" I motioned to my bare head and shrugged.

He laughed again. I would miss that sound when he finally left me in Olon Süme weeks from now, something that didn't bear thinking about. "You and I were both born with clots of blood in our fists. You will be my feet amongst the Onggud, but also my eyes, ears, and mouth." He licked his fingers, wiped the leftover grease on his *deel*, and stood. "It's only a matter of time until you determine how to best rule your new people." He stuffed the empty goatskin into the front of his *deel*. "And I'll be leaving Shigi with you, at least for the first few months while you settle in and before our conquest against the Tanghut begins in earnest. That way you'll have secret eyes of your own."

My father winked at me, then left to make his rounds among his men, clapping a hand on one of his general's shoulders and easily joining their conversation, even as my own food remained untouched. The enormity of what my father expected struck me then, making me want to gasp for breath and reminding me of the time Ogodei had thrown me into Older Sister Lake. I'd sunk for what seemed like forever before finally touching the bottom and kicking frantically to the surface, my lungs screaming and my eyeballs threatening to explode. I'd survived the experience, but barely.

I prayed I'd survive what my father required of me.

"It looks like you won't be going home anytime soon. Instead, you're stuck with me," I said to Shigi, expecting a witty rejoinder or conspiratorial smile. Instead he stared again in the direction we'd just come.

"It seems we're both stuck with each other," he said, giving a weak smile.

I knew not what troubled him, but I didn't have room in my heart to worry over Shigi's problems as well as my own. I was only a headstrong girl, not a conqueror who drew chiefs to me by the sheer force of my personality. I doubted whether I could rule my husband, much less a kingdom, in my father's name.

May the Eternal Blue Sky and the Earth Mother help me when I failed.

We traveled for six weeks across the Great Dry Sea, riding only at night to save the horses and ourselves from the scorching heat, although it was already well into autumn. I grew accustomed to our upside-down life, sleeping in the light and riding and hunting in the dark. Shigi taught me to play Sorkhokhtani's *buree* from my saddle, coaching my fingers on a song I'd often heard Toregene humming. We caught an occasional deer but mostly subsisted off dried milk paste and meat from the reserve horses we brought with us. There was no time to cook, nor would we have welcomed the additional heat from the fires, so we tucked the meat beneath our saddles and ate it raw and soft after the sun disappeared each night. I looked for the fabled Mongolian death worm, the *olgoi-khorkhoi*, a bright red creature as long as a man and reputed to spew yellow poison that could kill a beast on contact. The *olgoi-khorkhoi* eluded us, but we passed such strange sights that I began to believe my mind played tricks on me: eagles' nests made of sticks in a land without trees; duck hawks feasting on the flesh of a herd of dead antelope; and the strange bones of massive, long-dead lizards hidden amongst the dunes and blowing sands. I realized that the barren stretch of sands wasn't dead at all, for delicious water welled up from the earth at the edge of rocky basins, and jerboas with their long tails often leapt in front of our horses in the dead of night. I rode next to my father, listening to his tales of battle, but more important, to his stories of loyalty and honor. He recounted his early exploits against the Merkid and the Blood War against Jamuka, and although I already knew the tales, I listened now for the ways my father had woven men to him to create the Thirteen Nations. Finally, the Great Dry Sea's constant wind song faded from my ears and its dunes slipped away, diluted first by grasses, then shrubs, and finally the cool birch forests that reminded me of home.

Then one day as the sun was beginning to wake, we saw the black outline of Onggud walls on the horizon.

Olon Süme was stark and hard, an unnatural scar on the gentle swell of the earth, as if men had forced the settlement onto the Earth Mother's back. The city was surrounded by hundreds of grazing two-humped camels, more numerous than the blades of grass on the hills. I'd rarely spent much time around my mother's camels; we kept our horses separate from the awkward, humped beasts due to their natural animosity toward each other, but still, I'd never seen so many camels all together. I was accustomed to the smell of animals, but a foreign stench burrowed into my nostrils and made my gorge rise as we passed the shaggy beasts: human waste, accumulated years of animal dung, and the musk of too many unwashed bodies crammed together. I reared back like a whipped horse, wanting to bury my head in Neer-Gui's mane and gulp the hot desert air I had never thought to miss.

"The Onggud have herders who travel with the seasons, but most remain within the safety of the walls." My father's voice was soothing, and I recognized the tone he often used to calm frightened horses. "And there are treasures within those walls that will make up for the stink."

Still, I didn't move until Shigi cleared his throat. "Now would be a good time to avail yourself of your mother's gifts, Alaqai."

Panic made it impossible to speak, but I beckoned for my cart and opened the trunk that had been carefully sealed all this time against the desert sands. I'd overheard my father's men tell tales of Onggud women who had been fed perfumes since infancy so the bees and butterflies followed them, infatuated with their fragrance. Another story claimed their noblewomen painted their faces with yellow lead and their lips with the ashes of fragrant flowers. Their women were skilled at poetry and dance, song and a variety of musical instruments. I was only a girl expert with a bow and arrow, my father's blood in my veins my only commendation.

Inside the trunk was my meticulously folded red *deel*, and under it, the tall *boqta* I'd worn to leave my mother. I shook out the robe and slipped it over my travel clothes, the familiar scent of my mother's cook smoke making my eyes sting and my fingers fumble with the elaborate bone toggles, which resembled galloping horses. Already my neck ached from the weight of the headdress, and I could scarcely balance it atop my head as we finally approached the walls. Nervous herders scurried back inside the city at our approach, their camels unperturbed, and soldiers called down to us, their words a foreign jangle in my ears.

Turkic.

The Onggud lived at a crossroads of the steppe, between the Turks and the Jurched. While I had realized this, I hadn't thought to be entirely cut off from communicating with the people I would rule. Panic threatened to overwhelm me once again.

My father answered back in Mongolian, his command clear and steady. "Tell Ala-Qush, Prince of Beiping, that Genghis Khan is at his gates and requests admittance into the city of Olon Süme." He motioned with his scimitar behind him, his lip curving up in a dangerous grin. "And my men request admittance as well."

The soldiers scurried away like rats to do my father's bidding, and I

could almost hear their hearts pounding at the thought of the bloody conqueror at their gates. It was an image my father liked to propagate, to save
the trouble of unnecessary battles.

"Ala-Qush speaks our language," he said, eyeing me. "I have no doubt
that soon you'll speak all the Onggud languages. Shigi will help you."

It wasn't just Turkic I heard as people began to gather along the walls,
but a cauldron of strange tongues. All around, flat-faced people stared
down at us. Realization dawned in their curious eyes at the sight of this
strange girl in a *beki*'s headdress and her father with his sixteen hundred
men. The expressions of more than a few hardened into glares before they
averted their eyes.

I remembered my mother's words and tilted my chin, resisting the urge
to straighten the ungainly headdress. The chatter of its beaded strings did
little to drown out the furious whispers.

A soldier approached through the open gates, the tall wooden panels
carved with plodding tortoises, smaller relatives to the golden tortoise that
carried the earth on its back, and still another sign that the fire in my soul
would clash with these people I must now rule. "The Great Ala-Qush of
the Onggud, Prince of Beiping, bids you welcome to our city," he said, his
voice wavering. "He asks you to proceed to the Great House."

The walls closed in upon us as we entered and headed toward the
Great House. I expected a palatial tent like my mother's, large enough to
hold at least thirty men, but Ala-Qush's residence was smaller and built
from polished wood with a birch roof. Tiny weather-beaten houses huddled
around it like nervous old women, and a man almost Ogodei's size and
dressed in shimmering blue silk stood outside the door. Ala-Qush
stepped forward to greet my father, his arms outstretched in welcome even
as he stared at me from a face that screamed of his white-boned ancestry. I
refused to drop my gaze but clasped my pommel as his upper lip curled
before smoothing into a stiff smile of welcome.

I could see it in his eyes—Ala-Qush didn't relish the idea of marrying
me; he only wanted the alliance our union would bring. In that moment I
would have traded the stars in the sky to appear more like delicate Sorkhokhtani and less like myself.

"The Onggud welcome the Khan of Khans and his most esteemed daughter to our town," Ala-Qush said. I was a foreigner come to rule over them, to use them for her father's conquests, and I was under no illusions; one wrong move and they'd feed me to the wolves, then rejoin their ancient alliance with the Tanghut.

"Ala-Qush." My father remained on his horse, as befitted a Khan greeting his vassal. "It is with a glad heart that I bring you my favorite daughter. May the two of you cleave as one heart until the end of your days."

Ala-Qush offered a hand to help me from my saddle, but I swung my leg over and dismounted without assistance. His brows jumped in surprise, but I couldn't tell if he was pleased or not. If so, his pleasure wouldn't last long. "And it is with a glad heart that I shall take Alaqai Beki as my wife tomorrow," he said to my father.

There came a snort of derision from behind Ala-Qush. A sallow-skinned woman stood straight-backed, dressed in a *deel* that shimmered in the sunlight, although it was too rough to be silk. Two children flanked her, a boy with a thick nest of black hair and wide ears like a jerboa, and a thin-lipped girl almost my height. Both bore Ala-Qush's broad cheeks and flat nose and this woman's sharp chin. I wished I still sat astride Neer-Gui then, for my knees threatened to buckle under their scathing glares.

Not only had I supplanted this woman, but my future children would outrank hers. From her expression, I could guess that a bleak and possibly very short future stretched before me, one in which I had to fear a pillow over my face every night and test each bite of horsemeat or sip of goat's milk. It would take more than simply setting me above this woman for her to obey me.

"Shall you introduce me to your family?" I asked Ala-Qush, gesturing to the boy and girl.

Ala-Qush motioned stiffly to his wife, twice my age and with the leathery skin of the desert lizards I'd shot in the Great Dry Sea. Unlike in the stories, she wore no yellow lead on her face, but her skin was so pallid that the paint might have been an improvement. "This is Orbei, mother of my sons Jingue and Boyahoe."

Only one son stood on the platform now, but I didn't dare ask what had happened to the other. At least not yet.

"And your daughter?" I asked. "What is her name?"

Ala-Qush quirked an eyebrow at that, for it was uncommon to inquire about a girl-child. "She is called Enebish."

Enebish. The name meant *Not This One*, an entreaty to malicious spirits not to carry off a weak child. As the only girl, Enebish would have been seen as frail, although the young woman who glowered at me now seemed far from weak.

Ala-Qush's son reminded me of Tolui when he was about seven years old, with rosy cheeks and a shock of hair that partially obscured his eyes. His round ears only made him more endearing, although it would be unfortunate if he never grew into them. He was the only one to offer me a smile, revealing a chipped front tooth, at least until his mother's hand on his shoulder made him wince.

"Our firstborn is not here," Orbei sneered. "Jingue was called to leave Olon Süme in order to purify his mind."

Our firstborn.

His absence during my arrival was a slight no one could ignore. I wondered what heinous thoughts Ala-Qush's former heir needed to purge from his mind, whether they perhaps revolved around the heathen girl who had come to supplant his mother and bear sons who would replace him.

I fluttered my fingers in the air, seemingly unconcerned. "A shame. I'd thought to meet all of my husband's children today."

Orbei clucked sympathetically, but I wasn't fooled. "It's unfortunate when life doesn't adhere to your plans, isn't it?"

Some demon urged the next words from my tongue unbidden.

"Perhaps," I said. "Although I'm pleased I was able to meet my husband's *former* wife."

Orbei's eyes narrowed to slits and for a moment I feared she would spit at me. Instead, she drew back, and Ala-Qush's brow furrowed, his gaze skittering from me to my father. Better to do this right away, surrounded by plenty of witnesses.

"Surely you've already set aside your other woman, as I'm to be your first and *only* wife?"

Those words were a gamble that would alter the course of my life, although I didn't yet know it.

Enebish cried out at the insult to her mother, but my father didn't balk at the change of plans, and for that I loved him even more. He glanced at Orbei, then to Ala-Qush. "Or perhaps the Prince of Beiping has yet to do as I commanded?"

My future husband was pinned, surrounded by sixteen hundred of the fiercest warriors in the world. I could tell from his expression that he didn't relish the feeling, the hint of bloodlust in the air. Neither did I.

There was a rustle like whispers as Orbei shifted on her feet, the wattle under her chin twitching with anger.

"I don't recall being asked to set aside my wife." Ala-Qush's jaw clenched, but he dared not refute my father's supposed request. "Perhaps in my old age, I've forgotten the details of our negotiations."

I almost laughed at that. Ala-Qush had seen more than twice my years, but he was scarcely an old man. He'd have to find a better excuse.

My father dismounted and ran his hand down his stallion's muzzle, pretending to consider Ala-Qush's words. "I'm willing to overlook such a mistake, but Alaqai Beki is the key to our alliance."

I interrupted then, my mouth suddenly dry. "As such, tomorrow I'll become Beki of the Onggud, and your only wife. Or . . ."

I shrugged, letting him imagine my father's hordes pouring over the city walls.

"I see," Ala-Qush said, motioning to the men behind my father, all armed with spears and shields. "And I assume your men expect as much?"

My father stroked his mustache. "Naturally."

Ala-Qush straightened, and for a moment I wondered whether he could feel the daggers of his wife's eyes against his spine. "Then the woman who has served me these past years has done her duty." He clasped his thick belt with its ivory deer buckle, a meaningless gesture to those far away, but this close I could see the tension in his hands as he gripped the leather. "I shall take Alaqai Beki, daughter of Genghis Khan, as my one and only wife."

I knew not whether Ala-Qush was a man for revenge, but I had no doubt Orbei would find a thousand little ways to seek her vengeance for this. Yet without her husband's power behind her, her jabs would be toothless.

I should have felt flush with this first victory, but instead I felt only emptiness. I had won this battle, but the war had only just begun. I still needed to convince these people that I was able to rule them, and I knew one thing for certain as I looked at the hostile faces of Ala-Qush's wife and the Onggud around me.

The battle lines had been drawn.

Chapter 17

I spent the day after meeting Ala-Qush erecting my *ger*. Tradition demanded that my husband's family assist me, but I wasn't foolish enough to expect Orbei to offer her help. Mine was the only tent in this city of walls, setting me further apart as something different and foreign, yet I couldn't find it in myself to pack away my mother's felts and allow wooden walls to entrap me more than I already was. The felt panels of a *ger* represented the Eternal Blue Sky, its smoke hole the Golden Light of the Sun, and the floor the Earth Mother; without them I would be truly lost.

That night brought angry shouts from the Great House, eventually replaced with the grunts and moans of a rutting couple after most of the village had drifted to sleep and the stars glittered overhead. I punched my pillow until camel hair bulged from the seams and tried in vain to stuff my ears to shut out the sounds of Ala-Qush with Orbei. I contemplated marching over and demanding they stop, but the thought of Ala-Qush's wrath or, worse, their laughter kept me in my narrow bed.

That bleak night was the first time in my life that I'd slept alone, without even the snores of my father's men to carry me to sleep.

Night was painful, but the coming day was far worse.

Enebish came to attend me on the morning of my wedding, but her scowl was too much like Orbei's for my liking and I sent her away. Of all my clan, only Shigi would remain with me when my father left, but I could scarcely ask him to dress me in the silken trousers of my wedding finery or button my *deel* over my breasts. Instead I managed on my own, gingerly slipping into Ala-Qush's gift of a long yellow robe made of camlet and tying it with a red sash. This was the reason for all the camels we'd seen: the Onggud specialized in the production of silk woven with the finest camel hair, a material softer than the downy feathers at the bottom of a swan's nest. Orbei's robe from the previous day was made from camlet, and I'd later learn that her ancient family controlled the trade of the precious commodity and, thus, most of the economy of Olon Süme.

I wondered then if I'd done the right thing in insisting that my husband set aside his wife. Yet the deed was done.

I emerged from my *ger* to find my father waiting for me outside. The Khan of Khans wore a brown felt *deel*, and the curved sword in his belt matched the silver hairs threaded through the black of his braid. Even without his fur-lined helmet and the ragged bearskin draped over his shoulders, it would have been impossible to mistake him for anyone other than the leader of the Thirteen Nations. My father wore the bearskin only when dealing with potential enemies, relishing the image of the savage they all believed him to be and therefore making them more likely to capitulate to his demands. Yet this was a wedding between allies; I didn't know why he wished to intimidate the Onggud today.

It was only after he lifted his arms to embrace me that I noticed the smear of fresh blood on my threshold. It was bad luck to step on the exact border of a *ger* and infinitely worse to spill blood there. My father's eyes flicked to where Shigi shuffled off with something hidden in his arms.

"What is that?" I called to him.

"Don't, Alaqai," my father warned.

"I wish to know what was left on my doorstep," I said, storming in all my wedding finery to where Shigi stood, his back to me. I opened the brown felt blanket wrapped around the bloody gift, revealing a dead marmot.

I drew back, swallowing back bile at the stench and the flies feeding on the creature's eyes. "It was generous of Ala-Qush's wife to leave me such a gift on my wedding day," I said, covering my nose and waving the thing away. "Wasn't it, Father?"

My father drew my arm through his, his voice low. "The best revenge is success, Alaqai. I could kill Orbei for this or you could punish her, but it would be better still to conquer her people."

"As you did with Jamuka?"

He smiled. "Perhaps with less bloodshed. After all, the people of Ala-Qush's wife will be our people after today. And you must always serve our people faithfully."

I wondered which people my father meant: his or the Onggud. Perhaps both.

We passed priceless cauldrons stewing freshly slaughtered horses on our way to the Great House; both the iron pots and the meat were wedding gifts from my father. Most of the town had turned out to examine me, but there were no cheers or shouts of joy, only the sound of boiling water and the smell of horsemeat.

My father squeezed my hand and we entered the Great House together. I touched the emblem of Toregene's god at my throat, needing protection from all the gods and spirits to keep my stomach from rebelling as I faced the man who was about to become my husband.

Ala-Qush sat on the center of a wooden platform, flanked by various advisers and nobles. Orbei was conspicuously missing, prompting me to thank the Eternal Blue Sky for small miracles. Again I noticed the absence of my husband's eldest son, Jingue, and filed away the insult. There would be plenty of time later to sniff out the recalcitrant boy.

At home, my appearance as a bride might have prompted shouts and taunts about the upcoming evening in the bridal tent, but this ceremony was as silent as the winter sky. Ala-Qush scarcely looked at me when my father handed me to him, but I stood tall and arranged the folds of my *deel* while my gaze skimmed the heads of my father's entourage. I was thankful for Shigi's calming presence in the crowd; he stood serenely in his blue cap while others of my father's men jostled Ala-Qush's chosen representatives. If things didn't go well, my wedding might be celebrated with fights instead of songs and toasts.

My father began his speech, but I heard little of it until the end. "Now I give my daughter, Alaqai Beki, to Ala-Qush of the Onggud," he said, joining our hands together, "so they become two shafts of the same cart."

He presented Ala-Qush with the ceremonial arrow, smaller than a real quarrel, with a silver tip carved with a snarling wolf. I wondered if my new husband recognized the wolf as my father's totem, meant to convey my father's continuing protection over me. If Ala-Qush noted the symbolism, he hid it well. Instead, my husband removed my Mongol headdress and replaced it with the towering Onggud crown with its strange gold horn, likely removed from the bedside of his leather-faced wife only that morning. The beaver ruff's scent of mildew made my nose itch, and the strings of carnelian beads obscured my vision.

I was now Beki of the Onggud. A *beki* would never break, no matter how life strove to break her. Only one thought echoed in my mind as Ala-Qush wrapped an arm around my waist, claiming me as his own.

I would not break.

My resolution was sorely tested that night, but not in the way I expected.

There were no wild celebrations for my wedding, no merry dancing around campfires or impromptu wrestling contests in honor of the groom's virility. A late autumn wedding at home had meant that the colts were weaned and every guest could drink their weight in *airag*. Olon Süme offered only neatly stacked wooden casks of Onggud wine, served warm and meant to be sipped from tiny porcelain cups.

I watched my father and his entourage ride away on their open path to the Tanghut outpost of Wulahai, their cloud of dust finally disappearing over the horizon into the night, leaving me with only Shigi and a new title: the Princess Who Runs the State. I'd heard many soldiers comment on their eagerness to leave Olon Süme's walls and filth behind, and I wished I could join them. Instead, I retreated to my *ger*, where Enebish waited to ready me for my husband's attentions. I suffered her presence out of necessity, sure that Orbei had instructed her to spy on me. The weight of loneliness settled upon my chest then, and I found myself yearning for Sorkhokhtani's music or even my mother's lectures to distract me. I attempted a few notes on the *buree*, but my scowling daughter-by-marriage yanked off my headdress and the camlet robe and tugged the coils from my hair until they tumbled down my back like a black waterfall. I endured the pain with a tight smile when she pulled the tortoiseshell comb harder than was necessary.

I heard my husband coming before he entered, accompanied by a distorted voice and followed by a rude guffaw of laughter. Enebish bowed her head to him when he entered. "Rest well, revered father," she said, and he ruffled her hair with tenderness. The door closed and he turned to face me, although he didn't look pleased about it.

Toregene's advice about all the tricks and secret ways to pleasure a man crowded my mind and made me flush. I longed to put this night behind me and greet a new day.

"Good evening, husband," I said. I stepped close and ran a finger up his chest, my palm cupping his cheek.

He grabbed my wrist, so hard I winced. "I'm hardly your husband," he growled, shoving my hand away. He filled two fists with the camlet at my collar and ripped the robe open so it fell to the ground at my feet, exposing my nakedness. My cheeks flared and I shuddered with shame and revulsion, but his next words flared my fury. "I find myself saddled with a mare I never sought and now find abhorrent. I shall never call you wife."

I yanked my robe back up, ignoring the scarcely restrained outrage in his voice and not troubling myself over his rearranging the facts over who had sought whom. "If you think I'll let you speak to me like this—"

"I'll speak to you as I please," Ala-Qush said. "After all, I've bought and paid for you, haven't I?"

"I am your *beki*, not your slave," I said, hugging the camlet robe closed over my breasts. "No one speaks to the daughter of Genghis Khan in such a manner."

I knew they were the wrong words the moment they left my mouth.

"Your father's no longer here to protect you." Ala-Qush grabbed my wrist and twisted my arm behind my back. "Some of my nobles encouraged me to support your upstart father, yet still others desired an alliance with the ancient Tanghuts. I cast my lot with you, yet you and your father humiliated me before my people and made a spectacle of the wife who has served me for longer than you've lived. Everything about you heathens offends me, from your stench of sour milk and the filthy skins you wear to the way you cook your horses, eyeballs, assholes, and all." He stepped back and spat at my feet. "And above everything, you offend me most of all."

I tasted the copper tang of blood as I bit my tongue. I wished I had my father's power then, that I could make Ala-Qush cower before me. Instead I gave my husband the insult of my back, unwilling to let him witness the riot of emotions on my face.

"I won't listen to this," I said. "Nor shall I share your bed until you've apologized."

His cruel bark of laughter made me cringe. "No, Alaqai Beki, daughter of Genghis Khan, it is you who shall never share *my* bed. Not this night or any other."

I sputtered, then whirled around in time to see the door slam shut so hard the frame of my *ger* shuddered. A gust of cold air hit me in the face, almost guttering the fire.

My mind struggled to make sense of what had just happened; then I hurled the Onggud headdress into the opposite wall, followed by the silver bowls of wine left out for after the bridal bedding. I could imagine my mother shaking her head at me, the disappointment writ clear in her eyes. I gave a cry and flung myself on the bed, staring at the stars through the smoke hole and wishing I could burn all of Olon Süme to the ground.

It wasn't long before I heard the same grunts and moans from the night before, Ala-Qush and Orbei mocking me in my empty *ger*.

Only this time they were louder, so the whole town could hear them and know my shame.

In the days and weeks that followed, I recalled words my father once said when recounting the hardships he faced after his father's death at the hands of the Tatars.

"Life is like an arrow," he had stated, his features made sharper by the flickering fire. "Both must be pulled back before they can be launched forward. Remember that when you feel as if nothing shall ever be right again."

I understood what he meant now. My husband and I scarcely shared the same air, and if I happened upon him, he'd growl like a bear and order me away. More than once I heard the deep bellows of his men's laughter when he made some comment at my expense. After several days of this constant humiliation and nights listening to him with Orbei, I waited for him outside the Great House. He attempted to ignore me, but I used my tiger sword to bar his exit, earning a scathing glare that would have made even my mother quake with fear.

"Return to your tent, Alaqai Beki," he said. "My head pounds like the inside of a drum and I won't make it worse by listening to another of your tirades."

"This arrangement is unacceptable," I said, ignoring the men behind him.

His smile was icy. "I find it preferable to the alternative of locking you in a wooden cangue for the rest of your days. I believe your father withstood such a punishment once."

"You wouldn't dare."

"No?" He threw open his arms. "And who would stop me?"

It was a challenge, then, a test as to whether I'd invoke my father's name again. But even if my father weren't off campaigning, we both knew I wouldn't admit to being unable to manage my responsibilities as wife and *beki*.

"That's what I thought." Ala-Qush leaned in and I noticed his pupils were strangely dilated. "Now, run along and play with your bow and arrow, wife. I have a kingdom to rule."

My husband's advisers laughed and cast me withering looks, drawing the hems of their pristine robes close as they passed me. I forced myself to stand and watch them go, leaving me alone on the threshold of the Great House.

Something had to change. My husband despised me and refused to visit my bed, and his people loathed me.

There had to be another way to conquer the Onggud.

The idea came to me at midnight a few nights later, a time when restless spirits roamed the winds, looking for sleepless souls to torment. I should have known better than to trust a plan born of meddling shades.

Ala-Qush was gone again, seeing to the border patrols the Onggud had maintained for centuries. I'd thought to invite myself along, but the idea of spending a week with my husband sounded as enjoyable as having a rotten tooth removed. I'd already been rebuffed when I sent him a paper envelope stuffed with powdered gingerroot from Olon Süme's market. Shigi recalled that Toregene had once boiled the herb into a tea for him to alleviate a terrible headache. I felt an emptiness in my heart when I thought of Toregene and Sorkhokhtani, for without any messengers, it was impossible to know how they fared. "I miss them, too," Shigi assured me, and that night we poured a bowl of milk into the earth in a prayer for their health and happiness. Shigi, Toregene, and Sorkhokhtani didn't share the blood in my veins, but sometimes it seemed that they were more my kin than the brothers who'd been born from my mother's womb. I noted the way Shigi's eyes grew distant when my sisters and our home were mentioned, the way he seemed to retreat within himself as if pulling memories around his shoulders.

Still, although Shigi might not return home for several years, it was difficult for me to muster much pity for him, knowing that I might never see my family or former home again. And so I would continue to attempt to ingratiate myself with the Onggud and my husband.

Regardless of the efficacy of Toregene's herbs, Ala-Qush's messenger returned the package with a sniff of disdain.

"Ala-Qush, Prince of Beiping, does not require your dried weeds," he said, dropping the rumpled envelope in my hand before turning on his heel and stomping off.

Fine. Let the demon in my husband's head devour his skull for all I cared.

Now that Ala-Qush was gone, I planned a dinner for his children, masking the command that they attend in a polite invitation. I'd face them alone, although Shigi protested when I ordered him to leave for the evening.

"The Khan will never forgive me if something happens to you," he said, planting his feet while I worked to close the smoke hole against the night air. Two long-nosed dogs lay at Shigi's feet—Olon Süme was full of the flea-riddled beasts and I'd made the mistake of feeding these mangy specimens. My father had always hated dogs, so there were few in our camp when I was growing up, but I didn't have the heart to kick these ones away. It was quite likely they'd end up my only companions once Shigi left.

"I'm sharing dinner with children," I scoffed. "The worst they might do is spit in my food."

"Jingue is a grown man, not a child."

"It will be difficult for my husband's eldest to eat with us when he's not even within the city walls." I'd overheard Orbei tell Ala-Qush before he left that she expected Jingue to return over the coming days. She claimed to be toiling over a homecoming gift for her eldest son, likely another camlet robe, or perhaps a winter hat made from the stuff. I was heartily sick of camlet, the constant smell of camels, Onggud wine, and everything else that reminded me of this miserable new life of mine.

"You need to leave your tent more." Shigi fingered a gold hoop at his ear. "Jingue arrived this afternoon."

"What?" My arms fell to my sides. "And you're only telling me this now?"

Without Shigi and his ability to speak Turkic, I'd know little of what went on around me, a problem I sought to rectify by slogging through his lessons on how to speak the tongue-twisting language.

"He's here, although I haven't yet laid eyes on him." He swatted away the dog nuzzling his leg. "And Jingue aside, Enebish is only a few years younger than you, and you've publicly insulted her mother."

"I have my tiger sword if she threatens to kill me." I gave a mischievous smile. "Or in case she throws a bowl of millet in my face."

Shigi sighed, knowing better than to argue. "It would serve you right to get pelted with a bowl of that foul porridge they all love."

I wrinkled my nose. The boiled millet I'd been served when the sun had risen this morning hadn't been fit for a starving dog to eat. I knew, because I'd tried to feed it to the dogs, but they'd only growled at me.

A grinning Boyahoe and sulking Enebish entered my tent as the sun began to set, casting a glow of the softest gold on the walls of my *ger*. At first I thought perhaps Jingue had managed to avoid me yet again, but then a man dressed in a thick brown *deel* with close-cropped hair and a single braid down his back ducked inside. He was my age, perhaps a winter younger, with a narrow jaw and deep-set eyes. Unlike most men, he wore no sword, beard, or mustache, yet his bearing was regal. This was the heir I still hoped to supplant with my own sons, the man who would become Olon Süme's future Prince of Beiping if I failed.

I stepped forward, my hands tucked inside my sleeves. "You must be Jingue."

"I am," he said. His Mongolian was accented, but not unpleasantly so. His eyes flicked over me and I waited for him to speak again, or at least to bow, but he only crossed his arms, as defiant as his mother and sister.

"I see you share your family's manners," I said, giving him a false smile and taking some small satisfaction as his eyes widened. "Please," I said, addressing his siblings and gesturing to the feast Shigi and I had set out. "Sit with me and eat."

The Onggud delicacies of roasted bear paw, duck soup, and flat rice cakes pounded with bean sprouts awaited in golden bowls engraved with flowers and scrolls—a design Shigi had informed me was borrowed from the Tanghuts—along the low table. Only hooved animals should eat anything green, but the Onggud grew sprouts in their windows and sold them in the market, along with a foul assortment of sickly sweet melons, bushy stalks of celery that smelled like grass, and brown mushrooms with clods of earth clinging to their stems. I'd sooner starve than eat anything that grew from the dirt.

Boyahoe stepped forward first and sat on one of my mother's rugs, offering a chipped-tooth grin from one big ear to the other until his sister slayed him with a glare. Enebish looked to Jingue, then slowly followed suit at his stiff nod. I plastered a gracious smile on my face.

"Do you have rice balls?" Boyahoe asked after he and his siblings had prayed over their food, thanking the god of the cross for the meal they were about to eat while I sat silently. My husband's youngest son leaned forward with both hands on the table as he scanned the platters. His Mongolian was stilted but understandable. "Rice balls are my favorite."

"I don't think so." I glanced at the spread of food, wishing I'd thought to send Shigi to learn all their favorites. It was too late now.

I worried at Toregene's necklace against my throat, praying to her god and the Eternal Blue Sky to see me safely through this night without any mishaps on my part. Right now I'd welcome Enebish throwing a bowl of porridge and its opportunity to laugh with these hostile creatures my husband had spawned.

Jingue leaned forward, squinting as if nearsighted. "That emblem on your necklace," he asked. "You worship Christ?"

My fingers stilled. "I respect the god of the cross," I said, flustered by his question until I noticed a similar token at his throat. "As everyone should."

Unconcerned with talk of gods, Boyahoe shoved his hair from his eyes and stuffed a hand into his pocket. "Yesterday I ate so many rice balls that I was sick, but my mother made more this afternoon." He retrieved a ball glazed with what looked like honey and peppered with bits of wool lint from inside his *deel*. "Do you want to try it?"

"Boyahoe—," Jingue began, but I held up a hand to silence him, forcing myself not to cringe at the lopsided ball and managing to smile instead.

"It's thoughtful of you to share," I said, taking the sticky treat from him and taking a bite off the corner, doing my best to avoid the biggest piece of lint.

Suddenly Jingue lunged forward and knocked the remainder of the rice ball from my hand. "For the love of Christ," he yelled, his brows twisted in anger. "Don't swallow it!"

I stared at Boyahoe, then at Enebish's seething expression. A sudden burning on my tongue was followed by a burst of panic and a desperate roaring in my ears. I spit the half-chewed rice into my hand and dragged the back of my sleeve across my mouth. Horror clenched like a fist around my heart, and I shuddered at a sudden gust of cold air, as if death itself had brushed against me.

"It's rolled in *gu* poison," Jingue said. "Made from the toxins of a centipede and a scorpion after they've devoured each other. A single drop would be enough to make you ill; several would kill you."

And the entire ball had been rolled in the concoction. This was the fulfillment of the warning of the dead marmot on my doorstep.

I gulped wine and swished it round my mouth, spitting into a clean cup and repeating the process several more times to be safe. My tongue still burned, but that was better than my entire body feeling the lick of invisible flames. "How did you know?" I managed to gasp.

Jingue grimaced, his eyes hooded. "My mother happily informed me of your impending death upon my arrival. She meant it as a gift."

I almost laughed then, for the homecoming gift I'd overheard Orbei planning was no camlet hat or embroidered *deel*, but my still-warm corpse.

Jingue and his family had much to gain from me frothing at the mouth and vomiting up my lifeblood, but I didn't have time to ponder why he'd saved me. My tent door opened and Shigi burst inside, sword drawn. "Alaqai!" His chest heaved and he kept his blade tucked close to his body, ready to attack. "I heard yelling. Are you all right?"

"I'm still alive, despite Orbei's best efforts." I ignored his confusion and whirled on Boyahoe and Enebish then. "You both knew of this?"

Tears streamed down Boyahoe's face and he stared up at me with eyes like brown river stones. "I didn't know," he whimpered. "My mother promised me a whole plate of rice balls if I gave it to you. She made me swear not to eat it and set Enebish to watch me to make sure I followed her directions."

Because no one would suspect death delivered by a child with hair that fell constantly into his eyes.

Enebish remained silent, her insolent expression proving her guilt.

I looked to Shigi. "Bring Orbei to me."

He hesitated but gave a curt nod when my eyes flicked to where my tiger sword lay on my bed, partially hidden under a camel-hair blanket. Enebish stood to follow him, but I blocked her path. "Don't even think about it," I said. "You don't breathe unless I allow it."

Her hands curled into fists and I thought she might challenge me, but she resumed her place next to Boyahoe. A stifling silence filled the *ger*. Dampness spread under my arms and a strange kind of singing filled my ears, drowning out all other thoughts.

I could do this. I *would* do this.

Shigi reentered the tent, prodding a scowling Orbei before him. Her stiff-backed carriage reminded me of another woman, although that was where the similarities between Orbei and my mother ended.

"I understand you sent Boyahoe with a gift for me tonight," I said, keeping my voice level, as if discussing the quality of the lambs this year.

"I'm afraid I don't know what you mean." Orbei's children drew closer to her, like soldiers to their general.

"Don't play coy," I chided. "It doesn't fit a woman who dabbles in poison and murder."

"You poor girl," she said, her voice practically a purr. "I fear you must be addled as well as the daughter of a rampaging murderer."

"You sent Boyahoe here to poison me," I said, my voice rising.

She shrugged. "If I did, it would be a death you deserved."

"Perhaps, but I didn't die," I reminded her. "And in return, you'll receive only what you deserve. From this night on, you are childless, a barren spinster. No one will ever call you Mother, just as no one shall care for you in your old age."

It was the second time I'd wagered against Orbei, and I wondered whether it would be the last.

She gave a sharp inhale and glanced at me. "You won't lay a filthy finger on my children—"

"*My* children," I corrected her. "You forfeited your privilege as a mother tonight. You will return to the family of your birth. You shall approach the Great House only with my express permission."

I'd banish her to the Great Dry Sea if I could, but I knew my husband would never stand for that. There was a general outcry behind me, but I twisted Orbei's arm behind her back, surprised at her frailty. "Agree," I whispered in her ear, "else I'll slaughter your children one by one and send the bloody pieces of their bodies to you in carved golden boxes."

She craned her neck to search my eyes, as if seeking out the lie in my boast. I didn't know myself if I told the truth or not, but she needn't know that.

"It's your choice," I whispered amidst the cacophony of Enebish's yelling and the dogs' howling. Only Jingue remained stonily silent. "Tell them to do as I say and then leave the way you came. Otherwise, I can guarantee this will be the last time you'll see them whole."

"You filthy Mongol whore," Orbei hissed. "Ala-Qush will never stand for this."

"But he's not here now, is he?" I turned so my back faced the children. "I have more blades than you can count hidden in this *ger*," I lied. "And I won't hesitate to use them on your children."

The fire in her eyes banked and her body slackened. We both knew she had lost.

She stepped back, brushing her *deel* where I'd touched her, as if contaminated. "Our esteemed *beki* is your new mother," she said, her voice rising over the melee to silence Enebish and Boyahoe. "As such, you must forget your old mother. It is in all our best interests to obey the *beki* in this, as in all things."

I gave a minute nod. Her words were scarcely sincere, but they would suffice.

Enebish muttered something to Boyahoe, sullen but obedient. I was suddenly glad they were younger, lest I have a rebellion on my hands.

And then there was Jingue. He'd remained silent this entire time, standing almost a head taller than all the rest. I wondered if he'd curse his decision to save me one day, if perhaps he already wished he'd let me die.

Teb Tengeri had once called me a foot soldier of death, yet tonight I'd narrowly escaped losing my soul to the sacred mountains. Instead, I'd punished my greatest rival and succeeded in placing all the potential heirs to my throne under my control.

Now I just had to keep them there.

Chapter 18

"You did what?" Ala-Qush roared louder than a winter wind the following morning.

My husband had returned early from his supposed dealings with the border patrols, smiling and laughing with his men as he approached the Great House until his gaze fell on me leaning against its wooden wall and playing my *buree*. Enough shock flickered over his features that I wondered if he'd expected to return home to find my body already cold. His timing was both convenient and suspicious, giving me the strength I needed to withstand the onslaught of his fury as he dragged me into the Great House.

"Orbei had to be punished," I said after I'd recounted the events of the evening, shaking him off and lowering my voice so he had to stop blustering to hear me. I sat with my hands folded around the flute, wondering how much the walls of the Great House muffled the conversation for all those listening at the door. The two stray dogs sat at my feet, their unblinking eyes trained on Ala-Qush. "I am your wife and *beki*. It is my honor and duty to raise your children."

"You'll do no such thing." He slammed his fist onto the wooden table and I forced myself not to flinch. One of the dogs growled deep in his throat.

"I'll do whatever I please."

"I'll not have this strife in my household—"

"And I'll not fear poison at every meal!" My temper finally erupted. It was difficult to think straight after spending a sleepless night for fear of waking to find a knife at my throat. I'd lain with my tiger sword at my side and made the children remain in my *ger* so I might keep an eye on them, only to discover after I ordered Enebish to a makeshift pallet that Jingue had disappeared. I doubted whether I could have won a fight with Ala-Qush's eldest, especially as I owed him my life.

Anger rolled in thick waves from Ala-Qush, yet I pressed on. "I'm sure you knew nothing about Orbei's plot," I said. "Despite my death being a convenient solution to all your problems."

I waited for him to deny the accusation, to protest that he'd known nothing of Orbei's intentions, but he only leaned on the table, the tension in the room making it difficult to breathe. "I won't allow you to harm my children," he said.

"I'm nothing if not benevolent," I said, pausing. "Provided that there are no repetitions of last night. You'd be hard-pressed to explain my death to my father, especially after the account Shigi transcribed last night. Rest assured that word of recent events will make it to my father's camp if anything happens to me."

"Fine," he barked, then turned and slammed the door behind him. I waited until his footsteps had ceased pounding the earth, then slumped into a chair with my heart thudding in my ears. The dogs laid their heads in my lap and I stroked their ears with shaking hands.

Only sixteen, and I was already *beki*. And now I was a mother as well.

It was precisely because I owed Jingue my very breath that I sought him out that afternoon. I didn't care to be beholden to anyone, least of all the young man who stood to gain the most from my downfall.

I searched for him first outside the Great House and then traipsed down Olon Süme's narrow streets. Glaring mothers and wide-eyed children cowered when they saw the bow and the quiver of arrows slung on my back, and merchants turned up their noses at my plain *deel* and sturdy boots.

Craving air that wasn't tainted with the stench of unwashed humans, I rescued Neer-Gui from Ala-Qush's stable of long-legged horses and stalls of dirty hay. My poor gelding was unaccustomed to being penned, but I had no desire to let him roam free and find him on the doorway of my *ger* as I had the dead marmot. Together, we left the city walls and passed through the herds of straw-colored camels and into the hills. I snagged a handful of the season's last striped gooseberries from an obliging bush and let Neer-Gui graze below; then we left the established path to stalk hares with the first patches of winter fur on their clumsy back feet. I nocked my arrows with practiced ease and let them fly. I wished I could aim my bow straight at Ala-Qush's miserable heart, but unfortunately, starting a war with the Onggud didn't seem like a good way to please my father.

Toregene would tell me that her god had spared me from death for some greater purpose, and I chose to believe that purpose was tied to my role as *beki*, although I hadn't worked out exactly how. It seemed I was beholden not only to Jingue for my life, but also to Toregene's long-suffering god.

Neer-Gui and I returned from the hills with two rabbits strung on my saddle and a smattering of itchy pink welts on my neck that made me wish I'd thought to rub squirrel grease on my skin to repel the insects. My heart almost broke when I had to leave my horse in the stable, his eyes pools of sadness as he nuzzled my shoulder.

"I know," I said, stroking his mane. I'd taken it out of the leather thong Ogodei had teased me about and felt a pang of homesickness as I thought of my laughing older brother. "I wish we'd never come here, too."

Kicking pebbles from my path on the way to my *ger*, I passed buildings sacred to Olon Süme's people: squat Nestorian churches with rough wooden crosses nailed to their doors, a Saracen house of worship with men facing west on silken prayer rugs, and several dilapidated buildings where yellow- or red-robed children recited the wisdom of ancient sages in words I couldn't understand. Nothing here was familiar, certainly not the magnificent rooster that cackled as I passed its perch, and I found I hated the town more and more with each passing day. Even to my untrained eyes, the buildings looked worn and shabby, like old crones buffeted too long by life and the winter winds. The door to one cross-marked building yawned open and I peered inside, drawn by the melodious language spoken by the teacher.

It was Jingue.

He stood before the pupils—all boys—while reading a passage from an open book. He asked a question and the class answered in perfect unison, like a flock of geese flying south for the winter answering the call of their leader.

This was a world I would never belong to.

Jingue glanced up and his eyes met mine; then he raised his hand. I caught sight of Boyahoe as the children stopped their recitation, but Ala-Qush's youngest ducked his head as if hoping to become suddenly transparent. I stood rooted to the ground, my fingers still sticky from the gooseberries, my skin mottled with mosquito bites, and two dead hares dripping blood onto the ground from my belt. Compared to Jingue, with his freshly shaved face and spotless white robes, I was nothing more than a heathen from the steppes.

Jingue watched me for a moment too long, then said something in Turkic I wished I understood. The students all scrambled to their feet, but Jingue guided Boyahoe back to his bench and placed a blank paper and brush before him. The others smirked and continued to the door, until Jingue's harsh tone stopped them before they crossed the threshold.

Judging from the obsequiousness of their bows as they passed, he'd probably reminded them that their barbarian *beki* had a volatile temper and a quiver of arrows on her back.

"I'm glad to see that you're recovered from last night's . . . excitement," he said in Mongolian when the last boy had vaulted down the steps. I couldn't decide if Jingue's look of concern was true or false, but considering who his parents were, I guessed false.

"I'm still breathing, if that's what you mean." I didn't mention that the tip of my tongue remained numb from the *gu* poison, and instead I stood awkwardly, wishing I had something with which to busy my hands. Now I knew why my mother was always stitching, churning, or stirring a meal on the hearth—to give herself time to think in moments like this.

"Why did you do it?" I finally asked, fiddling with the roll of brushes on his table.

"Do what?" Now it was his turn to avoid my gaze.

I set down the brush and leaned back. "Stop me from taking the poison. It would have been the perfect way to send my body back to my father."

I waited for him to ignore the accusation as Ala-Qush had, but he only sighed. "I thought of that," he said, picking up a brush and twirling it between his ink-stained fingers. "But the Commandments forbid killing. And I doubt Christ would have taken kindly to the murder of one of his followers."

I flushed at that. "I respect the god of the cross," I said. "Yet I don't worship him."

"But you wear his emblem." Jingue's expression was lodged between bewilderment and anger. He likely would have let me die if he'd realized I worshipped the Eternal Blue Sky and the Earth Mother above all the other spirits.

"It was a gift from someone close to me," I said, covering Toregene's cross with my hand. "I'm learning to appreciate your god's powers, and I won't soon forget that I owe my breath to you both."

"I would hope not," he said. "Because of you, Enebish won't speak to me and my mother makes a sign to ward off demons when she sees me."

"They won't remain angry for long," I said. "Blood will always win out."

Unfortunately, no one here shared my blood. And too many others sought to spill it.

"It seems I owe you, then," I said, expecting him to demur. Yet Jingue rarely acted as I expected.

"It would appear that way," he said.

I scowled and pretended to peruse his open scroll. Shigi had taught me several of the strange symbols and I could now write my name in the new Mongolian script my father had ordered Shigi to create and also in Turkic, but the majority of these jagged characters still swam before my eyes. Jingue guided Boyahoe's hand to complete a line like a lightning bolt, although the character was already marred by countless inkblots. I took comfort in the fact that my letters were better than my seven-year-old stepson's. Not by much, but still.

Jingue tucked his arms inside his sleeves. "So am I to call you Mother as well?" His tone was mostly amused, but I detected a dose of annoyance, too.

"What year were you born?"

"The Year of the Iron Dog," he answered. "In the fall."

"So I'm your elder," I said. "Though only by a season."

"Then I'll call you Alaqai."

No one except Shigi had spoken my name in anything other than hatred since my father had left. I didn't know if I liked the sound of my name on Jingue's lips, but I admired his boldness.

"My mother—I mean, Orbei"—Boyahoe bit his lip at the error, considering I was now his official mother—"said never to call you Beki."

"What are you supposed to call me instead?"

"Heathen," he said, blithely unaware of the insult or his brother's sharp inhale. "Or Horse-Face."

Orbei's words in her son's mouth stung, but they weren't lethal, coming as they did from a viper without teeth.

"I've a feeling your mother has many more choice names for me," I said, wishing I could call Orbei a name or two. That cross-eyed camel should be kissing my feet for sparing her life last night, not filling her son's ears with insults against me.

Boyahoe offered me an innocent smile, then put the finishing flourish on his last character. Jingue relaxed and took the ink-stained brush from his brother, cuffed him affectionately on the chin, and herded him out the door.

"I didn't expect you to be a teacher," I said.

"Life is full of the unexpected," Jingue said as he watched his brother go, echoing his mother's sentiment when I'd first met her. "I certainly didn't expect you to be as you are."

"Is that a compliment or an insult?"

Jingue didn't answer. "You don't speak Turkic," he said after Boyahoe had disappeared around a corner. "Do you at least read it?"

An insult then. He and his family had expected an educated *beki* and had received an illiterate heathen instead. Fortunately, by now I was accustomed to disappointing people.

"It's a difficult language." I didn't tell him of my lessons with Shigi, tedious and painful as they were.

"You'll never gain our respect if you don't learn our language," Jingue said, letting the door close. Sound and sunlight penetrated the paper-lined window, but I still felt trapped inside. "And without that respect you have no hope of ruling us."

I wondered if he meant himself, his family, or the Onggud. Probably all three.

I crossed my arms and leaned against Boyahoe's desk, although the dead rabbits at my hip made that a bit awkward at first. "Why would you of all people offer me advice?"

He shrugged. "Once you have our esteem you might be able to do some good here, perhaps persuade my father to build more religious houses or a School of Healing to train physicians to minister to the sick."

I snorted at that. "I was once accused of being death's foot soldier. I'm undoubtedly the least qualified person in this town to help the sick."

Jingue dipped the used brush into a bowl of water, seemingly nonchalant about my protest, yet his shoulders tensed. Perhaps this was what he sought from me, although I was an unlikely candidate to build anything with walls. And Toregene was the healer, not me. Still, the idea was intriguing.

"I take it your father isn't well-disposed toward these projects?"

"My father believes that we are beset by enemies along all our borders. He cares only for his alliances and how much wealth he can accumulate to purchase them."

That explained why I was here, along with the carts of silks and weapons that had accompanied me. Jingue's black ink swirled like smoke in the bowl of water before it dissolved. "But you'll never get anywhere if you can't talk to the Onggud," he said. "Or understand what they say about you."

I untied the rabbits from my belt, dropped them on the table with a dull thud, and sat down. "Then teach me."

My father always claimed that one should know an enemy better than a friend, and Jingue still fell firmly in the camp of the former. Shigi could verify later that Jingue hadn't taught me to call his mother a snot-dragging yak instead of asking where to find the butter churn, but this was an opportunity I couldn't allow to slip away.

Jingue arched an eyebrow. "Is that an order?"

"Does it need to be?"

He tucked the wet brushes into their bamboo roll, then crouched and shuffled through a box of papers beneath the table, retrieving a sheet that bore creases from having been folded and unfolded many times.

He laid it before me, standing so close he almost brushed my arm. "What do you think it says?"

I pointed out several characters, the signs for daughter, son, and nation, triumphant in my newfound knowledge. I knew my identifications had been correct, so I was annoyed when he pursed his lips. "Anything else?" he asked.

I shook my head, irritated.

He pointed to the scrawl at the bottom. "You don't recognize your father's name?"

I almost laughed at that, but his expression was serious. "My father doesn't write," I said, ashamed of my father for the first time I could remember. I could only imagine the insults running through Jingue's head, cursing the illiterate infidels who'd usurped his kingdom, but he simply folded the paper.

I snatched it from his hand and stared at my father's name, overwhelmed by how much I missed him. "He might have dictated it," I said. "What does it say?"

"This is the letter in which Genghis Khan demanded that my father marry you."

My head jerked up at that. "It says no such thing. Your father wrote to mine, begging for the alliance our marriage would bring."

Jingue gave a harsh laugh. "Is that what you were told? That my father pleaded for the honor of demeaning his wife and disowning his children in return for a child bride?"

Suddenly everything and nothing made sense—the Onggud hostility upon my arrival and even my father's easy acceptance of my demand that Ala-Qush set aside his wife. But why would my father lie to me?

My emotions must have been writ plain on my face—confusion, anger, and embarrassment—for Jingue's tone was softer when he next spoke.

"Ask your Tatar scribe to confirm my claims," he said, taking the paper from me and returning it to its box. "Your father positioned you to fail, Alaqai. He knew you'd be loathed here."

"He wouldn't do that," I said, but my voice lacked conviction. I grabbed the clutch of dead rabbits, ignoring the smear of dark blood on Jingue's table. "I should go now, before the meat gathers flies."

It was a terrible excuse, but Jingue didn't challenge me. "Go in peace, Alaqai."

His words were a common farewell, for both the People of the Stone Walls and the People of the Felt were unwilling to bid final good-byes in case malicious spirits decided to make the words into a permanent parting.

Still, as I walked away, I was struck by the miserable realization that there wasn't a soul in Olon Süme who wouldn't rejoice if I left and never came back.

"Is it true?"

I stood before Shigi that evening, my two long-nosed strays sitting at my feet like silent soldiers. The dark obscured my accusatory glare while the autumn stars shone sharply overhead and the last of the faded leaves fell into the blackness around us. The children huddled in a firelit circle across the way, having been herded outside after Ala-Qush had joined us for a stilted dinner and then disappeared with the excuse that he needed to meet with the Jurched ambassador in the morning. That had left me to entertain his surly sons and daughter, and I'd ignored their glares when I harried them out to tell stories under the stars. I'd promptly dragged Shigi far enough out of earshot that no one could hear us, although not before whispering to Boyahoe that I expected a full accounting of his siblings' conversations when I returned. Still, I felt Jingue's gaze on my back while he pretended to listen to Boyahoe's tale of a one-armed shepherd and his lost camels.

Shigi patted the end of the merchant's cart next to him, but I refused to sit.

"You're an obstinate mule sometimes, Alaqai Beki." He sighed. "And yes, Jingue was right about the letter. Your father's message fell scarcely short of ordering Ala-Qush to marry you. I transcribed it myself."

"So he wished me to fail." I pressed the heel of my fist to my lips to keep from yelling in frustration. "And he lied."

"Your father took liberties with the truth," Shigi acknowledged. He shrugged off his wolfskin coat, a gift from my father, and wrapped it around my shoulders. I almost shoved it away, but it was so cold I could see my breath, an early warning of the winter yet to come. "But it was for your benefit."

"It was hardly beneficial to believe that my husband desired our marriage, when in fact he already despised me." I sat then, pulling the fur tight and inhaling its scent of animal musk and Shigi's inks. One of the dogs pushed his wet muzzle into my hand and I petted his head absentmindedly.

"How would you have felt to know you were marrying a man who was adamantly opposed to you?" He crossed his arms and the cart creaked as he shifted next to me. "And don't tell me you would have been imbued with eagerness and confidence."

I scowled, hating the truth of his words. My father's lie had allowed me to act the part of a *beki*, at least for a short time. Now it was up to me whether to continue the deception.

"If you hadn't demanded Ala-Qush set aside his wife," he said, "Orbei would have you scrubbing pots and opening the doors to the Great House by now."

"That doesn't excuse your complicity."

"Don't be ridiculous." Shigi draped an arm around my shoulder and squeezed me to him. "I value my head far too much to risk your father's wrath."

"I plan to give him an earful when I see him next."

"As only you could do, and survive to tell the tale." Shigi dropped his arm to lean forward, propping his elbows on his knees. "Or I could carry the message to him myself."

"You're leaving?" I'd known that Shigi wouldn't stay with me forever, but now I felt a surge of panic at the idea that he'd soon be gone.

He nodded, the gold ring in his nose reflecting the campfire's light. "Your father commands me to join the campaign before the snows render travel impossible. He wants me present to record his victory over the Tanghuts."

Something in the way Shigi spoke made me realize that he didn't wish to obey my father's summons. Yet I also had a feeling he didn't seek to remain at my side. "You'd rather return home, wouldn't you? There's someone you miss, isn't there?"

"I don't know what you're talking about," he said, stiffening next to me. "Of course I miss our family—"

"Don't lie, Shigi," I said. "You're not very good at it, even in the dark. I've seen the way you gaze toward home." I glanced at his profile from the corner of my eyes, decided to take the chance. "She must be very special."

I waited for him to deny it, but he only sighed. "She is."

I grinned at my victory and nudged my shoulder against his. "She's a lucky woman, to make you pine away so. I expect I'll hear of your wedding, then, after my father's campaign is over. And your tent full of precocious children reciting the wisdom of Tanghut sages."

It was a wedding I'd never see, and children I'd never meet. I sobered at the thought, but Shigi made a noise in the back of his throat, a sound devoid of all humor. "I'll never marry, Alaqai, nor will I have any children. My only legacy shall be the histories I write for your father and the records of his new laws."

"But I thought . . ." I watched Ala-Qush's children sitting in the firelight, while I tried to make sense of Shigi's words. "This woman—"

"Is married, Alaqai." Shigi stood and brushed his *deel*, as if brushing away our conversation. He looked at the stars, as if he might gather strength from them. "The Eternal Blue Sky is with us wherever we go, yet there are some things we can't have, regardless of where we are."

There was nothing I could do to dispute that; I wished for many things here in Olon Süme, and I knew enough now to realize that they might be forever beyond my grasp.

"Will you take Neer-Gui with you?" I asked Shigi, needing to fill the painful silence.

"Your horse?"

There was an old Mongol saying, that once a man has ridden a horse, it will never leave him. I loved Neer-Gui, but still I nodded, cursing the tears that welled in my eyes. "This is no place for him," I said, wanting to add *or for me*. "He needs to be free to run."

"I'd be honored to ride him as my own," Shigi said, squeezing my hand.

"I'll miss you," I said, my voice catching. I'd be friendless and utterly alone once Shigi left Olon Süme. Panic tightened my throat, and I knew I'd have to harden my heart even further when he was gone.

"You're stronger than you know, Alaqai. And you're not entirely without allies here, at least not if you choose to seek them out."

I followed his gaze to where Jingue sat with Boyahoe and Enebish, all singing a haunting sort of melody, like those Sorkhokhtani once played on her *tobshuur*. "You're wrong," I said, patting the flanks of both the mongrels at my feet. "These dogs might stay by my side, but Jingue would feed me to the wolves if given the chance."

Shigi rubbed his chin. "I don't think so, at least not anymore. Cultivate his friendship, for one day you may need it."

"I'd sooner eat that foul Onggud porridge."

Shigi laughed then, and I felt Jingue's gaze on us. "Who knows, little marmot?" Shigi said. "One morning you may wake up to find that you crave a steaming bowl of boiled millet."

Somehow I doubted that very much.

In the end it wasn't my loneliness that forced Jingue and me together, but his father.

"You drove away my wife," Ala-Qush said one cold morning almost a month later when I visited him in the Great House. I'd found him slurping gray porridge from a pewter bowl. "And now you chase off my son."

Shigi had left me before the first snows fell, riding east with Neer-Gui to rendezvous with my father. I'd stuffed his saddlebags to bursting with bean sprouts for the long journey, a final gift for the horse I'd likely never see again. When they'd disappeared, I was alone for the first time, surrounded by enemies and so isolated I decided I'd take Shigi's advice and cultivate Jingue's friendship.

But then I'd awoken one chilly morning to discover Jingue's horse tracks interspersed with those of a raven in the dusting of fresh snow, returning him to the Nestorian monastery to which he retreated from time to time.

"I did nothing to urge Jingue to leave," I said, restraining myself from dumping the extra pot of porridge over my husband's head.

"That's not what he claimed." Ala-Qush scowled, using his finger to lift the last drop of lumpy porridge from the bowl. "He couldn't have left any faster than if his horse's tail was aflame."

I didn't know why Jingue had left again, and I told myself that I didn't much care. My only concern at his absence was that it would be impossible to learn Turkic—and therefore truly rule the Onggud—now that both my teachers had abandoned me.

Then I realized there was another teacher right under my nose. I took advantage of the fair winter weather to instruct Boyahoe on riding and wrestling, and together we climbed the great oak tree that grew inside the city walls, shimmying along its thick branches to jump over the stone wall into drifts of snow on the other side. Ravens often paused in their digging to watch us, snow speckling their beaks and faces before they continued their search for food. At night, Boyahoe tolerated me peering over his shoulder as he practiced his lessons in my *ger* with my dogs at his feet, my stepson's tongue caught between his lips as he struggled to make perfect characters for Jingue to marvel over upon his return. We held competitions on who could master the most symbols each night, competitions I won as often as Boyahoe did, until at last I could read and write Turkic with some ease.

Life was dull but almost pleasant. How quickly things change.

A temperamental spring brought warm rains, and with them, my roof leaked and dampness seeped into the ground beneath my *ger*. My morning porridge remained uneaten and as gray as the weather outside as I locked away damp scrolls and rolled up sodden rugs while ordering Boyahoe to place every bowl and bucket at my disposal to catch the drips. A spotted ewe had dropped twin lambs early and I'd brought them inside to avoid the deluge, but their downy coats were drenched and they bleated at me in consternation. I cursed back at them and found myself wishing for a solid roof above my head for the first time in my life.

The door opened, bringing the sound of spitting rain, and my water-logged husband stumbled inside. His drenched hair obscured his face, and his boots squelched with each step.

"Have you come to help us, revered husband?" I asked over my shoulder. Ala-Qush rarely deigned to set foot inside my tent, and I awaited the inevitable comment about my living in filth and squalor while surrounded by muddy beasts, but he only mumbled something under his breath.

"Father?" Boyahoe's voice trembled and I straightened over the chest I'd been lugging away from the growing lake at my feet. I wiped the wet hair from my eyes and gasped in horror.

The flesh on the right side of Ala-Qush's face drooped like hot wax, and one of his pupils was dilated larger than during the worst of his headaches. He opened his mouth to speak, but the words were slurred to incomprehension. He fell to his knees with a muddy splash.

I abandoned the chest and wedged myself under his leaden arm, struggling to lift him until Boyahoe helped support his unaffected side. Together we scarcely managed to drag him to my bed. "Find a physician," I ordered Boyahoe. "Now!"

The terrified boy ran from my *ger* while I maneuvered Ala-Qush to his back. I didn't know what to do; I'd never heard Toregene describe an illness like this and prayed it wasn't the plague I shared a name with. Ala-Qush moaned and attempted to speak again, but I could only make out a few words in jumbled Turkic.

Pain.

Children.

Death.

"Don't you dare die," I said, jabbing a trembling finger into his chest. I was ambivalent toward the man who claimed to be my husband, but as his childless widow, I'd be cast back to my family. Unless the Onggud decided to dispose of me in some other way.

The rain slapped harder against my felt walls and the lambs bleated so loudly I threatened to turn them into stew before Boyahoe finally reappeared, trailed by Enebish and tugging the sleeves of a long-bearded physician. Enebish remained by the door, her eyes glistening. "What can we do?"

"Pray to every deity you worship." I rubbed my silver cross, worn smoother these past months, and flicked drops of milk from my porridge to the ground in an offering to the Earth Mother. "Pray for his recovery."

The physician made a great show of checking Ala-Qush's breath and pulse, even removing his curled boots to palpate his feet and using a silver hook to open his eyes. I expected Ala-Qush to react to the latter, but he just stared at the ceiling, unblinking and scarcely breathing.

"The Prince of Beiping has an imbalance of water," the physician declared, tucking his arms into his wide sleeves. "And it has caused his body to revolt."

"What can you do?" I asked.

The sage shrugged. "I may be able to alleviate the excess of fluids with my needles, but I believe the worst of the storm has passed."

By then my husband had fallen silent, his eyes closed in what appeared to be a restful sleep. Still, the right side of his face seemed untethered from the bone, and his arm hung slack at his side.

"Use the needles," I said, lifting his arm to lay it at his side. "And anything else that may help him."

The physician nodded, but he drew me away from the children. "I've seen this before, Beki. It is possible that the prince will never fully recover from this unfortunate episode."

"But will he live?"

"I believe so."

I offered a silent prayer of thanks to the Eternal Blue Sky. "Then do all you can for him."

I began issuing unnecessary orders to occupy the children and distract them from their father's condition. "Return the lambs to their ewe," I said to Boyahoe. "And these crates need to be taken to the Great House."

Enebish hugged herself, her lower lip trembling. She put on a show of being older than her years but was little more than a scared child. "And my father?"

"He'll remain here for the time being, until the physician deems him able to be moved."

"May I care for him?" she asked. It was the only request I could ever recall coming from her, and I knew it had cost her dearly to even ask.

I nodded, wondering if I'd regret my next words. "And bring your mother, if she'll come. We'll take turns tending him until he recovers."

"I'll fetch her right now," she said, as if I might change my mind. "Thank you, Beki."

It was the first time she had used my title without looking as if she might spit. Today was a day of tragedy, but also one of small miracles.

"Wait," I said, stopping her at the door. "Send a messenger to ride for the monastery. Jingue must return home."

"Of course," she said. My request seemed aimed to bring her family together in its time of need, when in fact, I was motivated by reasons far less pure. In the terrible event that Ala-Qush's spirit flew to the mountains, Jingue would become sole ruler of the Onggud and I'd be nothing more than a childless widow of sixteen winters. I couldn't afford to have him out rallying the surrounding towns against me, or worse.

Only time would reveal which role I would play in the days to come: *beki*, widow, or corpse.

· · ·

I'd prayed for my husband's survival, but death would have been a kindness.

Jingue returned while I was with his father in the Great House, a crick in my neck and my mouth half-open in sleep, a Turkic book on herbs under my face. The treatise was open to the page on the use of a woundwort infusion for weak hearts, and although it had taken me much of the night to puzzle out the full meaning of the entry, I doubted whether such a treatment would have any impact on Ala-Qush. When I wasn't in the Great House, I was often playing games with Boyahoe to divert him from the fact that his father could no longer eat, walk, or even relieve himself on his own. Ala-Qush's ruined face rendered speech impossible, but my husband had yet to use the paper and ink I'd suggested we keep nearby. Instead, he vacillated between raging in grunts and moans and throwing things at us with his good arm. I understood the black moods a ruined body could bring, but my temper was being worn thin.

"How is he?" Jingue startled me awake when he touched my shoulder, then knelt at his father's bedside, his expression pained. He still wore his heavy travel clothes, and he smelled of morning's crisp air and towering spruce trees.

"The physician's done all he can. Now we wait." I rubbed my tired eyes and twisted in my chair to find some relief for my aching back. I'd been indoors for so long I'd almost forgotten what the air outside smelled like, and my nose twitched from the stink of Ala-Qush's urine bucket.

"What do we wait for?" Jingue removed a carved wooden cross from his throat and laid it across his father's chest. "His last breath?"

"The physician says the danger of that has passed. That shall have to be enough, at least for now."

Orbei entered with Enebish then, both their noses wrinkling until their eyes adjusted to the dark and they saw Jingue kneeling next to me.

"Jingue!" Orbei pulled her eldest son to his feet and gathered him into her arms. Scenes between mothers and sons played out the same the world over, although I realized with a pang that I had little hope of ever clasping to me a son born from my own womb.

I busied myself emptying the urine bucket and folding Ala-Qush's blankets; where the Great House had once entertained Tanghut, Jurched, and Song ambassadors, now the dimly lit wooden house was only the sickroom for a broken old man. Finally, Orbei released her son and took up her bench by her husband, a wooden board and a bag of knucklebones on her lap.

"I thought I might entice him to play when he wakes," she said to me. Orbei and I had learned to speak civilly to each other while Ala-Qush slept, although our conversations were stilted and often more painful than slitting one's wrists. Enebish and I occasionally shared talk of the School of Healing and often spent evenings in companionable silence sitting with Ala-Qush.

"Good luck," I said.

Orbei set herself to the task of combing Ala-Qush's long hair, and for a moment I imagined her with my husband as a young bride, performing the same simple act on a bed fresh from lovemaking. My cheeks flushed and I beckoned to Jingue. "Will you walk with me?"

I was proud of myself for asking the question instead of commanding him, yet he only shrugged. "For a bit."

I swallowed my ire and swept past him, wishing I'd thought to wear something more intimidating than an old gray *deel* stained with my failed attempts at making Ala-Qush's ox broth. Enebish caught my arm on the way out.

"Be gentle with my brother, Alaqai," she whispered. I searched her eyes for malice but found none, only the stony set of her jaw. "His is a gentle soul, and I won't have your fire scalding him."

"I have no intention of harming your brother," I said. "Although he does try my patience sometimes."

Enebish smiled at that. "As you do with all of us," she said.

I chuckled under my breath, prompting Jingue to raise an eyebrow as he gestured toward the door. "I had no idea you and my sister were on speaking terms," he said, closing the door behind us.

"On good days," I said. But it wasn't Enebish I wished to discuss.

"How long to you plan to stay?" I asked, setting us on a path toward the tortoise gate and beyond that, the hills.

"For now."

"I'll need you here longer than that with your father in this condition."

Jingue shook his head. "There are plenty of people to care for him. My place is—"

"Here," I said, feeling a flutter of annoyance that this very man who'd proposed a School of Healing was, in fact, indifferent toward his afflicted father. "I'd not ask you to wipe the drool from his mouth or help him to his bucket, but—"

"I'm not so weak as to fear caring for the man who sired me," Jingue said, his voice harsher than I'd ever heard it. "But this hasn't been my home for some time now."

Since I'd come to Olon Süme. I recognized the accusation but refused to acknowledge it.

"You belong *here*," I said, "not in some distant monastery. Your father needs you, Jingue. *I* need you."

He gave me a startled glance at that, but I walked apace, making my husband's heir hurry after me. Olon Süme's walls retreated behind us before he finally spoke. "What do you mean, you need me?"

"I plan to build the School of Healing as you recommended," I said. "I always repay my debts."

"Of course." His face grew stony, the opposite of the reaction I'd expected.

We'd reached the hills and I tossed myself to the ground with a dull thud, plucking several blades of new grass and plaiting them together to help my concentration. Jingue stood nearby, as tall and silent as a birch tree.

"Your father isn't going to improve," I said, softening my tone. "No matter how much we may wish it."

Jingue sat and crossed his legs then, folded his hands in his lap. I imagined him this way at his Nestorian monastery, at peace with himself and the god of the cross. I cringed to think that I was ordering him to leave all that behind, but there was no way to avoid it.

"I know," he said.

"The taxes must still be collected and appropriated. The border guards must be paid."

"Life goes on," he said, his voice pained.

I dared touch him then, thinking of what I'd feel to face my father as a man broken by his own body, yet such a thing was impossible to contemplate regarding Genghis Khan. My fingers brushed Jingue's shoulder first; then I let my hand fall to join his. My heart tripped at the moment of uncommon intimacy and I waited for him to withdraw his hand, but he didn't move.

"I plan to allocate a portion of the tolls to build the School of Healing," I said, breaking the moment by clearing my throat and returning my hands to my lap. I stared at my palms, the innocent flesh and bone that had just trespassed against some invisible boundary. "I've been thinking about it since before you ran away to the monastery."

"I didn't run away." He looked askance at me then, and I saw the lie in his words. This was a man who might have walked calmly through any of life's storms, had I not enveloped him in my unique sort of chaos.

"That's not what your father claimed. He said you left to get away from me."

Jingue looked ready to deny it, then sighed. "You were far from what I expected. I found it difficult to hate you as I planned."

"And do you still wish you could hate me?"

"It would make things easier." Jingue stood then, as if he needed to put distance between us. I was struck then by his noble height and the way his white *deel* pulled tighter across his shoulders. I wondered for a moment what the muscles looked like underneath, whether they were hard and compact, or long and trim, and what they would feel like under my hands. A flush crept up my neck at the thought and I had to look away.

There was no one nearby, only the clouds overhead and the occasional chatter of a long-tailed ground squirrel. I was reminded of a similar grassy plain at my father's *khurlatai*, the last time I'd been with a man, and terrible laughter bubbled in my throat at how my life had changed since then. It was inappropriate to be here, alone with my husband's son, especially as my thoughts regarding Jingue at that moment were far from appropriate.

I scrambled to my feet and stalked down the hillside ahead of Jingue, the burning in my chest so strong that I expected to see flames on my flesh.

"You'll get your school," I threw back at him. "But I'll need your support for my decisions as *beki*, so long as your father lives."

"And after that?" he called after me.

I didn't answer. I'd make no promises about a future I couldn't see.

Chapter 19

1211 CE

YEAR OF THE WHITE SHEEP

We built the School of Healing and I learned to welcome foreign ambassadors in my husband's stead, entertaining the Jurched and Song ministers with anecdotes from my newly discovered favorite books on travel and medicine while negotiating higher tolls for the use of our roads to carry their priceless silks and spices to the West. The Onggud bent unwilling knees to me, a result of my continuing role as Ala-Qush's official wife, but it was Jingue's constant presence behind me in the Great House that dissuaded the Onggud from attempting to depose me. Despite my gains in their language and the building projects I'd undertaken, I was still an outsider set above them, and they loathed me for it.

Boyahoe I loved because he reminded me of a young version of Ogodei, and Enebish and Orbei tolerated me, but it was Jingue—the thoughtful religious scholar—who seemed content with me as I was. The longer I spent with Ala-Qush's eldest, the more I came to appreciate his quiet approach to the world, so different from my own quick-blooded temperament. I told myself it was only because I was lonely here in Olon Süme that I anticipated the sound of his laugh with such eagerness or enjoyed the hot thrill of his hand brushing against mine, but I relished them all the same.

We'd lived with Ala-Qush's illness for more than two years, and it was a fair autumn afternoon when I managed to drag Jingue from under his pile of books for an impromptu archery competition on one of the last warm days before the frosts came. The golden grasses rippled and the breeze played with his hair as he nocked a quarrel and sent it flying, narrowly missing the center of the rice bag we'd set dangling from a willow tree.

I smirked and drew an arrow from my quiver. "You realize you'll owe me an accounting of the tolls after I win this shot?"

"I'm still waiting for my pot of rabbit stew after I beat you last time." Jingue leaned against the tree, dappled sunlight playing on his face. "Although I'm not convinced you didn't let me win then."

I hadn't let him win. I'd only lost because I'd been more interested in watching him and had aimed my last shot so poorly I'd almost shot his horse. "Suit yourself," I said. "I warned you my cooking was more punishment than reward."

"I find it difficult to believe that a woman who can speak three languages, ride, and shoot as you do would be cowed by making a simple stew."

It was true that I now spoke Mongolian, along with passable Turkic and Khitan, yet I still struggled to make yogurt that wasn't too thin or cheese that wasn't so salty it puckered one's lips.

"I am a woman of many talents," I said. "Unfortunately, cooking is not one of them." A disturbance on the horizon saved me from saying anything else, a fast-moving rider coming from the roads that led to the west.

My father had finished his initial conquest against the Tanghuts, and his empire had prospered since, including the creation of the *ortoo*, an elaborate messenger system with a series of riders and relay stations to speed the transmission of information. I'd received a message bearing the sad news of Gurbesu's death from fever and a terse letter from Shigi in the spring carrying word that Sorkhokhtani had given Tolui a son named Möngke and that Toregene had gone on to drop another son for Ogodei. For his part, my brother had requested that a cart of as much wine as I could spare be sent to him across the Great Dry Desert as a proper celebratory gift. I'd sent the wine and my hollow congratulations, then returned to my empty *ger*.

I shielded my eyes against the sun. This was no common arrow messenger wearing an official silver *ortoo* badge at his waist and running at a pace to avoid tiring his horse, but a slight figure wearing a helmet topped with a horse's tail and bent over a lathered gelding that raced as if the steppes were on fire.

The rider veered toward us and brought the yellow gelding to a halt so hard it almost sat on its haunches. I recognized the delicate sweep of the rider's nose and her immaculate riding *deel* even before she dismounted and released a sheet of shiny black hair from under her helmet. Sorkhokhtani smiled at me, her cheeks ruddy from the ride, although the rest of her skin was still as soft and pale as the moon. "You look well, Alaqai Beki," she said.

It had been too long since I'd heard my family speak my name, and I welcomed the unexpected sound. "And you look perfect as always, Sorkhokhtani of the Kereyid." I pulled her to me in a fierce hug, feeling as if I were embracing a sliver of home. "The People of the Stone Walls welcome you," I said. "As do I."

"I bear warm greetings from your family, especially your mother. Borte Khatun is as strong and fierce as ever." Sorkhokhtani brushed her hair from her cheek, just under the mole she so hated, and looked to where Jingue stood, no longer leaning against the tree. "And is this your husband, Ala-Qush?"

Sorkhokhtani was as small as a weasel and just as sneaky, likely the most intelligent of all my father's sons- and daughters-by-marriage. Her eyes sparked so I knew that she realized Jingue couldn't be my husband.

"This is Ala-Qush's eldest son, Jingue of the Onggud."

Jingue offered her an elegant bow. "You are most welcome to Olon Süme, Princess of the Hearth."

I shouldn't have been surprised that Jingue knew the names of my family, much less their titles or relationships. I'd yet to find a topic that Jingue wasn't well versed in.

Sorkhokhtani gave a gracious smile. "I'm most happy to be here. This will be a welcome respite after many weeks crossing that infernal desert. It's been a long time since we've known shade, or a good bath or meal."

"We?" I asked, searching the horizon for the rest of her party.

"Your father sent me ahead with a message for you."

For my father to travel so far could mean only one thing, yet I didn't care to discuss so dark a matter, at least not yet.

Jingue caught the meaning in my eyes and swept up his bow and quiver before relieving me of my weapons. "You must be tired and hungry after so long a journey," he said to Sorkhokhtani. "I'll return to see that a feast and accommodations are arranged for you."

"I appreciate your thoughtfulness," Sorkhokhtani said to Jingue, enunciating each word in perfect Turkic. It was difficult to forget that this sister of my hearth had been raised as a Kereyid princess, more educated than anyone in my father's clan. Had it not been for the fact that she was already married to Tolui, she and Jingue might have made a perfect match. The very thought made me scowl, earning a quizzical expression from Sorkhokhtani.

"I look forward to meeting the rest of your illustrious family," she said to Jingue, arching a delicate eyebrow in my direction.

We watched Jingue retrace the path back to Olon Süme's tortoise gate. "That one seems quite dedicated to you," she murmured when he was out of earshot, although I could hear the laugher in her voice. "Toregene would ask if you've tumbled him yet, but I assume from the way you ogle him that you've only dreamed of him in your bed."

I gaped and slapped her arm. "I suppose it's a good thing Toregene isn't here, isn't it?" I ignored the heat in my cheeks and took the reins of her lathered horse to follow Jingue through the herds of camels and into the city. "You claimed my father sent you with a message. I'd ask why he didn't send one of my brothers, but I fear I know the answer."

"Jochi vanquished the northern forest people and fights the forty tribes of the Kyrgyz now," Sorkhokhtani said. The smile had left her voice and a frown took up an uncomfortable roost on her lips. "Chaghatai, Ogodei, and Tolui spend too much time drinking to remain upright in a saddle long enough to cross the Great Dry Sea."

I winced at the appraisal of my brothers, recalling the nights I'd watched Chaghatai come to blows while red-faced drunk, and Ogodei roaring with laughter while swilling from jugs of *airag* and Onggud wine, one right after the other. And Tolui, whom I last saw hiccuping and weeping like a woman until Ogodei led him away. "So you volunteered for the task?"

"I did, the better to survey the lands my son might one day rule." Sorkhokhtani spoke with the same certainty as if commenting that the sun would rise tomorrow or the mares would drop their foals in spring. I felt the hole in my heart grow a little wider; she and Toregene both had sons, yet I remained childless.

"How does Möngke fare?" The words tasted bitter, but I managed a smile. "I imagine everyone dotes on the Prince of the Hearth's little heir."

"They do, yet I try to curb the worst of their excesses, the golden saddles and constant parade of ponies. I'll raise my son to fill his grandfather's boots."

It was no empty boast, for as my father's youngest son and Prince of the Hearth, Tolui would inherit the lands of my father's birth. Sorkhokhtani seemed to sense my sadness and squeezed my arm in a rare display of tenderness. "Your arms won't always be empty, Alaqai. Your womb will fill with life when the time is right."

"That may be," I said, trying to keep the bitterness from my voice. "But I've accepted that I'll be an old woman hunched over my lonely hearth."

"If that were so, I'd ride to Olon Süme myself and steal you back to my *ger*."

"I don't doubt that you would." I chuckled then. "And I could entertain your brood with exceptionally poor *buree* music."

She brightened at that. "You learned how to play?"

"I take it as a good sign that the dogs have stopped howling when I practice. How does the rest of our family fare?"

"Yesui's daughter Checheyigen has gone to marry the Oirat prince and your father promised Gurbesu's daughter Al-Altun to Tokuchar, the Idiqut of the Uighurs. Tokuchar begged the Khan of Khans on his knees to become his fifth son. Your father might have refused the sable furs, pearls, and gold the Idiqut brought as the bride-price, but when Tokuchar paraded the white gyrfalcons and geldings before him . . ." She shrugged.

And so two more of my father's daughters would give him alliances and extend his influence. I wondered whether my father's skill as a conqueror lay in his ability to wage war or in his adroitness at spreading our family across the steppes, mountains, and valleys.

We approached Olon Süme's gate and Sorkhokhtani recoiled as the breeze ruffled the fur lining of her collar. I recalled my first impression of the city that was now my home, the way nothing could have prepared me for the stench and noise within its confines.

"It helps if you breathe through your mouth," I whispered. "At least for the first few days."

She covered her nose as we passed under the gate, her brown eyes wide over the green felt sleeve. "And you live like this?" her muffled voice asked.

"One does what one must." I was reluctant to venture into the real reason why she was here, but we'd lingered long enough on niceties. "So tell me, who does my father attack this time?"

She lowered her arm, but her nose remained wrinkled. "The Jurched."

They were our prestigious neighbors to the east, and many of Olon Süme's noble houses—including Orbei's—relied on the Jurched for the camlet trade as well as for the steady river of silk and spices as they traveled west. This latest conquest of my father's would prove more difficult to support than that against the Tanghuts. "When does the army arrive?"

"They're only days behind. I fear this campaign promises to be bloodier than even the Blood War."

Gooseflesh rolled over my limbs at her warning and the terrible realization it brought.

In mere days, war would surround us once again.

Time had ravaged my husband but scarcely touched my father. As he dismounted outside Olon Süme, I noted with new eyes that though he stood with bowed legs from his years in the saddle, he was still as solid as a boulder. Shigi had accompanied him and smiled down at me from where he sat astride Neer-Gui, dressed in his jaunty blue judge's hat. My gelding tossed his mane and I wondered if he remembered our wild chases over the steppes and the long journey together over the Great Dry Sea. I was glad to see him well cared for but saddened at the remembrance of one more thing I missed from my old life. The hills around Olon Süme swarmed with mounted cavalry bedecked with spears, bows, and gleaming cutlasses. Sorkhokhtani had told me that my father had integrated Tanghut engineers into his corps, that these learned men would build catapults and giant wheeled crossbows when they reached their destination. I'd shivered at her pen-and-ink sketches, for the drawings of the war machines were more menacing than anything I'd seen before. I was glad I wasn't amongst the Jurched.

"It's been a long time, *tarvag takal*," my father said, opening his arms and breathing deeply as he pressed his forehead to mine. My nose filled with the scent of horse and leather, and despite the way he'd tricked me before my marriage, for a moment I didn't want to let go.

But I was Beki of the Onggud, not just the daughter of the Khan of Khans.

"Father," I said, stepping out of his arms and gesturing behind me. "My family welcomes you, as do all the Onggud."

Part of my family at least. Ala-Qush sat in a cushioned wheeled cart that Jingue had fashioned to transport him about Olon Süme. Since his illness, my husband had shrunken into an old man and his braid had gone completely gray. His sons flanked him, Jingue dressed in his usual white *deel* and Boyahoe in a camlet robe of midnight blue tied with a yellow sash. Orbei and Enebish had asked to remain behind to ready the Great House for my father's arrival. I had granted their request, although I'd recognized it as a plot to avoid facing the Great Khan.

My father clapped Ala-Qush on the back as if they were old friends. For all that my husband bemoaned the crudeness of the Mongols, the protection my father had offered the Onggud had sheltered Ala-Qush's people from the ongoing saga of war and conquest.

Until now.

Ala-Qush's perpetual frown deepened and he used a piece of charcoal to scribble on the paper I kept tucked in his chair, then waved it in the air.

"My husband has lost his ability to speak with his illness," I told my father in a low voice, "but not his sharpness of mind."

Jingue intercepted the paper and his lip twitched as he scanned the message. I raised my voice so it would carry to the crowd. "And what does Ala-Qush, Prince of Beiping, say to Genghis, Khan of Khans?"

Jingue cleared his throat, his hands and the message behind his back. "Ala-Qush of the Onggud bids welcome once again to the Khan of Khans. In addition, he wishes to open his stables to Genghis Khan, for he knows that the great conqueror is also a great admirer of horseflesh."

My father roared his approval and a white-faced Ala-Qush gave an angry grunt. Jingue pressed the paper into my palm, and I read it before hastily tucking it into my sleeve.

Don't let the heathens eat my horses.

I smothered a snort of laughter while my father squeezed Sorkho-khtani's shoulder. "I see my daughter-in-marriage reached you," he said. "I trust she told you the reason for my visit."

I glanced at the crowd gathered behind me. There had been much debate in the days since Sorkhokhtani's arrival as to whether the Onggud—a people terrified of war—would support my father's campaign. The Jurched were Olon Süme's longtime allies, and many noble families had taken wives from them and relied upon trade with their eastern cities. Still others argued that my father's campaign against the Tanghuts had forced more luxuries to pass along our roads, resulting in increased tolls for our coffers. I'd reminded everyone that we had no choice but to ally with my father, yet it had taken messages of support from both Ala-Qush and Jingue before the debate had ended in the Great House. Still, the nobility seethed, and they'd be angrier still when they realized their taxes would soon increase in order to finance my father's conquest.

"May your campaign against the Jurched see them scattered to the winds," I said to my father. "Olon Süme shall provide you with the necessary supplies for your attack."

My father gestured toward the land of the rising sun. "My cavalry will travel east after we've rested. Our dried meat and reserve horses served us well in crossing the desert, but we require fresh water and horses."

"Our wells are sweet and our horses fast," I said, stifling a smile as Ala-Qush gurgled in protest about the horses. "Take all you need."

"This shall be a lightning campaign," my father said. "With my new weapons and the Mongols and the Onggud united as one, the Jurched don't stand a chance."

Robust shouts from his soldiers and lukewarm cheers from the Onggud met his proclamation. Yet within my heart, I recognized a familiar jolt, the same I'd felt when Teb Tengeri had touched me at my father's *khurlatai*.

The brush of death.

The day my father departed was drenched in gold, as if the sun itself fell to earth to bless his campaign, and yellow dust choked the air as the regiments of the Thirteen Nations departed Olon Süme on their way to the Jurched borders. I stood on the walls above the tortoise gate, dressed in a delicate Onggud camlet and my horned *boqta* as I nocked a specially crafted golden arrow against the smooth curve of my bow. It flew to the east in a flash of light, and I relished the reverberation of the horse-gut string through my shoulder long after the arrow had passed from sight. This weapon, tipped with the Golden Light of the Sun, would guide my father and his soldiers to victory.

The army's commanders scattered mare's milk into the earth and yellow linden leaves fell to the ground, tangling in horses' manes before they were trampled under the pounding of thousands of hooves. My father rode at the front of the line, dressed in an amber wolfskin and a black helmet trimmed with fox fur. Although I knew Sorkhokhtani traveled with my father only in her official capacity as his personal messenger, I felt a surge of jealousy as she nodded to me, riding on his right with Shigi on his left. Behind them came the oxcarts carrying supplies and physicians from Olon Süme's new School of Healing, their wheels creaking ominously. Despite Orbei's protests, Enebish had begun studying at the school under the guise of learning to better minister to her father, but her desire to put her new skills to use on the battlefield outweighed her revulsion against my family and I'd happily agreed when she'd asked my permission to travel east. I could set her free from Olon Süme, even if I remained trapped within its walls. She inclined her head to me from her cart, and behind her came the soldiers, saluting me as they passed on their shaggy horses.

The sun drenched the countryside in its final hazy light as the last regiments departed, mounted on horseback and carrying double slings of arrows on their backs—one of feathered whistling arrows that gave the enemy pause to determine the origin of the strange sound, and a second quiver of shorter quarrels that would deliver death to the stationary target. I waited until the final man saluted me before returning to my *ger*, despite the ache in my feet from wearing the thin felt slippers all the Onggud women wore instead of my sensible fur-lined boots. Olon Süme's streets were mostly empty, but to my surprise, Jingue fell into step beside me as we passed the empty market square. The flagstones of the butchers' section were permanently stained with blood, and the ground near the grain sellers was covered with pigeons seeking an easy meal. "You look as worried as I feel," he finally said.

"I just sent my father and sister, along with countless other men, to war."

"Your father will return victorious," he said.

I gave a wan smile. "I didn't know you'd become a seer."

Jingue smiled in the dark. "Genghis Khan may lose the occasional skirmish, but has he ever lost a war?"

"Never."

"Then I doubt he's about to start," he said.

"My father claims it's easy to conquer the world on horseback. It's dismounting and ruling that are difficult."

"Your father would know," he said. "However, I suspect the deeds of Genghis Khan will be retold around hearth fires and gilded palace halls for centuries to come."

"I think you mean the tales of his bloody conquests."

Jingue chuckled. "I rather believe your father enjoys that version of him, the image of the ruthless savage that has his enemies' knees quaking before he even reaches their walls."

I smiled at that, knowing that my father had relished the stories during the Blood War that his body was made from copper and iron forged so strong that no weapon could penetrate it. "Perhaps so."

"And you never know," Jingue said, "but perhaps one day songs of his daughter's deeds will be sung as well."

The uncommon praise caught me off guard. I'd done nothing to earn being compared to my father, had in fact failed at everything I'd been set to do.

"We'll soon have our own war to fight," I said, feeling suddenly awkward. "I fear the first battle shall erupt when we collect the taxes to pay for my father's supplies."

Jingue ran a hand over his close-cropped hair. "My uncle has already called me a coward for not arguing against this campaign."

I shrugged. "Camlet is a luxury item. Orbei's brother can make common felt if he prefers."

"He'd sooner cross the Great Dry Sea on his knees." He looked about to say more but sighed. "It may be a good idea to keep a blade on you, in case one of the nobles thinks you an easy target for revenge."

So I was to fear death in every shadow yet again. I was moved by Jingue's thoughtfulness and wished I could touch his arm, but the weight of my headdress stayed my hand. "I've slept with my tiger sword every night since I came to Olon Süme. And no one would dare attack me, not after seeing my father and his army in the flesh."

"I pray that you're right," he said as we approached my *ger*. "For all our sakes."

I watched him go, his words making me realize that my father's campaign endangered not only the lives of his men, but also those of my Onggud family.

Unfortunately, there was nothing I could do about that now.

It had been a week since my father had left Olon Süme, and despite Jingue's warning, the herders continued to graze sleepy camels in the hills and merchants still hawked their treasures of silk, tortoise shells, porcelain, and honey. I convinced myself that the Council of Nobles in their ridiculous red hats had realized their mistake and reconciled themselves to the higher taxes that had been announced, all with relatively little dissent. Now I stood on the walls dressed as the *beki* I wished to be, ignoring the pattering raindrops as I stared at the horizon and willed Sorkhokhtani or another messenger to appear. Darkness fell quickly those days, so I didn't question the extra torches being lit in the square across from the Great House. By the time I heard the rising voices from the same square, it was already too late.

First came the rumble of angry shouts like a coming earthquake, then the growing light and heat behind me, as if the sun had decided not to set but to rise again from the west. I turned to see the wildfire of torches below me, but it was the flashes of silver amongst the gold, like fragments of the moon upon the sun, that caught my eye.

Swords.

"There she is!" An Onggud noble dressed in black silk pointed his curved scimitar at me. Even without his official red hat, I recognized him as Orbei's brother, the loudest detractor against my father in the debates of the Council of Nobles.

From the numbers of men surrounding him, I guessed this had been planned for days, perhaps since before my father left. Thankfully, I'd taken Jingue's advice, and I unsheathed my tiger sword as the man in black charged up the steps two at a time. I didn't wait for him to reach me, but leapt off the wall and landed in a cart piled with oiled leather sacks of camel hair waiting to be sold to the weavers. I stumbled out, feeling the rain start in earnest and the fast-forming mud soak through my worthless felt slippers.

"Get her!" he screamed, shaking his sword at me. "All those who support the heathen Khan must die this night!"

In the distance, the School of Healing was in flames, as if the mob sought to destroy all I'd touched. I was thankful Enebish wasn't there, but instead safe with my father and his men. I fled then, quickly realizing I couldn't outrun my pursuers. Before me, a group of men herded stumbling people into the square—women screaming, children crying, and men mumbling prayers to whatever gods they worshipped. I knew them all as my supporters in the council debates, and their innocent families.

This was no simple mob, but a revolt.

I kept the tiger sword ready and ran like a shadow through dark alleys, winding my way through the warren of passages in Olon Süme's religious section. Angry voices and the flicker of torches threatened to head me off, and the copper tang of blood and screams of the dying chased me as I ducked into the first dark building.

The Nestorian school seemed blessedly empty at first, and I'd likely have missed the scuffed boot poking out from an overturned bench had it not been for the muffled whimper that came from that direction. Only then did I see the yellow puddle of urine, smell the acrid scent of a child's fear.

"It's all right," I whispered. "You can come out."

There was nothing.

"You can't stay here," I said. "They'll find you."

I gasped when Boyahoe's face appeared, cheeks streaked with tears as he launched himself into my arms. Small for his eleven years, he suddenly seemed as young as the day I'd met him and I clutched him to me.

"Where's Jingue?" I managed to ask. "And your father?"

"I don't know." Boyahoe hiccupped, still clinging to me. "Jingue was here when the fighting began. He told me to hide before my uncle came."

"Your uncle was here?"

"He asked Jingue to come with them."

My heart stalled. "And did he?"

Boyahoe nodded. "He said he'd be glad to serve his family. My uncle gave him a sword."

Glad to serve his family.

Jingue had feigned his friendship with me, had waited all this time like an adder in the grass, preparing for the right time to strike.

Boyahoe's words echoed louder and louder in my mind. Once I was dead Jingue could take his place behind his father's throne, a place I'd usurped with my father's forced alliance. The betrayal cut deep, but I didn't have time to think on that now.

I had only one thought in my mind at that moment: to survive.

I thought to leave Boyahoe in a barricade of benches, but the screams increased and blood spattered the paper windows from outside. Boyahoe cringed and buried his face in my shoulder. My greatest fear had come true; this walled city was caving in and threatening to kill me.

"I need you to run with me," I said, hauling him up. "Can you do that?" I knew Jingue would never harm his brother, but I couldn't be sure about the mob outside. At least with me, Boyahoe would have the protection of my sword.

He nodded and drew in a shuddering breath. "What about Jingue?"

I wanted to lie, to say that he'd be fine, but I couldn't find the words. "Pray for him," I said. "And for us."

His small frame melded to my side, we ducked out of the school. I managed only a few steps before I stumbled over something firm and wet. A body, slick with warm blood.

My stomach heaved, but I yanked Boyahoe away before he could see the gruesome face screaming up at us with glassy eyes. We crouched behind a wagon loaded with metal cauldrons and I prayed that the fire in my soul would protect us from the bonfire of death and flames closing in upon us. Wooden houses popped and hissed before they collapsed in showers of glowing sparks, and bodies lay outside the Great House, more familiar features twisted with death and many coated with masks of blood. Beyond that was my *ger*, now a fiery inferno. Then the door of the Great House opened and a man in a wooden chair wheeled out.

"Father!" Boyahoe yelled, but I clamped a hand over his mouth.

Stooped like a man twice his age, Ala-Qush jolted his chair to a stop, his eyes vacant and unseeing, as if in a dream. He trembled, not with fear but with shock, his bones unable to bear what his eyes were seeing.

No one had glimpsed my husband yet, but soon one of the rebels would sound the alarm. I could run up the stairs and push him back into the relative safety of the Great House, thereby exposing Boyahoe and myself.

Or I could do nothing.

"If it isn't Ala-Qush, the doddering Prince of Beiping." Orbei's brother and his supporters emerged from an alley just as I pushed Boyahoe under the wagon of cauldrons. They wiped stained sleeves across cheeks streaked with soot and blood, and I searched their faces in vain for Jingue.

Orbei's brother circled my husband, then gave his wheeled chair a shove. The wooden contraption careened down the steps, spilling Ala-Qush in a heap at the bottom. I moaned and covered Boyahoe's ears. "You should have died before bending a knee to the heathen Khan," the man in black said, leaning down to grab Ala-Qush by his *deel*'s collar. "You're a disgrace to the Onggud, weaker than an old woman."

I clutched Boyahoe tight, ensuring he didn't witness his father's last moments, but I forced myself to watch without blinking, hearing Teb Tengeri's accusation in my ear.

The foot soldier of death.

Ala-Qush remained kneeling on the ground, as trusting as a goat awaiting its slaughter. The knife across his throat flashed quickly, and his eyes grew wide as a flag of crimson unfurled down his chest. He fell forward onto the trampled earth and blood of his people, but Orbei's brother kicked him onto his back, then spat on his ruined face before scuttling away with the rest of the rebels.

The rain fell harder then, great, fat drops as if the Eternal Blue Sky wept at such senseless slaughter. I waited until the mob had moved on, holding my breath as they passed our hiding place under the cart, and then I crawled out on my belly.

"Run to the climbing tree," I ordered Boyahoe. "Faster than you've ever run before."

We left Ala-Qush behind in a growing pool of blood, my husband's frail body already being washed clean by the rain. We had only one chance to escape, and together we raced toward the oak tree that Boyahoe and I had climbed the first winter I'd spent in Olon Süme.

The spirits of the dead must have clouded the eyes of the living, or perhaps it was only the thirst for blood that blinded them to us, for we had to backtrack often and I dared not sheath my sword as I ran. Once we rounded a corner and came upon an Onggud woman removing the decorated leather boots of a fallen man. The boot came off with a wet squelch and the woman gave us a gap-toothed grin. I ran as fleet-footed as a fox down the opposite alley, dragging Boyahoe behind me.

Finally, the tree was before us with its spread of bare branches.

I unclasped Boyahoe's grip and pushed him in front of me. "Climb," I said, whirling around, my sword ready against anyone who might spot us. "Up and then along that branch close to the wall."

"I can't." His body shook violently and he started to cry, great, heaving sobs that obscured his ability to speak. Voices followed us, echoing off the thick walls and making my heart thump like a war drum.

"On my back, then." With great misgivings, I tucked the tiger sword into my belt as he clambered onto my back, smelling of piss from where he'd wet himself earlier, and his slight frame quaking with tremors so strong I worried he might shake himself loose. Slowly, one hand over the other, I hauled us up the tree, the dried bark cutting into my palms, yet I felt no pain despite the sensation of warm blood slick on my hands.

Once up the tree, I clung to the trunk and tested the branch with my foot, my heart falling as it creaked with the slightest pressure. It had gone rotten and was no longer strong enough to hold my weight, let alone that of myself and an eleven-year-old boy. This time of year there were no snow-drifts on the other side to jump into, nothing to soften our fall. Even the ravens had fled.

The rain obscured my vision, but a man on the other side of the wall stepped from the shadows and into the circle of light created by the conflagration behind us. I swallowed a sob and waited for the arrow's whistle that would end all this, but instead, a familiar voice called to us. "You don't have much time, Boyahoe." Jingue spread his arms open wide. "Leap like a flying squirrel, and I'll catch you."

Jingue wouldn't harm Boyahoe, regardless of whether he sided with the mob. "Do as your brother says," I murmured to Boyahoe.

The boy hesitated, then shimmied down my back. The branch groaned, but he leapt with the swift motion of a soaring hawk. Jingue caught him with a pained grunt and they both tumbled to the ground.

My stepson safe, I now had two options. I could follow him over the wall or scramble down the tree and try to find some other route to safety.

But there was no other route, and Jingue and I both knew it.

"Come, Alaqai," Jingue ordered from below. "They'll be here any moment."

My grave awaited me if I stayed within these walls. And although I'd ushered others to their deaths, I had no wish to join their spirits in the sacred mountains. Not yet.

I ran along the branch, then launched myself into the air and away from Olon Süme's fiery inferno as the branch finally groaned and crashed to the ground. The impact when I landed on the far side stole my breath, and I expected a sword at my throat as I struggled for air, but it never came. Instead, I scrambled to my feet and drew my tiger sword, pointing it at Jingue.

"What are you doing, Alaqai?" Jingue asked. His borrowed sword remained in his belt.

"I'm protecting myself from those who seek revenge against me," I said, echoing his earlier warning that I keep my sword close. "Boyahoe told me you joined your uncle to hunt me down."

He gave a strangled laugh. "After all this time, you still think I want you dead? Another dose of *gu* poison would have been far easier to arrange than torching all of Olon Süme and slaughtering my people in the streets." His fists clenched and unclenched uselessly at his sides, and I kept the sword pointed at his throat. "I joined my uncle so I could save you. Aside from the tortoise gate, this is the only escape from the city, so I knew where you'd be."

"So your uncle let you go?"

Jingue was silent for a moment. "Yes," he finally said.

"And your mother? Would you leave her behind?"

I dared not mention his father, knowing that Ala-Qush still stared up at the night sky, his body bloodied and desecrated by his own people.

"My mother's family will protect her, but my lot has been cast with you, Alaqai, for better or worse."

I recognized the truth in his words. I owed Jingue my life and had destroyed his yet again, but there would be time later to wallow in guilt. "Then you'll have to come with us to my father's army," I said, lowering my sword.

"The Khan will bring his wrath upon the Onggud," Jingue said quietly. "He'll raze what's left of the city and slaughter everyone taller than a wagon wheel to punish them for this revolt."

I had no desire to witness more death, yet there was nowhere else to go.

"We have to go, and now." I was already moving away from the city and its promise of death. "There's no alternative."

Jingue glanced back at Olon Süme and all that we were leaving behind. "The monastery is a day's ride from here," he said. "They'll have horses."

"We'll never make it there on foot." At least not before we felt Onggud arrows in our backs.

Jingue gestured toward the dark hillside. "No, but we have camels."

I'd forgotten the herds. There were no saddles, but fortunately the herders kept rope reins tied to the pointed wooden dowels strung through the animals' noses. The beasts were a gift from the Earth Mother, but it took us so long to persuade the frightened animals to let us grab their reins that I almost screamed.

"Boyahoe should ride with me," I said once I was on the back of a particularly ill-kept camel, its hair matted with dirt. My stepson was too frightened and exhausted to control his own mount. Jingue nodded but hissed with pain as he handed him up. It was only then that I noticed his tattered sleeve and the angry wound hidden beneath the torn fabric, a detail that had escaped my terror-stricken mind in the dark.

"What happened?" I asked, grabbing his wrist to inspect his forearm.

"It's nothing." Jingue tried to pull his arm back, but I held tight.

"It doesn't look like nothing," I said. The cut was long and straight, but not too deep. "This is a sword wound."

"A sword wound will heal as well as any other injury," he said, yet his gaze wouldn't meet mine. "But not if we get killed before we reach the monastery."

"Put pressure on it," I said. "I can't have you falling off your camel from loss of blood."

I let him go then, noting the dark stain of dried blood on his sword for the first time and wondering if I'd ever know what he'd faced while Boyahoe and I ran through Olon Süme's streets. Now wasn't the time to ask.

We rode side by side all night, haunted by the ghosts of the dead and terrified of the living who might be pursuing us. I waited to speak until

Boyahoe's head lolled against my arm in sleep and the only sounds were the exertions of the camels. "Your father is dead."

Jingue's jaw clenched in the watery moonlight and the vein in his temple pulsed like a tiny snake. "May his spirit rest well."

I couldn't relate the details, that I'd watched his father be butchered instead of saving him, had seen his body grow still as his spirit flew to the sky. I recalled Teb Tengeri's words from long ago.

You carry death in your heart, just like the vermin you're named for. Death's own foot soldier.

I said nothing else to Jingue, only prayed under the cold sweep of stars that we wouldn't soon greet Ala-Qush and the rest of the dead in the sacred mountains.

Chapter 20

The monastery gave us horses and supplies as Jingue had promised, and the three of us soon followed the trail of scorched Jurched villages left in my father's wake. Death blanketed the countryside; the only signs of life we encountered amongst the burned fields and broken pens were wild dogs and bent-necked vultures feeding on the waxy and bloated bodies and horse carcasses left to rot in the sun. Unfortunate Jurched corpses spilled purple intestines through bloody gashes, and others lay sprawled facedown with arrows protruding from their backs like giant porcupine quills. The stench of decomposing flesh burrowed its way into our noses and coated our tongues so I feared I'd never taste or smell anything save death.

Finally, we reached a town that had not yet been put to the torch, surrounded by a veritable city of felted field tents. The air was still and the wooden gates had been flung open as if in welcome, yet Mongol soldiers roamed the streets, relieving the abandoned countryside of its goats and pillaging anything that wasn't nailed down. There were no peasants around, and I wondered then if these lucky Jurched had escaped with their lives, fleeing their beds and hovels in terror at news of my father's approach. Instead, we'd later learn that they'd been captured and sent ahead with Sorkhokhtani's contingent to dig up boulders to fill the moat of Liaoyang, the nearest Jurched capital and my father's next siege target. The peasants were motivated to dig quickly, for my father threatened to use their bodies instead if there weren't enough stones.

I held my head high despite the caked mud and dried blood that still plastered my felts. One of my father's soldiers finally recognized me beneath all the grime, and my name was shouted on the wind, followed by waves of men bending their knees to me. I felt Jingue's gaze on me as I sat straighter in my saddle, proud of the honor paid to me by the people of my birth, although embarrassed that I'd never inspired such devotion from the Onggud.

My father emerged from his camp tent at the commotion, eyes hardening as he beheld the blood-spattered lot of us. "Greetings, Khan of Khans," I said, dismounting. "We come bearing news of your vassal state, the Onggud of Olon Süme."

"Unpleasant news, it appears," he said, crossing his arms over his stocky chest. I could already hear the thoughts in his head, his plans to besiege my city and lay waste to its fields. Still, he beckoned us inside his traveling tent, away from the ears of his soldiers. "Bad news is best served over a good meal, and I just ordered a particularly fat Jurched sheep slaughtered for my dinner."

The smell of boiling meat made my stomach growl in anticipation, and I filled the dented metal bowl my father offered me, pouring a bit of the mutton stew into the hearth fire for the spirits while Jingue and Boyahoe prayed over their food to the god of the cross. "Tell me what happened," my father said.

It took far less time to relate the horrors of the attack than it had to survive them, although I skimmed over the worst of the atrocities, both for Boyahoe's benefit and because I had no desire to relive them.

"The Onggud have served their *beki* and our vassal with treachery," my father answered as he drained the last of his broth, wiping his mouth on the back of his sleeve. "They must be repaid in kind."

And so Jingue's warning would come true. New rivers of blood would run through the streets of Olon Süme, and more bodies would be piled like kindling within its walls. Although they'd kept me an outsider during my time as *beki*, I had no desire to see them destroyed.

"The Onggud aren't a clan to be annihilated," I said, setting down my bowl. "They are my people."

And without them, I was no *beki*, only the failed daughter of a great conqueror.

My father scoffed. "You would show them mercy after all they've done?"

"A mother may punish her children, but only to teach them a lesson." I spoke slowly, forming the words carefully. I thought of my own mother, feeling in my soul that she would approve of this decision. "Give me a contingent from your army and I'll retake Olon Süme. But I will *not* raze it."

"They won't accept you," my father said, shaking his head. "They must be cut down, and their bodies burned so their ashes feed the grass."

With Ala-Qush dead, the rebels would need a new leader. Though bold, they wouldn't be so audacious as to place someone from outside my husband's white-boned lineage in the Great House. That left two candidates for the new Prince of Beiping. Fortunately for me, both were inside this tent.

"They will accept me," I said, squaring my shoulders, "if I marry Jingue."

Both men drew sharp inhales. I didn't have the courage to face the revulsion I might see in Jingue's expression, so I tipped my chin to my father, daring him to defy me. He only nodded after a moment, stroking his long mustache. "That is a sound approach."

"Boyahoe must remain with you while we march on Olon Süme." I wouldn't present the rebels with a choice of who might lead them, nor would I put my stepson in further danger.

"How old are you, boy?" my father asked Boyahoe.

"I've seen eleven summers." Boyahoe trembled in his seat, his eyes almost as wide as his ears over his untouched bowl of stew. My youngest stepson had been taught that Genghis Khan was a brutal and bloody conqueror, but he'd soon find my father was also a charismatic leader, a trait I hoped Boyahoe might one day learn to emulate.

"I'd say you're old enough to learn the ways of war," my father said, slapping his own knee while Boyahoe's eyes grew even larger. "I'd already killed my first man by your age."

I refrained from mentioning that that man had also been my father's brother. Instead, I dared to face Jingue, my heart thudding at his blank expression. "I'd have you, Jingue, son of Ala-Qush, as my husband," I said, drawing a deep breath. "But will you have me?"

The silence might have lasted only moments, but to me it seemed an eternity. Jingue finally sighed and rubbed a hand over his haggard features, his forearm still wrapped in a dust-stained bandage. "Life never brings the expected when you're around, does it, Alaqai?"

"You don't have to agree," I said, my cheeks flushing as my ire rose. "I'll ride on Olon Süme alone if I have to."

"I don't doubt that you would," he said, holding up a tired hand to stop my tirade. "But that won't be necessary. I'll take you as my wife, Alaqai, as you've commanded."

The smile that jumped to my lips died just as quickly at the emptiness in his eyes. Jingue would make a worthy Prince of Beiping, and I'd dreamed of him in my bed countless times, yet he agreed to marry me now only because he had no choice. The joy at what should have been a glorious moment fled, leaving my heart hollow. I turned to my father, my voice flat. "When will the men be ready to ride?"

My father laid his hands on my shoulders as he'd often done to steady me when I was young, then pressed his forehead to mine. "You shall have your men at first light, *tarvag takal*," he murmured. "But first we must see you married."

My first marriage took place under the shadows of lies and half-truths, my second under the stain of war and revolt. Yet despite the circumstances, I was determined not to come to Jingue dressed as a refugee.

I sought out Enebish amongst the other Onggud healers housed within my father's tents. She'd just finished packing Jingue's wounded arm with a honey poultice, and both of them glanced up with hooded expressions when I entered the healers' tent, a sure sign that they'd been discussing me.

"Thank you, sister," Jingue said, avoiding looking at me. He passed by me with the sweet tang of honey, and Enebish watched him go.

"Did Jingue tell you how he was injured?" I asked.

Enebish busied herself rolling a tidy pile of wool bandages and packing her box of ointments. "Only that he earned it during the riot, after our father's death." Her fingers stilled. "He told me he's to marry you tonight."

I hesitated, then sighed. "I hoped you might help me find something to wear." I gestured to my filthy *deel*. "I could just wear this . . ."

She folded her hands primly over her medicine box, her lips pursed. "I can scarcely see your face under all that grime. My brother should greet his bride swathed in silk, not wearing the blood of other men and a layer of dust from days spent traveling on the road."

I clenched my teeth. "Does that mean you'll help me or not?"

She closed her eyes, as if gathering strength for her reply. "Yes, Alaqai. It means I'll help you."

Together we spent the afternoon wandering through empty Jurched houses and rifling carefully through the many abandoned and brightly painted chests until we found what we were looking for. The green silk *deel* was wrapped in yellowing paper and embroidered with reclining dragons, and a cloud of dust and the hopes of a bride from long ago billowed from it when I shook it out.

"It's lovely," Enebish said, her eyes warm as she fingered the soft silk. "You'll make a beautiful bride for my brother. Once you've had a thorough bath, that is."

I almost dropped the *deel* at her compliment, but Enebish's expression was sincere. With a ragged fingernail I traced the silk dragons, their coiled tails and the fire billowing from their mouths. "I expected you to spit and hiss when you learned I was to marry Jingue," I said.

She acted for a moment as if she hadn't heard me. "Sometimes we're forced to make difficult decisions," she finally said. "I may not agree with all your choices, but this marriage will save my family and my people. *Our* people. That makes me happy, as I believe it does Jingue."

"You don't know your brother very well," I muttered, but Enebish only smiled. "Will you come with us back to Olon Süme?" I asked.

"If you think it best," she said, her gaze dropping.

"You'd prefer to remain here instead, to continue patching up my father's wounded soldiers?"

She lifted her shoulders. "Perhaps one day I'll ache to marry some noble dressed in camlet and bear his children, but for now I enjoy my work here, setting bones and sewing wounds for men who need me to save their lives, and not their vanity."

There was nothing else she might have said to convince me to let her have her way. I'd not deprive Enebish of her happiness in this life, especially as her work assisted my father. "Then you shall remain here," I said.

"Thank you, Alaqai." She gave me a mischievous smile. "I don't think I've ever said it before, but I'm sorry we tried to kill you when you first came to Olon Süme."

"I accept your apology, late though it is." I laughed. I knew not whether Enebish was more daughter or sister, but against all odds, she'd become a part of my family all the same.

"Now, go put this on," Enebish said. "And I'll find some hairpins for those stubborn tangles of yours."

Enebish rifled through more chests and I draped the emerald *deel* across my chest, a waterfall of green silk that ended in a froth of golden dragons. "Thank you for letting me borrow this treasure," I whispered to its unknown owner, wondering if she was still alive and on her way to Liaoyang, or beyond that, the Northern Capital. I would return the priceless outfit after the ceremony, and perhaps one day she would come home to find it folded differently than she'd left it, and scented with fresh hopes.

I prayed for victory and happiness with Jingue, yet I didn't discount the very real possibility of failure.

Enebish and I hummed traditional wedding songs while I tied the coordinating deep yellow silk sash around my waist in a simple knot and she plaited my hair into a makeshift *boqta*, an elaborate pile of coils my clumsy fingers never would have managed. Finally, I carried my tiger sword with me, for tomorrow I would be transformed from a bride into a warrior *beki* intent on reclaiming her right to rule.

My father was waiting when I emerged into the gray haze of twilight, his smile deepening the creases that fanned from the corners of his eyes. Shigi and the Four Dogs of War flanked him, and the purification fires burned as bright as the flames that had devoured my *ger* in Olon Süme. I was struck by the incongruity of a wedding on a field of battle, some grim joke of mischievous spirits.

"I wish your mother could witness this," my father said, low enough so only I could hear. "Instead, Shigi shall transcribe everything to share with her one day around the hearth fire."

Shigi beckoned for my sword then, and I cocked my head in question, but he only waggled his fingers in response. I relinquished the blade, opening my mouth to protest when he tucked it into his own belt. "You'll have it back come morning," he murmured, threading something in my hair. "Your very wise uncle doesn't want you to be tempted to use it on your new groom. After all, you do have your father's temper."

I made a face at that, then touched the new ornament he'd placed in my hair, trying to discern its design.

"A jade tiger," Shigi said. "It seems a fitting trade for your sword, at least for tonight."

"Go well, Alaqai," my father said, gesturing to the tall man who approached, dressed in a brown silk *deel* that had likely been pilfered from another obliging Jurched trunk. Even so, the sight of Jingue made my heart trip. "This man of yours is a good one."

"He is indeed." Yet I was far from good, forcing Jingue into this marriage. I offered a wan smile to my waiting groom and was surprised at the heat I saw in his eyes. Then he blinked, and the fire was banked as he held out his hand for mine.

Without a proper wedding tent, we walked between the purification fires and down the dusty path filled with thousands of soldiers' footprints. Jingue intoned a prayer to his god of the cross and I prayed to the Earth Mother before we entered my father's traveling *ger*, lent to us for the night before we rode for Olon Süme in the morning. There was no salt tea to serve to my father's Dogs of War, but I poured many mismatched porcelain bowls of wine, requisitioned by our soldiers from abandoned Jurched homes. Jingue and I drank from our own bowls first; then our fingers brushed as we switched and placed our lips on the imprint left by the other.

"Your bride looks weary," one of my father's Dogs finally said to Jingue, his voice too loud after several cups of wine.

"She'll be even more weary after the groom's through with her," a red-nosed general hollered, prompting a roar of laughter that might have been heard all the way in Liaoyang. I was no fresh-cheeked virgin, but still my face blazed. This celebration was so different from my first wedding, the merriment heightened by the threat of a battle yet to come. I wished to laugh with them like any other bride eager for her wedding bed. Yet I was no common bride, and this was no common marriage.

"Refill your wine bowls and leave us in peace!" I exclaimed. I craved a moment of calm to collect myself. I could have kissed the tops of Shigi's curved boots when he began ushering everyone into the night air.

The flap of the traveling tent muffled their voices, and I turned to find Jingue sitting on my father's narrow camp bed, elbows propped on his knees as he stared at the wine bowl between his hands. We'd scarcely spoken tonight—only our marriage vows—and I found myself light-headed from the wine and the sudden storm of nerves in my belly.

I turned my back and tugged with trembling fingers at the stubborn knot on my sash but was startled as Jingue threw a heavy felt blanket on the ground, causing the fire to waver and sputter before righting itself. "I'll sleep on the floor," he said, his voice cold and flat. "You take the bed and we can leave at first light."

My hand fell away and for a moment I could only blink. "You'd sleep alone? But I thought—"

Jingue laughed, yet the sound held no mirth. "You thought I'd force you to share my bed, even after you made it clear that you sought to marry me only because it was the best way to keep your *beki*'s headdress?"

Then I realized the truth, that Jingue had married me in name only, obligated to an alliance to save his family and people.

This was Ala-Qush all over again.

Jingue tossed the remainder of his wine into the fire so the flames hissed and spit; then he set down his bowl, hard. "Rest assured that if I ever come to your bed it will be because you want me there, Alaqai, not simply because you'll tolerate me there."

I stared at him, then burst out laughing. Once started, I couldn't stop, but I grabbed Jingue's hand when he cursed and moved to leave. He stopped when I fell to my knees. Never before had I humbled myself in such a manner, but I would do it now, for this man.

"I want you," I gasped, holding tight as he tried to free his hand. "I've wanted you since the day you returned from that cursed monastery of yours."

"Don't lie to me." He scowled as he pulled me roughly to my feet, but his eyes reflected his uncertainty in the firelight. "I'll stay here tonight and we'll leave in the morning—"

I let my hands drop. "I'll never lie to you, Jingue. I want you at my side in the Great House, and to share my tent as your wife. Most of all, right now I want you in my bed, even if it means I have to drag you there myself."

The silence grew too long, but then it was Jingue's turn to laugh, a deep, throaty sound that echoed in my heart as he crushed me to him. I inhaled his scent, fresh scrubbed from the river, but still with a hint of ink and horses—before he pressed his lips to mine for the first time.

It was a kiss that left me trembling, truly and gloriously alive for the first time in years.

I arched against him, my entire body tingling with the golden heat that spread from my belly and settled still lower. It had been so long since I'd been with a man, but this was a different kind of hunger, deeper and more powerful. I tugged away his *deel* and trousers and drank in the long brown lines of his body, the way the flames shifted shadows across the sinewy muscles of his chest.

Despite his bandaged arm, Jingue lifted me up and spread me across the bed, covering me with his body and caressing my cheeks. His eyes were the color of damp earth, the very element to calm the fire that always raged in my soul. I realized then that for all our differences, this quiet, thoughtful scholar was the man I could spend the rest of my life with.

"I love you, Jingue," I said.

He only smiled and brushed his lips against the sensitive skin at the base of my throat. "And I love you," he murmured. "In fact, I've loved you since almost the day I met you."

I shivered at the surge of pleasure his lips sent down my body, scarcely managing to gasp a single word. "Almost?"

He chuckled and lifted his lips, leaving me aching for his touch. "I *did* almost let you die of poison that first day."

"I'm glad you thought better of it," I said, drawing a sharp breath as he finally loosened my sash and opened my *deel*, his tongue teasing my nipples before he tugged the silk trousers from my hips.

"So am I." His arms were under me then, lifting me to him so there was nothing but our flesh and the perfect fit of our bodies together. I wrapped my legs around him, gasping as he filled my body and soul in the same moment. "And tonight I plan to prove it to you," he murmured.

And he did. Several times.

We spent the rest of the evening in each other's arms, then dressed in *deels* tightly woven with raw silk—the better to stop enemy arrows from penetrating our flesh in the battle to come—and the fur-lined helmets my father had left for us when the sky turned from black to gray. Together we stepped out of the silence of the tent, transformed into a single yoke in the eyes of my father and his men.

My cheeks were flushed with happiness, but I couldn't resist whispering a question in Jingue's ear as we walked past waves of bowing soldiers. "So, husband of my heart, will you take any more wives once we return to Olon Süme?"

"You foolish woman." Jingue chortled. "I waited all this time for you—what could I possibly want with another wife? Aside from peace and tranquility, that is."

I gave him a fierce scowl and a mock punch to his arm, earning still more laughter despite my relief. Nestorians didn't make a habit of taking more than one wife, but I'd worried that I might follow in my mother's footsteps, my heart broken as Jingue married more women, as my father had done. "I can scarcely handle you, Alaqai," Jingue said, "much less any other women."

"And I'd have you gelded if you did," I said. "I'm quite handy with a knife, you know."

Jingue threw back his head and laughed as we walked to where my father stood with Shigi and Boyahoe, our army of mounted cavalry fanning out behind them.

"It pleases me to see your happiness in this marriage," my father said to us, smiling before he motioned to where Boyahoe stood with Enebish. "When we've defeated the Jurched, this boy-soldier can return to Olon Süme or accompany me to the Khwarazmian Empire to conquer the lazy sultans in their palaces of gold."

"You never remain at peace for long, do you, Father?" I asked.

He harrumphed, sounding like an old man, but his eyes were as bright as those of a boy receiving his first horse. "There will be plenty of time for peace once my flesh feeds the earth."

I breathed the cool morning air on both sides of his leathered face while Jingue bid his brother and sister good-bye. "Thank you, Father," I murmured. "I'll see you soon."

"Indeed you shall, *tarvag takal*." He winked. "When next we meet we shall toast one another's victories with that fine Onggud wine of yours."

Shigi presented my tiger sword, freshly sharpened and polished, a knowing look in his eyes.

"It was good that you took this last night," I said. "You know me well."

He shrugged. "I've always liked Jingue. It would have been a shame to have to arrange his funeral today."

"Be safe, Shigi," I said. "Don't let a Jurched arrow find its way to your back."

He smiled, turning his palms over to reveal ink-stained fingers, so like Jingue's that I almost laughed. "I fight with brushes and ink, Alaqai Beki, not swords and spears."

And I was glad of it, for although he didn't share our blood, Shigi was as much a part of my heart as my parents, Toregene and Sorkhokhtani, and Jingue. I remembered his words before he first left Olon Süme and wondered if he'd fully reconciled himself to living without a wife at his side, if he still pined for his married lover. I squeezed his hands, then mounted my borrowed horse and lifted my tiger sword to salute my father, prompting cheers from the soldiers behind Jingue and me.

Despite the flush of excitement, I felt a flutter of dread at the uncertainty of what lay before us when we reentered Olon Süme.

My father pledged victories for all our family, but I could only pray that the Eternal Blue Sky would grant his promises.

With a contingent from my father's army at our back, we retraced our path through the skeletons of burned villages, listening silently as my father's soldiers recounted their execution of the Crow Swarm outside one barren Jurched town, the way their war drums had pounded and men galloped at once from all directions. They left only charred earth and fat crows in their wake, like a gaping wound in the earth after a lightning strike. Olon Süme would suffer the same fate if its people refused the demands that Jingue and I would set before them.

The air still smelled of soot and the oily stench of death when Jingue and I approached Olon Süme's carved tortoise gates, our army of cavalry and hastily constructed ballistas hidden in the hills on ground I'd recently sprinkled with fresh mare's milk, beseeching the Earth Mother for an easy victory. I prayed that the Onggud fear of war and the threat of mounted Mongols armed with catapults would induce Olon Süme to accept our terms. We'd been gone only ten days, but already the blows of hammers and chisels resounded, signs of a city being reborn. Freshly tilled soil outside the walls lent the impression of spring instead of autumn, but there were no seeds tucked into these furrows. Instead, the last open pit we passed held only corpses with bloated limbs and unrecognizable faces, too many dead to leave uncovered on the steppes for the foxes and vultures.

I stared at the walls ahead and prayed we wouldn't soon have more bodies to bury.

Several overdressed figures, all wearing the red hats of the Council of Nobles, hurried to the bulwark over the tortoise gate, now frantically closed to bar our entrance. I kept my hands clasped before me, searching for

Jingue's uncle and shocked when I didn't find him. Orbei stood stiff-backed amongst the nervous men, but her reptilian features sagged with relief when she recognized her eldest son riding next to me.

A reed-thin man I scarcely recognized from the council lifted his pointed red hat to wipe the top of his shiny head. "Jingue, son of Ala-Qush," he said, his voice trembling as he stared at me and then scanned the horizon. The man might be a coward, but he was no fool. "To what do we owe this honor?"

Jingue nudged his horse forward, but I held back. "May Christ rest my father's eternal soul," my husband said, ignoring the question. "With God's blessing, the noble lineage of Ala-Qush has ruled Olon Süme for genera-tions, and with his passing, I've returned as the eldest son and hereditary heir. I assume you'll open the gates and follow behind me as I claim the Great House as my own."

The men whispered amongst themselves, pointed red hats bobbing as their eyes darted to Jingue and me. It was no small thing to supplant their god's chosen leader, and well they knew it. "And yet you've brought the daughter of the Khan of Khans," the first man said. "Did you capture her as your uncle instructed?"

"I did not capture her." Jingue glanced at me, his eyes sparking. "I married her."

And now it was my turn.

"You, the Onggud of Olon Süme, have betrayed us. My father, the Great Khan, craves the blood of the Onggud for the insult you have of-fered his daughter." I turned in my saddle to wave my tiger sword at the hills. The metal captured the sun's light and threw the signal back to where our scouts waited with their catapults and the newly invented spiked shells that would wreak havoc on Olon Süme's walls. "Jingue, son of Ala-Qush, is the true Prince of Beiping, and as his first and only wife, I, Alaqai Beki, daughter of Genghis Khan, am Beki of Olon Süme. Together we make you a single offer to save your city and your souls."

Already the disturbance in the hills was being noted as our men moved the ballistas into position. The men on the wall muttered and crossed themselves.

"What are your terms?" Orbei asked, her voice rising above the men's panic. "Tell us, for we are listening."

Part of my heart cried out for revenge, for the Onggud to know the same fear I had faced as the fire raged around me and my people screamed in death and fear. But I was mother to these people. And no matter the crimes of her child, a mother never seeks retribution.

I drew a deep breath. "You know what trespasses you committed. Those stains will mark your souls until you draw your final breaths. We offer mercy in this life if you surrender and accept our rule. If you refuse, the full wrath of the Mongol army will rain upon this city, until only your ashes are left to bear testimony to its existence."

By this time, the hills were covered with the mounted soldiers borrowed from my father, their swords glinting in the sun. The loaders stood ready with the giant lethal arrows for the ballistas. Orbei stepped forward, the breeze ruffling tendrils of gray hair that had escaped from her severe braid. "And our daughter and youngest son?" she asked. "Will they be spared as well?"

"They remain with the Khan of Khans," I said. "Enebish wishes to continue her work as a healer, and Boyahoe is learning to soldier from the greatest conqueror of all." When Orbei didn't respond, I asked the question I needed to have answered. "Where is your brother, he who fanned the revolt that saw this once-great city reduced to rubble?"

"My brother's body lies beyond the walls now," she said, her face betraying no emotion. "He was killed during the Night of Flashing Swords."

The Night of Flashing Swords.

Suddenly I realized why Jingue refused to speak of his wound. "He was killed by a sword wound?"

Orbei gave a tight nod. "He was."

I glanced at Jingue, reading the truth in his eyes. My precious husband, who believed so deeply in the sanctity of life, had murdered his own uncle and then risked his life to save me. My throat tightened and it took me longer to find my voice than I would have liked.

"What is your answer to our terms?"

The huddle of men conversed with Orbei while Jingue and I waited.

Behind us in the hills, impatient warhorses threw their heads and men stood ready with the arrows for the ballistas. I prayed I'd soon give the order that would return them to my father.

Finally Orbei bowed her head to us. "All shall be as you ask," she said. "The Onggud welcome their new Prince of Beiping and his *beki*."

The tortoise gates creaked open on ancient hinges and the Onggud fell to their knees in the streets before us. I rubbed the golden tigers on my sword with my thumb, the victory ritual from my youth. Jingue and I had departed this city as fugitives, but now we returned as prince and princess. Together we would rebuild our broken city, tempered and made stronger for all we'd survived.

Against all odds, we had won. Together, we would prosper.

Later that night, I received yet another blessing.

In return for my mercy, the Earth Mother lifted the shadow of death Teb Tengeri had once claimed I carried. While I nestled in Jingue's arms before a roaring fire and safe under the peaked roof of the Great House, my husband's seed buried itself deep in my womb. Less than a year later, surrounded by Orbei, Enebish, and the sticky heat of the summer solstice, I gave birth to a squalling, red-faced son.

His name was Negudei, and the Earth Mother and Eternal Blue Sky decreed he would be the only child born of my womb.

In the days to come, he would be my most precious gift of all.

PART III

The Rose of Nishapur

Chapter 21

1221 CE
YEAR OF THE WHITE SNAKE
NISHAPUR, KHWARAZMIAN EMPIRE

The day my city was destroyed started as any other.

It was Farvardin, the first month of spring's delicate warmth and life's rebirth, when the black chaos of death descended upon our city like the blazing hellfires of Jahannam. In the days to come, we children of Nishapur—the astronomers and poets, mathematicians and philosophers—would fall for seventy years into the pit of everlasting hell. The nineteen celestial angels cursed those of us who weren't shattered to pieces with garments of fire and a perpetual feast of thorns.

We howled in pain for Allah to save us, to deliver us from our torment, but the One God was deaf to our prayers.

At the first light of dawn, yawning merchants pushed creaking carts of fragrant cinnamon and the last of the winter pears toward the bazaar, spotted flycatchers darted from stuccoed eaves in search of insects, and the pale blue sky was filled with the sun's shining light. My mother had named me Fatima for that light, and for the Prophet's revered daughter, who died a martyr for our faith. I had no wish to live a glorious life as my namesake had, or to die a venerated death, but sought only to live in quiet ease and beauty, to keep an elegant home for my husband to return to each night after he became governor of Nishapur.

Hidden behind the high walls of our garden, delicate tulips opened their faces to the sun and fragrant pink blossoms garlanded spindly quince trees. The kitchen slaves, mostly Christians and a handful of Zoroastrians, had chosen a haunch of fresh lamb still streaked with rubied blood and pearled fat from the butcher that morning and argued now whether to season tonight's stew with figs or dried limes. Thus the scent of blood was already in the air before the invaders poured into Nishapur.

I smoothed my hair under its veil and gave the girls a gentle scolding for raising their voices on so pure a morning, then made my way to the balcony that overlooked the garden, the treasure of our home. The scent of jasmine and freshly turned earth filled my nose, and I lowered my head to my prayer rug, its red and gold silk knotted by my mother's deft hands before she had departed this life, gathered into Allah's waiting arms as a result of my cowardice. The perfume of the flowers was the smell of my childhood, reminding me of my mother in the garden, arms covered in dirt as she divided tulip bulbs or transplanted rosebushes while purple sunbirds darted amongst the hibiscus. I'd never understood why my mother didn't allow our many slaves to tend her flowers and shrubs, but I'd listened with my head in her lap when she spoke in her smooth voice about the plants she loved. She knew which ones Allah had created only for their beauty, or which—like the chamomile and mint my father used to calm his often sour stomach—also possessed healing qualities.

A profound calm wrapped around me, as if the One God cupped me in his hand, when I knelt on the prayer mat facing Makkah. I closed my eyes to let my soul fill with the imam's clear voice rising from the main mosque, so beautiful the birds ceased their songs to listen to the call beckoning the faithful to prayer. This was one of my favorite sounds, and five times a day it filled my heart with joy and calmed my mind.

Allahu Akbar. Sam'i Allahu liman hamidah, Rabbana wa lakal hamd.
   God is most great. God hears those who call upon Him; Our Lord, praise be to You.

I imagined the men filling the mosque's dainty courtyard, pausing to wash their hands and feet in the delicate fountains and combing their dark hair flat against their heads. My father would be there with a crimson-and-gold prayer mat identical to mine, another gift from my mother. Mansoor would help him find his place and together they would honor Allah.

My marriage to Mansoor was arranged by our parents, of course, but my father had waited until I was nineteen—far beyond the usual age for girls to marry—to choose my groom. I'd been pleased to learn the art of love in my husband's patient arms, but the months had turned to years and my womb had never quickened with his seed. I had failed my husband, yet Mansoor refused to take another wife, something not even my father understood.

"What need have I for a child?" my husband asked once, kissing away my silent tears. "I have all I require in this life in you, dearest Fatima."

And so, unable to give my husband a child, I gave him everything else I could. I massaged his back with rose oil when he came home each night, served him his favorite lamb-and-mint stew on delicate porcelain plates from Cathay, and listened attentively to his talk of tax disputes and trade ledgers from Nishapur's lucrative turquoise trade.

This afternoon, after their prayers, my husband would lead Father to our home and I would oversee the slaves as they served my men the midday meal of sweet brittle bread and pomegranate soup.

Mine was a beautiful life, and one I'd been bred to live.

I lifted my voice in an ululating prayer for my mother's soul as I'd do until the traditional four years of mourning had passed. Once the last note had faded into the sky, I rolled up my prayer rug and padded back inside on bare feet, pausing to rinse my mouth with rose water and wincing at the lumpy silk bag that remained by the door, accusing me with its very presence. The poet narcissus bulbs inside were a gift from my father, culled from my mother's garden. I had promised my father I'd plant them, but in truth I couldn't bear to touch them without being reminded of the role I'd played in allowing my mother's soul to fall into the fires of Jahannam, imperiling myself at the same time. Instead, I nudged the bag behind the loom strung with the prayer rug I'd been weaving as a name-day gift for Mansoor, its vibrant red-tulip border meant to symbolize undying love. My husband appreciated beauty in all its forms, and so I'd wed a man who prized my weaving and calligraphy as much as he worshipped the curves of my body. I flushed at the thought of our lovemaking last night in the garden below, our skin damp from the heat and perfumed from the carpet of lilac blossoms we'd lain upon.

I tucked a stray tendril of hair beneath my head scarf and settled into Mansoor's favorite chair, vacillating between reading the illuminated verses of Nishapur's famous poet Omar Khayyám and dabbling with my brushes and ink while I waited for my men to return. The book and my writing remained untouched as my eyelids grew heavy and I drifted toward dreams, seeing Mansoor walking away from me with a sad smile on his face. My hold on the inkpot loosened, and the glass bottle fell and shattered, fingers of black ink spreading across the turquoise tiles. I stood to summon a slave to clean the mess but started as a feral scream rent the air, gooseflesh rolling down my skin as the terrible sound crescendoed like the trumpet blast that would herald the Day of Arising.

Heart pounding, I ran to the edge of the balcony. Our home sat near the city walls, perfectly situated to capture the cool mountain breezes in the summer, but now the streets were choked with people fleeing toward the center of town, veiled mothers tucking precious children under their arms and wives clutching their husbands' hands as they stumbled away from certain death.

Mongol horsemen, multiplied like locusts, swarmed over the hills.

And the walls.

Last winter we'd watched the Mongol hordes descend upon us as the trees shed their last leaves. The heathen warlords had demanded our empire's surrender before they shed our blood, but the sultan ordered the massacre of their first emissaries, and their second envoys were humiliated by having their beards shaved in the streets and the Khan's gifts of camels and silver seized. The third messenger from Genghis Khan bore only a letter of four words:

You have chosen war.

Still, we did not worry, for the Khwarazmian Empire was ancient and strong, surely more powerful than a group of filthy soldiers dressed in squirrel skins and reeking of horses. Then came the news that Genghis Khan had captured and executed the governor of Otrar, dragging him screaming from the city's citadel and pouring molten silver down his nose and throat. The Mongols had arrived at Nishapur soon after and demanded our surrender outside the great Gate of the Silversmiths with its massive panels of beaten metal and turquoise studs. During those tense hours, the words of Omar Khayyám's famous poem *Rubáiyát* had replayed over and over in my mind.

> *Awake! For morning in the Bowl of Night*
> *Has flung the stone that puts the stars to flight:*
> *And Lo! The Hunter of the East has caught*
> *The Sultan's Turret in a Noose of Life.*

At our refusal of their terms, the sun had swallowed the moon in a ring of fire and one of our soldiers launched the fateful arrow that lodged in the heart of a young Mongol general bedecked in a horsehair helmet. We learned later that he was the husband of Al-Altun, Genghis Khan's youngest daughter from a lesser wife, but the swarms of dreaded horsemen fled after his fall, leaving us in stunned peace. Afterward, Father claimed we should leave the city in case the Khan of Khans ordered the heathens to return, but Mansoor's position as vice-governor of Nishapur required his presence. I refused to abandon my husband or the city of my birth, to forsake my mother's grave and the memories of walking with her to the bazaar to buy saffron for the *ash-e* soup my father adored.

Nishapur had celebrated after the Mongols fled, people filling the streets and claiming that the moon was like the Mongol hordes, too small to swallow the sun of our turquoise city. We didn't realize then that the ring of sun fire wasn't a sign of our victory, but an omen of our impending doom.

My knees buckled as I realized we were under attack for a second time, and for a moment I thought to hide. Instead, I hesitated, running downstairs to order in a calm voice that the slaves go to the cellar. Then I vacillated over whether I should try to find Mansoor or bar the doors against the barbarian invaders. I moaned aloud to think of the Mongols in our house, stealing our silver candelabra, tramping across the silken carpets, and tearing apart the leather-bound Qur'an passed down through the generations of Mansoor's family.

But none of that would matter if I died. Or if Mansoor died.

The Mongols had already cut a bloody swath through Nishapur by the time I finally tripped down the stairs and burst barefoot into the chaos. The burly baker from the shop down the street knocked me into the wall, his arms coated with flour and eyes ravaged with shock and grief. I gasped to see his wife's broken body in his arms, her veil torn away and glazed eyes open in death. A boy stumbled past, holding his stomach as if about to be sick. He stopped, eyes unseeing as he grabbed my arm and bent double to cough. The spray of crimson that spattered my own veil matched the blood seeping between his fingers. I shook him off and fought against the current of terror to elbow my way toward the mosque.

Screams came from inside the tiled walls. I jumped back when the iron gates were flung open, and men in prayer caps were cut down by wild-eyed Mongols dressed in filthy furs and leather vests stained with years of blood. Pages of the Qur'an fluttered in the air, its sacred verses shredded by swords and spattered with crimson. I fell to the ground, feigning death despite my pounding heart, while men around me screamed to Allah and the Mongols barked unintelligible commands. I dared not move and give myself away. It seemed an eternity before the sounds of pounding hooves and swords against bone finally moved on and I was able to stumble to the gates amidst the groans of dying men. Inside, the sacred grounds were trampled with sacrilegious dirt and blood.

So much blood.

I recoiled from the unholy sight. Men lay sprawled on their prayer mats, limbs splayed, with arrows and spear shafts embedded in their chests. One man rolled in agony, frothy red bubbles at his mouth as he clutched his abdomen. A quarrel with spotted feathers protruded from his stomach, but his blood-slicked hands slipped as he tried to pull it away. I could feel the life draining from him, his tortured soul straining to greet Allah.

"Help me," he moaned. "Please."

I turned away, making the sign against the evil eye with one hand. I was a coward, unwilling to speed a dying man to his death. Instead, I ran through the mosque, my bare feet leaving a trail of red footprints in my wake, further desecrating the holy ground.

Every step brought me to a new body; every stranger's face twisted with death gave me hope that my father and Mansoor had escaped the carnage. Something caught my eye at the base of the mihrab, the tall arched niche directing the faithful toward Makkah and closer to Allah.

The dull gleam of red silk on the floor, interwoven with gold.

An animal moan escaped my lips and I fell to my knees, crawling toward the precious bare head scattered with brown spots and wisps of gray hair. My father's prayer rug was drenched with blood, his body laid out as if awaiting a shroud. The flesh at his neck had been sliced open so that his blood wrapped around his neck like a winter scarf and his unseeing eyes still stared in shock at the face of his killer. I pressed my fist to my lips, muffling my howl as I crouched low and rocked on my heels.

"Fatima."

I gasped and looked to the crumpled form that uttered my name. Mansoor lay curled on his side, face pale and body shaking. I crawled to my beautiful husband and pulled his head into my lap, my fingers fluttering against his chest. We had sat like this only days ago in the garden, a moment of everyday happiness among the jasmine and tulips. Now a nightmare surrounded us.

"I tried to help him," Mansoor said, "but it happened so fast—"

He was wracked with coughing, flecks of shiny blood spraying my yellow robe. An alarming trickle of red slipped down his lips to his chin, the same lips that had kissed me so tenderly only that morning.

"Everything will be all right." I glanced around frantically, but Mansoor's hand closed on mine, cold and clammy. I recognized the unmistakable brush of death from my mother's last moments.

"Run, Fatima," he whispered, more blood trickling from his lips. "Before the heathens find you. Hide in the cellar—you'll be safe there."

I shook my head violently, touching his lips with my fingers and catching the scent of the mint leaves he loved to chew, mixed with the copper tang of blood that made my stomach revolt. "I won't leave you."

"You must," he said, his hand brushing my cheek beneath my veil. "Live for both of us, Fatima, and I'll meet you in the gardens of Jannah."

"You won't," I sobbed, for, unbeknownst to anyone, I had damned my soul the night my mother died. It was not Mansoor and the gardens of Jannah that I would see in the afterlife, but the hellfires of Jahannam. "Don't you dare leave me."

But the life faded from Mansoor's eyes, his soul gathered into death's waiting arms to return to Allah's glorious light. And I was left behind, a widow wearing the blood of both my father and my husband, wreathed by a courtyard full of corpses and dying men.

I hid not in the darkness of our cellar like some hunted vermin, but instead, scarcely able to see through my kohl-stained tears, I stumbled up the steps of the minbar to where the cleric would lead the faithful in their prayers. The white-bearded imam was still there, his body sprawled facedown on the steps. I muttered my apologies as I stepped over him, then curled into myself at the top of the platform, shielding my ears from the screams of battle and the cries of dying men that filtered through the windows along with the sun. The world had come undone, but I would wait until darkness fell and then wash Mansoor's and my father's bodies so they would be prepared to greet Allah.

I wished for sleep, but grief and terror kept my body taut, leaving me to alternate between a terrible numbness and fearful tremors that threatened to crack my teeth. When darkness finally fell I picked my way over the imam to the fountains. Silence shrouded my once-proud city as if it had been abandoned, and the water had stopped for the first time I could remember. The Mongols had been known to divert entire rivers to besiege cities; they must have cut off Nishapur's water supply.

For a moment I almost despaired—the bodies of my beloved and my father must be washed and arranged before they could greet Allah. Yet gleaming at the bottom of the cheerful turquoise-and-white tiles was water not yet drained or evaporated, still containing the impurities and prayers of men now dead. I removed my head scarf and veil, letting them absorb the water and grimacing as my husband's blood seeped from my hands into the water, smoky red tendrils reaching out to brush the sides of the fountain.

I bathed my father and Mansoor as best I could, but none of my ministrations could wash away all the bloodstains and nothing could mend the wound in my father's neck to make him whole again. I kept the brush that I found in Mansoor's pocket, its wooden tip marred with sharp grooves where he'd bit it absentmindedly while reconciling accounts only last night. My father's pocket contained a small silk bag with the last of my mother's narcissus bulbs. The innocent blossoms would be downy white with a crimson-gold corona, and the fragrance when they bloomed seemed sent by the angels themselves. Yet the bulbs . . .

The bulbs of the poet narcissus were lethal, inducing vomiting with the slightest taste and death with the merest bite. I knew not when I would need them, but I recognized the gift from my parents and from Allah.

There was no linen with which to wrap the bodies, but I rolled my father and Mansoor onto their right sides toward Makkah and tore my veil in half to cover their faces, praying that Allah would forgive the hasty preparations as he'd done for the victims of the ancient Battle of Uhud. My men would have been dead a full day by the time the sun reached its zenith, the longest a body could be left aboveground without facing penalties in the hereafter. Surely Allah would show mercy on their souls.

The din of battle seemed to have died along with the sun, and I swayed on my feet to see the hungry flies gathered on the eyes and wounds of the dead. Standing under the empty dome of the mosque, I threw three handfuls of earth I'd stolen from under the rosebushes in the mosque's courtyard onto the bodies of my husband and father.

"*Inna lillaahi wa inna ilayhi Raaji'oon*," I said, intoning the prayer of death as the black dirt crumbled over their hearts.

To Allah we belong and to Allah we return.

The verse fell empty from my lips, but I repeated it until the words ran together and the leering moon crept from behind a cloud. Still, the words did nothing to lighten the weight of my grief. Trapped within the city walls and unable to leave the men I loved, I took up Mansoor's calligraphy brush.

I was still writing when dawn warmed the sky and footsteps entered the mosque, my delicate calligraphy made of their blood decorating the tiles around their bodies with the stories of their lives. Terrible laughter bubbled in my throat several times as I thought of how I must appear, my hair wild while I painted with blood, but I had nowhere else to go, nothing else to do. I stood on the precipice of madness, unsure whether to stay where I was or to jump into the yawning abyss.

The footsteps stopped behind me, but I cared little if a Mongol heathen stood poised to loose an arrow at me. I thought of Mansoor's final words, and at that moment, I knew not whether I wanted to live or to die.

The intruder hovered behind me and my every muscle tensed, waiting for the inevitable blow.

Instead, the man spoke to me in my native Farsi. "Stand," he ordered.

I didn't move. I recalled stories of cities vanquished by the Mongol horsemen, of the men slaughtered and women and children distributed as wives and slaves. The heathen repeated himself, but still I didn't move. It wasn't until the sharp tip of his hooked lance prodded my ribs that I turned.

There was not one man, but two, although the second was scarcely more than a boy, with his lanky arms and faint shadow of a mustache. The fur ruff on the first man's helmet stood motionless in the mosque's foul air, but the hoops in his ears and the golden ring in his nose gleamed in the moonlight. He poked me again and motioned toward the arched entrance.

"Come," he said, glancing at the two bodies behind me. "There's nothing more you can do for them now."

I looked down at my father and Mansoor, thinking to throw myself on the man's lance, but my insides turned to water at the thought of feeling the weapon lodge itself in my belly, the soldier yanking it out covered in my blood, laughing as I died.

I was a coward.

Panic threatened to bring me to my knees at the thought of leaving the men I loved, but the Mongol prodded me more gently. Later I would wonder whether it was the instinct to survive that moved me or whether divine grace—or perhaps punishment—kept me on my feet.

The soldier herded me into a deserted alley, but the younger one's face lacked conviction when he pointed his curved sword at me. A waterfall of early jasmine blossoms poured from a white balcony overhead, an oasis of beauty amidst the bloody chaos. At the end of the alley, another Mongol released his waters in a foul yellow stream, grinning widely.

He urinated on the body of a slain Persian woman.

The foul beast glanced at me and licked his lips over two rows of crooked teeth before he turned and continued urinating. The tall soldier pushed me out of the alley and into the soft spring sunshine, so at odds with the carnage all around me in the streets.

Bodies. The sight of bodies filled my vision, their blank eyes staring at me and skin shining like wax in the early sunlight.

I almost stumbled over a broken old man with limbs bent at wrong angles. I wondered fleetingly if some had managed to escape, but the images of the dead overwhelmed me so I could no longer think.

I looked to the sky then, letting the soldier prod me through the streets, past the blue-domed roof of the tomb of famed poet-astronomer Omar Khayyám, and up the steps to the city walls, snippets of prayers tumbling through my mind. My life was in Allah's hands now, as it had ever been.

We walked along the ramparts, the breeze lashing my tangled hair about my face and heavy with the smell of rain soon to come. We drew to a halt above the Gate of the Silversmiths, still studded with the scaling ladders the Mongols had used to penetrate the walls. Before me stood two commanders, their backs to us as they gestured to the plain before the city, situated between Mount Binalud in the distance and the pear and apricot orchards that bordered the walls. I saw then where the survivors had gone, not escaped but herded like beasts awaiting slaughter. The Mongols had taken Nishapur, but they weren't finished with it, or its people.

The soldier behind me spoke again, addressing the generals, and I would have gaped had I not already been so battered by the events of the day. These were no ordinary commanders, but women dressed as soldiers. One was scarcely more than a child, with high cheekbones and full lips, yet her belly was swollen in the final months of pregnancy and her eyes were hard under her furred helmet. The other was slight and closer to my mother's age, but I felt as if death wrapped its hand around my heart when she leveled her mismatched eyes at me; it was akin to staring into the gaze of an angry djinn.

The soldier repeated himself, but the pregnant one turned her back to us. The other lifted my hands to inspect my fingers, stained with blood.

"Shigi thought we might be interested in you," she said, her Farsi bent with the guttural consonants of the Mongols. I saw the intricate silver cross of the messiah Isa Ibn Maryam at her throat and wondered which conquered people she had stolen it from. "A Persian woman found writing over the bodies of the dead is a rare treasure indeed."

I was unaccustomed to such scrutiny from someone so obviously below me in stature, but I tipped my chin and said nothing.

"You have the strength of these mountains in your soul," she said, holding my chin and tilting it to see my eyes, then gesturing to Mount Binalud to the north. "That will serve you well in the days to come." The pretty one spoke over her shoulder, and the djinn answered in the mongrel tongue before letting her hand drop. "Al-Altun says I should kill you," she said to me, so that my heart lurched. "But I have need of a scribe."

"You mean a slave." I taunted her with my scalding tone, half hoping she'd stab me through the belly and end my misery. I recognized the name Al-Altun as Genghis Khan's daughter, the wife of the general who fell during the first Mongol raid against Nishapur earlier in the winter.

"I am Toregene, wife of Ogodei, the third son of Genghis Khan. I don't eat my slaves, wear their teeth as necklaces, or use their bones to decorate my tent, contrary to what you may have heard."

I'd heard all those rumors about the Mongols, but I only attempted to look down my nose at her, a difficult feat as we were the same height.

Her gaze flicked beyond me to the orchards and Nishapur's survivors. "You'll be treated well," she said in a tone of dismissal. "Shigi will take you to my tent now."

"And if I won't go?"

"You will," she said, "if only because a woman in your position has no other choice."

I didn't know if she meant that this regiment of bloodthirsty heathens wouldn't hesitate to rape me, or she guessed that, unlike my mother, I lacked the courage to follow my husband and father into the next life. I'd heard stories of the dreaded Khan kidnapping women from other clans, to marry them himself or wed them to his sons, and wondered if perhaps this woman had once been on the losing side of the Mongols' destruction.

It didn't matter what trials this woman had once faced. The Mongols were an abomination and deserved to writhe in the flames of Jahannam for eternity.

Toregene pushed past me, pausing long enough to linger at Shigi's elbow. She murmured something to him in the Mongol tongue, then gave a pointed look at the plains, covered with Nishapur's gathered sons and daughters.

"What do you say?" I asked, my throat constricting in fear. "What will happen to them?"

Toregene ignored me, and Shigi prodded me with his sword, guiding me down the wall and out the Gate of the Silversmiths. I swayed at the smell and the sight of the carrion crows gorging themselves on the bloated bodies in the moat and tried to keep the stench away with my sleeve, but it burned itself into my soul.

The turtledoves fell silent as I passed the smaller group of the walking dead, mostly women and children, and a few men I guessed to be scholars and artisans from their long beards and ink-stained fingers. The men wore the same vacant eyes and haggard expressions, their clothes spattered with the blood of their loved ones and their cheeks streaked with dried tears. The Mongols and their horses had trampled the ground, stripping the leaves from the apricot trees and tearing the grass from its roots.

Shigi urged me to hurry, but my feet felt like boulders, and we hadn't yet reached the largest of the white tents beyond the orchards when the screams began.

A gentle rain pattered down, changing the ground to mud. Horsemen pounded behind us, and I turned to watch in horror as people tried to escape, running as if chased by demons, only to be hunted by spears and stabbed by Mongol swords. Some were beaten back with fists and sword hilts, sometimes worse. I watched dumbstruck, unable to move, as if I was a sparrow in the shadow of a soaring hawk.

The Mongols struck down everyone who served no use to them—Nishapur's remaining men, the elderly, and the infirm were slaughtered like penned sheep. Shigi tried to push me into Toregene's tent, but I fought him until he let me stumble to the ground, rendered deaf and mute by the sight before me.

The killings went on until night fell, until the bodies outnumbered the stars in the sky.

Exhausted, I crouched in the mud, listening to the keening around me and wishing I could pray, but my mind was numb. The two women stood on the walls again, surveying the corpse of our once-proud city. Then the young one—Al-Altun—threw her head back and let out a battle cry of victory that chilled my very soul.

This woman had decimated my city, killed my family, and turned my dreams to dust. I knew then what it was to hate, to feel the lust for revenge settle like a vulture in my heart.

Later it would be said that seventy thousand of our brave soldiers lost their lives at Nishapur, akin to washing away all the grains of sand on a beach. Al-Altun left nothing alive inside Nishapur, for the Mongol swords cut down even the cats and dogs. I doubt the heathens left even a rat breathing within those walls.

Unable to do anything else, I beat my fists into the earth and screamed one question at Allah.

Why?

The next morning, the djinn from the walls roused me from the filthy blanket I'd fallen asleep on in her tent, dragging me from my nightmares of Mansoor's dying eyes and my father's broken body to a reality worse than any dream. Toregene had tried to press the woolen outfit of a Mongol slave on me, but I'd informed her that I'd rather die than leave my home dressed as a heathen, half hoping she'd order me killed where I stood. In-stead, she'd arched an eyebrow and ordered Shigi to find me a set of

Persian clothes. Alone in her tent, I set aside my ruined attire and stood naked for a moment, then ripped a part of the sleeve stained with Mansoor's blood from my old robe and tucked it into the pocket of my new clothes. That dark stain and his writing brush were all I had left from my husband, a bag of narcissus bulbs all that remained from my mother and father. And around my neck I wore something new: the silver medallion imprinted with Toregene's symbol of a tiger that branded me her slave.

I donned the robe and trousers, cringing at the inferior silk and almost gagging at the veil's smell of cheap violet perfume. Like the meanest *darvīsh*, I would learn humility, although unlike the pungent ascetics with their vows of poverty, I did not choose this. I had no kohl with which to paint my eyes, and my lashes were stiff with dried tears, but I took a deep breath and stepped outside under the same warm sun that had witnessed such slaughter only the day before.

Toregene was waiting for me, dressed as a warrior queen in an iron helm ruffed with black sable and a gleaming cutlass at her hip. "Follow me," she said. "And I'd suggest you keep your eyes on the ground."

But I couldn't ignore the death throes of my city. My courage had fled yesterday, but today I would bear witness to what had happened here. I would remember, for so many others could not.

Just as I'd been debased, Nishapur's towering gates had been stripped of their turquoise and precious metals so only the battered wooden planks remained. My city was a skeleton now, and corpses and the carcasses of horses littered the plains outside the exposed gates. The earth was greasy with human fat, and mountains of decapitated heads stood taller than the walls, their skin already rotting and shrinking in the sun with a stench that made me sway on my feet. The jaws hung open, frozen in silent screams as we passed.

Swarms of bowlegged soldiers finished pillaging Nishapur, loading our famed white oxen and the docile asses, each worth thirty marks of silver, with our remaining silk, steel swords, and filigreed books. One day, caravans would pass our broken city, its majestic mosques still bearing carved bands of calligraphy and arabesque, but robbed of its fabled treasures and deserted of its people. Would travelers pause inside our barren houses and ponder our stories? Would some linger and take up plows in our abandoned fields, or would our ruined city waste away, worn by the winds until it crumbled to sand?

I had never walked—or, more accurately, been carried in our curtained sedan—far enough from Nishapur that I couldn't turn and see its reassuring sprawl. Now I would leave behind forever its familiar skyline of minarets and turquoise-tiled domes that guided travelers from the Silk Road to us like an oasis. So, too, would I leave behind the graves of loved ones so that my heart shriveled now into some black, misshapen thing, saved from annihilation only by the glowing ember of revenge that burned deep in my breast under the silver slave's medallion.

My knees threatened to buckle, but Toregene's hand on my arm propelled me forward. I was reminded of Omar Khayyám's famous poem as my scalp prickled with the accusing stares of tens of thousands of sightless skulls.

> *Whether at Nishapur or Babylon,*
> *Whether the Cup with sweet or bitter run,*
> *The Wine of Life keeps oozing drop by drop,*
> *The Leaves of Life keep falling one by one.*

Toregene beckoned to where Shigi held the reins of a sleek brown stallion and a disreputable gray mare. Most of the Mongols walked bandy-legged, as if they were incomplete without a horse between their thighs. I, however, had never ridden one of the stinking beasts in my life.

Thus began my next ordeal.

"Surely the horse should carry something more important than a slave," I said, failing to sound demure as I'd hoped. "I shall ride in a cart."

"Carts are for invalids and old women," Toregene said, stepping into the iron stirrup with one foot and throwing her other leg over the wooden saddle, embellished with tooled leather and geometric bronze castings. "The mare is old enough for the stewpot; even a child could control her."

I prayed Toregene wasn't serious about cooking the horse, but the gray mare snorted and threw its head. The animal seemed more likely to trample me at any moment, and I'd not yet mounted her.

I struggled to maneuver my curved boot into the flat stirrup, then attempted to swing my leg up as Toregene had done. I flushed to my hairline when Shigi had to boost me over, his hands touching my waist and backside.

"This is your first time on a horse?" he asked, the corner of his lip quirking in amusement.

"It is."

"May your god protect you, then," he said.

I looked down my nose at him as he rifled through a nearby cart, then returned with something hidden behind his back. He revealed a small satin pillow with a gleam in his eye. "Mongolian saddles are comfortable for the horse, but not for the rider. You may soon find this more precious than gold."

I sniffed at his implication that I was somehow weak, but no matter how I shifted in the saddle, I could find no ease. I took the pillow and laid it in my lap, staring straight ahead.

"Where is Al-Altun?" I asked, although the name of my city's murderer was so bitter I could scarcely utter it.

"The Khatun of the Uighurs departed with her plunder while we slept," Toregene said. "She returns to govern her husband's lands."

And so, like a thief in the night, Al-Altun stole Nishapur's artisans and engineers, crates of pistachios and saffron, and skeins of silk embroidered with birds and beasts, also taking the opportunity for my revenge.

I swore in that moment that I would wait for her, that I would find her one dark day and watch the light leave her eyes just as it had faded from my husband's.

Thus we began our journey east, leaving my home and the splendid life I'd once lived. The stirrups were short—I'd later learn they were designed for riders who stood in the saddle while launching arrows—so my knees were bent at an awkward angle that already made my legs ache. We'd scarcely descended the first hill when my demon mare jerked to the left at a gallop, and I sailed into a bush of thorns, scraping the side of my face and narrowly avoiding the powerful hooves that threatened to crush my skull.

The thin silk of my veil hadn't protected my skin, so the flesh of my cheek wept blood, but the thick robe had protected my arms from the worst of the brambles.

"One end bites and the other kicks." Shigi offered me the reins of my ill-behaved horse from atop his mount. The triumphant mare snorted and grazed on dried brambles. I hoped she'd choke on them.

Toregene laughed again. "Just imagine how good this horse will taste in your soup when we return home to the steppes. Revenge is sweet, or in this case, it will be when flavored with salt and garlic."

My stomach turned at the thought of eating horse stew, and my eyes stung as I pressed my fingers against the scratches on my cheek, but I clenched the reins to gain control of myself. I longed for a lunch of courgette blossoms stuffed with soft cheese or veal served with olives and preserved lemons, but now I'd survive off whatever these heathens ate. Likely gristle and fermented blood.

I managed to mount again, this time with the pillow Shigi had given me, and Toregene distracted me by pointing out rocks and birds and teaching me their Mongol translations. The fresh-faced soldier from the mosque— Boyahoe—joined us, although he was interested only in the Farsi translations for weaponry.

"Boyahoe is my sister Alaqai's son and has spent these past years learning war from the Khan," Toregene said. "He was a reluctant warrior when he came to us."

"No longer." Boyahoe grinned, a chipped tooth marring the smile, but he sobered at my pained expression. "Being a soldier has taught me courage. I was skittish as a desert fox before the Khan took me in."

Shigi chuckled. "What Boyahoe means is that he'd have been killed when his people revolted. Alaqai rescued him from certain death, but we don't hold it against him."

Boyahoe's rather large ears turned red and he offered a sheepish smile. "I'm happy to learn from the Khan of Khans, despite these two brutes."

The three of them settled into conversation, but I reflected on Boyahoe's lesson. I, too, would learn from these Mongols, study their strengths and root out their weaknesses so that one day I might wield them as weapons.

We passed the towering green-and-white Solitary Tree where Alexander the Macedonian and King Darius had fought, before fording countless rivers and continuing to chase the rising sun. The endless expanse of the steppes made me feel lost and insignificant—something I'd never experienced before these Mongols came crashing into my life—cast adrift in these wild lands like a snowflake in a vast desert. The clouds hung heavy, like smudges of charcoal across a sodden sky, as if Allah had turned his back on this heathen world, and on me.

Many times I wished I'd died in Nishapur, especially when I lay shivering on my cold pallet at night and recalled the evenings I'd fallen asleep warm in Mansoor's arms, and when my hands grew brown and calloused from the reins I clasped tight every day, so I was beyond grateful for Shigi's gifted pillow, which allowed me to walk each night I dismounted. I almost fainted the first time I watched the Mongols eat, slurping their rehydrated milk paste and cramming their gullets full of raw meat tenderized under their saddles after a day of riding. One careless soldier lost his leather flask during a long gallop, and he remedied his thirst by piercing a vein in his horse's neck, drinking the blood straight from the animal, and then leering at me with teeth stained scarlet.

Each day was a punishment worthy of the meanest traitor on the Day of Judgment. And each morning I opened my eyes to live it once again.

We kept a brutal pace, for I soon learned that the harder a Mongol rides, the more he sweats and the less often he needs to empty his bladder. Each night I stumbled from my horse to the traveling tent I shared with Toregene, its thin felt walls replacing the elegant cornices and domes I'd once known. Often I woke to find her pallet empty, and I would set about boiling water for her salt tea, a skill she and Shigi had laughingly taught me the first morning on the trail. My cheeks had flared at the insult, but they had sobered to see my humiliation, both at the fact that I knew not how to boil water and because I'd been reduced to performing such menial tasks.

"Life isn't a placid lake, unchanging with the years and seasons," Toregene said, lifting the iron cauldron onto the metal spider while Shigi stoked the meager flames below. They shared a glance then, one that I might have called tenderness had it not been for the tears that blurred my vision.

"It's more like a river," Shigi said, straightening. "Sometimes frozen in winter, but more often diving and plunging over rocks, engorged with spring rains." He smiled and touched my shoulder, dropping his hand at my recoil. "Rivers change their course, Fatima of Nishapur, just as your life has changed its course."

Yet I wished and prayed for only one thing: the return of my old life.

We passed mounds of boulders that were littered with horse skulls—ancient burials, according to Shigi—and primitive stone steles carved to resemble men and scrawled with crude images of deer, before finally arriving at the base of the Altun Mountains. A camp of circular white tents lay cradled among the foothills, situated along a clear river filled with massive fish like overgrown eels that Toregene claimed no self-respecting Mongol would ever eat. She declared this was one of the most beautiful spots in all of Mongolia, but to me it was simply another desolate plain.

"Home awaits, whether we wish it or not." Toregene breathed a deep sigh worthy of an old crone's death rattle. "It will be good to see my sons again, especially my eldest, Güyük."

She spurred her horse ahead so I had no choice but to follow and weave my way through the labyrinth of ragged tents and mongrel dogs, past a dusty boy wearing only shoes and chewing on the end of a bone. I swallowed a screech of fear and clutched the pommel of my saddle. "What in the name of Allah is that?"

Toregene followed my gaze to where a herd of strange black-and-white beasts stood, the size of small elephants but covered with shaggy hair three hands long. She gave a low chuckle. "Yaks," she said. "They're the ugliest of the southern Five Snouts, but their hair is softer than silk."

But silk didn't share the same stench of dung and rotting hay.

Grinning fathers left our caravan to toss squealing children—some with bare bottoms streaked with mud and who knew what else—into the air, and teary wives with wide cheeks embraced husbands long feared dead. A few hopeful women searched in vain as the final carts creaked into view, but the bodies of their dead men had been left to rot aboveground, another savage custom I couldn't fathom. How could one leave a father, husband, or son exposed for wild dogs and vultures to tear apart?

I often doubted whether these Mongols were fully human; this was yet another proof that they were not.

I encountered still more evidence when a hunchbacked woman shook out an exquisite silk prayer rug, then trampled it with her muddy boots. I waited for Allah to smite her where she stood, but there were no bolts of lightning or sudden chasms opening below her.

Toregene scowled, but not at the woman desecrating the prayer rug. "That's odd," she said, shading her eyes from the sun. "There's someone else here."

I followed her gaze to where a cluster of carts and horses stood. To me, they looked no different from all the other dusty horses and rickety ox-carts, but Toregene's frown only deepened. "I'd thought Ogodei might greet us," she said, "but my husband is likely snoring under a table. Reconcile the ledgers for my carts—I don't want any of the men filching what belongs to my husband and sons. Find me in Ogodei's *ger* when you finish."

I looked around at the veritable city of identical tents, as bent and mean as a herd of old sheep. "How will I find it?"

"Listen for the loudest tent," Toregene said. "You'll find Ogodei inside."

I oversaw the unpacking of Toregene's carts while some men erected her tent. "Unload the scrolls first," I commanded, peering into a crate of yellowing scrolls from Nishapur's House of Wisdom with its ancient Babylonian tablets and Egyptian papyri. I prayed the illiterate Mongols wouldn't use the precious texts as kindling for their fires. The soldiers scowled and grudgingly followed my instruction, although I knew it was only because they'd overheard Toregene's orders. A pockmarked youth and a second boy with eyes that drooped at the corners wandered toward our commotion. The first picked up the occasional caged red falcon or glazed porcelain bowl before tossing them back into the crates. His flat face and wide cheeks marred any chance he ever had of being called handsome, and his leather boots and breeches smelled of a cow freshly slaughtered.

"Look what the sunrise brought." His gaze skimmed over my veil and travel-stained robe. "I've never had a Mohammedan in my bed before."

I recoiled at his ignorance and wished for once that I'd dressed as these heathens did. My fingers itched to slap him, or better yet—rip out his filthy tongue. The other slaves stopped what they were doing, but none spoke.

My skin crawling, I stepped closer to the repulsive boy, glad he was a fingerbreadth shorter than me. "I'd sooner slit my own throat," I murmured in Mongolian, "or skewer your manhood and serve it mixed with goat liver before I'd go to your bed."

His face burned like a furnace. "How dare you—"

"And you'll not speak to me again, lest you care to take up the matter with Toregene, wife of Ogodei."

"Toregene Khatun?" The fire in his face banked, and he grew sallow as I withdrew the silver tiger medallion from under my collar.

"Come along, Güyük," the second boy said. "Lest your mother find out what trouble you're causing."

Güyük. It took me a moment to recall Toregene's mention of her eldest son. I'd expected a young man with a smile like his mother's but instead confronted a foul demon whose white silk robe and gaudy green felt hat trimmed with ermine did little to cover his heathen stench.

"Keep your opinion to yourself, Kublai." Güyük grimaced, then stepped back and spat at me. The yellow glob of spittle spattered my hem and he stormed off, kicking up angry puffs of dust.

"My apologies for my cousin," the tall one said, tugging on the earflaps of his woolen hat. "He inherited his father's temper."

I watched them go, then turned to find Toregene's slaves staring at me. My glare scattered them and they continued unloading Toregene's leather saddles, embroidered pillows, and snowy oxen while I calmed my heart. Only once everything was situated did I seek out Ogodei's tent.

Smoke from the largest tent puffed into the air like steam on a winter's night, and a chuff of coarse laughter burst from inside, followed by trills of high-pitched giggles. Someone threw open the tent's door, snaring me in the shaft of light that poured from inside. I moved to retreat when I recognized the flat-nosed boy from the cart, but Güyük gave a feral grin and caught me by my wrist. "You won't get off so easy this time," he said.

He pulled me into the tent before I could protest. Soldiers dressed in stained leathers and ratty furs stood, sat, or sprawled wherever there was space, and the wine fumes on their foul breath could have felled a bear. I shirked their curious gazes and straightened my shoulders as if addressing my own slaves in Nishapur, praying to Allah that no one would notice the trembling in my hands or quaking of my knees under the pleats of my robe.

"Look what I found lurking outside," Güyük hollered. He dragged me before a huge man dressed in luxurious brown silk who reclined among overturned bowls in the middle of the tent. There was no denying their shared resemblance, although the son seemed a crude and misshapen shadow of his father.

So this was Toregene's husband, the son of Genghis Khan.

Ogodei's face was as ugly and pockmarked as Güyük's, his nose red and flat, and his arms were as wide as tree trunks. Yet he let out a ripe guffaw that made his mustache twitch, and his beetle black eyes sparkled with great mirth, as if he'd been blessed by Allah with all he could desire in this life. He clutched a drinking bowl in each hand—one of silver and the other of transparent yellow horn—and on his lap sprawled two women, both with matted hair and who seemed to have difficulty focusing their eyes. One draped her arm around his neck, pressing her breasts against his chest in a way that made my face burn, for I'd never so much as touched my husband outside the privacy of our own walls. Ogodei didn't seem to mind.

"This one has a tongue like a snake on her, Father," Güyük said. His friend Kublai sat next to him wearing the same apologetic expression he'd had at the cart. "Perhaps you should save us all the trouble and cut it out."

I didn't deign to acknowledge Güyük, and fortunately, neither did his father.

Instead, Ogodei shifted the women from his lap and balanced one elbow on his knee while a boy-slave filled his cup in the other hand. "If I cut out her tongue, she couldn't tell me where she's from, and I always like to know where beautiful women come from."

I glanced around for Toregene, but aside from a few slave-girls, all holding cauldrons and jugs of what I supposed was more alcohol, there were no other women among all these slavering men. This was the last place I wanted to be.

"I'd guess you're one of the slaves from Nishapur, or perhaps Otrar." Ogodei reached for one of the cauldrons and shocked me by withdrawing a soup bone. He cracked it in half over his knee, then dug inside before licking the marrow from his finger. He gestured with the bone to a place at his feet. "Sit, little rose."

Shigi cleared his throat, sitting cross-legged on a sheep-wool rug near the door. I hadn't realized he was here, although it appeared that he took dictation for Ogodei as I'd been told he had for the Khan.

"Her name is Fatima," he said. He glanced up from the papers in his lap. "You could claim her as your slave if you wish—"

This brought murmurs of approval and a few shouts of encouragement. I prayed for my legs to hold steady.

Shigi glanced at Ogodei. "But any man who touches her will have to deal with your wife."

"Which one?" Ogodei sniffed. "Toregene?"

Shigi nodded. "She's partial to this slave."

Ogodei recoiled from me as if I'd suddenly broken out in boils. "I try never to cross that wife."

I glanced at Shigi, but he had eyes only for his paper. I didn't care to be indebted to him, but it was better than being claimed by Ogodei. "I'll leave you to your wine, then," I said to Toregene's husband.

"Stay," Ogodei said. "And join us." He thrust his silver wine cup at me, golden rings on every finger, so the woman on his left pouted and the other scowled in my direction. "There's nothing in life that can't be improved with a bit of *airag* or a bowl of wine," he said. I expected his teeth to be brown and rotten, but they flashed white under his smile as he nudged the blade-thin man snoring on the floor with his boot. "Except perhaps my brother Tolui here."

The Qur'an forbid alcohol, but most Persians circumvented that law by boiling wine down until it grew thick and sweet. The pale yellow liquid in my hand was unboiled and unclean, yet I couldn't appear weak before this man. I took a long draft, then spat it onto the packed earth, wincing at my own crassness. Ogodei stared at me, but I shrugged. "I tasted finer in Nishapur," I lied.

His women looked at him as if waiting for him to explode, but his booming laugh threatened to bring down the felts. "Don't tell my little sister that," he said. "She brought that wine herself today, said she planned to drink an entire jug herself when she married again."

The wine's acrid taste clung to the insides of my mouth, and I longed to wipe my lips on my sleeve. Al-Altun was the blood daughter of Genghis Khan, the only daughter I was aware of, and therefore also Ogodei's sister. Hope flared in my chest that Al-Altun had come here instead of returning to her husband's lands, that I would meet her and see justice done for my family. "Your sister is here?" I asked.

Ogodei nodded, his eyes closed as the ragged women nibbled on his drooping ears. I averted my gaze, wishing for something to scrub the ghastly image from my mind. "An unexpected visit from her and her sprat," Ogodei said. "But necessary after her husband's death."

I stood suddenly. "I must go," I said. "Toregene will be expecting me."

"A pity," Ogodei said. "Feel free to visit us anytime, Rose of Nishapur."

"And send us any girls you see along your way," one of the men called. "Or perhaps a goat for Güyük!"

I would have smiled under my veil at the insult, but Güyük's glare stabbed me as I ducked outside, glad for the clean air that filled my lungs. Autumn would come soon, and with it, the need to plant the narcissus bulbs I kept tucked into my belt before they withered and spoiled. I had plenty for Al-Altun now, and with spring would come the opportunity to harvest and split the new growths in case I had need of them beyond tonight.

I pushed past bleating goats and sidestepped the occasional flea-bitten dog until I arrived where Toregene's white tent stood proudly among the now-empty carts. Her wooden door was carved with the head of a single snarling tiger and painted with vibrant hues of yellow, green, and blue, yet the workmanship was inferior to that found in the meanest shop in Nishapur.

I expected to find Toregene and Al-Altun inside, but instead I discerned three women wreathed in smoke as my eyes adjusted to the murky light. Al-Altun faced away from me with her head pillowed on a stranger's lap, and Toregene stirred a boiling cauldron over the new hearth fire. My hand tightened on the bulbs in my belt. I would have to find an excuse to chop them up, to stir them into the foul-smelling stew boiling atop the metal spider.

Al-Altun made a sound akin to an ox's snort. "I held him in my arms," she said, her voice quavering. "And then his battered soul slipped through my fingers."

Her words caught me in their wintry grip, the image of Mansoor's final moments filling my mind. I smelled the copper tang of death again and heard the shrieks of the grieving on the wind. I would avenge his death before I left this tent, despite the consequences to my already-stained soul.

Al-Altun heaved a shuddering sigh, sobs wracking her body. "I keep thinking of what I might have done differently, how I might have saved him."

Toregene rose from the fire, then knelt next to the grieving woman. "There's nothing you could have done," she said, clasping the woman's hands. "Jingue had his father's sickness."

Jingue. But I recalled Mansoor and my father discussing the first battle of Nishapur, when the Mongols had retreated. Al-Altun's slain husband had been called Tokuchar.

My heart fell and the visions of Mansoor fled as I realized that this grief-stricken widow wasn't Al-Altun at all.

"Join us, Fatima," Toregene commanded before I could gather my thoughts. "Alaqai, sister of my heart and eldest daughter of Genghis Khan, has received a terrible blow and traveled to our camp to recover."

Eldest daughter. So the bloodthirsty invader had sired more than one daughter.

The weeping woman sat up and wiped a sleeve across her nose, leaving behind a smear of tears and snot as if she were three years old instead of thirty. She was beyond the first flush of youth and her features were too strong to be called beautiful, yet a face such as hers would always draw attention. There was intensity in her every movement despite her puffy and bloodshot eyes, as if a gust of wind and burst of fire had somehow been trapped beneath her skin.

Toregene offered me a bowl of stew from the fire, a mix of greasy meat and gristle with several strands of goat hair floating on top. I'd never cooked a meal in my life—that's what slaves were for—but even the thorns served to those unfortunate souls in Jahannam would be a delicacy compared to this. I shook my head, my stomach threatening to revolt as she pressed it into my hand. "Alaqai made it," she whispered. "Eat, or she's likely to start crying again." She addressed the other two. "I claimed Fatima at Nishapur after she lost her family. She's a talented calligrapher."

After she lost her family.

I'd lost my husband and father only because these women's sister had ordered their slaughter.

Alaqai glanced at my bowl of stew and her lower lip quivered as she turned her glistening eyes toward me. "You don't like the stew?"

Toregene gave the bowl in my hands a pointed glance. I tipped it back and managed to gag down a mouthful without it coming back up. I'd never survive a second bite. "I should reconcile the ledgers," I lied, for I'd checked the accounts until I knew they were pristine. "I don't wish to intrude."

"You'll do no such thing," Alaqai said, her tone exactly as I imagined a queen's in a crowded throne room would be. "After all, you've also lost a husband, haven't you?"

My husband, and most of my heart.

"I thought so," Alaqai said, reading my expression and flopping down again. The woman whose lap served as her pillow was a tiny thing with a mole high on her cheek, and she possessed the skill of fading into the background so I'd almost forgotten she was there. Or perhaps she disappeared simply because the overwhelming force of Alaqai's presence pushed all others into the shadows. "One widow knows another," Alaqai said. "Toregene's first husband passed to the sacred mountains before she came to us, so only Sorkhokhtani here has been spared that particular grief."

"True," the tiny one said, her soothing voice reminding me of the call to prayer. "But only because I've also avoided the burden of love."

"Sorkhokhtani is Princess of the Hearth," Toregene said quietly. "She received news of Alaqai's impending arrival and traveled to meet her in my absence."

I nodded distractedly as I sought a way to empty my bowl without Alaqai's notice. If only I could throw the stew onto the fire when she wasn't looking, but the fumes would likely kill us all.

"My first marriage spared me love and also joy, but my second gave me love and my hellion of a son," Alaqai said, staring at the hole in the ceiling. "I once scoffed at Gurbesu for her three weddings, but only the gods know what my third marriage shall bring."

"Third?" I choked at both her blasphemy and the idea of taking three husbands, thankfully not at the same time, although I wouldn't put even that past these heathens.

"Alaqai weds Boyahoe in the morning," Toregene said calmly. "Although I've asked her to wait for the arrival of her mother. I'm sure Borte Khatun would wish to see you off."

"A widow is weak and broken in the eyes of the Onggud." Alaqai gave a derisive snort. "Despite my ten years being married to Jingue and the prosperity they brought to Olon Süme, they believe I can only be whole again once I marry a boy almost half my age. I cannot wait for my mother."

"Boyahoe had grown into a capable soldier," Toregene chided, "and a good man."

"I know, but he's not Jingue." Alaqai drew a shuddering sigh, pressing her fist into her heart. "No one can ever take his place."

"Of course not," Sorkhokhtani said. "But you must do what's best for Negudei now. Your son and his lands must be your main concern."

Alaqai sat up, rubbing her temples. "That's why I'm here. Negudei is all I have left of Jingue," she said, her lip trembling again. "That boy is wilder than I was at his age, yet every glimpse of him reminds me of his father. I'd do anything for that child, yet I can't help wondering . . . Teb Tengeri once told me I carried death in my heart. I've outlived two husbands and I have no desire to outlive a third. Not only that, but I'd wish for more for Boyahoe than to marry his brother's old widow."

"You're hardly old," Toregene said. "For if you were, that would make me a crone."

"I'm thirty-one," Alaqai said. "I'm old enough to be Boyahoe's mother."

"His very *young* mother," Toregene corrected, a smile playing at her lips. "You're only nine years older than Boyahoe, and he's no longer a fledgling falcon whose feathers are still gray. Many women would tremble with anticipation at having such a young man in their bed."

"You have your son and your kingdom," Sorkhokhtani said, changing the subject while her fingers stroked Alaqai's hair as if she were playing a lute. "In the absence of all else, our children still give our lives meaning."

I was glad for the darkness that hid my face then. I had no parents, no husband, and no children, nothing to keep me tethered to this life, save my desire for revenge.

Alaqai seemed to sense my sadness and leaned toward me. She removed a comb from her hair and tucked it behind my ear. I touched it, trying to make out its shape with my fingers.

"A jade tiger," she said. "A gift from one widow to another, so we never forget that we're not alone."

"Thank you," I said, almost stuttering the words. "But I have nothing to give you."

She smiled then. "You ate my stew. That's gift enough for me."

I listened with one ear as Alaqai lay down again and the women talked of Genghis' latest forays into Persia and plans for the coming winter. I kept my fingers and my imagination busy assembling a platter of soft cheese and wine to replace the inedible slop Alaqai had tried to poison us with, even as my guts protested over the lone bite—I doubted whether even pigs would eat the gray swill.

Only once Alaqai had drifted into a fitful sleep and Sorkhokhtani had slipped away to take her husband to their tent did I find Toregene at my elbow.

"Did Ogodei offer to sleep with you?"

How does one answer a woman when asked about her randy bull of a husband's lewd propositioning? I checked Toregene's expression for venom, but her features were as placid as if she'd just commented on the existence of the sun. I hesitated, then decided to tell her the truth.

"He did," I said, wondering whether I should tell her of Güyük's offer as well. No woman wanted to hear that a son of her womb was a womanizing wretch, so I spared her. "But I refused."

Toregene shrugged. "Ogodei can be terribly charming when he chooses. Few decline his advances." She spoke detachedly, as if she didn't care how many women her husband took to steed, but it seemed contrived. "Ogodei isn't as wily as his father, but neither is he stupid. If he bides his time, one day he'll be Khan."

I wondered if we were speaking of the same man. "How can you be sure the Khan won't choose one of his other sons?"

She ticked off the other possible heirs on her fingers. "Jochi and Chaghatai are the elder brothers, but they got into an awful brawl over that very question and each threatened to cut down the other if he was named the successor, so Genghis named Ogodei instead. That was years ago, but Jochi doesn't share the Khan's blood, and Chaghatai is a brute known for riding his horses to death and raping his soldiers' women. And it won't be blubbering Tolui—even Sorkhokhtani knows that." Toregene seemed far away for a moment. "No . . . it must be Ogodei."

I almost felt pity for Genghis then, to be saddled with such miserable sons that the great lump of flesh I'd encountered tonight was the best of the lot. I had difficulty imagining bellowing, red-faced Ogodei as Khan and cringed at the idea of Güyük one day becoming leader of the Mongols. Genghis Khan's son would direct the empire of horsemen to raid only those cities with extensive vineyards, while his grandson would surely inspire hatred both within and without his empire.

Perhaps it was the black and withered fruit of Genghis' lineage that would finally cause his empire to come crashing down and free the world from his terror.

I smiled at the thought. There was nothing more I wished to see than the utter destruction of these people. And when it happened, I would crow with victory just as Al-Altun had on the walls of Nishapur.

Chapter 22

1226 CE

YEAR OF THE FIRE DOG

Without my permission, the days turned to weeks and months and then years. I soon realized that these Mongols were fearsome warriors because everything in their lives, from the food to the weather, was raw and harsh. The summer was transient; blistering heat often followed torrential downpours, but as the winter snows fell I'd have given anything for the summer mud that seeped underfoot in Toregene's *ger* during the worst of the rains. Even worse were the mosquitoes that feasted on me every time I walked outside to fetch water or lay cheeses out to dry.

I awoke each winter morning to a water bucket frozen solid and a thin sheen of ice on my upper lip from my breath. At Toregene's urging, I'd taken instruction from Shigi in recording the events of the Golden Family, but during the winter we were unable to do even that, for the ink froze as hard as a rock and our fingers became cramped and brittle from the cold. The days grew shorter and there was no fruit to eat on the winter solstice, no dates or even dried apricots as we used to nibble long into the dark Night of Birth, as we'd done at home. I survived what I thought was the worst of the cold, but after the winter solstice came the season of the Nine Nines, nine sets of nine days so frigid I'd have wept if it wouldn't have left ice on my cheeks: the First Nine, when a pail of water thrown into the air freezes before it hits the ground; the Third Nine, when the horns of a four-year-old ox freeze; and the Seventh Nine, when the hilltops blacken. During those months, I'd have given my soul for a sweet desert breeze with its scents of sand and saffron, or better yet a bag of dried cherries.

But my soul was doomed the night my mother died, so I went without fragrant desert breezes or dried fruits. This was the end of the Ninth Nine, when the air no longer bit my face, and I was glad to enter the season of the White Moon after the winter solstice, when the Mongols roused themselves from their snow-covered tents to traipse from *ger* to *ger*, stuffing their wind-burned cheeks with fresh white curds, *buuz* mutton dumplings, and sheep-tail fat—a so-called delicacy I refused to touch, much less swallow. Shigi had delighted me with a precious gift of dried apricots, saved in a pewter tin since autumn, when the last of the caravans had passed our camp.

My ever-present grief for Mansoor had dulled with the passing months and years, even as my recollection of my husband's chiseled cheekbones and his almond eyes grew dim. Part of my heart was forever lost, yet I found that I enjoyed Shigi's quiet companionship while I adjusted Tore-gene's ledgers and he worked on recording the actions of the Great Khan. Perhaps I spun fancies from the air, but I thought he might enjoy my company, too.

"You seem to have found some peace here, Fatima of Nishapur," he had said one day, finishing his writing and wiping his hands on a bit of damp felt. I resisted the urge to bid him to use sesame oil to scrub away the ink stains, for that was something I'd once told Mansoor. Also, I'd yet to see a drop of sesame oil since I'd left Nishapur, something my chapped hands could attest to.

"Not peace," I had said, hiding those hands in the sleeves of my woolen cloak, sewn by my own hands in the draping Persian style along with a new veil and head scarf. I'd long ago folded away the clothes I'd worn from Nishapur, burying the robe and veil in the bottom of one of Toregene's trunks so I wouldn't be reminded of the day I'd left my old life. Part of me wished to burn the borrowed silks, yet I also wished to have something from home in case I ever returned. Or at least so I might be buried in proper clothing and not a *deel* stinking of wet sheep. "No, not peace at all," I murmured. "More like resignation."

Shigi had set down the cloth and stared at me for a moment, the corners of his eyes crinkling. "Perhaps that was it at first, but I've seen your eyes light with a smile when you think no one is watching."

I felt my cheeks flush at the realization that *he* had been watching me. Here in the vast emptiness of Mongolia, I was caught between trying not to draw attention to myself and also refusing to become a ragged heathen. Of everyone, it seemed only Shigi understood my desperate need to cling to the remnants of my former life. It was he who brought me volumes of poetry stolen by Mongol raiders and a blank record book in which he urged me to write an account of my life. The words I read and those I wrote allowed me to escape this new life of mine, and against my will I felt my heart softening toward Shigi, that softening always followed by a wave of guilt, as if my very thoughts made me unfaithful to my dead husband.

Shigi reached out then and touched my hair, his touch simultaneously shocking and pleasing. "This comb is familiar," he said. "Did Alaqai give it to you?"

"She did," I answered, hating the way my voice caught. "How did you know?"

He smiled. "I gave it to her, on her wedding night."

"A very thoughtful gift," I said, remembering what Alaqai had said when she gave it to me, *a gift from one widow to another*. Yet here I was, sitting beside a handsome man who was decidedly not my husband.

"Actually, I only gave it to Alaqai so she wouldn't kill her husband with that tiger sword of hers," Shigi said, rising. "It's a long story, perhaps one you'd care to hear during the feast tonight?"

"Perhaps," I answered, unsure whether I spoke the truth. During the recent solstice celebrations, I had tried not to remember similar feasts with my family during Ramazān nights, my father's jokes and Mansoor's slow smile as we filled our empty bellies after a day of fasting. But those celebrations were only faded memories now. After three days of celebration and drinking enough wine and *airag* to fell a herd of oxen, the Mongols would stumble back to their tents, there to remain until fresh shoots of grass speckled the melting snow.

And when spring came, I'd wait for the narcissus outside Toregene's tent to emerge from the frozen earth. I always split the narcissus bulbs under spring's first full moon, keeping them in a hammered-bronze chest until I could replant them each fall. Narcissus flowers ringed Toregene's tent every spring, their delicate white faces nodding in the breeze.

A circle of beauty that still held the promise of revenge.

I waited for Al-Altun to travel to our camp, but she remained in the west, controlling the Uighur people alone with the authority claimed by a child of Genghis Khan. We received news that Alaqai ruled the Onggud while Boyahoe carried out the Khan's orders to expand east toward the lands of the Song.

I spent the endless march of days recording for Toregene, preparing her bowls of salt tea, and arranging platters of famed Basra dates when the traders came from the west as the snow melted. Toregene taught me about the plants and herbs native to the steppes, and I traded the knowledge my mother had given me about our garden, although I kept secret the lethal qualities of the narcissus bulbs planted outside her door.

Tonight the sliver of the White Moon shone overhead as I hurried down to the frozen lake to relieve myself, burrowing deeper into my layers of rabbit fur and brushing aside shadows like cobwebs. Toregene had long ago stopped teasing me each time I bundled myself up for the long trek, for many Mongols in the winter scarcely poked their bare backsides out of their tents to relieve themselves.

Although I was forced to live among animals, that didn't mean I would debase myself to act like one.

I grimaced and picked my way around newly revealed piles of old horse dung in the dirty snow, my face flushing at the moans and other sounds of lovemaking that drifted from several tents while the happy couples inside took advantage of the White Moon to plant new seeds. I felt my loneliness keenly then, recalling the way I clambered into my pile of freezing blankets each night and shivered myself asleep. Through the bare trees, the moon's curve glowed on the lake's glistening ice, and clouds the color of ink swirled above in the dark sky. Snowflakes swirled down in mad patterns, like calligraphy drawn in the air with bits of ice. Although I'd never admit it aloud, this land had some beauty to it, and the dainty lace of snow that clung to my sleeve reminded me of the delicate silver filigree that decorated the interior of Nishapur's mosque. I'd expected the lake path to be empty, but someone stood at the edge of the ice, her white hair gleaming down her back like an errant shaft of moonlight.

The woman didn't acknowledge my presence. Despite her age, there was only one woman in camp who stood as tall and straight as a minaret.

The weather had warmed enough that Borte Khatun had traveled to the camp of her third son for the White Moon festival. Genghis Khan had chosen his lesser wife Yesui to accompany him as he campaigned against the troublesome Tanghut, leaving the administration of his homelands to Borte. Ogodei had managed to stay sober long enough to welcome his mother and then had outdone himself drinking and carousing. Over the past few days, Borte had visited Toregene's tent several times in the full regalia of the Khatun, and I'd found her milking goats and boiling yogurt while still wearing her towering green headdress, but tonight she wore only a wool robe. The Khatun plucked a handful of the alder catkins Toregene sometimes boiled into a bitter tea, tasted one, and then tossed the lot to the ground. "His shade won't protect us much longer," she mumbled to herself. "Jamuka has abandoned us."

"Borte Khatun?" I spoke hesitantly, not wishing to startle her. A recent rebellion in Rus had been crushed—the majority of the rebels had been cut down and the two Rus princes had been stretched out under boards and suffocated while the Mongols stood on the wooden planks during the victory banquet—but news from the north had come only weeks ago that Borte's eldest son, Jochi, had died, leaving his sons Orda and Batu to lead the White and Blue Hordes.

The Mother of the Mongols whirled around, her wide eyes reflecting the white snow. The Khan's senior wife stood taller than me, but without her headdress she seemed stooped and frail. It occurred to me that perhaps the Khan had traveled to conquer the Tanghut without his chief wife because she lacked the strength for such an ordeal. "The storm gathers tonight," Borte muttered, but she stared right through me. "And nothing shall shelter us from its destruction."

I glanced at the night sky, as placid as the frozen lake. "I don't think we have to worry about any storms tonight."

She blinked and her vision seemed to clear. "Fatima. I didn't realize you were there." She reached out a hand to steady herself, swaying on her feet.

"Are you well, Borte Khatun?" I said.

"For now," she said, offering a wan smile as I took her arm. "Although I fear that shall not last long. You were not bred for a life such as this, were you, Fatima of Nishapur?"

She patted my hand when I didn't answer. "Neither was I, my child. I tried to avoid it, for my mother proclaimed in my youth that I would usher in a war of blood and destruction. Mine was only the beginning of our epic tale, the start of this quest for a mighty empire. I must be content with the choices I've made, and the knowledge that, although the *tobshuur* players will long sing of our family around the hearthstones, I won't live to know the ending." She sighed. "We must all suffer in this life. You've suffered more than most, but I fear neither of us has reached the end of our travails."

I opened my right hand to ward off the evil eye, wishing for a handful of esfand seeds to burn over a charcoal brazier then—two staples of any proper Persian home—with their tiny explosions and fragrant smoke that warded off malevolent spirits. Borte's words reminded me of the fortune-teller my mother had once asked to visit her sickbed, a silk-clad woman who carried a little bird to pick snippets of illuminating poems from a box, and who, for an added fee, read the dark dregs of my mother's tea. Yet Borte Khatun's warning seemed to carry more import than the fortune-teller's prophecy that my mother should throw lentils in a rushing river to rid herself of the pain that had only just started to gnaw at her bones. I glanced down at the snow so Borte couldn't see my face. "You've lost your boots," I said.

The Khatun's bare toes poked out from under the snow-crusted hem of her *deel*. She lifted a gnarled hand and caressed my cheek. "So I have, my dear," she said. "And I shall soon lose so much more in the days to come."

I watched Borte shuffle back the way I'd come. Perhaps it was how she carried herself, or the air of fragility that followed her, but the Khatun of the Thirteen Hordes reminded me of another woman on a different winter's night. It seemed a travesty that the innocuous weapons of illness and old age could bring such strong women so low. "Are you sure you'll be all right, Khatun?"

She stopped and nodded. "Of course, Fatima of Nishapur. But I shall rely upon your strength in the days to come."

A shiver of foreboding curled down my spine as she retreated, and I saw her footprints in the snow, each step tinged with blood.

All that spring we endured poundings of hail, another abuse particular to this wretched land, which flattened the new grass so the horses and goats starved. Bolts of rotten silk arrived from Cathay riddled with moth holes, and the expected camel caravans laden with packs of Persian limes and dates failed to materialize, leaving me aching with dusty memories of home.

On the day the storm unleashed itself, Toregene had disappeared somewhere and I sat with Borte, sewing marten fur into Toregene's winter robe while the Khatun churned butter. Despite the fact that Borte owned the finest of wooden churns, the Khan's senior wife claimed the best butter was shaken in a sheep's stomach so it tasted of grass and red clover. I enjoyed watching her work, be it churning butter or shaping giant blocks of cheese curds to dry in the sun, her old hands conveying peace and wisdom to everything she touched. But as a rider approached, she dropped the bloated sheep stomach to the grass and rose on unsteady legs, her face as pale as the moon.

I set aside my sewing as the rider dismounted and fell to his knees before her. "Borte Khatun," he said. "I bring you news from the lands of the Tanghut."

Borte trembled so violently I thought she might collapse. "What is this news?" she asked.

"It's the Great Khan . . . He is dying." The messenger bent his head as if awaiting the Khatun to unsheathe a sword and strike him dead.

"What happened?" she asked. Her voice was strong, but she still shook like a leaf in a storm.

"The Khan of Khans stopped to hunt wild horses while crossing the Great Dry Sea. His favorite horse, the one the color of red earth, threw him when the herd charged." The messenger swallowed hard, glancing up and wringing his hands. "A fever consumed him, but he insisted on continuing with the campaign against the Tanghut. The sickness has overtaken him, and he is making his way home."

"He's coming home to die," Borte whispered. She spoke to herself, but the messenger nodded.

"It's unlikely he will survive the journey," he said.

"Then I will meet him." Borte spoke as if merely ordering a cart to felt wool for the day, rather than commanding an entourage to escort home the conqueror of almost the entire world. "Order my horse, Fatima. Inform Toregene and Sorkhokhtani of the circumstances so they may accompany us."

Despite her recent frailty, the wife of Genghis Khan was a great woman, a queen who might have been at ease at the elbow of any shah or emperor the world over.

Yet she was about to be widowed, a fate I'd not wish on any woman. I prayed she was strong enough to endure the coming days.

The Khan of Khans was still alive when we met his caravan, but barely.

I expected my first glimpse of Genghis Khan to make my knees tremble with fear, but the scourge of the world resembled neither the epic Persian hero Rostam nor Ali ibn Abi Talib at the Battle of the Camel, but instead a grizzled old man strapped into his saddle so he wouldn't topple over and be trampled underfoot by his reddish-gray warhorse. Dressed in a boiled-leather vest over a black robe, he surveyed us from under a silver helm rimmed with mangy black sable, his long, graying beard tied with a worn leather thong and a gleaming cutlass slung at his hip. He looked as raw as I imagined did Kaiumers, the first shah of Persia, who dressed in ragged tiger skins and lived in mountain caves. This was the beast that had stood on the steps of Otrar's famed mosque after pouring molten silver down the governor's throat and claimed to be the flail of Allah, sent to punish us for our sins. The winds whipped about the whispered cries of the countless souls that clung to the Khan of Khans, cut down before their time by this bloodthirsty warlord.

"You should ride in a cart," Borte berated him, but Genghis' eyes lit at her approach and he offered her a grimace that might have passed for a smile.

"And greet my Khatun like an old woman?" He reached out an arm for her and she was at his side in an instant. "Never."

They dismounted and I busied myself with ordering the building of Toregene's tent, thankful to be off the cursed beast that had carried me for the past week but unwilling to reconcile the idea of this heathen conqueror who was capable of tender feelings toward his wife. All around me, a city of tents sprang up, the family and advisers of the Thirteen Hordes of the Golden Family.

They had all come to bid farewell to the Khan of Khans and to scavenge the pieces of his empire like carrion.

Borte had hoped that Toregene's herbs and healing hands might drive away the Khan's deadly fever, but it soon became apparent that we were fortunate to have reached Genghis while he still drew breath.

His body crippled and his voice cracking, the Great Khan begged the representatives of the People of the Felt to help the children he left behind, implored his sons, daughters, and grandchildren to remain united. The fastest riders in the empire carried messages to bring Genghis' daughters, but the Onggud and Uighur lands were too far for Alaqai or Al-Altun to make the journey in time. One by one, Ogodei and Toregene, Tolui and Sorkhokhtani, and all their sons bent over his bed and pressed their foreheads to his, then formed a ring around the edges of the tent while a fire blazed under the smoke hole.

"Stay," Toregene whispered to Shigi and me when we tried to leave. "So you can write about this in your histories."

I trembled at the oppressive weight of death that made it difficult to fill my lungs, the same lingering heaviness that had pushed upon my chest when my mother lay dying. Shigi's arm brushed mine, and for once I let myself be comforted by his touch.

"The world shall not forget this day," he murmured under his breath. "Nothing shall be the same once the Khan flies to the sacred mountains."

Tolui fumbled with the wax seal on a jug of wine, and Ogodei roared for his wives to bring his horse and the cart of *airag* he'd ordered specifically for this journey. The Khan's sons were ill equipped to rule the world they were about to inherit.

"Nothing good shall come of your splitting your lands amongst our sons." The Khatun whispered the bitter words while I held the useless bowl of ox broth she'd ordered for the Khan. She clutched her husband's hands as the last threads of air were pulled from his beleaguered lungs. "Our realm will shatter into a thousand pieces like jade trampled by the hooves of wild horses, and our peoples shall be scattered in the eight directions, fragile as dried leaves in the wind."

Genghis Khan, the man who had united the Thirteen Hordes through spilled blood and the sheer force of his will, used his remaining strength to brush a strand of white hair from her temple. "You must hold them together, Borte Ujin," he whispered. "Just as you always have, my stubborn little goat."

In later years, travelers and foreign diplomats would speak of the Khan's death in hushed voices and strange tongues, telling how Genghis died after taking an arrow to the knee or being struck by lightning, drinking poison hidden in his nightly cup of *airag*, or being tormented by the black curse of an enemy king. One particularly creative story claimed a captured foreign queen inserted a hideous device into her woman's flower so when she seduced him, the Great Khan's sex organs were ripped off and he died in agony, bleeding on a pile of black sable furs while the queen laughed over him.

There were those who believed the foul tales rampant in every corner of the empire—many of which he'd propagated himself—and who wished their gruesome revenge upon this famed scourge from the east. Since they could not conquer him in life, the Khan's enemies sought to send him into the next world in as painful a way as possible. But those princes and ambassadors underestimated the love that the spirits held for their favored son.

My eyes stung and tears fell freely down my cheeks when Borte pulled the Khan's head into her lap, her voice lifting in a soothing melody. I'd heard Toregene speak of the song of the dead, and I'd imagined it as rough and grating, similar to everything else about these Mongols. Instead, it reminded me of the hymns I sang while grieving for my mother and the prayers to Allah that I'd chanted over Mansoor and my father. I touched the narcissus bulbs I kept hidden in my pocket, carried here in the vain hope that Al-Altun might travel to bid her father farewell on his final journey.

Genghis Khan had been a brutal and bloodthirsty warrior who slaughtered hundreds of thousands of innocent souls. I knew this in my mind, but as his soul fled now, all my heart felt was that he left behind a grieving widow, a woman who had loved him with all her soul. Now she—as we all must at one time—would face the world alone.

The Khan of Khans died the peaceful death of an old man, in the arms of the woman he loved.

Now only one question remained.

Who would take his place?

The Khan had ordered Borte to hold united the empire he left behind, but the lands he'd cobbled together began to fracture as soon as her husband lay on a simple wooden cart, dressed in a white robe and wrapped in a snowy felt blanket stuffed with sandalwood and secured with three golden straps. His face had been frozen in a stony glare as if staring down death in his final moments, but the Thirteen Hordes would never again hear the Khan's bloodcurdling battle cry.

The evening after Genghis' death, I came upon Shigi sitting alone as the sun set over a hill scattered with boulders shaped like pale, sleeping grizzlies. He gazed up at the moon in the night sky, reminding me of an astronomer charting the stars, and I recognized the jug cradled in his lap as one filled with Toregene's famed *airag*. In all my time with the Mongols, I'd never seen Shigi's lips touch a bowl of wine or that foul fermented milk. I hesitated to approach, but he looked up and gave a wan smile.

"I'd understand if you preferred not to spend your evening with a scowling scribe," he said, moving on the boulder so there was space for another. "But I'd be glad of your company tonight, Fatima."

And I, the woman who had resigned herself to a life of loneliness, felt something flare deep within my withered heart as I sat next to him, allowing Shigi's warmth to seep from the stone through the thin silk of my robe.

"You were well loved by the Khan, were you not?" I was terribly aware of Shigi's closeness and the scent of the inks that always clung to him. I'd never seen him angry or upset, but tonight his grief seemed to thicken the very air around us.

"When I was a child, the Khan spared me when he might have had me killed," Shigi said, his fingers tracing the top of the wine jug. "He gave me to his mother to raise and elevated me to record the history of his Golden Family. I have much to be grateful for."

I clasped my hands before me. "And yet it was he who ordered the destruction of your people."

Shigi offered the remnant of a smile. "As he did yours."

His words were true, yet it was Al-Altun whom I held responsible for the death of my family. And it was another of the Khan's daughters who had saved me, leaving me ambivalent toward Genghis Khan himself. I drew a deep breath and dared to let my hand touch Shigi's. "Still, I'm sorry for your loss."

Shigi stared at our hands for a moment, and I withdrew my fingers, my bravery gone as quickly as it had come.

"Thank you," he said, slowing the words as if he'd drunk too much from the wine jug. "But it's more than the Khan's death. We are neither of us happy, Fatima, you and I. With Genghis' passing, Ogodei shall wear the Khan's helm and take with him my only chance at happiness."

I pondered what he meant, but he lurched to his feet. "I fear I'm poor company tonight," he said. "Go in peace, Fatima of Nishapur."

With that, he strode down the dark path toward the encroaching darkness, leaving me with an empty boulder and a jug of wine, wondering if perhaps the wine had loosened Shigi's tongue and caused his erratic behavior. I was surprised to find the clay seal on the jug intact, its contents untouched.

And I was still alone. Always alone.

Somber soldiers dressed in their finest silks and furs escorted Genghis' body to the land of his birth, then to the base of Burkhan Khaldun, the holy mountaintop so high it grazed the belly of the sky. The men's voices rumbled deep in their throats, rising in the wind only to plummet back to earth and settle amongst the steppe's emerald grasses. I walked with Borte behind the Khan's Spirit Banner, followed by his riderless reddish gray horse with its empty saddle. The same writers who speculated over the Great Khan's death pondered over his burial, claiming that his funeral escort was slaughtered to keep his grave a secret and a river diverted to hide the sacred site. While the Khan's favorite horses and many hapless souls who wandered across the entourage were killed, the Khan's sons and grandsons—Ogodei, Chaghatai, Tolui, Güyük, Möngke, and Kublai—laid him at the foot of the mountains where he had spent his youth, bringing the world's most brutal conqueror to the end of his journey.

Borte's hands hadn't stopped moving since the Khan's death, be it sewing, milking, or churning, and Sorkhokhtani's mournful music filled the night air. Toregene was nowhere to be found the evening of the burial— the latest in a string of many disappearances. I assumed she was off gathering plants, for she'd mentioned that her columbine and chamomile supplies were low.

I took pains with my appearance that night, silently rebuking myself for my absurdity as I applied kohl to my eyelids, slipped the jade tiger comb into my hair, and straightened my veil before Toregene's copper mirror. Tonight I would tell Shigi of my burgeoning feelings, of my hope that together we might carve out some small piece of happiness. The idea of speaking thus to a man was foreign to me, but after these past years as Toregene's slave, I knew I couldn't face the wintery desolation of a lifetime alone. While I would never love another as I had Mansoor, I hoped I might find some purpose in this life if I could learn to love again. I smiled at the thought of Shigi, of his refined nature and elegant ways, so familiar to me, as if we were meant to be together.

I was glad for the light of the half-moon and the clean air as I stepped outside and headed for Shigi's tent. There was no smoke coming from the smoke hole, and when I peered inside it was to find everything dark, his orderly bed and the neat line of gilded chests, which I knew were filled with pens and ink, volumes of precious books and stacks of untouched paper. I walked toward the hill of grizzly boulders then, thinking to find him alone again, yet he wasn't among the stones.

I would take the long way back to camp, through the thin excuse of a forest and along the creek. My hope waned and my nerves calmed, for more than likely, I'd return to my cold mattress in Toregene's tent as I'd done every night since Nishapur.

I hadn't gone far when I noticed movement across the way, two figures pressed against the base of a great fir and shielded by several scrubby birch and alder trees. Despite the chill of the night air, the woman's *deel* was rucked around her waist, her legs wrapped around the man as their bodies moved in rhythm together. A braid hung down the man's back, and moonlight glinted off the gold ring in his nose.

I stared for a moment, horrified and entranced as I recognized the woman, her head thrown back in ecstasy.

Toregene. And Shigi.

It took a long moment to realize the emotion that stabbed my heart and ripped the breath from my lungs.

Jealousy.

I ducked behind an alder bush, hiding like the humiliated carpenter in my father's illuminated book of fables, concealed under the bed while he listened to his wife and her lover above him. I wanted to scream at Toregene, the woman who had saved me from death and who now dug her fingers into Shigi's back as his lips brushed the hollow of her neck. The depth of my envy and loneliness made me moan aloud, the black emotions overwhelming the walls I'd erected around my withered heart. I'd dared to dream of happiness while allowing Toregene's and Shigi's kindnesses to chip away at my defenses, but now I was betrayed.

Not betrayed, some small voice reminded me. Neither Shigi nor To-regene knew of my feelings or my hopes. I recalled their closeness on our return from Nishapur, the way Shigi sometimes lingered when he brought Toregene rare herbs purchased from passing caravans and how they often laughed at some secret joke, their heads bent together.

I pressed my fist to my mouth, turned on my heel, and raced back up the path. I was almost to Toregene's tent when Ogodei emerged from a copse of trees, retying the belt on his trousers amidst the smell of fresh urine.

"The Rose of Nishapur, returning from a midnight tryst?" The moonlight reflected off his crooked grin.

"Ogodei," I stammered, resisting the urge to look over my shoulder. "I didn't expect to see you here."

"This is my *ger*." He glanced beyond me, and for once I couldn't smell any alcohol on his breath. "Where is my wife? I've become accustomed to seeing you in her shadow."

My heart stalled and I shook my head, seeing again the terrible image of Toregene entwined with Shigi against the tree. I was glad for my veil when Ogodei's eyes narrowed to slits. The man was a drunk, but he was no fool, and he would be the next Khan. "I believe Toregene is sitting with Borte Khatun," I said.

Ogodei's grin widened. "My wife has found a faithful servant in you, Fatima, but you need not lie for her. She's not with you, so that means she must be with Shigi just now."

I stared at him, dumbstruck. "I don't know what you mean," I stammered.

He tsked me under his breath. "You can't fathom the idea that I might know of—perhaps even condone—my wife's love of another man, can you?"

He was right. In Nishapur, a woman caught with a man other than her husband would be publicly stoned to death for adultery. And yet here even Ogodei knew of Shigi and Toregene's relationship, while I alone had been blind.

"I was once infatuated with Toregene, caught under the spell of her strange eyes," Ogodei said, running a hand over his thinning hair. "But that was many years ago. She gave me the heir I needed and runs an efficient camp while I drink and carouse. In return, I allow her happiness with our family's very talented scribe."

"You are indeed generous and magnanimous," I muttered. My soul was stained with my mother's death and my lust for Al-Altun's blood, but just when I thought I'd discovered the furthest limits of these heathens' degradation, they surprised me yet again.

Ogodei laughed at my sour expression. "And you, Rose of Nishapur, were it not for my wife's protection, would find yourself the subject of my ardent pursuit."

"What?"

He chuckled, but then sobered. "Toregene tells me your heart will be forever buried with your husband." He reached out as if to touch my veil but dropped his hand. "He was a lucky man to have inspired such devotion from such a woman as you."

"I—"

I couldn't find the words to agree with or rebuff Ogodei, or anything else for that matter. He gave me a sad smile. "Have no fear, Rose of Nishapur. I've never taken an unwilling woman to my bed, and I'm too set in my ways to start now. You're safe from me, and from any man, as far as I'm concerned."

After a moment, he gave a harrumph and adjusted his belly over his belt. "Tell Toregene when you see her that I seek her advice," he said. "And I don't care to wait long for it."

He lumbered back up the path, and I stood staring after him, my jaw slack.

Why was nothing about these Mongols as it seemed?

"When were you going to inform me of your relationship with Shigi?" I glowered at Toregene, fists on my hips as she closed the door behind her, filling her tent with the scent of the crisp night air and something else that almost brought me to my knees.

Happiness.

She shrugged out of her fur wrap and busied herself unlacing her boots. "The cold must have addled your mind," she said, but I cut her off.

"I saw you with him tonight." My tone was biting, petulant even to my own ears as I threw off my veil and the tiger comb. "I'd like to think you both drank too much wine out of grief and realized afterward the weight of your mistake, but I doubt that's the truth."

"I'm sorry, Fatima." She heaved a wretched sigh. "I thought about telling you several times, but I couldn't bear to hurt you."

"Hurt me?" Was it possible my thoughts toward Shigi had been so transparent? "What do you mean?"

Toregene traced the spine of my thick blue record book, identical to the one Shigi used to record his version of the Golden Family's history. "I believed you might have feelings for Shigi. I didn't wish to cause you pain, but Shigi and I . . . We've loved each other for a long time."

"I see." I wanted to howl with my suffering, but instead my eyes burned with unshed tears and I cleared my throat. "How long?"

"Since almost the day Genghis brought me to the Golden Family."

"What?" Such a revelation was almost more shocking than what I'd seen tonight in the woods.

"Borte took me in, but it was Shigi who helped me see the sunlight in each day after all the darkness I'd witnessed during the Blood Wars. We never acted on our feelings, for I knew Borte wished me to marry one of her sons. I married Ogodei and then Genghis took Shigi on the campaign against the Tanghut."

"Because he suspected you?"

She shrugged. "Perhaps. Yet I was a good wife to Ogodei, running his household and giving him Güyük. It wasn't until more recently that anything happened."

My hands fluttered helplessly at my sides; I didn't care to listen to the details of Toregene's love for Shigi, but she looked beyond me now. "Shigi first kissed me one night not long after Nishapur," she said, tucking loose strands of hair behind her ears, her expression taking on a dreamlike quality. "I thought everyone would know my heart didn't belong to Ogodei then, but no one noticed, or if they did, they didn't care. We tried to fight our feelings for a long time, but . . ."

She shrugged and I thought then of one of my favorite verses in the beloved old volume of ancient poetry I'd left behind in Mansoor's library, wondering if perhaps it was still there now, forgotten beneath a layer of dust or perhaps long since burned in some marauder's fire. I spoke aloud:

> *"Did my Beloved only touch me with his lips,*
> *I, too, like the flute, would burst out in melody.*
> *But he who is parted from him that speak his tongue*
> *Though he possess a hundred voices, is perforce dumb."*

Toregene smiled at my recitation. "I knew you'd understand."

I swallowed a swell of sadness, struck silent at how I'd misread the entire situation. Perhaps I did understand Toregene, but only because I'd experienced such a love with Mansoor. My own battered emotions aside, she was still Ogodei's senior wife and a member of the Golden Family. "Don't you worry what people will think?" I asked.

"People see what they want to see. No one expects a woman with gray in her hair and a face as plain as sand to love the Tatar brother of Genghis Khan."

"Ogodei knows."

That seemed to catch her attention. "Does he?"

"It doesn't seem to bother him."

She offered me a meager smile. "Ogodei ceased caring for me once my mismatched eyes and the curves of my body lost their newness. But Shigi loved me long before I married Ogodei. He'll love me until the day I die."

My brittle heart threatened to crack at her words, but I gave a weak smile, until her next words stole away my breath.

"Enough of all this talk of love," she said. "We have much to do to prepare for their arrival."

I blinked hard. "Whose arrival?"

"I saw the riders on my way back from the . . ." Her voice trailed off and she had the decency to look embarrassed. "Alaqai and Boyahoe will be here tomorrow. Al-Altun won't be far behind them."

Al-Altun.

I'd thought that perhaps I might fill my life with love, but I recognized this sign from Allah. With tonight's discovery, I now knew it would not be love that gave my life meaning, but something else entirely, something I'd silently nurtured as I had the narcissus bulbs, and that now overshadowed my desire for love.

Revenge.

I avoided Shigi in the days to come, reconciling myself to the fact that he was a man I might have loved had I been given a chance. Yet that was never to be. Sleep eluded me as I imagined Al-Altun's return, and I wove plot after plot to ensure my success. When I did sleep, it was to dream of my father and Mansoor, their eyes hard and accusing after all the years I'd squandered without avenging them.

One raw and soulless night, I dreamed of my mother, blood dribbling from her lips. "Kill Al-Altun as you killed me," she whispered. "Give her the narcissus bulbs as you did me, and end her life."

I woke from that dream gasping and with tears streaming down my face. The shadows under my eyes deepened to the color of fresh bruises, so it was the first thing Alaqai mentioned as she dismounted her red-and-white horse.

"Has Toregene been beating you?" she asked gaily after she'd greeted Toregene, crushing me in a hug that threatened to break my ribs. "Or merely keeping you up all night working on her ledgers?"

"It's my own fault." I waved away her concern, feeling both Toregene's and Shigi's gazes heavy on my back. "Too many thoughts in my head."

"You must learn to think less, then," Alaqai said, releasing me. "And learn instead to enjoy life."

Boyahoe had already dismounted and was speaking in earnest with Ogodei, although the future Gur-Khan only roared with laughter and clapped Alaqai's husband on his back, gathering the tall young man at his side into his free arm and tousling his hair. Toregene clasped her hands before her and smiled. "It seems you and your family have found happiness once again, Alaqai."

Alaqai's gaze strayed to her husband and the boy who bore a striking resemblance to her. Her eyes sparkled. "I never expected it, but I think Jingue's spirit would smile upon us."

"The Khan always said Boyahoe made a fine soldier," Toregene said. "I'm glad to hear he makes a good husband as well."

Alaqai laughed at that. "Boyahoe is more my son than husband, but he's as fine a father to Negudei as I could ask for."

Toregene glanced at Boyahoe, then back to Alaqai. "Then you're not . . ."

"By the Earth Mother, no." Alaqai made a face. "Boyahoe has his other wives for all that, and ruling the Onggud and raising my wild hellion leaves me no time to ponder my cold bed."

A smile played on Toregene's lips. "I'd have thought a cold bed would have been a greater hardship than you could bear."

"And once I would have agreed with you." Alaqai laughed. "Yet most nights I fall asleep before my head hits my pillow. I don't know how my mother managed with all of us."

"Borte Khatun will be pleased to see you," Toregene said. I hoped she was right, for since the Khan's death, Borte had scarcely left her tent. In truth, I'd avoided the Khatun these past days, terrified that she might see into my shriveled heart and discover the hot fire of revenge burning there.

Toregene gestured to the path leading to Borte's tent. "I'll take you to her."

Alaqai followed but paused before me and clasped my hands. "I meant what I said," she whispered. "We widows can choose the easy path and allow grief to consume us, or we can find a new purpose in this life, Fatima of Nishapur. Our hearts are forever scarred, but in living life we might honor our husbands."

I stared at her, Mansoor's final words expanding and filling my mind as Alaqai squeezed my hands. She kissed my veiled cheek, then swept away like a hot desert wind.

Live for both of us, Fatima, and I'll meet you in the gardens of Jannah.

Yet I was never destined for the paradise of Jannah, not after I'd helped usher my mother to her death.

Alaqai didn't need to know that I'd already found a new purpose in life.

Al-Altun didn't make it to the Khan's deathbed, but Ogodei ordered a feast in her honor when the Khatun of the Uighurs arrived at our temporary camp at the base of the Altai Mountains, come to pay her respects to the man who had sired her. My hands trembled as she approached on horseback, only growing calm when I touched the silk bag of narcissus bulbs hidden within the folds of my robe.

Patience is bitter, but it has a sweet fruit.

And tonight, under the silver light of the moon and the golden glow of countless cook fires, I would have my revenge.

The Khatun of the Uighurs hadn't changed since I'd seen her at Nishapur, and my throat tightened at the remembrance of her on my city's walls, grinning wildly at the carnage spread before her. My gaze lingered on the gleaming hilt of the sword slung in Ogodei's belt, and I wondered if perhaps the price of slitting Al-Altun's throat in full view of the Golden Family might be worth the consequences.

I knew what I had to do. And I wouldn't allow myself to fail.

Most of the Golden Family had already disbanded and left the Altai Mountains, deciding that the arrival of Genghis' youngest daughter wasn't incentive enough to linger away from their homelands any longer. Alaqai and Boyahoe cited their need to return to the Onggud before the snows flew, and Borte remained in her tent, claiming Al-Altun could meet with her later that evening if she wished.

The camp felt strangely silent without the energy Alaqai and her family had brought, but I was thankful for the emptier paths with fewer eyes to discern my true motives tonight. I elbowed my way past several scowling generals in their whispering silks and creaking leather to where Al-Altun exclaimed loudly over Ogodei's new Great White Tent, its size and the team of twenty snowy oxen that could pull it across the steppes. Unlike his father, who lived in a simple *ger* all his days, Ogodei reveled in ostentation. Hidden in the shadows, I doubled back to where Al-Altun's slaves were assembling their hearths and her modest traveling tent. The air was warm from the roaring fires with their massive cauldrons and the stench of boiling horsemeat, and a cook in a stained *deel* supervised the flurry of slaves. He whirled about when he saw me, his face turning redder than it already was in the heat.

"Get out," he ordered, a single glance taking in my foreign robe and veil. "The only slaves allowed in my kitchen are the ones I've ordered here."

"You'll have to explain that to Ogodei and his senior wife," I said. "They sent me to supervise this meal, and they outrank the Khatun of the Uighurs."

The cook's eyes narrowed to a squint at my lie, but he threw his hands in the air with a curse in Uighur. "Fine," he said. "But stay out of my way or I'll see to it that you accidentally run into one of my carving knives."

I scowled over my veil despite my nerves, remembering the foul language and threats I'd often heard my head cook in Nishapur mutter under his breath. Perhaps the heat and smell of blood made cooks a permanently surly sort. Yet I didn't have time to parry with this man.

"Fine," I said. "Where are you preparing the Golden Family's food?"

The cook jerked his head toward several smaller metal *kazans* set over a trench dug in the ground, merry fires blazing underneath with rice cooking inside. And on a low table nearby, piles of chopped carrots and yellow onions waited to be mixed into the tasteless Uighur dish of *palov*. No one would notice the addition of my narcissus bulbs.

"Ogodei is a cultured man whose cooks hail from the farthest reaches of Cathay," I lied. "He won't be impressed with this slop you plan to feed him."

The cook's nostrils flared. "I'll have you know that the Uighur aqueducts bring pure water from ancient glaciers, proof that my people are more civilized than the bowlegged creature you serve. My family has been making *palov* for generations—"

"I don't care if your family served *palov* to the Prophet," I said, cringing at my blasphemy. "Where are your spices? Ogodei's favorite spices must be added so that he and the Golden Family can choke down this swill."

The cook's glower would have stopped a fainter heart than my own, but he dug under his collar, then flung a key at me. "The chest is there." He spat the words. "And you'll account for every grain of salt and flake of pepper you use."

The drums outside Ogodei's tent began their steady beat as the cook stormed away. I hadn't much time. I rifled through the man's impressive store of spices, removing garlic cloves, lumpy gingerroots, and a packet of black pepper. The paper of the narcissus bulbs crackled beneath my fingers as I removed them from my pocket. One had rotted on the journey, but the remaining three were white and only slightly wrinkled underneath, no longer smooth from their long absence from the earth. I cut them as quickly as I could with my knife, palming them and letting the fire devour the evidence of their papers and tiny root clumps.

I made a great show of grating the priceless gingerroot, while next to me, the Uighur cook supervised the filling of golden bowls of varying sizes, all hammered with scenes of daily life in the various khanates. The largest must be for Ogodei, decorated with crude scenes of horses, mountains, and even several tents; another showed the familiar domes of my homeland. The smallest bowl depicted camels traveling through the Silk Road oases of the Uighur kingdom.

Al-Altun's bowl.

But I had to be sure.

"Which is your khatun's bowl?" I asked the cook. "I'll not waste precious spices on her Mongol tongue, accustomed as it is to boiled horsemeat and bland rice."

The cook growled at me like a dog about to attack but jerked his thumb at the camel bowl before turning his back on me with a curse.

Allah had heard my prayers. This was my chance.

I opened my hand, marveling for a moment at the chopped narcissus bulbs and the power I held in my palm. My heart pounded so loudly in my ears that the skies might have thundered and I'd have been oblivious to the storm.

I was so absorbed in what I was about to do that I didn't notice the shadow that fell over the bowls before me.

"Here you are," Toregene said. Her hand on my shoulder startled me so I almost cried out. "I've been looking all over for you."

Without hesitating, I dropped the narcissus into the golden bowl of steaming rice, praying that she wouldn't realize the crime I'd committed.

"What are you doing?" she asked.

"I thought I'd help prepare the meal." My voice was smooth, but the blood rushed in my ears.

"But you can scarcely boil water." Her brow knit as she studied the chopped bits of poison in Al-Altun's bowl. "Is that garlic?" She took a bit out and sniffed it. "It doesn't smell like garlic."

I didn't think when she lifted the poison to her lips, but grabbed her wrist and flicked the narcissus back into the *palov*. "Don't," I said. "Please . . ."

Her eyes narrowed. "What are you doing, Fatima?"

"Correcting a wrong from long ago," I said. "Since Nishapur."

Horror dawned in her eyes. I waited for her to shriek at me, but instead, there was a flash of gold like lightning as she shoved Al-Altun's bowl to the ground. Immobile, I watched helplessly as meat, rice, and precious bits of narcissus were strewn across the earth.

Then came the unexpected bolt of pain at my temple, and I staggered back at the impact of Toregene's open palm across my face.

"Idiot!" she screamed. I gaped at her and clutched my cheek as slaves scurried to clean the mess.

"What's going on?" The cook was purple faced at the sight of the overturned bowl, growing more livid as he looked from Toregene to me.

"My fool of a slave knocked over Al-Altun's bowl," Toregene said, grabbing my arm so hard I scarcely resisted the urge to rake my nails across her face. My promise to Mansoor was gone, scattered across the trampled earth, and it was all her doing.

The cook lunged at me. His fist made contact with my other temple, causing a second explosion of pain and a ringing in my ears. "I'll have your hide for this, Saracen!"

I steeled myself for the next blow, but Toregene yanked me away from the cook before it could land. "Throw some fresh rice in a pot," she tossed over her shoulder. "I'll skin this slave myself." She hauled me away from the cursing cook and his fires, dragging me out of camp until we'd reached the river. Perhaps she'd drown me now; she was within her rights to do so.

Instead, she whirled me around. "Christ's wounds," she cursed, her chest heaving. "Have you taken leave of your senses?"

"Al-Altun deserves to die a thousand deaths for what she did in Nishapur." My veil had come loose in the fight and I ripped it off, waiting for Toregene to hit me once more, to rail at me for my disloyalty or perhaps find a guard to order my execution, but she only grabbed me by my shoulders and gave me a shake.

"Only God can judge Al-Altun, or mete out her punishment." She held my shoulders and drew a ragged sigh. "Just as only he can judge you."

I recoiled at her words. My mother's death had been a murder of mercy, but Al-Altun's death would have been a crime borne of revenge. Yet she would walk free after tonight's dinner, oblivious to how close she'd come to dying.

I'd failed completely.

The sob that escaped my throat took me by surprise, and it required every shred of my willpower not to lash out, not to scream with fury at my impotence. What sort of wife and daughter was I that I couldn't even avenge my family?

"I know something of what you're feeling, Fatima," Toregene said. I shook my throbbing head and lurched away when she tried to touch my hand.

"You know nothing," I yelled, and then I was overcome with uncontrollable sobs. I wanted to throw something, to inflict this searing pain on someone else, but instead I closed my eyes and clamped my lips tightly to smother the sounds of my misery. My eyes snapped open when Toregene drew me into her arms, and I stiffened at the embrace. It had been so long since anyone had embraced me, but then I let her hold me, silent tears streaming down my cheeks.

The river muffled the sounds of my hiccups, and when I stepped back it was to find Toregene staring past me at something only she could see. "I *do* know what you're feeling," she said slowly. "For I watched the first son of my womb and my husband being cut down like terrified horses in the midst of a midnight raid. Another son, too, still a babe at my breast."

"What?" My pounding head could scarcely make sense of her words, yet one look at her pale face and haunted eyes told me she spoke the truth. "When?"

She blinked as if she'd forgotten I was there. "It was years ago, during the Blood Wars and before I came to Borte's tent. My second son was scarcely a season old, and Genghis brought me to Borte with sour milk still staining my *deel*. For years after that, I dreamed of killing the Khan."

"The Khan?" I struggled to make sense of this new tragedy, hidden for so long. "You mean Genghis?"

She nodded. "He led the final raid against the Merkid. I imagined all the ways I might kill him, envisioned stabbing him in the stomach or slitting his throat while he slept more times than I could count."

"Why didn't you?" My hand had been stalled by distance all these years, but the flame of revenge in my withered heart had never died. I couldn't imagine the temptation of sleeping in the same tent with my family's murderer, or watching him laugh over a bowl of stew cooked by my own hands.

Toregene opened her palms in a gesture of submission. "Borte loved the Khan, and I love Borte. I couldn't cause her to suffer my same pain." She clasped my hands. "Al-Altun sought revenge on Nishapur because your city killed the husband of her heart. Her mother was long dead, and as the daughter of a lesser wife, she was never needed by her father and the rest of the family. Her husband was all she had. Isn't it possible that you'd have done the same in her place?"

I saw the simplicity of her logic but also its inherent flaw.

"My family—my people—didn't deserve to die," I said. "And neither did yours."

"But they *did* die, and one day they will greet us when we've glimpsed our last of this world. You shall see them again, Fatima. I promise it."

I looked into her eyes then, one glowing gold and the other like burnished copper. "That's why you saved me, isn't it?" I asked, wiping my eyes. "In Nishapur?"

She gave a sad smile. "I've often wondered if perhaps it would have been kinder to let you die instead. But yes, Fatima, I saved you because I saw echoes of myself in you." She stepped closer, touching my collar and withdrawing the chain that held the silver tiger medallion that marked me as her slave. "And now I'd like to do something I've been considering for a long time." She lifted the necklace over my head, placed it in my palm, and folded my fingers over it. "I give you your freedom, Fatima. You are no longer my slave, but I would be honored if you choose to stay by my side."

Freedom. I could leave here, return to Persia, and make a life for myself.

But there was nothing left for me in Persia, no family or home.

I stared at the medallion with its image of a snarling tiger, more tears stinging my eyes. I'd reconciled myself to the fact that I would endure the remainder of this life alone, no parents, husband, or children to fill my days. Even my hope for revenge had been destroyed, but before me now stood a woman, an unexpected sister who had rescued me more than once.

The jagged outline of the Altai Mountains was black against the twilit sky, a dragon's back as wild and fierce as these lands I'd always hoped to leave. Toregene had given me my freedom tonight, and perhaps more, yet I wondered if one day I might regret my decision to remain at her side.

"I'll stay," I whispered, the words catching in my throat. "For now, at least."

I was bound to this woman by the bonds of life and death, ties closer perhaps than those that bound sisters of the same womb.

Against my will, Toregene had become my family.

Chapter 23

I avoided Al-Altun until she left our camp, spending my time in Toregene's tent either working on my record of the Khan's death or bent over a
prayer rug, begging Allah to heal my battered heart. Perhaps the One God
heard my prayers, but he ignored the other broken heart in our camp.

Each month after the Khan's funeral found Borte more deteriorated.
She still rarely left her tent, and while I'd assumed the night at the lake
had been an isolated spell brought on by some terrible dream or a way-
ward djinn, instead the Khatun's fits of forgetfulness increased and her
thoughts became so tangled that her mind was more often lost than present
among us.

The light in Borte's eyes finally grew dim, and she ceased recognizing
Toregene and Sorkhokhtani. On her worst days, the Khatun sobbed over
terrible memories she couldn't share, fighting with the strength of a tiger
as I tried to calm her, screaming the name "Chilger" as she bucked against
me. I sent the fastest arrow messenger available to summon Alaqai again
and prayed that the only daughter of Borte's womb would be able to cross
the fabled Great Dry Sea in time. Finally, the Great Khatun fell silent,
calling out in her dreams to those who had long since turned to spirits.

Gurbesu.

Jamuka.

Temujin.

"I'll care for her," I told Toregene one day. Sorkhokhtani was brushing the cascade of Borte's hair while the Khatun sat motionless in her bed. Both Toregene and Sorkhokhtani had much to attend to, assisting their drunken husbands as they attempted to hold together their father's empire and garner enough support to call a new *khurlatai* to proclaim the next Khan, while still arguing amongst themselves over who that would be. For now, tradition dictated that Tolui, as Prince of the Hearth, hold the position of regent, despite the fact that Genghis had intimated his preference for Ogodei. No one wished to see Genghis' eldest son, Chaghatai, wear the Khan's headdress.

"The Khatun gathered us all to her," Toregene said, her gaze faraway. "Like lost cranes, we were tumbled about by an autumn storm and so broken she feared we might never be whole again. Now it is her daughters' privilege to care for her."

I sat back, stung. "I didn't mean to presume—" Anger tightened my throat. "Of course you and Sorkhokhtani must care for her. And Alaqai, when she arrives."

Toregene blinked and patted my hand absentmindedly, watching as Sorkhokhtani styled the Khatun's white hair, as thick as a sheep's fleece. "You are one of Borte's daughters, Fatima. The last, in fact."

Chastened, I fiddled with the silver bangle on my wrist. "She suffers," I said. "It's difficult to watch."

Toregene stood and rifled through a box of herbs she'd taken to leaving in Borte's tent, retrieving a small glass vial filled with a murky brown liquid. "Willow bark might ease the worst of her pain."

I turned over the vial in my hand before tucking it into my waistband, knowing that willow bark would be useless in the face of such a terrible fight. "There's something else," I said, the words lodging in my throat. "Narcissus bulbs could speed her toward peace."

A cold hand tightened around my heart, but it was too late to take back the words. My narcissus bulbs would no longer be a secret, but I couldn't watch Borte's long and futile struggle against death when it was in my power to end it.

"Speed her toward peace?" Toregene asked. "Or would you use your narcissus bulbs to usher her toward death? Is that what you planned to use on Al-Altun?"

I avoided her eyes and her questions. "Are peace and death not one and the same?"

"The god of the cross forbids such a crime," Toregene answered. "As does Allah, if I'm not mistaken."

Allah forbade suicide, but my soul was forever stained from feeding my own mother the narcissus bulbs she'd begged for when her body became too ravaged to bear any more pain. I touched Toregene's hand. "Our gods forbid it," I said. "But Borte's does not. My father's brother lingered like this for many more years, lost between life and death."

Toregene pursed her lips, her eyes shining with unshed tears. "We'll make no decisions until Alaqai arrives. I'll not deprive a daughter of her final chance to see her mother."

I recalled Alaqai's comment the first time I'd met her about carrying death in her heart. I doubted whether she'd see Toregene's decision as a kindness.

Alaqai arrived with her son, both swathed in black, with the bloodshot eyes of the grieving. Although she hadn't yet seen forty years, the Khatun's daughter leaned heavily upon her adolescent son, as if the burden of life had grown too heavy for her now.

"Boyahoe was killed in battle against the Song," she said, closing her eyes as if to steady herself. "We received your message about Mother and left before his funeral feast. I couldn't even give him the proper forty-nine days of mourning." Alaqai's voice quavered as her expression hardened. I recognized the mask of hidden sorrow, for it was one I'd perfected long ago, as effective as the veil that covered my face today. Alaqai whispered something in her son's ear, and he scampered off, likely relieved to be free of his mother's grief, even for a few moments. "Boyahoe's life was too short," Alaqai said, stomping her foot. "It's my fault he's dead, for I let him go off to prove himself in battle. I'm done marrying. I won't curse another husband with an early death."

"Our entire camp will feast in Boyahoe's honor, even the dogs," Toregene said. "Together we shall celebrate his life."

"He'd have liked that," Alaqai said. "I think his happiest time was here, in the army with Father. Now they're both gone, and Mother . . ." Her eyes filled, but she drew a ragged sigh and blinked back the tears. "How is she?"

Toregene gestured for me to answer. "Borte Khatun is much changed since you last saw her," I said. "The men are with her now."

"I want to see her," Alaqai said. "And then I'll visit Father's bones."

Borte's blue seer's door stood proud and defiant as Ogodei and Tolui stumbled outside, both dressed in rumpled *deels*. Shigi stepped out behind them, upright under his blue judge's cap as he tucked his arms into his sleeves. I'd seen Toregene slip into his tent the night before and wondered how he could share the same air with Ogodei the morning after making love to his wife. I'd convinced myself that it was only my loneliness that had made me yearn for Shigi, yet my continuing bitterness toward him hinted otherwise.

"The Khatun rests now," Shigi said, his gaze briefly meeting Toregene's before flickering away. It was a tender expression of concern, but so brief no one else seemed to notice. "Her sons may have exhausted her with their reminiscing about the Great Khan."

Tolui's nose was redder than normal and he wiped it with the back of his sleeve, leaving a shiny trail of snot like a slug's path. He gulped air, showing off his missing tooth.

"Go with Ogodei," Sorkhokhtani said to Tolui, cupping his cheek with her hand. Sometimes I still had a difficult time reconciling graceful Sorkhokhtani with her coarse, and typically drunk, husband. "We'll sit with the Khatun."

Ogodei's great bulk almost swallowed Alaqai as he pulled her into a tight embrace. "It's good to see you, sister," he said. "Perhaps with you here, our mother may yet win her battle over death."

I exchanged a look with Toregene and Sorkhokhtani, feeling the terrible weight in my pocket. My mouth went dry and my underarms grew damp. If all went as we'd discussed, today I would become a murderer a second time over.

Alaqai's fingers threaded through the Spirit Banner outside Borte's *ger*, the tail of her father's favorite warhorse. "I miss you, Father," I heard her whisper. "One day we'll race each other on horseback again. I might even let you win."

Then she stepped inside. I'd never grow accustomed to the stench of burning dung inside all the Mongol tents—more like a stable than a home—but despite my veil, Borte's tent smelled also of Toregene's freshly ground herbs and the insidious smell of death that grew stronger every day. Alaqai wavered and I guided her inside, toward the bed her mother hadn't left for so many months. Borte's brown eyes were blank, as they always were, her mouth slightly open. I might have thought she'd already passed to the next life had it not been for the gentle rise and fall of her chest and the sound of her labored breathing. "You've faced battles with flashing swords," I whispered to Alaqai. "And watched three of your husbands leave this life. Let those trials give you courage now."

She worked to swallow, and it took a moment before she managed to speak. "How long has she been this way?"

"A full season," I answered. I opened the smoke hole in the top of the tent wider to let in fresh air and removed my veil, since I was safe in the company of women. "We feed her broth and milk, bathe her from a bucket, and move her to avoid sores on her skin."

Alaqai pressed her knuckles to her lips and squeezed her eyes shut. " 'Two queens—one grown stooped and the other like a child—shall part once more with tears in their eyes.' She foretold our final meeting, but I never imagined it like this."

Toregene and Sorkhokhtani were at her side with a rustle of silks, bolstering her with their strength. "Just as she cared for us when we were young, now we care for her," Sorkhokhtani said.

"She once spent an entire afternoon spoon-feeding me mutton broth when I fell ill with a fever," Toregene said. "It is an honor to do the same for her now."

"She often used to sing Tolui to sleep," Sorkhokhtani said. "Now I sing to her each night."

"She's so broken," Alaqai whispered. "Even more than my father, my mother was always the strongest person in any room."

"She might yet linger like this for months, even years," I said.

Tears finally spilled down Alaqai's cheeks, and she knelt at her mother's side. "She'd hate this slow death."

I swallowed hard, prompted by Toregene's nod. "With your permission, we would speed her on her journey."

"Speed her?" Alaqai gave a sharp intake of breath. "You mean kill her?"

"Borte Khatun is already gone," Sorkhokhtani said. "This shell of flesh and bone isn't the woman who rode out to save her husband from the Tatars, or who rescued the People of the Felt from Jamuka's plots."

Alaqai touched the wolf-tooth necklace at Borte's throat, the necklace that Toregene had insisted I tie around her neck each day despite her chests of silver and jade. "I can't imagine a life without my parents. Yet it seems I have no choice."

"Borte Khatun was ill before your father died," I said. "I fear his death sped her illness."

"And there's nothing more to be done?"

I shook my head. "We've tried everything. Her spirit has already fled."

She nodded and drew a deep breath. "How would you . . . ?"

I dared to touch her hand, relieved when she didn't draw away. "Narcissus bulbs," I answered.

"Will it be painful?"

I couldn't lie; death by poison was rarely an easy way to leave this life. "It will be quicker than this."

Alaqai nodded, squaring her shoulders as she clutched the bed. "She'd want me to say yes. But I need to say good-bye first."

"Of course."

Sorkhokhtani slipped silently outside, and Toregene and I sat on a woven silk rug near the door as Alaqai whispered to Borte while the sheep bleated outside, Alaqai occasionally chuckling over some shared memory from long ago while she brushed her mother's hair and arranged her hands over her chest. I remembered my mother's hands as she lay dying, their delicate webbing of veins and perfectly trimmed nails. Those pale hands had taught me the graceful curve of calligraphy and wiped the tears from my cheeks when I pricked myself with my sewing needle. Yet it was what Sorkhokhtani held that stole my breath now, as she slipped into the tent with an armful of rainbow-hued wildflowers. The vivid colors of the blossoms robbed me of my voice, and I heard my mother's final words in my mind.

"There are so many colors," she'd gasped, her eyes staring unseeing toward the ceiling. Blood and vomit trickled from the corner of her lips. "Colors like our garden in spring."

She drew a last tortured breath and then her soul burst from her body, freed of the sickness that had ravaged her, leaving me clutching the remnants of the narcissus bulbs that still bore the marks from her teeth. I threw them across the room, but the touch of the bulbs polluted my palms, their fire increasing as I listened to my father wail at my mother's bedside after he found her body stiff and cold.

He was so overcome with grief that he never noticed me burying the mangled bulbs in the garden or scrubbing my hands until the water in the porcelain ewer was cloudy with blood.

"Fatima?"

I looked down to see Sorkhokhtani staring at me, a strange expression on her usually placid face. "I asked if you knew where Borte kept a ewer for the flowers."

"They're beautiful," I managed. "I'll find something to put them in."

Sorkhokhtani padded past Alaqai, but I decided against a ewer and instead spread them like a wreath around the edges of the bed. I knew not whether the Khatun noticed them, but Alaqai's eyes gleamed even as more tears spilled down her cheeks. I shivered to realize Borte had foretold this very moment and waited for it all these years.

I removed the bag of narcissus bulbs from my pocket, then ground them to a pulp with a heavy stone and stirred extra willow bark into the mixture with a silver spoon engraved with tigers and dragons. I'd always envisioned the bulbs as a weapon with which to murder Al-Altun, but now they'd become an instrument of mercy. Alaqai reached out a trembling hand for the bowl. "Give it to me," she said. "I'll do it."

The temptation to hand the poison to her was overwhelming, yet I shook my head. "No," I said. "A daughter should never be the instrument of her mother's death."

Sorkhokhtani looked at me with sad eyes. "You say that as if you know."

"I do," I said. "And my soul has already been damned to Jahannam for it."

Sorkhokhtani gave a small smile. "We should not presume to know what any god—the Earth Mother, Christ, or Allah—intends for us. They may yet surprise you, Fatima of Nishapur."

Alaqai looked as if she might still demand the poison, but after a moment her hand fell to her side. "Thank you," she whispered to me.

I drew a deep breath, wondering if I imagined the smell of campfires and rushing rivers as I spooned the mixture onto Borte's tongue. I worried that perhaps the Khatun lacked the strength to swallow, but her eyes met mine for a brief moment and then her throat worked.

I gave her a second spoonful. And another.

We took turns bending over the Khatun and breathing deeply, sharing the remaining fragments of Borte's soul among us. Sorkhokhtani began to sing then, her voice as clear and strong as any imam's, and the rest of us joined in, my voice mingling with Toregene's deeper timbre and Alaqai's husky tone. It was our voices that would send Borte's soul to Jannah's waiting rivers of wine and honey tonight.

I wondered then whether it was flowers Borte saw—or perhaps the campfires of her many children or her daughters gathered around her—as I felt her soul slip from her body, hover for a moment above us, and finally fly free into the waiting sky.

Chapter 24

The leaves unfurled and changed, fell, and grew again while Genghis' sons fought among themselves for their father's position. The flesh fell from the Khan and Khatun's bodies and the sun bleached their bones white, abandoned to the steppes they'd fought for. Before Alaqai returned to the Onggud, I'd helped her, Toregene, and Sorkhokhtani erect Borte's *ger* in an empty valley within a day's walk from Ogodei's camp, a sort of shrine packed with the Khatun's butter churns, cheesecloths, and even a finely wrought silver cradle that Tolui and her grandchildren had once slept in. Her spirit would linger there, and Genghis' spirit banner now waved outside Ogodei's Great White Tent. As Borte had foretold, the Great Khan's empire fractured the moment he drew his last breath, a precious piece of jade splintering from within. Yet it took longer to discover the fracture within Ogodei, despite his place at the head of the Thirteen Hordes.

The clans gathered for a *khurlatai* to confirm Ogodei as Khan, but not everyone agreed that Genghis' third son should succeed his father. Hot-headed Chaghatai refused to partake of the proceedings and took his people and his vote with him back to his lands in the west. Finally, after ritually declining the nomination three times, Ogodei bowed his head and accepted the helm of the Khan. His first act was to seize the lands along the

Tuul River, the verdant valleys gifted by Genghis to his wives Yesui and Yesugen. Because the women were only secondary wives and had no sons to stand for them, the rest of the Golden Family ignored the bloodless conquest.

Ogodei took to passing out pearls and gold coins to his people and wearing a golden robe both day and night. It seemed a shame to waste such good silk dressing an ox, but if people grumbled, it was only to mutter that Genghis' third son was becoming a soft man of easy pleasures.

Not only soft, but sedentary.

After seizing Yesui and Yesugen's lands, Ogodei slaughtered half a herd of sheep and summoned the Golden Family to his newly erected Great White Tent for a feast. I accompanied Toregene, who wore Borte's tall green *boqta* as befit her new station as the Great Khatun, and ignored the churning in my stomach as the Khan tore into greasy haunches of mutton, licking his fingers and belching so the air grew thick with sour fumes. Sorkhokhtani sat with her sons, silently picking at her food while Tolui's place beside her remained empty. Everyone else shared bowls of golden wine between them, but I'd overheard Sorkhokhtani forbid her sons to so much as breathe too deeply near a bottle of wine or jug of *airag*. Given their father's example, I couldn't blame her.

Pieces of gray meat fell from Ogodei's mouth as he revealed the full reason for his celebration: a proclamation that he would build a permanent capital to replace his father's wandering circles of tents.

"Our new city shall be the envy of the world," he boasted, after rambling on about his great *ger* and plans for the city's earthen walls. "Artisans and architects will compete to live there, to show off the splendors commissioned by our empire."

I gave an audible scoff, earning a scathing glare from Güyük.

"Let me guess," Ogodei's son snarled. "The imperious Persian slave doesn't believe my father can accomplish such a feat?" Güyük rose, his skinny fingers curled into fists at his sides.

"Be seated, Güyük," Toregene said to her son. "Fatima hasn't been my slave for some time."

I shrugged, arranging my silver slippers with their curled toes beneath the hem of my new crimson robe. "What do you Mongols know of beauty?" I asked from beneath my veil.

"We've conquered the world over," Güyük sputtered, ignoring his mother's command to sit. "If anyone can build the world's greatest capital—"

"It is not you Mongols," I finished for him. "Instead, you and your kind destroyed countless beautiful cities from Persia to Cathay." Güyük was a petulant child trussed up in a man's body; I sometimes wondered if perhaps Toregene had mistakenly lain with a demon to conceive him.

"How dare you speak in such a manner?" Güyük demanded, but his father's hand clapped down hard on his shoulder.

"Let her continue, boy," Ogodei growled. "You speak as if you think you were Khan. Yet you're only a lamb who has yet to fight his first battle."

Güyük flushed, his face as red as a misshapen radish, but he obeyed his father. Ogodei leaned back on the long bench of his carved Horse Throne— the same one that his father had once sat upon, although Ogodei had ordered it gilded over with gold—and traced the rim of his wine cup with his thumb. "Tell us, Rose of Nishapur," he said, "what you would recommend so that our city rivals the splendor of Baghdad and Samarkhand."

I stood, ignoring the nervous flutter in my belly. "First of all, no ruler of any civilized people sleeps in a tent, no matter how grand. You must build a palace."

"I'd as soon take up a plow and eat grass like cattle as I would sleep within walls," Ogodei said. "A Mongol doesn't live within stone."

"But your city will have a wall around it, will it not?" I countered.

The Khan scratched his chin. "We have made many enemies over the years. My architects insist on having walls to guard the treasures within."

"And you must have a palace to showcase those riches. Else all those kings and foreign ambassadors will forever see you as a marauding heathen."

Of course, the rest of the world would always view these bloodthirsty horsemen as savages who stunk of leather and dung, but I needn't mention that to Ogodei.

Even Toregene gasped at the audacity of my insult, and Güyük looked as though he might strangle me then and there. But Ogodei only nodded slowly. "We shall add a palace, then." His gray eyes glinted mischievously. "Although I hope you don't expect me to sleep there."

"Sleep where you will," I said. "But you must receive your subjects in a throne room decorated with gold and jewels."

"I see why you keep this one close to you, wife." Ogodei glanced at Toregene, then dropped a stack of drawings in my lap. "She hides a ready mind behind that veil. What else should I build, Rose of Nishapur?"

I tapped my chin, pretending to ponder his question as I scanned the ink sketches of buildings. There were districts for homes and markets, and an impressive array of houses of worship. "Thus far, your city has storehouses and guard towers, four gates, two Saracen mosques, twelve temples, and too many Nestorian churches to count."

"My city shall be a tolerant place," Ogodei said, pride evident in his eyes.

"Yes, but it still has nothing to awe its visitors," I said. "No statues or art to make jaws drop in wonder when they enter its gates."

"Like Nishapur's famed turquoise domes," he said.

I felt a pang of remorse then, that I was here, prodding the Great Khan to build a capital to rival the city of my birth, while so many others had met their deaths at the end of Mongol spears and swords. No town could be as lovely as Nishapur, but perhaps I could help this new Khan build a fair city in which his conquered peoples could come together, to live in a place of beauty and art, of stars and poetry. Perhaps Ogodei might learn to take more interest in building cities instead of destroying them.

"Like our domes," I said. "And the Gate of the Silversmiths."

"Everyone out except for the Rose," Ogodei roared, his mustache twitching over his smile. "Send for my architects!"

I started at being singled out, but Toregene's imperceptible nod encouraged me to stay. Güyük shot me a glare and leaned toward me. "You'll pay for making me look the fool," he snarled, his breath hot and damp on my ear. "I have plans for you, Fatima, and one day my mother and father won't be able to protect you. Then what will you do?"

Fortunately, I was saved from responding when Möngke and Kublai each grabbed Güyük by the arm and dragged him outside with talk of a horse race. Still, he twisted to glance back at me, his eyes afire with fury and some other emotion. Sorkhokhtani trailed behind them, as silent as ever.

Once the door closed, Ogodei patted the seat next to him on the golden bench. He blew an exasperated puff of air through his thick lips when I hesitated. "You'll lecture the Great Khan on his building follies, but you cringe at sitting next to me? Perhaps you're not so brave as you seem."

I sat then, enveloped by the male smell of him and that of his priceless perfume—a rare scent that originated from tiny black spheres of deer musk. The pungent balls fell from the glands of a diminutive fanged Kashmir deer and were collected from the forest floor before camels carried them to wealthy buyers along the Silk Road. Ogodei smiled. "Now, listen well to these architects and artisans from Cathay and your Khwarazm lands, Fatima. You'll help decide what other splendors my city needs."

I spent the remainder of the evening listening as architects proposed all manner of things to decorate Karakorum's imaginary flagstone streets—giant tortoise statues to stand sentry at the main gate, a pond stocked with swans and koi fish, and palace pillars carved with dragons whose tails wrapped around the base of marble columns. I finally left the Khan's tent under a moon that shone brighter than a thousand candles, with orders to return again in the morning. Still, an unwelcome thought stole away my euphoria.

These Mongols were the scourge of the earth, brutal warlords and murderers, adulterers and thieves; yet Borte, Toregene, and Sorkhokhtani had shown me true kindness. Alaqai had sacrificed her happiness several times to rule her people, and Shigi was so refined he might have graced the court of the Shah. Even Ogodei strove to build cities of everlasting beauty and had recently ordered that all Mongols set aside a two-year-old wether—a castrated ram—each year to help feed the poorest among them.

I wanted nothing more than to revel in what had once been a pure and simple hatred toward these uncouth infidels. But that was becoming more impossible with each passing day.

Ogodei's building plans were temporarily forgotten when death revisited the Golden Family. Ogodei had turned his eyes to the east and taken Tolui with him to finish their father's conquest against the Golden King of

Cathay. Their first forays were successful, and Toregene received a messenger who claimed that dead Cathay soldiers littered the land like rotting trees. The men then stopped on the Yellow Steppe, and Ogodei fell ill. Shamans divined the meaning of horse entrails on the earthen floor of the Khan's tent and proclaimed that Ogodei might be saved if someone from his family offered his life in his place. And thus Tolui committed the lone act of bravery in his life, claiming that without Ogodei, the Mongol people would be like orphans and the people of Cathay would rejoice. He offered to die so that Ogodei, his chosen older brother and the Great Khan, might live.

"Let my elder brother Ogodei determine how to care for my sons and widow, until my orphan boys reach manhood," Tolui said, raising a wine jug and swaying on his feet. He sat down hard, a lopsided smile on his face. "I'm drunk."

Perhaps it was the copious amount of wine Tolui had already guzzled that evening that infused him with rare courage for so selfless an act. The shamans sang their songs lauding his great sacrifice, and Tolui continued drinking, swilling enough wine to fell twenty soldiers while the bearded men conjured their devilry. The moon had scarcely moved from its notch in the sky when Tolui stumbled to his feet, burst from the tent in a drunken tirade, and breathed his last.

Now Sorkhokhtani, too, had become a widow. It seemed we women had two choices in life: death in childbed or widowhood.

Shortly after the funeral cortege arrived from Cathay, Toregene and I knelt in Sorkhokhtani's tent, preparing Tolui's body, when Ogodei came to comfort his brother's widow. The Great Khan had recovered from his illness shortly after his brother's demise and insisted on traveling home with the sledge bearing Tolui's corpse. Mongols rarely cried for the dead, for they believed that the tears of the grieving became an ocean of trouble for the dead. Yet, while Sorkhokhtani's eyes were dry, Ogodei's were bloodshot to match the ruptured veins that flared across his nose and cheeks.

"Tolui was the bravest of my brothers," he muttered. "While Jochi and Chaghatai argued between themselves for my father's favor, Tolui always stood steadfast by my side. He died for me and thus honored you, Sor-khokhtani, and your sons."

Sorkhokhtani accepted the Khan's condolences in silence. I should have known something was amiss when Toregene excused herself, claiming she needed more sandalwood although a basket of the fragrant bark sat at Tolui's feet.

"You must be provided for, Sorkhokhtani," Ogodei said. His collar was folded under and his sleeves pulled back, another superstition to confuse any malignant spirits that lingered near the dead. "I will not have it said that my father's Princess of the Hearth has been neglected or mistreated."

"Your family has always cared for me," Sorkhokhtani said, folding her hands demurely in her lap. Tolui's body lay between them, his torso covered by a white silk shroud. His eyes were closed, his face pale and stiff. I'd had to fight down the panic that welled in my throat when we first began to purify him, to quash the remembrance of Mansoor and my father as they lay in the mosque courtyard. It had been years since that fateful day, yet I would never escape from its shadow.

"I would ensure that we're always in a position to see to your well-being," Ogodei said. "That's why I would urge you to marry Güyük after the forty-nine days of mourning for my brother are finished. It was your husband's wish that I provide for you and your sons."

Sorkhokhtani's face remained as aloof as ever, but a mixture of disgust, revulsion, and horror flashed in her eyes before she dropped her gaze to stare at her hands.

"Tolui's body is scarcely cold," I said quickly, giving her time to gather her thoughts. "Perhaps you could discuss this some other time." Sor-khokhtani may not have loved Tolui—it was difficult to imagine such a proud woman caring for such a weak excuse for a man—but marrying Güyük would be a fate worse than death.

But Ogodei's next words stopped my heart. "Güyük asked first to take you as his wife, Rose of Nishapur," he said to me. "He claims he's thirsted for you since the day his mother brought you to our camp."

"Toregene would never allow it." Yet even as I said it, I wondered at the truth of the words. Toregene indulged her son in everything, and although

I was no longer her slave, I couldn't guarantee that she wouldn't give Güyük my hand if he demanded it.

"It matters not what the Khatun feels about the match," Ogodei said. "It only matters that *I* will not allow the marriage."

I breathed a silent prayer to Allah, promising the One God my eternal obedience. "Instead, I must see the Princess of the Hearth provided for," Ogodei said to Sorkhokhtani.

"My sons will provide for me," Sorkhokhtani said slowly, lifting her chin to reveal a woman once more in full control of herself. "I thank you for your thoughtfulness, but as the widow of the man who saved your life, all I ask is to grieve in peace and retire quietly with my sons."

Ogodei's eyes narrowed and he studied her for a moment before giving a curt nod. "You were a good wife to Tolui, and he was the best of brothers to me," he said. "For no one else would I entertain such a preposterous idea, but I will honor your request."

"Thank you," she whispered. She bowed her head, and I wondered for a moment if it was to hide her relief.

Sorkhokhtani and I had escaped Güyük and the intrigues of the Golden Horde, at least for now.

We wouldn't always be so lucky.

"The Oirat lands that belonged to Checheyigen should be mine now," Ogodei said to Toregene one day shortly after Tolui's funeral feast and Sorkhokhtani's retreat to the north. Toregene hadn't spoken to Sorkhokhtani since the morning Ogodei had proposed she marry Güyük, and I'd listened to her rage that night about how Sorkhokhtani should be honored to marry her son. Toregene was an intelligent woman, but she was blind to her son's many faults.

Now Ogodei shifted on his tasseled cushions, his councilors' heads bobbing like the ostriches I'd once seen in Nishapur's zoo. "My father would want me to bring the Oirat firmly under the Mongol yoke again, and not let them be ruled by an untried girl-child."

"Oghul Ghaimish is not just a random child. She is Checheyigen's daughter, granddaughter to Genghis Khan, and your niece," Toregene said calmly, despite the advisers' murmurs of agreement. Checheyigen had been Yesui's daughter and therefore Ogodei's half sister until her recent death, although I'd scarcely heard her mentioned before now. The entire clan seemed to pretend that Genghis' lesser wives and children simply didn't exist. "It's unfortunate that Checheyigen died of the tumor in her belly, yet the fact remains that her daughter is now the rightful ruler of the Oirat."

I set down the artist's plans in my lap, although I found them far superior to the talk of the Oirat and Ogodei's plans of conquest. My hopes that Ogodei's love of building would replace his desire for conquest had failed to materialize, and instead he'd commanded all his nobles to send their eldest sons to siege Ryazan. Jochi's son Batu commanded the attack, joined by troublesome Güyük and Sorkhokhtani's eldest boy, Möngke. Of course, Batu hadn't been thrilled at being saddled with Güyük, but it was better than having Güyük here with us.

"The Great Khan was quite clear on the matter of succession before he died," Toregene said, glancing up from accounts of the recent tribute from Cathay. "You were given your own lands, and your sisters were to keep the lands from their marriages."

"The Oirat won't welcome you," I said. "They're already ruled by your father's blood through Oghul Ghaimish." I thought Ogodei would let the Oirat matter drop in the face of reason, but I should have known that was folly. Ogodei was never ruled by reason.

"I care little for what the Oirat want," he said, pulling on his rabbit-fur-lined boots and stepping outside. He groaned with pleasure as the stream of his waters hit the ground, and I wrinkled my nose in distaste. "I'm Great Khan now," he said through the wall, "and I will consolidate my father's holdings and expand his empire, taking the Oirat lands just as I did with the Goryeo peninsula."

I didn't respond to that. Ogodei's early campaigns against far-flung Goryeo, also known by the Mongols as the Rainbow Land of the Son-in-Law Nation, had brought him a train of spoils that included ten thousand otter pelts and bolts of silk, twenty thousand horses, and ten children from the

Goryeo noble houses given as hostages. His more recent offensive had resulted in widespread Goryeo resistance, the torching of their land, and their wholesale starvation and slaughter. Of course, Ogodei had crowed about his success in both instances, and the campaign had whetted his thirst for conquest and the need to prove himself equal to his father.

The Khan scratched his chin. "And perhaps after I conquer the Oirat, I'll head south and persuade the Uighurs to accept my rule as well."

The Uighurs were Al-Altun's people.

The very thought of Genghis' youngest daughter brought my dreams of murder and poison flooding back, along with the memory of her crowing with pleasure along the ramparts of Nishapur.

"The Khatun of the Uighurs has consolidated her power in recent years," said one of Ogodei's advisers. Korguz was a Uighur himself, covered with dark hair like a monkey, and one of Ogodei's favorite councilors due to his ability to match the Khan's drinking and carousing. I loathed the little man.

"Too much power for a woman, if you ask me. Especially one whose very name means *subordinate*," Ogodei drawled, chuckling at his wit. "And her lands are not impregnable."

"Not at all," Korguz said. "In the face of your war machine, they would likely fall in a matter of months, if not weeks."

The hairy ape-man dared not even stand up for his people, but offered them on a platter to Ogodei. His next words were even more repulsive. "I'd be happy to act as an intermediary once Al-Altun capitulates to your demands."

Ogodei stroked his chin. "Perhaps. Your assistance might prove valuable, and in return, I shall soon have need of a governor of eastern Persia."

A grin spread across Korguz's face and I scarcely managed to mask my anger. Perhaps I'd cultivate extra narcissus bulbs next spring to ensure that such a foul ape-man never set foot in the lands of my birth.

Ogodei's attack against the Oirat was like a lightning strike in a forest of dried trees, and equally destructive. After their capital fell and Ogodei's niece, Oghul Ghaimish, had been taken prisoner, Ogodei's arrow messengers flew in all the eight directions to spread word of his destruction of the Oirat, and to strike terror into the hearts of his enemies. His treasure this time wasn't hostages and furs, silk and horses, but instead the Mongol army raped almost a thousand Oirat girls, claimed them as slaves or wives, and brought them back to Ogodei's burgeoning capital, where screams of terror and terrible sobbing replaced the constant sound of hammers and chisels on the night of his return. The moon shone down upon the foundations of the palace and the skeleton frames of the warehouses being built near the boundary stones of the ancient city of Khar Balgas.

"Ogodei hasn't heard the end of this," Toregene promised, pacing the length of my tent. She'd built the fire up so the crackle of flames would drown out most of the Oirat screams and help her sweat out the illness she hadn't been able to shake these past weeks. The Mongols' ineffective cure for everything was to eat more meat, so strings of sausage, haunches of horse, and even a ram's head hung from Toregene's rafters. The sheep's sightless eyes seemed to watch my every movement until I'd covered the carcass with a tattered felt blanket. "The clans have condemned his betrayal of his father's laws."

"But Ogodei doesn't care," I said.

"I know. All he would speak of tonight was his victory, and Güyük."

"Güyük?" I failed to see the connection of one disaster to the other.

"My son is here, recalled from the Siege of Ryazan by his father."

"May Allah help us," I muttered.

It made sense that Ogodei had demanded the return of his son. Spoiled and drunk, Güyük had argued with his elder cousin Batu at a victory banquet after one of the main cities of the Rus wild lands fell, claiming Batu was an old woman with a quiver, although Güyük had failed to take down even a single goat kid. When his cousin calmly ignored him, Güyük rode away cursing and knocking down the *gers* of his own soldiers.

"Ogodei threatened to have Güyük executed." Her voice was calm, but her sudden cough caused the pot she set over the fire to spill its water. The liquid splashed into the flames with an angry hiss, dissipating into steam that spiraled up to the top of the tent and out into the night. "He railed against my son so loudly that the Muscovites in the west might have heard him."

For my part, I wished Ogodei *would* execute his son and save all of us a lot of trouble. Yet despite Güyük's many faults, Toregene still loved her son. "What happened?"

"Güyük promised to do better next time."

"And Ogodei forgave him?"

"Of course. Ogodei seeks to bolster his power, in more ways than one." Toregene cleared her throat. "He's arranged Güyük's marriage to Oghul Ghaimish."

I stared at her, sure I had heard wrong. Yet she didn't repeat herself.

"Checheyigen's daughter?"

"The very same."

Ogodei's niece and granddaughter of Genghis Khan. In marrying his son to the last link to the Oirat ruling family, Ogodei would proclaim to all his enemies what would happen should they refuse to obey him: their lands destroyed, their men killed, and their girls absorbed into the Mongol Empire.

It was cruel, but also genius.

"Güyük asked to marry you again, Fatima, but Ogodei and I refused to allow it. I told him I agreed with Ogodei that he should marry Oghul Ghaimish instead."

I sagged with relief, and then guilt assaulted me, that this girl who'd already endured such horrors would now be subjected to Güyük for the rest of her life. It was a fate perhaps worse than death.

Then I remembered Güyük's words from the day in Ogodei's Great White Tent.

I have plans for you, Fatima, and one day my mother and father won't be able to protect you.

Gooseflesh rippled up my skin and I shivered in the sudden cold. "Why did you refuse?"

"I know you'll never love another man, Fatima." She smiled. "And I don't care to share you, not even with my son," Toregene said. "I fear you're saddled with me until the end of my days."

I smiled at that, but still my heart was heavy with guilt.

"Oghul Ghaimish's life was just destroyed. Surely Ogodei can be persuaded—"

"Ogodei is emphatic that the marriage take place tonight." She sat down, folding her legs so her chin rested on her knees. "Someone must prepare the girl."

"I'll find her and bring her here."

It was the least I could do, to help this broken princess who was taking both my place and Sorkhokhtani's.

Only how I would find the callousness and the strength to deliver her to Güyük tonight, I didn't know.

I discovered Oghul Ghaimish crammed in a corral with many more Oirat girls, their colorful silks stained a dull brown from the dust of the journey here and their hair matted in tangles like birds' nests. However, it wasn't their clothes that worried me, but the emptiness in their eyes, as if their souls had long since fled and left behind the hollow husks of their bodies.

I called Oghul Ghaimish's name as I passed the moonlit corral. The carts bearing silks and silver had been unloaded, but these unclaimed girls had been left to bear the brunt of the autumn winds in tattered silken shifts, guarded by the same men who had followed Ogodei's nefarious orders to rape them all. I'd never thought of myself as lucky, but it occurred to me that things might have been much worse for me at Nishapur had Toregene not chosen me.

"Come to choose a girl for a slave?" One of the soldiers hollered the question at me, then licked his lips. "They're docile, already broken, if you know what I mean."

I gave him a withering glare. "Open this corral," I said, but he didn't move. "Now! By order of the Khatun!"

He muttered under his breath and shuffled toward the gate to remove the wooden bars. I expected the girls to flood out onto the grass, but they remained rooted to the ground, like caged doves suddenly set free and unsure where to go.

"Which one of you is Oghul Ghaimish?" I asked them. At first no one answered, but finally a woman nudged the wraith of a girl next to her, her face obscured by lanky hair.

"She is Oghul Ghaimish."

I recognized the same flat face that Ogodei shared with his father, but there the similarities ended. The princess' eyes were so empty I felt as if I were looking at one already claimed by death, and she smelled of feces, as if her bowels had turned loose after all she'd survived.

"Come with me," I said, then turned to the guard. "Get these girls food and water and blankets. They'd better be fed by the time I return or you'll have to deal with the Khatun."

The man grumbled under his breath as Oghul Ghaimish tried to step regally from the pen, but she tripped on legs bruised and too long unused. I crouched to help her, shooting a scathing glare at the laughing guards as I looped my arm around her frail shoulders.

"This Oirat girl marries Güyük tonight, and may well be your Khatun one day," I said, swallowing back the bile in my throat at the implication of Güyük becoming Khan. The laughter fell from their lips and I gave a wicked smile. "I'm sure she'll one day remember all the kindness you offered upon her arrival. Perhaps she'll repay you with ordering a spear lodged in your stomach while you sleep."

The guard blanched the color of milk, and Oghul Ghaimish quivered in my arms like a feather in the breeze. She hiccuped as I led her toward Toregene's tent, but otherwise she was silent.

Toregene's tent was ablaze with the light of a roaring fire, and a red felt headdress lined with black sable and dangling strands of gold coins and turquoise had been laid next to a red felted dress. Toregene straightened and cast a horrified glance at us. "This is Oghul Ghaimish?"

What was left of her, at least.

I nodded. "Daughter of Checheyigen, blood leader of the Oirat."

"Then we shall have to make her look like it."

I expected Oghul Ghaimish to let us peel the ruined silk from her thin frame, but the moment we touched the fabric she gave a screech like giant claws ripping the air and attacked us with some hidden well of strength. Her nails tore away my veil and sliced open my cheek so I felt the slick warmth of fresh blood on my skin.

A fighter, then, but only once cornered.

It took both of us to subdue the frightened animal of a girl, pinning her to the ground with the full weight of our bodies. "Wine," I said to Toregene. "A full bowl."

She nodded and maneuvered herself off Oghul Ghaimish, leaving the panting girl pinned beneath me. "Drink," I said, as Toregene tilted her head forward and pressed the golden bowl to her lips. "It will make things easier."

I'd have plugged her nose so Toregene could pour the wine down her throat, but Oghul Ghaimish opened her mouth and gulped the ruby-hued liquid like a fish left too long out of water. Toregene and I sat back on our haunches, flushed from the fight.

Oghul Ghaimish held out the empty bowl, entranced by the ram's head hanging from the ceiling, its blanket fallen to the ground in the melee. "More."

I arched an eyebrow and replaced the blanket, but Toregene filled the golden bowl to its rim and handed it back to the girl. Letting Oghul Ghaimish drink herself into oblivion likely wasn't the wisest strategy for her wedding night, and I wondered with a fresh pang of guilt what she'd do once she'd met her husband. All the wine in the empire wouldn't be enough to drown her misery then.

She thrust the bowl back at me when she finished, a red tinge of liquid glistening on her upper lip. I shook my head. "You can have more once you've let us clothe you and dress your hair."

Oghul Ghaimish studied me, her scrutiny disconcerting. "You told the guard I might one day be Khatun. Is that true?"

Toregene's eyes widened, but she was seized by a coughing fit from her lingering illness and the exertion of the fight. I nodded to Oghul Ghaimish. "You'll marry the Great Khan's eldest son tonight," I said. "Güyük may one day become Khan."

May Allah strike us dead before that happened.

Oghul Ghaimish seemed to ponder that, scratching at a bleeding patch of skin on her neck and staining her nails scarlet. "You may dress me, then."

I stoked the fire, ready to pin Oghul Ghaimish to the ground again as we stripped her, but this time she didn't fight. I cringed when she finally stood naked before us. What might have once been a slight and pretty young Oirat girl was now a ghost of a child, stinking of old urine with feces and blood matted in the hair between her legs and the stench of fear clinging to her like an invisible cloak.

We scrubbed her gently, washing away the evidence of her ordeal, although I knew there were other invisible wounds that would never heal. She moaned several times, and her eyes fluttered open to reveal the whites of her eyes and swollen pupils.

"Are you sure Ogodei won't change his mind?" I whispered, but Toregene shook her head.

So we trussed up Ogodei's broken niece to sacrifice her to Güyük. She greedily slurped down one more bowl of wine before stepping from Toregene's grand tent.

Oghul Ghaimish held her chin high as she greeted Güyük outside the wedding tent erected on the banks of the artificial river being dug. The felt walls were darkened by the shadows of what would one day be the Khan's palace, and during the ceremony Oghul Ghaimish bit her lip so a thin ribbon of blood unfurled down her chin. Güyük didn't seem to notice, for his eyes remained on me for the whole of the ceremony. He strummed his fingers impatiently against his leg while the shaman intoned a blessing and Toregene invoked a Christian prayer for her son and new daughter. I was glad for the barrage of throat singers, lutes, and horsehair fiddles that burst into sound at a flick of Ogodei's wrist, the cacophony of music ringing in my ears and making it impossible to think of what I'd done to this frail girl.

Toregene beckoned to me when Güyük and his new bride walked between the purification fires, pressing into my hand a rumpled paper that had been folded and refolded many times. "I've had a message from Al-Altun," she whispered. "She claims to have need of Ogodei's army to quell resistance from her own people."

My mouth went dry as Oghul Ghaimish stumbled, then hesitated at the entrance of her new *ger*. "Will Ogodei do as she asks?"

"It may be a trap," Toregene said. "She likely heard of Ogodei's plans to wage war against the Uighurs and thinks to lure her brother to her and then destroy him. She may have massed superior forces against us."

"Or she may need him."

Toregene shrugged. "Either way, Ogodei has already agreed to ride for the Uighurs. This time we'll both accompany him—"

"You're not to leave the borders of this camp," I said. "Not until you've recovered from your illness."

"I'll be fine. I won't allow Ogodei to treat the Uighur women as he did the Oirat."

Güyük and Oghul Ghaimish entered the wedding tent then amidst shouts of joy and drunken laughter. Ogodei and his people wrestled, drank, and feasted so loudly that few heard the bride's screams later that night as the stars danced merrily overhead.

Chapter 25

The wind's cold breath screamed down from the snowcapped mountains to cut through our felt cloaks and steal the feeling from our fingers and toes. I reproached myself every day for abandoning Oghul Ghaimish to Güyük while we traveled to Al-Altun's lands, but I'd made Toregene swear to leave behind a contingent of soldiers to guard the Oirat princess. I prayed to Allah every night that Oghul Ghaimish's heart might heal even as Toregene's illness worsened and the bones in my legs threatened to collapse from the frantic pace Ogodei insisted we keep.

Finally, the Mongol army came to a stop outside Al-Altun's walled city of Gobalik, yet the town remained silent, as if it had already been abandoned. Only gray wisps of smoke and the occasional snorts of horses and oxen brought inside for safekeeping betrayed the presence of life. As night fell on the empty plain, Ogodei discussed plans for a siege, instructing his engineers to strip the surrounding countryside of its trees for catapults and battering rams so he might better conquer his half sister and her people.

Instead, Gobalik's gates creaked open and a boy on horseback cantered out, flanked by twenty of the largest guards I'd ever seen, all Uighurs with white felt hats rimmed with thick sable. I felt for the protective dagger Toregene insisted I wear in my boot, but then I recognized the arrogant sweep of the child's cheekbones and his full lips. The leather of my gloves creaked as I gripped my pommel.

"Welcome, Khan of Khans," said Al-Altun's son to his uncle, his voice high with boyhood and his smooth chin tilted with the pride granted only to the privileged and powerful, a conceit I recognized from my own youth.

"My mother asked that I apologize for her absence." The boy hesitated and received an indecipherable nod from the man at his right. "The uprising on the frontiers became critical and she rode out to contain it only days ago."

The councilor at the boy's side urged his horse forward and spoke. "Al-Altun bids the Gur-Khan, the Golden Family, and their soldiers welcome to the fair city of Gobalik," the Uighur said, but his speech was quickly interrupted.

"If I am welcome," Ogodei growled, "then why are the gates barred to me?"

"We are honored by your presence, but the foundations of our meager city would crumble beneath the hooves and boots of your great army." The man held his pommel lightly, but his posture was rigid. "Surely the plains have everything you require to pitch your tents and pasture your animals?"

"I am impatient to greet my sister," Ogodei said, directing his horse to trot around the man and Al-Altun's son. I could hear his mind calculating how simple it would be to seize his sister's city while her back was turned. "When do you expect her homecoming?"

The councilor lifted a hand to his heart and bowed over his saddle. "Al-Altun anticipated the Khan's wrath at her absence and thus left behind two contingents of her own men. Our soldiers would be honored to travel with you to launch a winter campaign against Wien while you wait for your sister's return."

The name Uighur meant *united*, and it appeared that Al-Altun's people had rallied together to thwart the Great Khan and his ambitions, knowing that he wouldn't be able to resist the generous bone they threw him in the direction of Wien, also known as Vienna, and, beyond that, the Great Sea.

"Al-Altun plays a dangerous game," I muttered to Toregene under my breath. She gave a tight nod in reply.

Ogodei had sent Korguz to oversee Persia—much to my dismay—and ordered Güyük in Karakorum to oversee the remainder of the building projects, so now he beckoned to Shigi and his newest adviser, a sallow-faced Christian who had forgotten what it was to bathe. It was rumored that the Englishman had forced his sovereign, King John, to sign a charter stripping away the crown's power and then traveled through the Holy Lands before seeking out the Khan of Khans. He had a knack for languages after his itinerant traveling, and thus Ogodei had plucked him into his service despite his ragged nails, grime-coated ears, and ever-present stench. Now the Khan leaned toward him, his black eyes gleaming. "First I shall conquer Wien with the help of my sister's forces," he whispered. "And then we shall seize Al-Altun's holdings out from under her."

I was under no illusions that the Khan would stop there; he'd soon turn his eyes to the only lands still outside his grasp, those belonging to Alaqai and Sorkhokhtani.

"Do you think it wise—," Shigi began, but Ogodei cut him off.

"Let my half sister play the warrior and stamp out her insurrection," the Khan said. "Once she's returned, she must meet me outside Wien."

Once I would have cackled with glee to watch Ogodei and Al-Altun destroy each other. I no longer burned with a desire for revenge as I had in the early years after Nishapur.

Instead, I worried that their desire for power and conquest would destroy us all in the process.

Winter followed us across the plains, but the chill was almost pleasant compared to the misery I'd survived during winters on the steppes. The barren grasslands gave way to rugged valleys, snow-smeared mountains, and fallow fields with fences and idle irrigation ditches. The horses grew thin from the lack of grasses, and the animals learned to give wide berth to the leafless bushes that sometimes hid venomous blunt-nosed vipers. A hapless mare's scream when she was bitten by one of the serpents brought back flashes of Nishapur, made worse when Shigi speared the mare to put her out of her misery. A second spear killed the striped gray viper, but for days after that I started at every rustle of grass. Nothing good could come of such a vile and barren land.

Hunger gnawed at my stomach so fiercely that I deigned to eat plates of greasy boiled meat after the reserve horses were butchered. Toregene laughed at me from beneath the cocoon of blankets she now required to keep her teeth from chattering, for I refused to eat with my hands like a common soldier. Instead, I became adept at using two daggers to both cut the foul meat and eat it. It was better than starving, but only just.

Finally, we neared Wien with its gateway toward the Great Sea. Mongol scouts prowled over the city's outlying districts, causing the pale-skinned Viennese to flee behind the supposed safety of their walls. They raided us only once, killing a handful of Mongol archers and capturing the sallow-faced Englishman. I was almost relieved to hear of the Englishman's death, for now he had a reasonable excuse for subjecting us to his pervasive odor, but Ogodei roared with anger when messengers brought news of the man's demise. I gritted my teeth as he raged against the Viennese, for Ogodei's anger stemmed not from the needless bloodshed or even from the loss of his valuable adviser, but instead because he'd been deprived of his rare toy. This entire campaign was only a game to Ogodei, a giant checkered board of *chatrang* scattered with us, his pawns, while he attempted to checkmate the queen and end the match.

Still, the Khan ordered more horses butchered despite the damp air that seeped into our bones and loosened the men's bowstrings. Tempers flared until the blare of countless curved horns interrupted the soldiers' grumbles and the whine of the winds, the *burees* announcing the approach of the Khatun of the Uighurs. It was Azar, the ninth month in the Persian calendar, which was named in ancient days for the time of worshipping fire, yet the youngest daughter born of Genghis Khan's seed was more destructive than any flames.

Al-Altun arrived amidst the razing of several tall pine trees and the steady scrape of saws and pounding hammers, for Ogodei's men were busy building ballistas and catapults to bring Wien to its knees. Genghis' youngest daughter dressed not as a warrior that day, but as a perfumed and harmless queen. She wore a crimson robe in the Uighur style with white braid down the front and thin sleeves, and a red scarf wound around her head that fell to her feet, topped with a gold crown resembling a boat with high points fore and aft. I waited for the surge of hatred at seeing my husband's murderer again, but I felt only its dull flicker deep in my heart, surrounded by a deep well of emptiness. Toregene drew closer and clasped my gloved hand with her own, as if sensing my sadness.

"You've done well, brother," Al-Altun said, grasping Ogodei's hands. She stepped back to survey his fine silks and his double chin. "At least when it comes to seizing the larders of those you've conquered."

Several Mongols gasped, but the Khan threw his head back and roared with laughter. "I'm surprised these Uighurs haven't relieved you of that sharp tongue of yours yet."

"A situation I'm sure you would have rectified long ago," she answered, rare dimples cleaving her cheeks, although I saw the way her eyes lingered at the golden dagger tucked into her brother's belt. There were no guarantees that she wouldn't find the weapon buried in her heart before this night ended.

"And Toregene Khatun," Al-Altun said, careful to emphasize Toregene's new title as she clasped her close. "I heard of Borte's passing. May her spirit continue to guide you in your new role as Khatun of the Thirteen Nations."

Toregene arched an eyebrow, but the effect was ruined as she bent double in a coughing fit. Tonight I would make sure she had a draught of columbine and chamomile, despite our dwindling herb supplies. "As I hope the spirit of your father, the Great Genghis Khan, guides you as well," she said.

I prayed that the spirits of Genghis and Borte protected their family even now, so far from the windswept plain where they'd been laid to rest.

Al-Altun shrugged. "The Golden Family rarely paid me much heed in life, except to marry me off to the first man who offered our father a profitable alliance. Why should things change in death?"

I realized then that Al-Altun was a bitter woman, grown from the bitter and abandoned daughter of Genghis' least important wife, but that did little to soften my heart toward her.

To me, Al-Altun paid no attention, but I preferred that she ignore me rather than remember me from Nishapur.

"The glorious Golden Family shall once again dine together," Ogodei announced. "In my Great White Tent, as my siblings and I used to do when we were children in my mother's *ger.*"

I wondered if Ogodei's slight was intentional, for I knew from To-regene that Al-Altun had rarely been included in anything having to do with the Golden Family. Even I was aware that Ogodei had created his own camp before Al-Altun's birth. Their age difference and their different mothers meant that this dinner tonight might well be only the second time the half siblings had shared a meal together, aside from Genghis' funeral feast. Of course, there was the chance that Ogodei was truly so oblivious as not to realize the insult.

"I shall be glad to join you after I've seen to my own tent," Al-Altun said, withdrawing from her brother's touch and hiding her arms inside her wide sleeves. Her sharp chin jutted toward Ogodei's Great White Tent. "Not all of us are fortunate enough to have our *gers* hauled fully assembled across the empire."

Ogodei wrapped his meaty arm around her slim shoulders, his free hand on the hilt of his dagger. "Nonsense, sister," he said, pulling her to him as if he might ruffle her hair. "My slaves will erect your tent. You may join us right now."

No one could mistake the command in his voice, and not even Al-Altun dared contradict the Khan of Khans. "As you wish, brother," she said. "I believe we even have an oxcart of Alaqai's famed Onggud wine."

Ogodei grinned at that. "I believe you've just become my favorite sister."

Al-Altun smiled, but the expression didn't reach her eyes. "I always thought Alaqai was your favorite sister."

"You may be right. But for today I believe you're my favorite sister." Ogodei led Al-Altun toward the looming Great White Tent. Toregene and the Khan's advisers followed, and I trailed in their shadows.

The Great White Tent smelled of burning dung and quickly filled with a fug of smoke and the odor of too many unwashed bodies. The thick haze from the center fire stung my eyes as I found a seat near the door while Ogodei settled his great girth on the golden bench, brought all the way from Karakorum. A parade of food arrived moments later, the usual mutton and boiled horsemeat, but also fresh venison and roasted hare dressed with juniper berries. Slaves filled the Khan's iron bowl, a cauldron large enough to hold a full-grown goat. The gorge in my throat rose when Ogodei scooped up the rice and meat with his dirty hands, shoveling them into his mouth, while Al-Altun speared tiny pieces of horsemeat onto her knife. Countless jugs of Onggud wine splashed into Ogodei's golden bowls, and he slurped them down with relish.

"There's my Rose of Nishapur," Ogodei hollered, his words already slurred as he beckoned to me with the greasy haunch of what appeared to have been a lamb. Tiny pearls of sweat beaded at his temples from the heat, and wine stained the front of his golden *deel*. "Come and tell my father's daughter of the wonders being created in my new city, the capital that shall dominate the world in culture, art, and beauty!"

I wished a djinn might steal me away then, so I might avoid sitting next to the woman I'd once tried to kill. But one could scarcely disobey the Khan's direct command.

"It will indeed be a beautiful city," I said as I took my chair, arranging the pleats of my skirt and avoiding looking at Al-Altun. I waved away the bowl a slave offered me and leaned away from the Khan, trying hard not to breathe in his sour smell. Toregene picked at her food as well, as if the family strife had driven away her appetite.

"I doubt it could rival Nishapur." Al-Altun squinted at me so I wondered for a moment if she was nearsighted. "I remember you from atop the walls, as your city fell to its knees."

I didn't wish to discuss the fall of my city. I'd fought hard these many years to let go of my hatred and make a new life for myself. Al-Altun's careless words threatened to destroy all that, leaving my hands shaking with fresh anger and bitterness.

"The Great Khatun saved my life," I said between clenched teeth. "I was one of the few to survive that day, and for that I owe her my gratitude."

Ogodei licked the last grains of rice from his fingers and smacked his lips. He banged his wine bowl on the table upon discovering it was empty. "More wine!" he bellowed.

"Have mine, brother," Al-Altun said. "I've never cared for Alaqai's Onggud brew."

"No?" Ogodei chuckled and reached past me to take the still-full bowl from his sister. "And I always believed you to be an intelligent woman."

Al-Altun chuckled at that, but the way she watched her brother as he slurped down the wine made my flesh prickle. The Khan belched and pounded his chest with a fist, then motioned for the slaves to refill his bowl and downed that as well. I was almost ill when he used his knife to pick the grime from beneath his nails, bits of dirt being flung about the wooden table.

The evening dragged on, Ogodei slurring his words and sloshing wine from its bowl as the tent grew ever hotter. Through it all, Al-Altun sat and endured her brother's insults, occasionally offering a barbed retort that made Ogodei either frown or roar with laughter. Despite the sweep of stars overhead, the Khan dismissed no one, and soon more than one courtier fell asleep where he sat, slack-jawed and drooling on his platter.

I remained stiff in my chair despite the snores, for being in Al-Altun's presence was akin to sitting next to a hive of wasps. Ogodei was in the middle of recounting the oft-told story of his bravery against the Water Tatars when he suddenly lurched to his feet, sending wine bowls clattering to the ground and spilling the crimson liquid into the earth like some offering to his heathen spirits. The Khan moaned and clutched his belly, and then stumbled to heave the contents of his stomach into the giant bowl that had earlier held his *palov*.

There was no doubt that the ruler of the largest empire in the world was a drunken fool, and an embarrassment to his family, for I'd lost count of the times I'd watched Ogodei vomit up copious amounts of wine and *airag*. However, once the Khan voided his stomach, he usually gave a lopsided grin and stumbled to his bed. This time he retched again and again.

"Out!" Toregene finally yelled when it became apparent that Ogodei wouldn't regain control of his stomach. "All of you!"

Heads jerked up and men stumbled to their feet and out the door. Al-Altun paused over her brother's heaving form. "*Bayartai*, brother," she whispered, patting him on the back.

I watched her go, troubled by her words. She didn't bid Ogodei to go in peace, but instead offered him the final Mongol words of farewell. Perhaps it was a slip, but I doubted Al-Altun did anything without forethought.

Ogodei continued to retch into the bowl, until there was nothing left in his stomach. I drew back in alarm to see a thin stream of blood slip from the Khan's lips down his chin. Toregene touched the ribbon of scarlet, her eyes widening at its stain on her fingertips. "No," she whispered. "It can't be."

I knew then that Al-Altun had poisoned Ogodei. The foolish Khan had drunk like a fish dying of thirst—at least ten bowls tonight—swallowing enough of whatever poison his sister had brewed to fell a bear. Toregene had once stopped me from taking Al-Altun's life, and now the treacherous Khatun of the Uighurs would kill Ogodei and plunge the Mongol Empire into chaos.

I hurried to where Shigi stood by the door, ignoring Toregene's panicked calls at my back, but Al-Altun had long since disappeared.

"Seize Al-Altun," I ordered Shigi. "Haul her back here before she can rejoin her army."

Shigi looked past me to where Toregene yelled for both of us now, but I grabbed his arm. "There's no time to waste."

He must have seen the truth in my face, for he gave a tight nod. "It shall be done."

I returned to find Ogodei on his hands and knees, his round face pale and glistening with sweat.

"Everything's spinning," he gasped, reaching out an unsteady hand for Toregene. "As if I were the center spoke of a wheel."

Toregene whirled on me, her face a deathly shade of white. "Tell me this isn't your doing."

I shook my head, my mind racing. "It's Al-Altun; I'm sure of it. If only you'd let me kill her after Genghis' death."

Ogodei's eyes widened and the muscles in his jaw twitched. "My Rose of Nishapur tried to poison my sister?"

"Long ago," I answered. "Toregene stopped me."

"Pity," he croaked. "I might have made you a queen if you'd succeeded."

Toregene looked at me helplessly. "Without knowing which poison she used . . ."

"It may be snake milk," I said. I thought of the viper that had killed the mare on our journey, the tales I'd heard since then of Uighur shamans milking their venom. "Probably hidden in the wine."

I remembered the greedy way Al-Altun had watched Ogodei slurp down her wine. I wouldn't have put it past her to poison her own cup, knowing that her glutton of a brother would drink it as well.

"You'll finally be rid of me, wife," Ogodei managed to get out. His words were becoming slower, and more blood oozed from his lips, but he seemed to uncover some hidden well of strength. "You can grow old with Shigi, as you've always wished."

"Hush," Toregene said, but he took her small hand in his large one, despite the violent tremors that shook his entire body.

Ogodei coughed, the bloody sputum further staining his ravaged *deel*. "There's something else . . ."

Toregene clutched Ogodei's hand, but he handed me something with his other hand.

The golden dagger from his belt.

It was me, and not Toregene, whom the Khan addressed. "My half-blood bitch of a sister must die for this."

I exchanged a glance with Toregene. "She will," I said. "I swear it."

Ogodei's final moments were so painful that, despite his crimes and transgressions in this life, I wished for Allah to hurry and claim him. The Khan lay on his side, panting like a dog on a hot summer day while a never-ending stream of blood slipped down his chin to pool under his face. Finally his chest rose, then fell with a rattle of phlegm.

It didn't rise again.

Toregene felt for a pulse, pressing two fingers into Ogodei's thick neck, then sat back to stare at him in stunned silence. It seemed impossible that this ox of a man, so loud and brash, was suddenly dead.

"Everything changes now," she whispered. "For better or worse, nothing will be the same."

I didn't have time to contemplate that, for Shigi and the guards soon returned. The soldiers recoiled at the sight of the dead Khan and the mess of his blood and vomit. "Al-Altun fled," Shigi reported. He avoided looking at Ogodei and addressed Toregene instead. "But the Khan's soldiers found her and dragged her back."

Toregene nodded slowly and rose, leaving her dead husband on the ground. I wondered if the funeral procession would make its way back to the Altai Mountains so Ogodei could join his father, or if his bones would be laid out in some farmer's field here so the siege of Wien might continue. Either way, Al-Altun's bones would soon join his.

Toregene moved to follow the guard, but I stopped her. "Do you wish to greet her this way?"

Toregene looked down, staring at her blood-streaked palms and *deel* for a long moment, as if she hadn't realized she wore the remnants of her husband's death. She shook her head. "Better that everyone see me this way." She glanced at me, her mismatched eyes gleaming with molten copper and gold. "Both of us, actually."

I hadn't realized that I, too, was spattered with Ogodei's blood, vomit, and wine. So much changed in so little time.

I averted my eyes when Shigi bent to whisper something in Toregene's ear, his hand brushing the small of her back to guide her forward. The rumble of angry voices outside swelled as the door opened, growing louder as we stepped from the Great White Tent. Al-Altun stood surrounded and outnumbered by Ogodei's guards, her own men held at bay by a ring of gleaming swords as Toregene stepped forward, palms open like a supplicant and adorned with the Khan's blood.

"Soldiers of the Golden Horde." Toregene threw her voice so those closest quieted to hear. "I come to you wearing the lifeblood of your Khan, Ogodei, third son of Genghis Khan and ruler of the People of the Felt. Tonight our Khan of Khans has passed to the sacred mountains, slain by the venom of a vile serpent."

I detected a flicker of triumph over Al-Altun's features, but it was short-lived when our guards grabbed her arms and dragged her toward us. There was an audible gasp, followed by more angry shouts.

As I'd seen Borte do many times, Toregene raised her hands for silence, and the mob settled, although their faces still seethed with anger. "I shall not allow the criminal responsible for this to go free while my husband's body grows cold." She turned now to stare down Al-Altun, leveling her full fury at the woman Ogodei had hoped to destroy. Instead, Al-Altun had destroyed them both this night. "Al-Altun, Khatun of the Uighurs," Toregene said. "I do hereby charge you with the heinous murder of the Khan of Khans."

A deep rumble erupted from the crowd. Genghis Khan's legal code required the trial of members of the Golden Family for any wrongdoing and forbade their execution. According to the law, Toregene might lock Al-Altun within the wooden planks of a cangue, or perhaps banish her to the far reaches of Siberia. Al-Altun seemed to know this, yet she didn't even flinch at the announcement, only smiled. "You have no evidence," she said, almost shouting to be heard.

"You poisoned the Khan of Khan's *airag* this night with venom milked from a viper," Toregene said. "Thus we pronounce you guilty of murder and treason. You shall be stripped of your land and titles, and you shall be dragged back to Karakorum, there to remain bound in a cangue until the end of your days."

Al-Altun opened her mouth to argue, but I stood behind her then, the point of Ogodei's dagger against her back.

"In order to save your son and avoid a war that will decimate your people," I whispered in her ear, "you will tell your soldiers to march home without further bloodshed."

She stiffened in my arms. "And if I refuse?"

"You'll watch your son's lifeblood soak the ground, and these men will siege your cities, slaughter your soldiers, and claim your women, just as you did to Nishapur."

She twisted so she could look me in the face, but her eyes were flat. "You've waited a long time for this moment, haven't you, Rose of Nishapur? I doubt you'd find the courage to kill me." She gave a strangled laugh. "And even if you did, at least I won't be alone in the sacred mountains, as I've been every day in this life since your foul city murdered my husband."

"Did you love him very much?"

She pursed her lips. "I did. He was all I had in this life after my mother died, slighted and ignored as I was by the Golden Family."

I felt Toregene's eyes on us, heard from far off the murmurings in the crowd. A girl without a mother, her husband killed . . . I almost lowered my knife, but Al-Altun's next words poured molten iron into my veins.

"And I'll die content," she said, "knowing I avenged his death when I saw your city slaughtered."

Perhaps my desire for revenge had simply lain dormant all these years, or perhaps I'd have been satisfied to hear that Al-Altun had died an old woman warm in her bed, yet I sensed the One God's hand in all this. It was possible that Ogodei's death was penalty for his earlier treatment of the Oirat, and Al-Altun's punishment was divine retribution for Nishapur. Only Allah knew.

"What is your answer, Al-Altun of the Uighurs?" I pressed the blade into her spine so hard she gasped.

"My people," she said, her voice as strong as any Khan's. "I submit to this fair judgment in exchange for the Khatun's promise of your safety and that of my son. Do not fear that I shall be harmed, for in his Jasagh the great Genghis Khan forbade such treatment of a member of his family."

Al-Altun was thoroughly mistaken if she was convinced that the words of her father would protect her now. I'd thought this woman was like me, but I was wrong. Had I a son with Mansoor, I'd have done anything to protect him, to *live* for him. Perhaps Al-Altun believed she'd done her best to save her child, but she'd condemned the boy to a life alone, the same as she'd lived.

"Command them to leave," I growled.

"Go home and return to your fields," she said, a smile in her voice. "Remember me, but do not mourn me, for I shall live a long life."

Her men cast yearning looks at her, and for a moment I thought they might rebel, but one by one they saluted their Khatun, then turned and walked away. I kept my blade pressed to Al-Altun's back all the while, imagining her people mounting their horses and riding away, believing their ruler cowed but protected by the decree of a dead Khan.

How wrong they were.

Toregene stood as straight and rigid as the Solitary Tree while the

Uighurs trickled away, her arms tucked into her wide sleeves. Now she turned and offered me an almost imperceptible nod.

"The Khan of Khans commanded your death," I said to Al-Altun, reaching one arm in front of her chest. "Such was his dying wish, and so it shall be."

In one fluid motion, I spun Al-Altun around and plunged the knife deep into her stomach. She gasped and her body lurched in my arms as I twisted the blade, jerking it up before pulling the knife out in a torrent of guts, her blood spraying like a fountain in the air.

I waited for the surge of triumph I'd yearned for all these years, but instead I watched in horror as Al-Altun clutched her belly, crimson blood and lavender entrails spilling between her fingers. Blood seeped from her lips and she slowly slid to the ground. I'd once hungered to watch the light leave her eyes, but instead it was as if I was in the courtyard of the mosque once again, the slick feel of Mansoor's blood on my hands, at the scene I'd relived so many times in my nightmares.

"I, too, sought revenge for my beloved," she whispered up at me, her bloodstained lips opening and closing as she struggled for breath. "I forgive you, Fatima of Nishapur, for what you've done this night. For I shall greet my husband soon, while you—" She gasped and her pupils widened as if finally seeing death. "You shall remain here, alone."

She grew still then, and I imagined her battered soul seeping from her body, leaving behind a heart long since shattered. Another of Omar Khayyám's poems floated to my mind, long forgotten, but almost making me weep now with its truth.

> *Khayyám, who stitched the tents of science,*
> *Has fallen in grief's furnace and been suddenly burned;*
> *The shears of Fate have cut the tent ropes of his life,*
> *And the broker of Hope has sold him for nothing!*

I had sought Al-Altun's death, but so, too, would I die one day. I might have plunged the bloodied knife into my own belly then, had Toregene not taken it from me.

"Remove the body," Toregene commanded one of the guards, gathering me into her arms as I began to tremble, silent tears running unchecked down my face as I muttered in Farsi the prayer for the dead over Al-Altun's corpse. "It's finished, Fatima," she whispered, her frame shuddering with exhaustion. "It's over, and we've survived unscathed."

But I wasn't unscathed.

I wanted to forget what had happened here tonight, as I'd often wished I could forget Nishapur. Yet I'd done this, not Allah or the heavens, and I knew this night would be added to my nightmares, to be endured again and again.

Chapter 26

Toregene recalled Ogodei's forces from the banks of the Danube River, and together our somber funeral procession retraced the path back to Karakorum. The winter journey was treacherous, and anyone who sought to follow us would need only trace the trail of broken carts and horse carcasses that littered the frozen grasslands behind us. Toregene's illness worsened, buffeted as she was by the winds and snow. Shigi and I demanded that she travel by oxcart, wearing her down with our pleas until she finally relented. I watched as he handed her up into the black cart, one hand lingering on her back while he tucked a stray tendril of hair behind her ear. Toregene clasped his hand to her cheek, closing her eyes and leaning into him. It was a rare moment of intimacy and one that wouldn't have been possible only a few days ago, so powerful that I had to turn away. I'd reconciled myself to spending the remainder of my days alone, save my sisterhood with Toregene. Still, it was painful to see what I'd lost.

I felt a touch at my elbow and was startled to see Shigi standing there, his face tired and drawn but wearing a puzzled expression. "You've left off your veil today, Fatima of Nishapur."

My gloved fingers touched the exposed skin of my cheeks. With the murder of Al-Altun, I had severed the ties to my past and forced Allah to abandon me. It had seemed only fitting to leave behind the protective veil

that I'd clung to all these years, setting me visibly apart from these murderous Mongols. And so I'd burned the delicate rectangle of silk in my
hearth this morning, watching the flames devour the fabric. "So I have," I
said to Shigi. "I'm no longer the same woman who walked through the
gates of her conquered city."

"Veil or no, you will always be the Rose of Nishapur," he said. "The
Golden Family was blessed by all the gods the day Toregene saved you."

While it was true that Toregene had claimed me, it was Shigi who had
found me in the mosque and brought me to her. Our lives were inextri-
cably bound together, their threads woven in a complicated pattern no
mortal eye could discern.

"Don't let her leave that cart today," he said, his gaze straying to Toregene. "She's more deteriorated than she looks."

I glanced to where Toregene sat, directing orders to a slave struggling
to carry a wooden crate. "We both love her," I said to Shigi. "I won't let
anything happen to her."

Shigi smiled. "I know you won't. And I'm grateful for it."

I watched him make his way to where the horses waited, then mount
his brown stallion in one fluid motion, before I turned back to the cart.
Toregene's capitulation to travel in the wagon was a double boon for me,
for it meant I would ride beside her and forgo the wretched ride on
horseback that left me bowlegged and aching for days.

"I once told you carts were for old women and invalids," Toregene said,
scowling as I stuffed fire-heated stones wrapped in wool blankets at her
feet. Soon the drifts would grow so deep that we'd be forced back to our
saddles, but I hoped that a few days in a cart would help her regain her
strength. "It seems my words have returned to torment me."

"You are neither old nor an invalid," I said, but neither was true.

"I need your strength, Fatima," she said, worrying the new golden
bangle at her wrist. The bracelet was a gift from Shigi, embossed with two
devil masks and a phoenix, so that between that and her silver cross, Toregene might always be protected from malevolent spirits. "There's no one
I can trust other than you and Shigi. Güyük must be proclaimed Khan in
a *khurlatai* when we return to Karakorum."

I could scarcely fathom the idea of spoiled, craven Güyük ruling the Mongol Empire. I tucked the wool blanket around her legs. "Perhaps it would be premature to call a *khurlatai* yet."

Toregene bit her lip, the skin chapped and as pale as the rest of her. "You think we lack the support to nominate him?"

If a *khurlatai* were called today, I doubted whether Güyük would receive more than a single vote, and that would be the one his mother cast for him. I loved Toregene, but she remained oblivious to her son's cruel streak.

"You ruled alongside Ogodei, did you not?" I asked, settling beside her, although she insisted on taking the reins. "Perhaps you should guide the empire now, at least until the issue of Al-Altun's execution dies down. Sorkhokhtani holds the east, Batu the north, Chaghatai's widow the west, and Alaqai the south."

"You sent an arrow messenger to Olon Süme?" Toregene interrupted, her teeth chattering. "Alaqai's the only one I can trust to administer the Uighur lands as well as her own."

"I did," I said, holding tight as the cart lurched forward. "And you could reign over all of them as Great Khatun, as Borte Khatun did while Genghis Khan was out conquering the world."

Toregene sighed. "You may be right, at least for now. After all, my eldest son is not without his faults—"

The world might have been a better place if Toregene had drowned Güyük at birth, but I held my tongue.

"But Güyük is still young enough to learn how to rule. If I assume the regency, we shall groom him to become Khan one day."

She paused, looking at me as if for my approval. Her eyes were wide and glassy with her illness, mismatched pools reflecting a lifetime of joys and sorrows. She'd grown so frail since we had started this journey, and she might grow weaker still before we reached the walls of Karakorum.

"If Ogodei managed to stay sober long enough to oversee the conquests of Rus and Goryeo and build a new capital, I suppose there's a chance for Güyük as well," I said, praying Allah would turn a deaf ear to my lie and not smite me where I stood. "But it may be that your regency shall be necessary for months, if not years."

My throat tightened to realize that Toregene might not live that long if her illness didn't abate. I pushed away the thought, for I couldn't imagine a life without this sister of my heart.

"Ogodei's councilors won't tolerate a woman set above them for so long," she said.

"Dismiss them." I waved away her concern with a gloved hand. "Consolidate your power immediately so their distaste for a woman as ruler is no longer an issue."

Toregene gave a slow smile. "Who knew my docile calligrapher could be so vicious?" Her eyes regained their old warmth, but her face remained wan. "Together, Fatima, we'll gain control of this unruly empire and ensure Güyük's succession."

I couldn't promise that I'd work to support Güyük's claim to the throne, but next to Toregene, I would help govern the largest empire the world had ever seen. The thought both thrilled and terrified me.

Dawn warmed the sky like a pale bruise over Karakorum upon our silent arrival. Herds of shaggy horses outside the walls nudged the snow with their noses, searching in vain for shoots of early spring grass. Implacable stone tortoises stood sentry at the main gate and the palace loomed tall, finished in our absence and decorated with painted roof tiles incised with grimacing dragon faces. Three stories high, its white exterior was accented with fluted red trim in the style of Cathay, and blue flags atop its roof honored the pagan sky spirit. The pieces of the palace had been named according to the colors of the empire—the Golden Ordu for the sun, the Green Courtyard for the grasslands, and the Yellow Pavilion for the wildflowers that dotted the countryside each summer.

We entered through the west gate and waded through its sheep and goat market, on our way to the main street through town, passing the domed mosques of the Saracen quarter. Outside the courtyard sat a *darvīsh*, his ragged beard and oft-stitched robe bespeaking his holy vows to Allah. I dropped a silver coin into the iron bowl in his lap, then pressed another into his hand. "One for the mosque," I whispered in Farsi to the ascetic. "And one for you to buy bread for yourself."

The man's eyes widened, but he avoided my gaze. "You wear no veil, lady, but speak the old language. I fear I hardly recognize this new world the Mongols have forged."

"I would be honored if you prayed to Allah for me," I said. "For I fear he no longer hears my prayers."

I stood before he could reject my pleas, imagining for a moment that we might be home in Nishapur, but the illusion was ruined by the dirty snowdrifts outside a nearby pagan temple and its cloying smell of incense that spilled into the air amidst the angry snorts of several nearby yaks. Few people were out in the streets in the blowing snow, but those that were exclaimed over our arrival in a medley of languages: Mongolian, Mandarin, French, English, Hungarian, and even Farsi. The city still smelled of freshly hewn lumber and newness, its bright colors gaudy and all for show. Beyond the metal shops with their steaming domed forges and smelting furnaces, four lurid silver lions reclined at the base of the Silver Tree, and heated *airag* flowed freely from their open jaws. The French goldsmith Guillaume Boucher had designed the masterpiece; he had been captured during the campaign against Belgrade and conscripted into Ogodei's army of craftsmen to turn Karakorum into a cosmopolitan city. Gems hung from the tree's branches and four golden serpents climbed up its towering trunk, their eyes studded with rubies, while four filigreed branches poured wine, clarified mare's milk, and warmed rice mead into silver basins. I dipped a hesitant finger into the last basin, smiling at the sweet *bal*, a honeyed milk that Mongol children lapped up like starving kittens. Beyond the Silver Tree was a man-made river, mostly frozen. We passed through courtyards shoveled free of their snow and filled with herds of the Five Snouts, each lazy beast marked with a golden tag in its ear to denote its ownership by the Golden Family.

I was reminded of the interior of the Great White Tent when the palace's towering door thudded closed behind us, blocking out the wind, although smoke from the torches permeated the air. Beneath our feet, stone ducts guided heated air into the room—a recent innovation brought from Cathay—but despite the decadence that Ogodei had sought when planning his capital, the simple elegance of the meanest villa in Nishapur might have rivaled all this.

Güyük found us in the main corridor, dressed in cloth of gold like his father, his beard crimped and a foreign shah's turban on his head. Oghul Ghaimish stood behind him, her braids pinned in two giant loops around her ears and decorated with a plethora of silver bells and ivory animal combs. A child with dried milk on its upper lip clung to the embroidered hem of her *deel*.

"I'm glad to see you returned safe, Mother." Güyük gave a deep bow, his face a perfect mask. "It was with great sorrow that I heard of my father's passage to the sacred mountains."

This dutiful son was hardly the man I'd expected to find upon our arrival, a stranger wearing a familiar—if unwelcome and still pockmarked—face.

"The Great Khatun is weary from her long journey," I said when Toregene didn't respond. Instead, she stared at her son as if confronting a stranger for the first time.

"When will you call a *khurlatai*?" Oghul Ghaimish's whine was followed by the escalating whimpers of her child. Despite her tasteful attire, angry red scratches poked from the collar of her *deel*, although I couldn't tell if they were put there by her own nails or someone else's. She picked at her scalp, as if there were nits hidden beneath her oiled braids. "Güyük promised me a green headdress when you returned."

A green headdress. The Khatun's *boqta*.

I wondered if Güyük had already promised to make Oghul Ghaimish the Great Khatun. Borte would writhe in her grave to see such an unstable young woman crowned as Mother to the People of the Felts.

"Perhaps you should return to our chambers and rest for a while, wife," Güyük said gently, his hand on the small of her back. "And take our son with you."

"Your son." Welcome color blossomed on Toregene's cheeks as she stared down at the child cowering behind his mother's legs. "You made me a grandmother while we were away?"

"I did indeed," Güyük said, beaming like any proud father. "And my second wife is ready to drop a foal any day."

Toregene exclaimed over that, but I continued to study Güyük. Perhaps fatherhood had calmed his violent streak, or perhaps that was only what he wanted his mother to believe. I knew not what game he played, but I wasn't convinced by his act.

Oghul Ghaimish slunk away, taking with her the sound of tinkling bells and the child's cries as she disappeared around a tiled corner. Toregene patted Güyük's hand. "I worried when your father chose Oghul Ghaimish as your wife," she said. "But you've done well by her. Treat her gently, and I'm sure she'll reward you with her loyalty and many more children."

Güyük followed us back outside and to the Golden Ordu—the white velvet tent held up by pillars plated with gold—inquiring politely about our journey and whether there were plans to return to Wien for a second siege. "Also," he said, "Sorkhokhtani and her eldest sons recently arrived."

"Good," Toregene answered. "Fatima sent a message requesting their presence in the capital upon my return."

Güyük's eyes darkened at that, but then he offered his mother a polished smile. "I'm pleased to hear they obliged, especially considering all the times Sorkhokhtani defied my father."

"Sorkhokhtani desires a quiet life," Toregene answered as we approached the doors of the Golden Ordu, fluted at the top in the Persian style but carved with dragons and horses in the style of Cathay. Like his people, Ogodei's palace was a conglomeration of styles from around the world, and I found the mix jarring and disconcerting. "Yet she is grown almost as old as me and has served our family well since Tolui's death. She understands her duties as Princess of the Hearth."

It seemed Toregene had forgiven Sorkhokhtani her rejection of Güyük, perhaps because she realized she'd now need the support of Tolui's widow.

Güyük didn't have a chance to answer, for the doors were flung open at Toregene's gesture. Inside, Ogodei's former councilors milled about, as did various members of the Golden Family, the men standing to the west and the few women to the east as if this were still a humble *ger* that stunk of wet goat wool instead of the grand throne room of the most powerful family on earth. I nodded to Sorkhokhtani, recognizing her sons Möngke and Kublai across from her.

At the opposite end of the room, two sets of stairs formed an inverted V, and atop them sat the Horse Throne. Gilded chairs set along the stair's wooden platforms awaited the members of the royal family.

The hum of conversation quieted and I felt a surge of pride as Toregene lifted the hem of her *deel* and mounted the stairs. She didn't hesitate when she reached the pinnacle, but ignored the Great Khatun's stool to take her place on the Horse Throne.

"My dear Khatun," a councilor shouted. It was Korguz, Ogodei's ape-like scribe, recently recalled from Persia at my behest, although he didn't realize that. "We offer our condolences for the loss of your husband." Yet his face showed no sadness as he separated himself from the crowd, daring to stand on the bottom step of the dais unbidden. "We assume you've come here today to share with us the name of the Khan's chosen successor."

"Did Ogodei name Güyük as his heir?" another yelled.

And still another, "Or perhaps Möngke or Batu?"

Toregene held up her hands. "My husband neglected to name an heir, as he neglected many things in this life." She sat straighter and I feared she might be seized with a coughing fit, but she only rested her forearms on the wide armrests of the throne. "For now, I shall sit upon the Horse Throne."

"But that is impossible," sputtered Korguz. "A woman cannot—"

Toregene leaned forward. "The great Genghis Khan often left Borte Khatun to administer his empire in his absence. Do you believe our great ancestor was mistaken to do so?"

"That was a time of war. Surely now we must have a new Khan—"

His words hung in the air as Sorkhokhtani picked herself up and mounted the stairs, trailed by her sons Möngke and Kublai. They took their seats beneath the throne, gazing out impassively at the lower ministers in challenge. To my consternation, Güyük emerged next from the crowd, followed by his younger brothers by Ogodei's lesser wives.

A heavy and uncomfortable silence fell. It seemed none of the white-beards wished to challenge the Golden Family, yet they weren't quite finished with Toregene.

"Why was the Khan not better protected when he was in Wien?" yelled another of Ogodei's ministers, an elderly Buddhist dressed in an orange *deel*.

"The Khan was protected, but Al-Altun poisoned her own wine and gave it to our husband," Toregene said calmly. "She paid for that decision with her life."

More shouting broke out until Kublai stood up, craning his neck to better see the Horse Throne. "Great Khatun," he said. "The mandate of Genghis Khan forbade the execution of any member of the Golden Family. Yet Al-Altun was still put to the sword. Why?"

Sorkhokhtani stood abruptly, leveling a scathing glare at her son. "My apologies for my son, Great Khatun," she said. "He is still young and has yet to learn when his opinion is warranted."

But Toregene smiled down upon them both. "Young Kublai's question is a good one. The Great Khan did decree that those who carried his blood were beyond the reach of the law. Yet I determined that Al-Altun's crime was so great that her death was the only proper penalty."

"A prescient move," Güyük agreed, one hand over his heart as he inclined his turbaned head in Toregene's direction. "I commend my mother for her decisive action against so treacherous a woman."

There were grunts of approval at that and many nodding heads. Still, Sorkhokhtani pressed her son into his seat while Toregene surveyed the pillared hall. "My husband's bones shall be laid to rest in the mountains before the sun sets tomorrow. As Ogodei's Great Khatun, I shall rule as regent until an appropriate time can be determined to call a *khurlatai*. I thank my husband's advisers for their service and hope they may now enjoy their retirement. Going forward, Shigi, adopted brother of Genghis Khan, and Fatima of Nishapur shall serve as my eyes and ears in Karakorum."

The dismissed advisers stared in shock, some openly gaping. Korguz leapt to his feet, his hairy fists clenched at his sides. "But, Khatun—"

Güyük crossed his arms before his chest. "Do you wish to contradict the Great Khatun?" he interrupted. "If so, perhaps you'd wish to follow in Al-Altun's footsteps?"

"There is no need for threats," Toregene said calmly. "It is the simple truth that my husband spent extravagantly, and I can no longer afford to pay the extensive list of advisers and artisans he employed."

I'd seen the palace accounts myself; it was true that Ogodei had squandered every gold coin he came across, but with the impressive tax revenues from the trade routes and the tribute sent every year from the empire's vassal states, Toregene could afford as large a retinue as she liked.

Korguz stormed to the door of the colossal tent. "I shall not suffer this humiliation," he said. "This empire shall crumble while you or your brood sit upon that throne."

Toregene ignored him to address the remaining advisers. "I thank you for your service to my husband, gentlemen. You have served your empire well."

At her nod, the advisers filed reluctantly from the Golden Ordu. I'd ensure that each—including miserable Korguz—was sent a sizable gift to soothe any ruffled feathers.

Shigi's brush flicked over the book in his lap, recording all this for his history of the Golden Family, and my fingers itched for my own pen and ink. Of everyone left in the tent, Toregene's lover and I were the only people without either the blood of Genghis Khan running in our veins or the ability to claim one of his descendants as a child of our bodies. Everyone else was a member of the Golden Family, either by blood or by marriage. "Borte Khatun, the Mother of the Thirteen Tribes, foretold that this empire would fracture after Genghis Khan's spirit fled for the sacred mountains," Toregene said. "I am not prepared to watch that happen. I ask for your support as I keep watch over the Horse Throne and guide the empire until we are ready to proclaim the next Khan."

Sorkhokhtani stood. "You have the support of the Toluids," she said. "But my sons and I would ask your permission to return to our lands."

Toregene gave a terse nod, and I wondered if she'd expected this from Tolui's widow. "You may go," she said. "And I thank you for administering Karakorum in our absence."

Sorkhokhtani bowed over her hands. Möngke opened his mouth to protest but closed it at his mother's sharp glare. The sons of the Princess of the Hearth would either be well equipped to withstand this family's travails or they would be weak-willed men cowed by any woman they met. The royal family began discussing plans for Ogodei's funeral, a mix of pagan and Christian traditions that made my skin crawl. Ogodei's body had been wrapped in scented felts on the night he died, but then he'd been dragged from one end of the empire to the other. Now his spoiled corpse would be blessed and hidden on some mountaintop, yet even the vultures would forgo such a desiccated feast.

I followed Sorkhokhtani and her sons into the corridor, catching her in the midst of berating Kublai for speaking out of turn.

"Fatima," she said when she saw me. "How may I assist you?"

"Can't you see that you should stay?" I asked her. "Toregene needs your help now more than ever."

Sorkhokhtani waved her sons away. "It is true that Toregene navigates uncharted lands," she said to me. "Dangerous even."

"Yet you abandon her." My accusation was tinged with anger, but she appeared not to notice. Sorkhokhtani might have made a fine Khatun, for not even the most skilled courtier could discern her true feelings.

She tucked her hands in her sleeves. "Toregene's every move will be scrutinized from this moment forward and her every decision endlessly debated. I, on the other hand, shall fade away as I've always done, disappearing into the shadows." She leaned toward me, as if taking me into her confidence. "The interesting thing about shadows is that while they are ever present, few notice them."

I didn't have time for nuances and hidden meanings. "Toregene plans to give the throne to Güyük one day."

"Then Batu was right in not coming." Her fingers fluttered at my questioning glance. "Jochi's son feared that Toregene might call a *khurlatai* for Güyük today."

"She thinks Güyük may be able to one day replace her. Not even Ogodei supported Güyük," I muttered.

Sorkhokhtani gave a delicate sniff. "Then Ogodei and I agreed on one thing in this life."

It was the closest I'd ever heard to Sorkhokhtani declaring her opinion on something. "Is there nothing I can do to persuade you to stay?"

She gave a sad shake of her head. "Toregene must make her own way. And I will do as I've always done: protect my sons and ensure they always have their father's lands to rule."

I gave a wan smile. "Go in peace then, Sorkhokhtani Beki," I said. "May Allah watch over you and your sons."

She pressed her forehead to mine. "And may he watch over you as well. I fear you'll need the gift of his divine guidance in the days to come."

Toregene's breathing grew easier in that spring and summer, but fall's dampness and winter's cold made the air crackle in her lungs, and her constant cough battered her ever-frail body. The scent of honey clung to her, for she swallowed a spoonful of the golden nectar with each meal and drank infusions of columbine tea to soothe her raw throat, but neither had any effect on the miasma that had settled in her lungs.

Shigi and I shivered with our backs to the hearth fire in her Great White Tent one afternoon, chuckling with Toregene over the proposition sent to the Golden Family by the Christian pope in faraway Rome. Innocent IV had sent a Franciscan monk to ask that the Mongols be baptized and to insist on their submission to the Holy Father's authority. I found it easy to be with Shigi these days, united as we were in assisting Toregene, and imagined that the calm affection I now felt for him was what I might have felt for an older brother, had Allah chosen to bless me with one.

"Heap honors upon this monk," Toregene said, a faint smile hovering on her lips. "But this pope knows little if he thinks I would force one religion on my people."

"He knows you are Christian. And he seeks to"—I cleared my throat—"'admonish, beg, and earnestly beseech you' to desist from your assaults of Christian people. Thus, you can unite with him to defeat the Saracens in the Holy Lands."

"Which we shall not do, of course," Toregene said, smiling at me over her bowl of tea.

"I do like the part where he mentions how we 'rage indiscriminately against all with the sword of chastisement,'" Shigi remarked. "Very well said." He smiled, but his worried gaze lingered on Toregene as she coughed at her latest herbal infusion, a mix of nettle, garlic, and something that smelled strongly of urine.

"The pope may rest assured that we shall not invade Wien again," Toregene wheezed. "Güyük has his eyes set upon Goryeo again, and I would rather expend my energies on my monasteries. Inform Innocent that we can't fathom what he means about the recent destruction and massacre of Europe, tell him to submit to us, and then give it to Güyük to sign."

I grimaced at the mention of Güyük. I'd write the letter later, but for now I set aside the pope's missive with its colossal red wax seal and took up the plans for Toregene's latest project, a Taoist monastery in Cathay. Despite her favoring the crucified prophet Isa Ibn Maryam, Toregene had encouraged the growth of a variety of religious houses in Karakorum and beyond the capital. Most Mongols had a queer belief that the majority of religions had an equal chance of being effective, and both Genghis Khan and Ogodei had asked Christians, Taoists, Saracens, and Buddhists to pray for them. I saw Toregene's building projects as a friendly competition among her and her sisters, for Alaqai often sent word of her latest monastery funding and Sorkhokhtani had recently founded on her sons' lands a school based in the teachings of Muhammad, prompting me to send a letter of gratitude to the Princess of the Hearth.

One of my slaves—a daughter of Goryeo's noble houses, sent as a hostage after Ogodei's last campaign there—entered and hurried to my side, her whisper in my ear making me frown. My scowl deepened as I read the letter she pressed into my hands.

"What is it?" Toregene asked.

"Korguz is causing trouble again," I answered. "This message from him to the governor of Otrar was just intercepted. He encourages the governor to revolt against your rule and to withdraw support from anyone you would nominate as the future Khan. He also speaks against Güyük's plans for a third invasion of Goryeo."

While once the idea of the Persians rising against the Mongol horsemen and Güyük's long absence while he subdued the Goryeo peninsula would have pleased me, I found I no longer had the stomach for bloodshed. Al-Altun's execution had cured me of that.

"Korguz has spoken against you and Güyük since the day you claimed the regency," Shigi said to Toregene, scanning the letter. "This is the first time he's put such ideas into writing."

"Thus he'd never broken the law," I said. "Until now."

Toregene sighed and rubbed her eyes. Lines had lodged themselves there and around her lips, too, etched deeper by the thinness of her skin and her sunken eyes. "I grow weary of hearing Korguz's name and his challenges to my rule." She gestured to the paper and brush at my elbow. I'd long since worn out the bristles from Mansoor's old brush and kept it in a wooden box inlaid with pearls and jade, a gift from Toregene. The box also contained Alaqai's tiger comb, a scrap of silk now black with my husband's blood, and my silver slave medallion. They, along with the narcissus I continued to plant outside my window box and around Toregene's Great White Tent, were the only surviving reminders of my past. Next to the chest was the book I'd kept since I'd first come to the steppes, each page covered with my meticulous recordings of the life of the Golden Family, from Nishapur to this place. My past and my future, forever intertwined.

Toregene cleared her throat with a rattle of phlegm, and I dipped the brush into the inkpot so I might take down her words.

"I, Toregene Khatun, Great Khatun of the Thirteen Tribes, do hereby order the execution of Korguz, former scribe of Ogodei Khan, for his treason against the People of the Felts."

I stared at her, my brush suspended in the air. Droplets of black ink fell, ruining the paper. "His sentence shall be carried out this fourth day of the ninth month," Toregene said. "In the Year of the Wooden Snake."

"Is it wise to order Korguz's death?" I asked, choosing my words carefully as I set aside the marred paper for a fresh sheet.

Toregene stood abruptly and began pacing, although she had to stop often to catch her breath. "I've worked since our return from Wien to strengthen the foundations of this empire. I cannot allow Korguz to threaten it all." She paused, coughing violently into the silk cloth she kept tucked in her sleeve. When her lungs calmed, she stuffed the white hand-kerchief out of sight, but not before I saw the spatters of blood. Shigi guided her back to her seat, the anguish apparent in his expression.

Toregene had been coughing up blood for some time now, but each fit grew bloodier. Our friend—sister and lover—was dying before our eyes, and nothing we could do might save her.

We exchanged pained glances, and the abject sadness in his face was almost too much for me to bear. "I cannot allow Korguz to continue slan-dering the Golden Family," Toregene said through gritted teeth. "We shall silence him and then we shall call the *khurlatai*. Our family must nominate someone to replace me before I die," she said angrily, slamming her bowl of tea down so hard that the porcelain cracked. Brown liquid leaked out, slowly at first and then in a torrent, and Toregene's eyes welled with tears as Shigi gathered her frail form into his arms. I looked away, cleaning up the mess with a silk towel.

"You'll nominate Güyük, won't you?" I finally asked, already knowing the answer.

She nodded, in control of herself once again. "He is the only choice."

Güyük's behavior since Toregene's assumption of the regency had been exemplary, and he and his wives had dutifully produced the next gener-ation of the Golden Family. In fact, he was absent from the Great White Tent today so that he could visit his second wife, who had just borne him a daughter. Oghul Ghaimish was also pregnant again.

"Are you sure his actions haven't simply been a show for your benefit?" I asked, ignoring Shigi's motion that I keep quiet. I wouldn't agitate To-regene further, but it was imperative that I know what she planned, mostly so I could assess the coming disaster.

"Not even Güyük could maintain such a farce for this long." She shook her head. "No, he's changed since his return from Rus."

"So you'll order the *khurlatai* and hand over the empire to him?"

"I'll continue to wear the Great Khatun's headdress, to write decrees and allow time for Güyük to find his legs."

That was all well and good for a newborn colt, but Güyük was no horse. Kings and shahs were taught to rule from birth, but Güyük had spent his early years learning only to surpass his father's depravity.

"And you think the Golden Family will wish to see Güyük don his grandfather's helmet?"

"I don't care what they wish. They must come to Karakorum," Toregene said. "Every last one of them."

She gnawed her nails, the tip of her thumb already bleeding. I stood and covered her hands with my own. "I'll send the command," I said.

"I want the pope's monk in attendance, and the Seljuk sultan and the princes of Europe as well. They must bow before my son."

"And Korguz?"

Toregene rubbed her temples, then took my pen, dipped it in the ink, and signed her name in the sprawling Mongol script. "I cannot fight a war on two fronts. Execute him and be done with it."

I bowed over the blank paper that would soon send a man to his grave. I backed away, leaving Shigi behind Toregene and rubbing her shoulders as the doors closed.

I disagreed with Toregene's decisions, but I did as she bade. At dawn the next morning, Korguz was arrested and the commands to attend the grandest *khurlatai* since Ogodei's installation as Great Khan flew like birds to the four corners of the empire.

I attended Korguz's gruesome death in Toregene's stead—she was too ill to rise from her bed that morning—and forced myself to watch as Ogodei's former adviser was dragged into Karakorum's main horse corral, screaming his innocence to the gathered crowd. I anticipated that he would fight his sentence, but I didn't expect that his pleas for mercy would be directed at Allah as the soldiers tied him to a waiting post.

"Korguz converted to the teachings of Muhammad in preparation for his post in Persia," Shigi whispered from his seat beside me, wearing his blue cap and serving in his official capacity as chief judge.

I nodded, making the sign against the evil eye. I'd set aside my veil, yet I would only ever pray to Allah, although I was sure he had forsaken me.

Korguz was as practical as the Mongols when it came to religion, but it jarred me to hear him begging for the One God to spare him. Even more disconcerting were his frantic pleas when his gaze fell on me.

"Please, Fatima," he begged, his eyes wild. "Intercede on my behalf with the Khatun. As a fellow Saracen—"

But I was not in charge of the proceedings. Güyük rose from his makeshift throne and motioned to the guards. "There shall be no intercession on your behalf, Korguz of the Uighurs," he said. "The Khatun has ordered your death in return for your treason. As punishment for your crime, you shall be stoned until you choke to death."

At his signal, two guards stepped forward, hefting a silver cauldron between them filled with smooth river rocks, clean and polished. I felt a flash of pity as a dark stain of urine spread down Korguz's trousers.

Güyük smiled as his fingers danced over the cauldron. He chose two pebbles and tossed them in the air, catching them neatly before handing them to the guards. "Start small," he said. "The criminal deserves a long and painful demise."

One soldier held Korguz's head steady while another plugged his nose to force open his mouth. The scribe tried to wrench his face away, but the brawniest soldier tilted his chin up and forced his lips shut over the rocks. The apple of Korguz's throat moved as he swallowed them; then the soldiers forced his jaw open and shoved more pebbles inside, his teeth smashing down on the rocks with a sound like a cart driving over gravel. One of the stones fell from his lips, along with a dribble of blood and tiny shards of white.

His teeth.

More stones were shoved into Korguz's mouth, and the punishment continued until the scribe's mouth was a mash of pink and red pulp, fragments of his teeth clinging to the spittle on his lips.

Güyük turned to me. "You choose next, Fatima. Just a small one, though—we wouldn't want him to expire too quickly."

I stared at him in shock as the guards hauled the cauldron before me. I could refuse to obey the future Khan and earn his further enmity, or I could do as he ordered and become his accomplice. Güyük's face was as smooth as polished marble, but his eyes glowed with pleasure.

I suppressed a shudder of revulsion and chose a stone the size of a grape, palming a second rock the size of a peach pit, large enough to lodge in the throat of any man. My gaze flicked to Güyük, but neither he nor his soldiers seemed to notice. Shigi's eyes grew wide as he realized what I intended, and he shook his head in warning. The guards waited expectantly, but I ignored them and ducked between the rough-hewn planks of the corral. Korguz sobbed quietly to himself, smelling of fear, urine, and the cloves he must have chewed that morning before his arrest. I touched his face, but he reared back at the sight of the stone in my hand. "Swallow it," I whispered. "Swallow it and all this will end."

Tears trickled down his cheeks, but he obediently opened his ruined mouth. I placed the stone on his tongue and recited the Qur'an's prayer for the dead.

"Inna lillaahi wa inna ilayhi Raaji'oon."

To Allah we belong and to Allah we return.

It was the same precious verse I'd said over the bodies of my mother and father, Mansoor and Al-Altun. Korguz's eyes shone with gratitude. "Thank you," he whispered.

Then he swallowed.

I expected Korguz to sputter or gag, but he only opened his mouth in a silent plea for air. His eyes bulged as death swooped down to claim him, but I dropped my gaze and turned my back, unwilling to watch the light fade from another man's eyes.

When I'd steadied myself enough to lift my gaze, it was to find Güyük's face contorted in anger. The gleam of fury in his dark eyes almost made me cry out, but I forced myself to duck back out of the corral and walk away from him. I stopped only when I reached the walls of the palace, my chest heaving and my hands as cold as ice as I cursed myself to Jahannam and back, recalling Güyük's words from long ago.

I have plans for you, Fatima, and one day my mother and father won't be able to protect you.

Fool and coward that I was, I'd thought to outwit Güyük, to demonstrate that while I might not challenge him outright, I wouldn't partake in his lust for cruelty. Instead, I'd only succeeded in reaffirming an enemy today.

And that enemy would soon be the most powerful man in the world.

I relived Korguz's execution over and over in my mind in the months to come, wondering what I might have done differently, yet each night I retired to my cold chambers in the palace to pray to Allah, although I never received any answers. The flash of cruelty I'd witnessed in Güyük that day had evaporated, replaced with the caring and dutiful son who had become a fixture at his mother's side. Even Shigi seemed won over by the idea of Güyük's ascension, although I suspected his agreement likely stemmed from a desire to lift the weight of the empire from Toregene's fragile shoulders. And while it took much cajoling and many threats and negotiations written to some members of the Golden Family, finally Toregene received enough confirmations to formally order a *khurlatai*.

And so, on a spring day when new grass covered the terraced hills outside of Karakorum, the Golden Family and its people gathered to crown Güyük as the third Great Khan of the Mongolian empire. Unlike his father, Güyük ignored the tradition of declining the silver helm three times, likely because he feared it wouldn't be offered again if he refused.

I looked out over the crowd of brown Mongols, interspersed with its conquered Persians, Uighurs, and the occasional pale faces and blue eyes of the European envoys. At least three thousand members of the world's royal families—all bearing carts of gold, silk, and furs in tribute—had traveled to witness Güyük's election in Karakorum's Yellow Pavilion. The only missing member of the Golden Family was Jochi's son Batu, who claimed illness, although he had made no secret of his distaste for Güyük after their fight in Rus. Still, this was a very different *khurlatai* from the one that saw Ogodei installed as Great Khan. In the place of Genghis' four sons now stood four women to represent their husbands' khanates: Chaghatai's bent-backed widow for Kashgar, Sorkhokhtani for the east, Alaqai for the south, and Toregene for the capital and the central lands extending to Genghis' birthplace. A disheveled Oghul Ghaimish sat with Güyük's other wives on the dais below as Toregene placed the Great Khan's helm upon Güyük's head. Oghul Ghaimish giggled into the silence, then swayed in her seat. Allah forbid that woman should ever wear the green headdress of the Great Khatun.

The night degenerated into the usual depravities of drinking and brawling, and I found myself craving the comfort of my new room in the palace and the crate of books Toregene had recently directed my way. Toregene had chosen to raise her tent within the palace compound, its new panels woven with white velvet so glorious as to make the sun weep and the moon sulk with envy. It had been too many years since I'd lived within proper walls, and although I still found the palace to be a crude attempt at beauty, I'd decorated my stone chambers with decadently soft silk rugs, delicate blue-glazed Ikanid ceramics, and even a bronze peacock oil lamp purchased from a Khorosan merchant that reminded me of one my father once had. I'd often stay up long into the night, writing in my book of histories by the flickering light of that lamp, finding satisfaction with each word I transcribed. Still, it would be many hours before I could curl up with my freshly printed volume of Rumi's poetry or record the events of the *khurlatai*, for Toregene ordered the festivities into a red velvet tent for a feast of roasted camel hump, an assortment of various sausages and white foods, and birds' nest soup—a foul Cathayan delicacy—inviting the ambassadors, who were unused to such unabashed revelry.

I, of course, didn't eat.

"The new Great Khan seems a robust young man," said the man on my right. Grand Prince Yaroslav of Vladimir-Suzdal strolled next to the Seljuk sultan, the latter as graceful as a wisp of smoke next to a man who lumbered like an ill-mannered yak. The sultan's eyes flicked to where Güyük stood near one of the tables heaped with food, stripped almost naked and awaiting his next wrestling opponent.

"Indeed." The sultan sniffed.

The royal entourage remained in the crimson feast tent until early sunlight overpowered the flickering light of the torches, drinking rivers of *airag* and wine gathered by slaves from the Silver Tree. One by one, the courtiers stumbled to their chambers in the palace, or to the tents they'd erected outside Karakorum's walls, leaving behind only a few scant members of the Golden Family. Shigi had excused himself, ostensibly to record the day's events in the quiet of his own tent, and Güyük stood with Möngke and Kublai. I remained with Toregene, Alaqai, and Sorkhokhtani, glad to have a chance to sit with all of Borte's daughters once again.

"It's been too long since we've been together," Alaqai said. Her son, Negudei, had recently been killed in battle against the Jin, another capable young man dead before his time. That painful loss, the worries of ruling two kingdoms, and the deaths of three husbands had etched themselves deep into her face. Still, next to Toregene, she looked vibrant and full of life.

"Much has happened since Borte's passing," Sorkhokhtani agreed. "I often find myself wishing we could ask her for guidance."

They continued to reminisce about the past, about the first *khurlatai*, when Genghis was proclaimed Khan of Khans and Alaqai had dressed as a man during the wrestling tournament—she claimed she could likely still beat Güyük—but the discussion came to a halt at a rumble of footsteps from the bottom of the dais. Alarm flickered in Toregene's eyes as more than a dozen guards marched up the stairs, their swords pointed at us.

"What is the meaning of this?" Toregene asked, rising from her gilded bench. "Put down your weapons."

"My men are acting on my orders, Mother." Güyük stumbled on the bottom step, his eyes glazed and words slurred so for a moment he might have been his father. Then he leered at me.

"They're here to arrest the piece of filth who sits at your feet and claims to serve you," he said, leveling a malicious glare at me even as his sneer revealed teeth already tending toward brown. "Hand over the Mohammedian bitch now, Mother."

I stared at Güyük, my stomach crawling into my throat with fear, but Toregene stepped between us. "You will not address Fatima in such a manner," she said to her son. "Fatima has been my most faithful adviser these past years, the sister of my heart."

"I don't care if she shared the same womb as you," Güyük said, wiping the back of his sleeve across his lips. He was so drunk I doubted whether he'd remember this confrontation in the morning. Still, my heart thundered. "She used the witchcraft of her god to bewitch you into an unnatural love. The Mohammedian is a murderer and a traitor, and she deserves to rot on a pike for all to see."

I was as terrified as I'd been when the first Mongols poured over Nishapur's walls, but I was no longer merely a pampered wife. I'd survived much over the course of my life, and this spoiled man-child wouldn't be the end of me. If the world was fair, come morning Güyük would find himself castrated, his tongue removed, and his helmet confiscated. I burned to spit those words in the drunkard's face but bit my tongue to save my head.

"Return to your rooms, you drunken fool," Toregene said, her voice so low I strained to hear her. "Lest I reverse my decision to give you that helmet."

Güyük's face grew blotchy with anger, almost curdled. "So you insist on protecting the Persian whore?"

Whore. I'd only ever known one man in my life. My fingers itched to wrap around Güyük's throat. Yet if I went for him, I'd find my throat stuffed with stones like Korguz and the camp dogs would feast on my corpse before the sun finished rising.

Alaqai stood then, imperious and snarling like a tiger. "Be glad that your grandfather and father are already dead, for they would disown you for your behavior this night," she said. "You wear the Khan's helmet, but you act like a bare-bottomed child."

Güyük's hands curled into fists, and a thick vein at his temple pulsed angrily, but Alaqai waved him away as if he were only a fly. "Will you order your guards to drag me away as well, your aunt and the last surviving daughter of Genghis Khan? What about your mother? Shall you arrest her, too?"

Sorkhokhtani rose, her very calm dispelling some of the tension. "Möngke," she called to her eldest. "And Kublai. The Khan requests your assistance."

Her straight-backed sons approached Güyük. "Come see the new stallion I brought as tribute for our new Gur-Khan," Möngke said, as smiling and jovial as ever, yet he looked upon Güyük with distaste. Another emotion filled his eyes when he glanced at me.

Pity.

"Leave the women to discuss their felting and sewing," he said.

Güyük opened his wine-sotted mouth to argue, but Kublai wrapped a strong arm around his shoulders. "Come, Güyük. I'm sure we can find a pretty slave or two eager to please the Khan of Khans."

We watched them go and Alaqai gave an angry grunt as the soldiers retreated and the door to the crimson tent closed behind them. "I love you, Toregene," she said. "But that whelp of yours is a miserable excuse of a man. You must rein him in or we'll all suffer."

Toregene turned to me, her pale face cracking so all her emotions shone through her ever-expressive eyes. "I'm so sorry, Fatima."

I drew a deep breath. "Thank you."

"Why in the name of all the gods would you thank me?"

"For not handing me over." A wild laugh bubbled in my throat. "I've been waiting for this day since the first time I met your son, after we returned from Nishapur."

Toregene's face melted and tears welled in her eyes. "Oh, Fatima." She clasped my face between both of her hands. "Did you think I might surrender you to him?" She stepped back and offered a watery smile. "Despite your disdain and pretensions, I love you, just as I love Alaqai and Sorkhokhtani. You are the sisters of my heart."

Words abandoned me. Childless, and without a mother, father, or husband, I had no one in this world. Yet Toregene had been by my side for half my life, a sister not of blood, but of circumstance.

And yet Allah might take her from me as well.

"Fatima should leave with one of us," Sorkhokhtani said, smoothing her silk *deel* as if discussing the rising sun. "It's not safe for her here."

"I agree," Alaqai said. "Güyük drank enough wine tonight to drain a lake, but he can't be trusted not to try this again."

"I can control him," Toregene said, but Sorkhokhtani cut her off.

"If you can't, it will be Fatima who pays the price," she said.

"Perhaps I made a mistake in choosing Güyük," Toregene said. She looked so fragile, her cheekbones chiseled like ivory and her wide eyes glassy from her illness, that no one contradicted her.

"What's done is done," Alaqai said, patting Toregene's hand and rising stiffly to her feet. "Now Fatima must decide whether to stay and face Güyük each day, or leave Karakorum to seek refuge with Sorkhokhtani or me."

"It's your choice," Toregene said.

I had no desire to run from Güyük, but neither did I wish to live in constant fear of the sound of guards in the palace corridors. I studied Toregene for a long moment, the signs of her illness writ plain on her face.

"You could come with me," I said to Toregene, but I knew her answer even before she shook her head.

"I swore to protect this khanate," she said. "I'll spend the rest of my days here, ensuring Güyük doesn't destroy the empire his grandfather and father forged with blood and steel."

I contemplated leaving Toregene alone to face her son and rule the kingdom with only Shigi at her side. Yet as I looked at her now, I realized that my main source of joy since Wien, or perhaps even since Nishapur, had been my sisterhood with this woman. Toregene had saved me—from death and myself—many times, forging a bond deeper than blood.

For many years now, Toregene had been my family. Despite the very real possibility that Güyük would continue to torment me, I couldn't leave her, especially now when she needed me most. Borte had died of a broken heart and Al-Altun had committed terrible acts in the name of love; surely I could sacrifice my comfort and safety for the sister I loved.

I had survived Nishapur, traveled halfway across the world, and been the instrument of three women's deaths. I would not allow Güyük and his threats to frighten me.

"I'll stay," I said. "Of course I'll stay."

Toregene gathered me into her arms in a rare display of tenderness. "Thank God," she breathed. "I don't know what I'd have done without you."

Regardless of what lay ahead, we'd face it together.

As I'd hoped, Güyük remembered nothing—or at least pretended to remember nothing—of the night he tried to arrest me, and the masses that had gathered for the *khurlatai* departed over the coming days, like thousands of yellow leaves dispersed and quickly forgotten after an autumn windstorm.

"Are you sure you won't come with me?" Sorkhokhtani asked on the morning of her departure. A messenger had requested Shigi's presence in the treasury, so he'd already bid the royal women farewell and Alaqai had already left, taking with her carts of books and Toregene's famed blood sausage, but I only shook my head as Sorkhokhtani mounted her mare.

"I can't leave Toregene." I swallowed around the lump in my throat, straightening my shoulders despite the knot of tension in my muscles there. "Her cough worsens, and I'm not sure she'll make it through another winter."

"Send for me if you need me," Sorkhokhtani said. "I'll ride through the night if necessary."

"Thank you," I said. I rarely cried, but my eyes stung at the thought of the ordeal Toregene would face when the weather cooled again this autumn.

"Toregene is fortunate to have you," Sorkhokhtani said. "I hope that perhaps together you can rein in the worst of Güyük's excesses."

I watched her nudge her mare's ribs and canter away, straight spined and melded to the back of her horse, leaving Toregene and me to face the Khan alone.

I prayed that Sorkhokhtani might be right, yet like the two sides of the moon, the *khurlatai* drew clear lines on Toregene's waning influence and Güyük's waxing power. Toregene had thought to guide her son while he settled into the Horse Throne, but our new Khan had no intention of sharing his throne with his mother.

As the sun found its notch in the sky that same day, a young slave waited outside Toregene's tent, bent over to sniff the fresh narcissus blooms I'd planted for Toregene last fall. I'd buried the bulbs around her tent and the Golden Ordu, and even throughout the palace courtyards in the months after our return from the Viennese campaign, feeling my mother's hovering spirit as I knelt in my silk robes with their knees stained with dirt. I thought of my mother often these days as I watched Toregene deteriorate, wondering if she waited for me in the abyss of Jahannam, and if perhaps I might be called upon once more to send a woman I loved to death's welcome release.

The girl scrambled to stand as we approached and offered a deep bow to Toregene, revealing the gold medallion around her neck that bore the imprint of Oghul Ghaimish's name on one side and her symbol of a fox on the other.

"Great Khatun," she said, her eyes darting from us to Toregene's guards. "I bear a message from the Khan's wife."

Toregene glanced at me, then gave a slight nod to her guards. "You may join us inside, and then you may tell us of your mistress's message."

The slave bowed her assent, her movements as graceful as a blade of summer grass. We entered the white interior of the tent and arranged ourselves around the hearth, then waited for the girl to speak.

"My mistress, first wife of the Great Khan, seeks your assistance," the slave said, her whisper weaving into the crack and hiss of the fire.

I waited, expecting tales of madness or secret plots, but she lowered her gaze, her hands fluttering like sparrow wings. "Last night, my mistress angered the Khan because she dropped his platter of lamb on the ground. He beat her, kicked her in the stomach. It has already been a difficult pregnancy, and my mistress fears that if this continues . . ."

Toregene rubbed her temples, her face stricken. "Tell Oghul Ghaimish that I will see my son about this right now. He shall not lay another hand on her, or I'll have him beaten until he glimpses death."

Toregene meant what she said, but Güyük was no child, easily disciplined with a harsh word or a whip. He was the Great Khan, and although Toregene had yet to realize it, he could do as he liked to his wife—or anyone—without repercussions.

The girl scrambled in the dirt to kiss Toregene's hem. "You are a merciful Khatun," she said. "May the Earth Mother bless you."

Toregene lifted her up. "And may she bless your mistress with a healthy child."

"I'll accompany you," I said as she scurried off, but Toregene shook her head.

"You've managed to avoid a confrontation with Güyük since the *khurlatai*. He's liable to be upset over my meddling—I don't want you caught in the middle when the storm breaks."

Part of me agreed with her, but another part balked at hiding from Güyük. Toregene must have read my expression and clucked her tongue.

"I'll return shortly, Fatima. You're welcome to peruse the crate of books Shigi just purchased from the new bookbinder in the market. I'd thought to save them for you as a gift during the Festival of Games, but you may as well read them now if you'd like."

There was no contest between reading Rumi's latest verses and listening to Güyük rant and rave. Toregene was welcome to her son.

Toregene swept away with Oghul Ghaimish's slave trailing after her. The top of the tent was open to the bright blue sky, and the crate of books waited by the door, their pages crisp and still smelling of ink. I tried to settle in to read the *Safarnama*, an account of Nasir Khusraw's travels during the sacred hajj, but the lingering calls of returning geese overhead scattered my already fragile thoughts.

I snapped the book shut when the door creaked open, expecting Toregene and startled to find Oghul Ghaimish instead. Güyük's wife hovered at the entrance, barefoot and as thin as ever, save her swollen belly. Her slave claimed that Güyük had beaten her, but she bore no bruises or cuts. Perhaps they were hidden from view, like the injuries inflicted on her mind during Ogodei's rape of the Oirat girls.

"Welcome, Oghul Ghaimish," I said, rising and gesturing her inside. "Toregene went to meet with Güyük, but you're welcome to wait for her return with me."

She nodded, reminding me of a kingfisher bobbing its head for tadpoles. Her lank hair was stringy today, threaded through with jade and turquoise beads. "Peace shall reign again," she mumbled. "I know it."

I waited for her to continue, but she only stared at the patch of sky overhead. The geese still circled there, reminding me of vultures over a battlefield. A tremor ran up my spine. "Where is Toregene?"

Her eyes darted to me and she licked her cracked lips. "In the Golden Ordu with Güyük," she said. "She sent for you."

"Now?"

She gave me an absent stare and shrugged. "I believe so. She said she needed you."

I pushed open the snarling tiger door and forced my steps to an even gait, following the short path beyond the Blue Fountain and through the palace's grassy courtyards to the Golden Ordu. If I hadn't been so absorbed in my thoughts, I might have noticed the lack of people in the courtyard and the stillness in the air.

I stepped inside the Golden Ordu, anticipating the fight within. Instead, silence greeted me.

Güyük looked down on me from the Horse Throne, and in the center of the tent and tied to a thick spruce pole was Toregene.

"Leave while you still can, Fatima," she wheezed. "Go now."

"Release her!" I lunged forward, but Güyük's guards grasped me from behind. I clawed and bit at them, but they held me fast. A thick tangle of hair obscured Toregene's face, but already a purple bruise blossomed around her right eye and blood dribbled from the corner of her mouth. "What have you done to her?" I screamed.

I'd worried that Güyük might continue to hunt me; I'd been a fool to think he wouldn't turn on his own mother.

Güyük leered at me, then leapt out of his chair as fast as a tiger. He leaned in so close I could smell the ginger on his breath. "It's you I wanted, Fatima of Nishapur. *I* should have ruled these past years, but instead *you* sat by her side and whispered poison against me into her ear. Do you know what she said when she came in here? That I should never have been crowned Khan. Where do you suppose she got that idea?"

Perhaps some demon possessed me then, for my fury boiled over. "You come from a line of vile conquerors, but your mother was too softhearted to see you for what you were: a foul, conniving beast unfit to gather dung, much less rule an empire."

I should have expected the blow, but the white surge of agony at my temple made me stagger and I'd have fallen back had it not been for the guards holding me. Toregene screamed something at Güyük, but I couldn't make out her words over the Khan's bellow.

"Take her away," he yelled. "The Saracen bitch shall suffer for her crimes against me. Tear her apart bit by bit until she begs for death!"

I struggled and Toregene screamed, but the last thing I saw as they dragged me away was the delicate ring of poet narcissus I'd planted outside the Golden Ordu, their innocent white blossoms stretching toward the sky and tinged with the color of blood.

PART IV

The Princess of the Hearth

Chapter 27

1248 AD
YEAR OF THE YELLOW MONKEY

I was born on the blackest winter night during the new moon and thus had been content to spend my life in the shadows cast by those around me.

Until now.

My entire world had been consumed with pulling my sons up to the height of great men. I was the daughter, wife, and mother who played music and clasped her opinions tight to her breast, but in truth, my *buree* and my horse-head fiddle kept me from going mad all these years, watching my husband drink himself to death while first Ogodei, and now Güyük, corroded the majesty and might of the Mongol Empire.

I crumpled Shigi's hastily scrawled message in my fist. I'd not cried when Tolui had gone to the sacred mountains—my husband's death had been a blessed relief—but this news from Karakorum threatened to bring me to my knees.

I'd spent the day alternating between playing my *buree* to clear my mind and wearing out my knees before the gold cross in my traveling chapel tent. My sons and I respected all the major religions of our people, the followers of Abraham, Buddha, and Muhammad, but it was Christ's waters that I'd accepted at my baptism years ago. I still hoped to one day convince my sons to convert, but for now there were more pressing issues.

I hadn't prayed like this since the day I'd rejected Ogodei's proposal that I marry Güyük. Christ had guided me then, and he guided me now.

We were halfway home after leaving Güyük's *khurlatai.* Now I wondered whether I'd ever again see the familiar hills and valleys of our lands.

I stood and stomped my feet to persuade the blood to move in my legs, then crossed the well-worn path from the holy tent to my own, pausing only briefly to wave to my sons sitting outside their own *gers,* the smoke from their wives' cooking fires climbing lazily into the sky.

Möngke set down the stick he was whittling and ambled over, trailed by Kublai. Mothers aren't supposed to have favorites among their children, but every woman knows that to be a lie. Kublai was my secret favorite, the son most like me. I would have Möngke as Great Khan, for he was the first to fall from my womb, but all my sons would receive worthy holdings.

Möngke settled next to me, sitting a head taller than me, with his thick eyebrow quirked in question. My eldest son was not a pretty man, but he had a solid mind, as did all my children. Teb Tengeri, Genghis Khan's shaman, had seen great things in store for my firstborn and had named him for the eternal stars, but it was Borte Khatun who had seen the entirety of my sons' stories in her cracked bones and the flames of the fire.

"Keep this one close," she had said, pressing Möngke into my arms after his birth, his skin smeared with blood and dark clots from my womb. "But raise all your sons well. One day they shall rule all the lands under the Eternal Blue Sky."

And so I had waited all these years. Now our wait was over.

"What's happened, Mother?" Möngke folded his legs beneath him, while Kublai drifted over. Patience did not come easily to my eldest, but I'd managed to beat a little into him, as a good mother should.

I set about warming a bone cup of goat milk over the fire. "What makes you believe something has happened?"

"Your scowl has scattered the clouds," Möngke said, gesturing upward.

A glance overhead revealed an empty sky as blue as an agate stone. It might have hailed grasshoppers or rained fire and I wouldn't have noticed.

"Also," Kublai said, his lips curled in the crooked grin I loved so much,

"I told Möngke that an arrow messenger delivered a letter to your *ger* this morning."

I chuckled at that. Kublai always had a joke on the tip of his tongue, but his eyes were as sharp as those of a Kazakh eagle on the hunt.

"I must return to Karakorum," I said, lifting my palms to stifle their protests. "Güyük has arrested Fatima, and Toregene . . ." I drew a steadying breath and handed over Shigi's crumpled message. Kublai smoothed it on his lap and my sons quickly scanned the slanting Uighur script. They'd have understood a letter written in any of the empire's nine languages, for I'd insisted that my sons be able to read and speak Mongolian, Uighur, and Mandarin, yet it didn't escape my notice that Shigi had chosen to write his letter in Uighur, the language Güyük was least likely to intercept and read.

"Toregene Khatun is missing?" Möngke's features twisted into a scowl. "I don't understand."

"I don't either," I said. "Shigi rides to warn Alaqai, and I must write to Batu—we may need his support if Güyük has overstepped himself."

Yet according to Shigi's message, my nephew had already overstepped himself, committing terrible atrocities against Genghis Khan's mandates. After Korguz's death, Toregene had dismissed the laws forbidding torture and executions, and now it seemed she and Fatima had suffered the consequences.

"I will write to Batu," Kublai said, "and we can travel together to the capital."

I gave a derisive scoff. "*We* will do no such thing. The letter to Batu must come from my hand so as not to cast a shadow on either of you."

Batu Khan was Jochi's only surviving son, the eldest of Genghis Khan's grandchildren and the respected leader of the Golden Horde. Like me, my nephew had wisely chosen to remain in his lands, patiently consolidating his power and biding his time. Childless and tainted by Jochi's impure blood, Batu had pledged his support for my sons and withheld his presence from Güyük's *khurlatai* based on that pledge and his loathing for Güyük after their fight in Rus. If the time came, I knew I could count on Batu and his Golden Horde for assistance.

Kublai crossed his arms before him. "So you will write to Batu and then remain content to spend your days making cheese and beating felts?"

I arched an eyebrow at him, a smile playing on my lips. "No," I said. "I shall return to Karakorum to see for myself what Güyük has done."

"Absolutely not," Möngke argued. "It's far too dangerous."

"I have outlived my husband and all the rest of the sons of the Great Khan, and most of his daughters, too," I said, my cup of milk forgotten beside me, growing cold as my tone gained heat. "I am not about to perish in Karakorum."

"And if Güyük decides to arrest you as well?"

"He won't."

Möngke pounded his fist onto the earth beneath him. My overly cautious son. I hoped such a trait wouldn't hinder his rule. "You can't know that. At least promise you'll take a guard with you."

"If it will soothe your worries, of course." I crossed my arms before me, under the flat breasts that had once suckled my sons, and drummed my fingers over my arm. Outside of my chapel tent, a Spirit Banner of black horsehair twitched in the breeze. As Princess of the Hearth, I'd guarded the Spirit Banner of Genghis Khan since Borte had flown to the sacred mountains. Oghul Ghaimish had demanded the banner after Ogodei's death, but I had claimed an angry wind spirit had carried it away. Her glaring lack of intelligence, and her husband's negligence, had showed themselves when neither questioned my claim.

"I know that look," Kublai said, his face mirroring my smile. "It means that our mother will soon get what she wants."

"I will indeed." I looked up at the red dusk striding across the sky. "It's time to gather Batu and your brothers. The final fight for this empire is about to begin."

I whipped my horse until a thick lather covered her flanks and my bones threatened to shatter beneath my skin. At my back, my golden saddle arch was decorated with two hares, the rabbits symbolizing the long life and legacy my sons would continue long after my death. The guards and I passed a herd of wild horses on the way to Karakorum, a lone *takhi* stallion with his mares and foals galloping free along the grasslands and making my own mare pull against her reins as if challenging them to a race. Farmers from Cathay, Persian merchants, and Mongol herders all streamed away from the capital with burlap sacks strapped to their backs or pushing carts piled high with saddles, basins, and food.

"You're going the wrong way," one called to me, a merchant dressed in emerald silks coated with dust from the road. His wives trailed behind him, all covered by veils that reminded me of those Fatima used to wear. "Turn around now, while you still can."

"What do you mean?" I asked.

"Haven't you heard?" He shook his head. "The Great Khan seeks to purge his court of his mother's influence. There have been many executions; the capital is no longer safe."

I'd spent much of my time as regent fostering agriculture in my sons' lands, making our holdings self-sufficient and endearing the Toluid family to the people through their full bellies. Güyük was a fool to drive away all these people; Karakorum already required cartloads of food to be delivered to it daily to sustain its populace, but now those herders and farmers were fleeing. But that was the least of my problems.

I entered Karakorum to find the city whipped into a wild frenzy, like a bruised and drunken army still awake on the dawn after a brutal victory. Leering soldiers skulked in doorways, and monks slammed the doors of their temples when my shadow fell across their thresholds. A Saracen made the sign against the evil eye when my gaze met his, a motion I'd seen Fatima make countless times.

Angry red sparks flew into the air as I passed the city's forges, and beyond them, shop windows boasted recent shipments of blue-and-white pottery glazed with images of cranes and fire, the symbols of longevity and destruction. The guards outside the palace allowed me entrance when I announced myself, and I continued past the Silver Tree toward the Golden Ordu, my old bones aching from the long ride even while the blood coursed hot in my veins. The comforting smell of horses and hay soothed my nerves as I dismounted at the palace stables. Slaves stepped forward to take my mare and I paused to stretch my back.

My spirit leapt from my flesh and I almost screamed when someone grabbed my hand and pulled me into an empty stall.

The face that stared down at me was ravaged by both grief and time, grown horribly older in the days since I'd seen him last.

"Shigi," I breathed, my hand on my heart. "You scared the breath out of me."

He held a finger over his lips, his sunken eyes darting from me to the door. "I didn't think you'd come in time," he whispered.

"In time for what?"

"She's waiting for you," Shigi said, glancing behind me. "I'll take you to her before Güyük realizes you're here."

"Who do you mean?" I crossed my arms before me. "Your message was vague."

"It had to be," he said. "Lest Güyük find out I was sending missives to you."

"You said you were riding for Alaqai."

He shook his head. "That was before . . ."

"Before what?"

"Toregene," he said, the misery in his face somehow expanding. "She's dying, Sorkhokhtani."

So she was still alive, despite my worst fears. Toregene had been ill for so long that I wished to wave away his concerns, but his face told me something was different this time.

"Take me to her," I said.

We ducked outside and past the slaves brushing down my weary mare, keeping to the shadows as we continued toward Toregene's Great White Tent. I'd always found comfort in shadows, but now I felt as if hidden eyes were watching us from dark alcoves as we raced toward death. Shigi hesitated when we reached Toregene's *ger* with its snarling tiger door, as if he needed to gather strength to face what waited there.

"Where is Fatima?" I asked. I imagined her inside, bickering with Toregene while urging my heart-sister to drink an infusion that smelled of rotting earth and foreign spices. The very idea made me smile.

"Dead," Shigi said, his gaze falling to the ground. "She breathed her last yesterday."

"No." I shook my head. I'd seen the elegant Persian only days ago, dressed in sumptuous silks and wafting the scent of rose with her every movement. "Not Fatima."

Shigi's jaw clenched. "After all she suffered, I promise you that her death was a release."

He didn't give me a chance to ask what he meant, only turned and pushed open Toregene's door.

As much as Shigi had been battered by recent events, they had broken the woman who lay in the bed across from us. Toregene's eyes were closed and her arm hung uselessly by her side, her chest neither rising nor falling. She might have been dead had it not been for the movement of her head as Shigi approached her bedside.

"Toregene," he whispered. "Sorkhokhtani is here."

She turned to face me, a fragile smile lighting her pale face despite the florid bruise around her eye. Her lips were stained with accumulated blood, and crimson-stained cloths littered the ground. Her fingers fluttered to beckon me forward, their deformed tips and purple nails swollen from her illness.

"Toregene," I said, my voice thick with emotion. "I left only days ago . . ."

"The world can transform in only a few days' time," she murmured. "As you well know."

She was right. My life had changed the day my father agreed to marry me into the family of Genghis Khan, and the Great Khan's mighty empire had begun to fracture the moment he breathed his last breath. So the world had changed, and now it would do so again.

"Your son—," I started, but she didn't let me finish.

"Güyük is no longer my son," she said, her thin lips twisting with pain and revulsion. She fiddled with the gold bracelet at her wrist, the gift from Shigi embossed with a phoenix and demon masks. Unlike the phoenix, I knew Toregene wouldn't rise from this day of fire and ash. "I rue the day I brought him into this world. It would have been better if that demon had died lodged in my womb."

"Then you would have died, too, sister." I settled on the side of her bed and took her hand. Her silks were ruined with blood and old sweat stains, and a sheen of cold perspiration lingered on her palm and at her temples. My heart-sister wasn't long for this world.

"Did Güyük do this to you?" I asked, but she shook her head.

"This has been a long time coming," she said, pausing as a fresh cough overtook her. My heart ached, for it was as if her lungs were saturated with blood, and a fresh stream of crimson flowed down her chin before she finished. I wiped away the blood, remembering all the times she'd nursed me when I was ill.

"My only regret in dying is that I won't live to see my son and his foul wife toppled from their dais." She clutched my hand, her eyes glazed with fever. "Güyük and Oghul Ghaimish must pay for their crimes."

"Their crimes?" I knew then what Shigi had meant outside. "Do you mean their crimes against Fatima?"

Tears welled in her eyes, and from the door, Shigi motioned for my silence. "Toregene." Shigi's voice was as hard as stone. "You need to rest."

But Toregene ignored him.

"Güyük murdered Fatima," she whispered to me, squeezing her eyes shut against the pain. "He claimed she'd bewitched me, that she'd used sorcery to influence me and keep him from the throne all these years." She stopped for air, her breathing coming in short and labored gasps. "He charged her with trying to overthrow him and ordered her execution, just as I once ordered Al-Altun's execution."

"Fatima wasn't a member of the Golden Family," I said gently. "He could have ordered her execution even without Al-Altun's precedent."

"But he mightn't have ordered her torture." Toregene's shoulders shook with silent sobs, but she pressed a fist to her lips to regain control of her breath. "He claimed he wouldn't spill her blood, but he tortured her for days," Toregene whispered, tears flowing freely down her cheeks.

"And he forced you to watch," I said, understanding dawning. Güyük was a demon from the furthest reaches of hell, inflicting pain upon his mother to speed her death, while murdering his greatest opponent. He'd been denied Fatima once and couldn't bear to have a woman like her influence his mother, and so he'd sought her destruction the moment the Khan's helm was placed upon his head.

Dread unfurled down my spine. I, too, had once denied Güyük my hand in marriage. I wondered what penalty he thought to inflict upon me—or worse, upon my sons—for my repudiation of his offer.

Toregene gave a weary nod. "When he was done, my son ordered her thrown into the river—"

She was overcome with a coughing fit so strong I thought she might die, drowning in a sea of her own blood. Shigi pulled her into his arms, stroking her hair and wiping her mouth as she was seized again and again with the bloody coughing. Through it all, I clutched her hand, willing her to stay. Toregene would soon be free of this world, but I wished for peace in her final moments, that her last thoughts might be of Shigi and all those she'd loved in this life, of the scent of grinding herbs and the sweet sound of music.

I sagged with relief when the coughing eased, only to find it replaced by heart-rending sobs.

"I killed her, Sorkhokhtani," she moaned. "I should have sent her with you—"

I stroked her thinning hair. "You gave Fatima her freedom long ago, and she could have left you at any time. She knew the risks, but she chose to stay with you. She loved you, just as I love you and Alaqai loves you, and as Borte loved you. Forget about the recent days, and think of the times when we were together."

She closed her eyes then, and I took the tiny *buree* from my pocket, the carved ivory flute almost identical to the one I'd given Alaqai when she'd first left for the Onggud a lifetime ago. The melody I played was soothing, like the whisper of wind rattling the leaves of a birch tree in autumn. Borte had once told me that I had air in my soul, and that was why I loved music.

"The air is often so calm that no one notices its presence," she had said, smiling while I played my flute. "But given the right force and direction, it makes beautiful music. It can also come screaming down from the mountains, overturning great spruce trees and tearing down *gers* in its fury."

My days of calm were coming to an end.

I looked up from the flute to see Shigi check Toregene's throat for a pulse. He closed her mismatched eyes and let fly a tortured sob, his frail shoulders shaking with grief.

Toregene had been well loved in this life, but now her soul gathered strength and soared to the sky, where I imagined her greeting Borte and Fatima in a tearful reunion.

First we became widows. Now, one by one, death claimed us, until only Alaqai and I remained.

One day, we, too, would join them. But not today.

"Shigi," I said, my voice firm but gentle. "We loved her, and we will honor her. But if we do not move quickly, Güyük may yet win."

He lifted his head and blinked away his tears, then nodded. "Tell me what to do, and I'll see it done."

"You must take Toregene's body to the mountains," I said. "And her Great White Tent must be dismantled."

"My slaves can see to the tent," he said, his voice wrought with emotion. "I'll carry her to the mountains myself."

"Good. Have your slaves inform Güyük of her passing, but they must wait to deliver the message until you're well outside the city walls." I glanced around the empty tent, then dropped my voice. "You must gather Alaqai. Both you and she must ride for the camp of Batu and the Golden Horde."

Shigi gave a weary nod. "You plan to depose Güyük, don't you?"

"I plan to do much more than that." I tucked my flute back into my wide sleeve and hesitated only long enough to press my forehead to Toregene's, feeling the warmth still there. Then I straightened and squared my shoulders. "Where did they take Fatima?"

"To the river outside the walls, downstream from the artificial river. Where all the city's filth is dumped." His gaze met mine. "I wanted to stop Güyük then, but I feared he'd turn on Toregene as well. I pray Fatima can forgive me."

"Fatima forgave much more than that over the course of her life," I said gently. "She was doomed from the moment Güyük took the throne, but we were too blind to see it." I wrapped one of Toregene's discarded shawls around my graying hair and picked up an old woven basket. "I'll see you in Batu's camp. Go well, Shigi."

"Go well, Sorkhokhtani Beki," Shigi murmured as Toregene's tiger door closed behind me.

I retraced my steps as quickly as I could, stopping for a moment in the stables to gather the necessary tools, then leaving behind the Silver Tree and the palace walls, and finally the whole of Karakorum. No one dared question an old woman on foot headed toward the river. The basket under my arm was heavy, but I managed.

I almost expected a crowd at the site of Fatima's execution, but instead the Orkhon River was deserted, as if both the living and the dead were offended by what had happened beneath the Earth Mother's sacred waters.

I didn't have to go far before I found her.

A large felt bundle was submerged beneath the surface, tied tight with rope and weighted down with many heavy stones. The water was bitingly cold, and it took several attempts before I could wade in and roll the stones away, then drag the muddy bundle out of the river. I panted from exertion and trembled from the cold, unsure whether I wished to face what lay inside.

I wouldn't cower from what I was to do in the coming days; I couldn't hide from this either.

The knots were too waterlogged to untie, so I used the knife from the basket to cut them loose. Closing my eyes, I gently peeled back the wet felts with their pervasive stench of wet wool and the lingering scent of terror.

Then I opened my eyes.

I lurched back and stumbled to the grasses, the earth spinning beneath my feet as I retched, gasping for air.

Nothing could have prepared me for the brutalities visited upon this woman who, in life, had moved with such grace, whose silks were always gently perfumed, and whose mind was seeped in poetry and beauty.

River water had bloated her naked corpse, the skin on her torso and limbs riddled with burn marks from branding irons. Still worse was her face; the nose, mouth, and eyes had been sewn shut with jagged stitches.

The golden silk thread was stained with blood, its decadence garish against so monstrous a backdrop.

I didn't need to inspect the rest of the body to know that Güyük had ordered her every orifice sewn shut to prevent her spirit from escaping her body. He meant to punish Fatima in this life and the next, too.

Kneeling in the grass under a sky throwing shadows dark with grief, I retched until my stomach was empty, rare tears pouring down my cheeks.

There was nothing left of Fatima's earthly body to save, but I might still salvage her soul.

Fatima was a Saracen, and according to her beliefs, she must be buried before a full day had passed since her death. I recalled her words at Borte's deathbed, claiming that her soul was already damned to the fires of hell. Yet I doubted whether any god would punish a woman of such loyalty and dignity as Fatima of Nishapur.

The stench of death was overwhelming, but I cut the stitches on her face with trembling fingers, pulling away the hated golden thread. The deceptive silk stitching had been done with a careless hand, each stitch doubled over so Fatima's soul had no hope of escape.

Until now.

I imagined her soul flying into the sky, returning to the gardens she had so loved. I had no doubt that her god would gather her to him and allow her to spend eternity in the paradise of Jannah, reclining on couches inlaid with gold and surrounded by fountains scented with ginger while watching rivers of pearls and rubies flow past.

I turned to the basket I'd brought, retrieving the shovel taken from Güyük's stables. Pausing occasionally to catch my breath, I dug a shallow grave for Fatima as dusk blanketed Karakorum.

"I have no bolt of silk for your shroud," I murmured to Fatima, forcing myself not to recoil as I smoothed the hair back from her ravaged face. "But I promise I will make this right."

I wrapped her again in the felt blanket, then dragged her broken body to the edge of the grave and gently laid her inside, making sure she lay on her right side facing Makkah. I tucked the dark earth over her, then arranged a wreath of red poppies and yellow wildflowers along the edges of the grave, as she'd once done around Borte's body.

The sky had grown dark and the stars shone down on this bleak steppe. I hoped that by now Shigi had managed to take Toregene to the mountains, and that perhaps these two sisters, joined not by blood but by life and love, could now greet each other with light hearts.

Their work on this earth was done, yet mine had just begun.

"*Bayartai*, Fatima and Toregene," I whispered. "I shall greet you one day in the sacred mountains, with many stories to tell."

I passed under Karakorum's main gate, guided by the moon and stars and perhaps the spirits of the dead. My footsteps joined those of few others out on the limestone cobbled streets that led to the palace, and the dark figures all shrank back at the sight of a woman covered with filth and reeking of death. I slipped in silence to where Toregene's Great White Tent had stood, already dismantled by Shigi's slaves, and dug in the soft dirt outside the ring of trampled earth until I found the gift Fatima had left behind. Smooth and white, with the promise of fresh life.

Or the ability to end life.

I recalled the narcissus bulbs Fatima had used to shepherd Borte toward the long sleep of death. I shoved the bulbs into my pockets, wiping away the clumps of black dirt that clung to my palms. I knew not what Güyük had planned for me now that Toregene had been consigned to the earth and Fatima destroyed, and while I considered fleeing, I knew Güyük would hunt me down and destroy me if he chose, and my sons in the process.

The time for retreat had ended. Now was the moment I'd waited for all my life.

Güyük's guards tried to bar my entrance into the Golden Ordu after I'd exchanged my ruined clothes, claiming that the Great Khan was in mourning for the death of his mother, but I gave them my most scathing glare. "I am Sorkhokhtani Beki," I said. "The Princess of the Hearth and Mother of the Toluids has come to visit the Great Khan. I demand to be presented to Güyük Khan, firstborn son of Ogodei Khan and Toregene Khatun."

Grudgingly, the guards stepped aside. Güyük reclined on the throne high atop the dais, staring intently at a yellowing scroll spread across his knees with the heavy copper treasury stamp next to him. I waited a moment, then cleared my throat.

He glanced up, then blinked and offered a slow grin. "Sorkhokhtani Beki, we are honored at your unexpected presence. I'd have thought you'd have been halfway to the barren lands of your sons by now."

I bowed so he couldn't see the hatred burning in my eyes. "I returned when I heard of your mother's ill health. I'm most distressed that I was too late to help her," I said, daring to glance up to gauge his reaction. "May I offer you the deepest of condolences, from myself and my loyal sons."

Güyük waved his hand, whether dismissing Toregene's death or my groveling, I couldn't tell. "My mother was ill for some time. Both she and the empire received a great boon when she passed to the mountains today."

If there was any justice in the world, a bolt of lightning would have struck this demon where he sat, but instead, Güyük only yawned and set aside his scroll. "I would send you with a message for Batu when you leave Karakorum."

I lowered my eyes, a demure matron. "And what message would that be?"

"Batu was the only member of the Golden Family not present at my *khurlatai*. I command his immediate presence in Karakorum, to demonstrate his acceptance of my rule."

"And if he refuses?"

"Then I will destroy him, just as my father destroyed the rebellious Oirat and Uighurs."

It was Toregene who had ordered Al-Altun's execution, and Ogodei had destroyed the Oirat at great cost to himself. Yet I held my tongue.

"I shall carry the message as you ask, but I would request one favor of you, Great Khan."

Güyük rolled up the map of Goryeo, pinching the paper between thick fingers. "And what might that be?"

"On my way to Batu, I would erect your mother's *ordu* next to Borte's. Your revered grandmother would wish Toregene's spirit to be nearby."

Güyük hesitated, and I could almost hear him mulling this over in his mind. "The winds will destroy that old tent in the months to come. You may do as you wish with it."

I neglected to mention that my sons and I repaired Borte's felts every spring and cleared away its spider webs, and would do so for Toregene's as well. A third tent would soon join those two, but Güyük need not know about that either.

"You are a great and noble Khan," I said through gritted teeth. "The Golden Family and your people are already speculating over which lucky woman you shall make your Khatun."

The Great Khan leaned back against his throne. I had been a great beauty when I first married Tolui, but now Güyük's eyes appraised my flat breasts and thickening waist, the hips that had carried my sons and the gray that had spread from my temples to cover most of my hair. His lip quivered with disgust, but a slow smile spread across his lips. "I could still marry you, Sorkhokhtani Beki. Absorb your lands into my own."

I'd sooner die than let that happen. Better yet, I'd see him die.

I answered with a frown. "You would gain nothing save an old woman in your bed, for I'd come to you empty-handed. My sons are no longer children; they rule their father's lands and provide for their widowed mother."

Güyük stood and descended the dais stairs, bringing the parchment with him with its dark outline of the Goryeo peninsula. Perhaps he thought to continue the conquests of his father, first attack Goryeo and then move against the territories of the Golden Family.

"You may be right, Sorkhokhtani Beki, and I've no need of a withered old woman in my bed," he said. "Not when I might have my pick of any ripe young woman the empire over. I could take as many wives as I'd like, and install Oghul Ghaimish as Khatun."

I shook my head. "Her mind is unstable. I fear she would anger your enemies and alienate your supporters. Better to leave the Khatun's head-dress empty than to let Oghul Ghaimish wear it."

Güyük stroked his chin. "Then I'll take another wife to be Khatun."

I feigned nonchalance. "My son Möngke would be delighted at the idea of a union between our two branches of the family."

Güyük practically salivated at the idea, whether gaining power over my dead husband's lands or marrying a fresh young girl. Or both. Of course, no one in my family would let him come within a day's ride of any of my granddaughters. However, I needed to assure Güyük of our family's loyalty, at least for now.

"Your proposition may prove favorable," Güyük said, flicking his wrist to indicate my audience was at an end. "I shall guarantee you safe passage across the steppes and you may depart with my permission to broach the subject with your eldest son. Of course, you'll speak to Batu first."

"All you ask shall be done," I promised, taking the oblong copper medallion he proffered. The slanting script down its center read, *By the order of the Eternal Blue Sky, Güyük, the Khan of Khans, decrees that all Mongols shall submit to the bearer of this medallion.*

If only things were that easy. I tucked the medallion into my sleeve, made my obeisance, and backed out of the Great Khan's presence for what I hoped was the last time.

I hoped never to see Güyük again. At least not alive.

I was eager to be gone from Karakorum, to return home and surround myself with my music, my prayers to the god of the cross, and my sons. My plan to topple Güyük must succeed, lest I find myself dragged back here to repeat Fatima's fate.

On my way from the Golden Ordu, I passed the open door to Oghul Ghaimish's tent. Güyük's wife wore jewel-studded hairpins shinier than a fly's body and her white silks from the *khurlatai*, but the underarms were stained from many days' use, and around her neck she wore a tangled necklace of yellow horse vertebrae.

"Sorkhokhtani," she said, offering me a gap-toothed smile and pulling me into her *ger*. The stench of stale urine and the pile of bowls with fluffs of gray mold growing out of clumps of curdled milk almost made me void my stomach again. Yet among the filth was also beauty: a porcelain lion figurine glazed in a pale blue that matched the sky and a polished copper mirror inscribed with two antlered stags standing under the sun. "I didn't realize you'd returned to Karakorum."

"Briefly," I said, trying not to breathe. I recalled the rape of the Oirat girls, that Ogodei had plucked Oghul Ghaimish from their number and ordered his son to marry her. For a moment, my heart surged with pity for this broken woman, but her next words robbed me of my breath.

"You missed Fatima's execution." Oghul Ghaimish pouted, rubbing her forefinger over the bones in her necklace. She hissed in pain when one sharp edge sliced open her finger, and she sucked away the blood before pushing her matted hair behind her shoulder. A fresh set of golden stitches ran along the ruined seam of the garment's neckline, the crisscross pattern an exact match of the jagged stitches on Fatima's face.

I swayed on my feet at the remembrance of Fatima's tortured body, her lips and eyes . . .

"The Rose of Nishapur deserved to die." Oghul Ghaimish grinned, her teeth streaked with blood. "I helped lure Toregene away from her and watched her breathe her last."

I'd thought Güyük had acted alone, but Oghul Ghaimish had helped torture Fatima. She continued to grin, a child proud of her accomplishments.

"Güyük was pleased with my role during the interrogation," Oghul Ghaimish said, her fingers—the same delicate fingers that had sewn golden thread through human skin—fluttering at her neck. "I wish she could have died a thousand deaths."

"You are indeed a dedicated wife." I blew a puff of air between my lips, my next words weaving a snare I knew Oghul Ghaimish couldn't help but stumble into. "I'd hoped to offer my congratulations upon your ascension to Great Khatun, but it's unfortunate that Güyük doesn't wish for you to wear the *boqta*."

My words had the desired effect.

"But I've earned the green headdress!" She stomped her foot and began to pace, then whirled upon me, her eyes narrowed with suspicion. "Is that why you're here?" She picked at the skin of her throat above the mended collar. "Has he offered to take you as his wife again?"

I shook my head ruefully, my mind racing. "I'm an old woman now. My only worth is my grown sons and their many children." I offered a reassuring smile, although my heart felt as cold as fresh snow. "I return to them now, and leave you to your husband."

She gave a wet sniff and her eyes shone bright, tears threatening to overflow.

I turned to go, then snapped my fingers. "I almost forgot," I said, pressing Fatima's gift into her hand while keeping some back for myself. "I wished to leave these with you."

She opened her palm, her breath heavy and foul. "What are they?"

"The bulbs of a rare flower," I said. "The poet's narcissus."

"I care little for flowers," she said, turning away.

I kept my voice light. "Plant them if you wish," I said. "The blossoms are exquisite although the bulbs are sometimes mistaken for garlic. Fatima once told me they can kill a grown man if eaten." I gave a girlish giggle. "I certainly wouldn't want to be responsible for anyone's accidental poisoning."

I strode from her tent then, not daring to look back. It was only after the door closed that I heard the lilt of a woman's smothered laughter.

The sweet sound of victory.

I hitched the black camels to a cart and directed Shigi's silent slaves as they finished loading it with the felts and poles from Toregene's *ger*. Even the animals seemed eager to leave, braying and pulling on their harnesses. I would ride straight for Batu and then my sons, following the path of the arrow messengers and pausing along the way to let the camels graze. There was only one stop I would make, a debt to be paid.

Flicking the reins to urge the camels on, I cursed myself at least a hundred times each day as the cart crawled toward my nephew's lands. I'd have preferred to ride by horseback, but that was impossible with the felts and disassembled poles of the two *gers* I pulled behind me. I was on the road for only two days when I noticed a disturbance on the horizon behind me, in the direction of Karakorum, and instinctively touched the medallion hidden in my sleeve.

My thoughts flew to Güyük, that perhaps he'd changed his mind and decided to have me arrested. I traced the bulges in my pocket, a gift from a brave woman. I would carry the narcissus bulbs with me until Möngke's rule was assured. I'd sooner die than fall into Güyük's clutches.

I spurred the camels on, but the cart and its precious cargo weighted us down like a boulder. The disturbance on the horizon grew nearer until I could discern two mounted riders when I glanced over my shoulder. I almost cried out in relief when I recognized them.

Shigi and Alaqai reined in their horses on their approach, both animals beginning to lather and their riders wearing thick coats of dust along with the swords strapped to their waists. I stepped down from the cart on unsteady legs as Alaqai dismounted. She pulled me into a tight embrace, and I breathed deeply of the familiar scents of horse and leather. "Shigi told me about Toregene and Fatima," she murmured. "I wish I'd known—I'd have ridden a hundred horses into the earth to get there in time."

"They're finally at peace," I said. "That's all that matters now."

"We're in this together, Sorkhokhtani," she said, releasing me with a fearsome grin that might have been stolen from her father. "Come what may."

Tears stung my eyes, but I tilted my chin. "I would be honored if you would help me raise their *ordus*."

She stood back, blinked several times, and drew a ragged breath. "Of course. Then together we shall travel to Batu's lands and gather your sons. It shall fall to Möngke and his brothers to unite this empire once again."

"So it will," I said. "And so they shall."

I turned to Shigi. "You've done well, Shigi. Thank you."

He bowed, his face grizzled from time and grief but still regal. Shigi had served Genghis Khan and Borte, then Alaqai, Toregene, and Fatima, and now me. He was a greater treasure to our family than Karakorum's Silver Tree with its fountains of wine and *airag*, a man whose name should be venerated around hearth fires for generations.

He felt in his saddlebags and withdrew a heavy book bound by a blue leather cover, the Eternal Blue Sky and its clouds brought to earth. I recognized it as one Fatima had carried with her almost everywhere, her pen scratching over the pages during Ogodei's *khurlatai* and Toregene's assumption of the throne.

"Fatima's history of the Golden Family," I murmured, and Shigi nodded.

"I saved it from her chambers before I left Karakorum," he said. "Her final entry was a description of Güyük's *khurlatai*. I give it to you now, that it may always be safe."

I flashed a wry smile. "Keep it for a while longer, my friend. Our story is not yet done, and I would have you write its ending."

He hesitated, then bowed again. "As you wish, Sorkhokhtani Beki."

Beki. Unlike Borte and Toregene, I, like Alaqai, would never be Khatun. Instead, my sons would mend this empire and ensure our family's rule for generations to come. That would be my legacy.

It took many more days for us to close the distance to Borte's lonely *ordu*. Once there, we spent the afternoon with only the howling wind for company, raising Toregene's Great White Tent to the east, and next to it, a more diminutive tent for Fatima. I wondered what the proud Persian would think to know that her final monument in this life was a plain Mongol *ger* on the outside, the inside bedecked with sumptuous silk carpets and wall hangings from her homeland.

I stood alone inside Toregene's tent after I had finished securing the felts with river rocks around the base. The rope that controlled the smoke hole dangled listlessly and the hearth lay dark and empty. The cold breath of air that made me shiver might have been Toregene's spirit, the shadow cast in the corner her shade.

I breathed deeply, imagining the scent of the herbs that always clung to Toregene's felts and wishing I had a fragment of her soul to carry with me. Instead, I had only memories.

I shut Toregene's tiger door quietly behind me, pausing for a moment to trace the snarling wooden face. Angry gray clouds had followed us from Karakorum, but now the dappled sun shone down upon the three *gers* and illuminated the door's vivid greens and reds, bringing the tiger to life.

Alaqai straightened in front of Fatima's *ordu* and brushed the dirt from her hands. I'd given her two of the remaining narcissus bulbs, knowing that Fatima would have appreciated seeing a piece of Nishapur blooming outside her tent each spring. Shigi sat in the grass near the camel-cart, writing in the blue-and-white history book. From the way he paused now and again to wipe his eyes, I guessed he was recounting the recent tragedies since Güyük's *khurlatai*.

Alaqai fell into step beside me and we entered Borte's tent together, the ancient felts still stained with the black smoke of her hearth fires. I wondered what message the divining bones would hold if she could scry for us now, if she would see our victory or our ruin.

"Give us your strength," I whispered to the spirits of the three *ordus* as Alaqai clasped my hand.

"They'll watch over us," she whispered. "As they always did in life."

I prayed she was right.

The night sky was black when I made out the fires of Batu's new capital of Sarai on the horizon, like the dull embers of charcoal. We had traded the camel cart for fresh horses at one of the *ortoo* messenger posts, and now I urged more speed from my stallion, flanked by Alaqai and Shigi. Together, we drove to the outskirts of the Golden Horde's capital, following the ruts of wagons come before us and passing between larch trees and two colossal tablets bearing the laws of Genghis Khan. Batu had once murdered a Rus prince who had refused to do obeisance to the tablets and a statue of Genghis, thus earning my nephew the further respect of every Mongol from Persia to Goryeo. I bowed my head to Genghis' scowling statue and continued down the newly laid streets, halting outside the largest tent as scouts recognized us and ran to alert their khan. I hesitated before dismounting, muttering curses against my stiff joints and sore bones.

"Sorkhokhtani Beki." Batu Khan's voice boomed out across the night, and I looked up to see him dressed in simple felts and furs, his only adornment the House of Batu's great copper dragon insignia on his belt. He grinned under a thick beard in the Rus style and his strong hands whisked me down as if I were a young girl, reminding me of when I'd greeted the Great Khan for the first time. Batu chuckled under his breath as a crowd gathered round. "Your arrival tells me that I won't spend this winter building my capital and tending my herds."

"Life on these steppes is never dull," I said, keeping my voice light. I was old enough to be Batu's mother, but the man would have made my blood run hot in my youth. With shoulders wider than an ox's, a crooked grin, and a shock of hair as black as a bear, the man had his share of female admirers, but he remained faithful to his wives. Despite that, the men held him in as high esteem as they had his grandfather. It was only due to his father's dubious parentage that Batu could never seize power himself, for no man would ever follow a man with Jochi's muddied blood.

Jochi. *Guest.*

Not for the first time, I wondered at Genghis Khan's wisdom at saddling his firstborn with such a name. Things might have been so different if Jochi had been named Khan instead of Ogodei, if Güyük had never sat upon the Horse Throne.

Men might not accept the Khan's helm on Batu, but they'd go where he led.

"Alaqai and Shigi," Batu said, acknowledging the remainder of Genghis' family. Beneath all the dust from the road, Shigi wore the blue that denoted his station as supreme judge and scribe of the Golden Family. Next to him, Alaqai's white hair was twisted under a headdress shaped like two yak horns and dangling with gold coins and carnelian beads. She looked so much like Borte that for a moment I thought I viewed a glimpse of the spirit world. "I'm pleased to see you join us," Batu said.

"You should be," Alaqai said, looping her arm through his. "As we've come to rid our empire of the scourge of Toregene's son."

I followed them into Batu's Great Tent, feeling the heat radiate off my nephew like a small sun in the dark. His first wife scurried about like a plump brown shrew, offering us cups of salt tea and bowls of steaming stew. I forced myself not to wave her away, and instead accepted the meal on a wooden tray carved with wildflowers.

"You should eat," Batu murmured when I didn't touch the food. "Milk paste and raw meat softened under a saddle grow old after only a few days."

"We scarcely stopped even for that," Alaqai said. "Sorkhokhtani sets a hard pace."

"Your wife's cooking is renowned," I said, giving Batu a pointed look. His mouse of a wife still bustled around, but he quickly caught her attention and sent her outside with an excuse that our horses needed tending.

"We've just come from Karakorum," I said, once the door was closed. Propriety demanded that we eat first, and then discuss the meaning of our journey, but decorum would have to wait until after the empire was righted. "Güyük requires your presence in his capital."

Batu laughed at that, a deep, booming sound that made the walls of his tent flutter. "And if I refuse the imbecile's demands?"

I shrugged. "Then he'll march against you."

Batu set aside his soup. "I'm no fool. Güyük will either march against me or he'll greet me with an army outside Karakorum. It was always going to come to this."

"Of course he thinks to fight you," I said, although I didn't mention that I hoped that wouldn't happen. "Better to draw the bear out of his den, don't you think?"

Alaqai snorted at that. "Güyük is no bear. More like a saw-toothed weasel."

"I shall be happy to meet Güyük on a field of my own choosing." Batu ground one fist into his palm, and I could well imagine what went through his mind then.

"And after?" I asked.

Batu relaxed but leaned forward so his elbows rested on his knees. "I keep my promises, Sorkhokhtani. Möngke fought well with me on the Ryazan campaign and I swore a blood oath that I'd support your sons in a *khurlatai*. Tell me you wish to gather the clans for Möngke's nomination, and the Golden Horde will be there."

I filled my lungs with my nephew's scent, then pressed my forehead to his for a moment. "Thank you, Batu," I said. "I can never repay you."

"Don't thank me until the Khan's helm sits upon Möngke's head." He chuckled. "Although I will say, you and I make a decent team for the son of a bastard and the widow of the drunken Prince of the Hearth."

"You are a good man, Batu Khan," I said, brushing off the skirt of my *deel* to hide the heat in my cheeks. I was overcome with weariness, yet there was still much to do. "When will your army be ready to move?"

Batu's teeth gleamed in the firelight. "They'd march tonight if I told them to."

I chuckled. "Tomorrow will suffice, Batu Khan."

Tomorrow I would ride with Batu's army toward this empire's destiny. By this time next month I might be the mother of the next Khan.

Or I might be a corpse, sharing a grave with those who surrounded me this night.

The army's pace was almost relaxing after our furious push from Karakorum, laden as we were with reserve horses and Batu's ten thousand men. As we realized that the coming battle would be the decisive fight, the sun seemed suddenly brighter, the wind crisper, and the calls of the cranes overhead sharper.

We gathered my sons and their smaller contingents of soldiers from their wives and hearths, and I watched in silent pleasure as Batu and Möngke greeted each other like reunited brothers, roaring with happiness as they clapped each other on the back, comrades in arms from the siege against Ryazan. Together, our expedition passed the three *ordus* that Alaqai and I had erected, and halted the entire army so that Batu, Möngke, and Kublai could seek blessings of our family's matriarch. My throat tightened when each of Batu's soldiers bowed their heads as they passed the three tents.

Shortly after, we entered a town where I'd funded the building of a Saracen school and were received warmly by the governor. I'd appointed many officials during my time as regent of Tolui's lands, and those officers now clamored to see my son on the throne. However, we learned as we changed horses that Güyük had left Karakorum and was preparing a great army to meet us outside the city.

"Güyük is smarter than I thought," Batu said from his saddle, a piece of art with its golden-clawed dragons. "He must have realized I'd refuse to greet him without a fight."

"Move slowly," I counseled Batu. I knew not whether Oghul Ghaimish traveled with her husband, but I wished to allow her every opportunity for revenge before our two sides clashed on a battlefield. So few of us were left who recalled the early days of the Blood War, before Genghis Khan's own *khurlatai*. I remembered, though, and I had no wish to water the steppes with the blood of the Thirteen Tribes.

Only Güyük's.

. . .

We waited for word from Güyük, but Karakorum was strangely silent. The reason why was revealed soon afterward, as a lone rider galloped from the direction of the capital, sending up puffs of fireweed cotton in the wind. News of our army had certainly reached the Golden Ordu by now, but at the sight of us the rider hauled back on his horse's reins so hard that the animal reared up.

"I'll go to him," Alaqai said. "No one will fear an old woman."

Kublai chortled. "He should when that woman could hit him with an arrow from a hundred paces." Alaqai gave a bark of laughter, but her lips curled up in a proud smile.

"I'll join you," I said, nudging my horse's ribs before my sons could protest. This messenger likely carried news about Güyük, and I wished to be among the first to hear it.

Alaqai was right—the rider urged his horse forward, then dismounted and fell to his knees at the sight of the Khatun of the Onggud and the Princess of the Hearth. I recognized him as one of Shigi's slaves, left behind in Karakorum. He wore a gold medallion at his throat now, marking him as a slave of Güyük's house.

"What news have you from Karakorum?" Alaqai asked.

The rider looked up with bloodshot eyes and a face creased with black grime from many days on the road. Whatever message he carried must be an important one. "I have word of Güyük Khan, son of Ogodei Khan and grandson of Genghis Khan," the slave said, his hands trembling in his lap.

"Does the Khan wish to negotiate with us?" I asked, gripping the horn of my saddle. "Or shall we meet in a field of blood?"

"Neither, Sorkhokhtani Beki," the man said. "The Great Khan is dead."

"Dead?" Alaqai glanced at me. "How can that be?"

The man bowed his head again. "Güyük Khan stopped with his army to hunt. They took down a great herd of deer, but after the feast that night, he fell ill. He lingered for a day in great pain, and then his spirit flew to the sacred mountains."

I turned my horse, ready to gallop back to Batu and my sons with the news of our victory, yet there was one more thing I needed to know.

"And Oghul Ghaimish?" I asked over my shoulder. "Did the Khan's first wife travel with him on his expedition from the city?"

The messenger nodded. "She did. It was the Great Khatun who sent me to ride for your army, to thank you for the gift you gave her, and to spread news of her ascension to the Horse Throne."

I whirled around at that, my horse prancing beneath me. "What did you say?"

The slave cringed at my tone. "Oghul Ghaimish has claimed the green headdress of the Great Khatun and the regency as well." He rifled through his saddlebags, then produced a crumpled paper. "She's proclaimed the family of Tolui to be outcasts of the Golden Family and offers a reward for anyone who would bring the heads of Möngke and Kublai to her."

My heart ceased beating and ice flowed through my veins. I glanced back to where my sons waited with Batu. Only Möngke and Kublai might challenge Oghul Ghaimish's right to rule, or her sons' eventual succession, so of course she would seek to rid herself of that threat. "Then you've come to kill my sons?"

The slave shook his head. "I served Shigi and Toregene Khatun faithfully, and witnessed the purges ordered by Güyük Khan and the glee with which Oghul Ghaimish carried out his commands. I wish only to continue in peace with the rest of my mission."

"And what might that be?" Alaqai asked.

"I'm to travel west with the proclamation of Oghul Ghaimish's coronation, and from there to the court of King Louis IX, to demand that the French king come to Karakorum to surrender to her, and to bring crates of silver and gold to ensure her goodwill."

I laughed aloud at the audacity of the mad bitch and the lunacy of her demands of the far-flung kingdom of France. It would take years for the slave to deliver his message to King Louis and return with an answer. No wonder he was content to leave us and continue on his way.

Next to me, Alaqai snorted in derision. "You'd best go, then. Be well, messenger."

The slave mounted his gelding, offering bows to both Alaqai and myself before kicking his horse and galloping onward.

"What do we do now?" Alaqai asked.

I stared in the direction of Karakorum, where a crazed woman now sat in the Golden Ordu.

"We call a *khurlatai*," I said. "And then we ride on Karakorum and remove Oghul Ghaimish from my son's throne."

We made good time as we took a circuitous route back to our homelands, following the network of supporters I'd carefully cultivated over the years. As word of the impending *khurlatai* spread, in each camp I was hailed as the mother of the future Great Khan. Most of the *gers* held felt effigies of Genghis Khan, and it was a simple matter to remind the people that the great conqueror's blood ran in my sons' veins. The years of bowing my head and trying to remain unnoticed disappeared into the past, and instead I sang Möngke's praises until he might have rivaled Abraham, Christ, or Muhammad. I never spoke Oghul Ghaimish's name aloud, but it was a simple matter to place the blame for our crumbling empire squarely on her lap by raising questions about the sharp rise in our tribute taxes while spreading word of her involvement in Güyük's bloody purges.

It was with a glad heart that I oversaw the preparations for the *khurlatai*. Our paddocks were overrun with animals, most of which would be slaughtered to feed the visiting guests. Girls worked under the stars to prepare vats of fermented mare's milk, uncaring of whether the colts cried for lack of their mothers' tits. Within a few days both would be butchered, and blood and milk alike would feed the earth again. A new wrestling ring had already been constructed and targets had been drawn and stuffed with fresh hay for the archery competitions. I imagined a similar *khurlatai* presided over by another mother. Borte Khatun had been mother to the Golden Family and also to the People of the Felts. Now, I, the lowly Princess of the Hearth, would repair this shattered jade realm. All that remained was for the guests to arrive, to cast their vote with their presence and proclaim my firstborn as the new Great Khan.

The first to appear were the twin crones, Yesugen and Yesui, ignored wives of Genghis Khan. Dressed in matching yellow cashmere *deels* and flowing robes of leopard and tiger skin lined with sable, bent and stooped with hands like claws, Yesugen had grown half-deaf and Yesui was as blind as a newborn pup. Their lands had long ago been confiscated by Ogodei, but they were the last of the old generation of the Thirteen Tents.

"Mother Yesui." I clasped her hands, gnarled with brown spots like rotted berries but with nails neatly trimmed. "And Mother Yesugen. You honor us with your presence."

"Horse manure," Yesugen said, almost shouting. "We came to see the end of this saga."

"*You* came only for the food," Yesui said to her sister, her rheumy eyes staring past me. Her clawlike hand clasped my forearm and she pulled herself taller so she might whisper in my ear. "I came to see Oghul Ghaimish swept from the Horse Throne."

Her words caught me off guard, for Yesui was Checheyigen's mother, and therefore, Oghul Ghaimish's grandmother, although I doubted whether the two had ever met. Yesui must have sensed my thoughts, for she patted my arm. "A mother knows when she's whelped a mean runt, and will often suffocate the little beast before he ruins the litter. My Checheyigen was a good girl, and Oghul Ghaimish might have been, too, had Ogodei and his ilk not ruined her. Toregene should have destroyed Güyük before he had a chance to suckle, but she didn't, and thus my granddaughter has paid for it. By all reports her mind is broken, and she will destroy what remains of this empire if she remains upon the Horse Throne. You've raised your sons well; I only hope they can repair the damage."

I laid my hand over hers, wondering if she'd be so composed if she knew what lay in store for her granddaughter. "I hope so, too, Yesui. I pray for it every day."

More members of the Borijin family—Chaghatai's grown sons and even the sons of Ogodei's lesser wives—came to pledge their support for Möngke, pitching their tents until the steppes were dotted with a sea of white like cotton flowers in spring. The numbers gathered at our camp were overwhelming, a huge show of support lacking only Oghul Ghaimish.

And so, on the first day of high summer, dressed in a flowing robe of leopard skins lined with sable and wearing a towering headdress as befit the mother of the Great Khan, I felt a surge of triumph as the Gur-Khan's helm was placed on Möngke's head. Christian and Saracen prayers choked the air of the Great White Tent—its felt panels sewn together by my own hands—and blue-robed shamans poured offerings of milk to the Earth Mother.

Möngke would be an able administrator and a steady presence to guide his brothers when I was no longer there to do so. Our family had spent decades waiting for this moment, but our work was not done.

"Send a message to Oghul Ghaimish," I said to Shigi, "commanding her to step down. And a second letter authorizing Batu to arrest her when she refuses."

Shigi stared at me for a moment, understanding dawning in his weary eyes as he set up his paper and ink. "You've been using her as a pawn all along, haven't you?"

"I'll beat her at her own game, if that's what you mean." I opened his inkpot, blue glass from Cathay blown into the shape of a tortoise. I recognized it as a gift from Toregene. "It's what she deserves."

"This shall be my last official act as scribe and judge to this empire," Shigi said, his voice resigned. "Then I would like permission to leave Karakorum."

"And do what?" I could scarcely fathom leaving the capital now that the transfer of power was almost secure, akin to leaving the battlefield in the middle of a fight. But Shigi had served the Golden Family well, acting as its judge in the early days of Genghis' ascension and then recording the family history until Fatima took over the role of scribe.

"I would live a simple life for my remaining days," Shigi answered. "Away from the intrigues of the court that has stolen so much from me."

So he would spend his last few years grieving for Toregene. I might not have experienced such a love, but if anyone deserved to spend his final years in peace, it was Shigi.

"Justice will be done," I said, clasping his hand. "I swear it, Shigi."

He gave a tight nod and I watched as his elegant script filled the paper with my demands, informing Oghul Ghaimish of our recent *khurlatai* and ordering the madwoman to leave the Golden Ordu. The ink seeped into the paper and the shiny black letters grew dull as Shigi blew on them. All that remained was to have Möngke sign the orders.

It was only a matter of time before Oghul Ghaimish was arrested. Then I'd see her pay for what she'd done to Fatima, and to Toregene.

It took almost two months, but Batu brought Oghul Ghaimish to me, just as I'd known he would. As the leaves dropped from the trees, the mad Khatun was dragged before us, shrieking like a magpie and covered in stinking layers of her own filth. Her bloodied scalp showed through patches of matted hair and the skin at her neck was raw and more bloody than ever.

Möngke looked out at the sea of his people assembled in the center of his Great Tent. "People of the Thirteen Tribes," he said, his strong voice calming the flutters of conversation like the shade of a hawk over the chatter of squirrels. "Oghul Ghaimish, wife of Güyük, no longer reigns as Great Khatun over the steppes. She has committed many evils against our people, and for that she must be punished. My mother, Sorkhokhtani, shall preside over her judgment." He gave a curt nod in my direction, then took a seat upon his throne to watch the proceedings.

Oghul Ghaimish cowered on the ground before me with her hands and feet bound, and so close I could smell the piss that stained her felts. She mumbled something incoherent and I wondered if her reason had finally fled completely. I didn't relish what I was about to do, but it was necessary, the final step to securing my family's safety.

"Oghul Ghaimish," I said, letting the breeze catch my voice, "you have been charged with conspiring against the Great Khan—"

I didn't get to finish before her piercing cry cut the air, like the scream of a panther about to kill and just as terrifying. I lurched back before steeling myself against the sound.

"You gave the poison to me," she screamed. "You wanted Güyük to die! But it's Möngke who should die, the imposter who sits now upon the Horse Throne!"

"Silence!" Möngke yelled.

"You'll never be the Great Khan," Oghul Ghaimish shrieked. "For I am Great Khatun. *I* wore the green headdress! *I* demanded the surrender of the king of France!"

"Restrain her," I ordered, and two guards rushed to do my bidding, but she bit at them. Finally, two others held her down while the first stuffed a rag in her mouth and tied it with horse rope. She sputtered against the gag, the whites of her eyes ugly with blood and rolling in terror. My foot itched to kick her mouth, to watch her spit out her teeth, but instead I stared down upon her. "You have been charged with conspiring against Möngke, Great Khan of the Mongols, and also of using black magic to murder Güyük, son of Ogodei Khan and grandson of Genghis Khan," I continued, although Güyük's name left a sour taste in my mouth. "Do you admit your guilt and repent your sins?"

Oghul Ghaimish glared at me from her knees, her brown eyes flashing as if she were possessed by all the demons of hell.

I bent down so only she could hear me. "Do you repent your crimes against Fatima of Nishapur?"

She stared at me, then gave a defiant shake of her head. Beneath the gag, she smiled, thus sealing her fate.

I could still release her, but then Möngke would forever be looking over his shoulder for this mad bitch who had proclaimed herself leader over the Mongolian Empire, however briefly. I would make one last sacrifice for my sons and then leave them to their rule.

"Since you do not admit your sins," I said to Oghul Ghaimish, "we shall see if you face your death as bravely as Fatima did. Evil shall be punished with evil."

I nodded to the guards behind me as I took my seat. "Take her to the river," I said. "She shall be drowned in a manner befitting the most vile of traitors."

The acrid scent of fresh urine filled my nose and I recoiled from the foul yellow liquid streaming down Oghul Ghaimish's legs to form puddles on the packed earth. It seemed Oghul Ghaimish would not greet her fate with defiance.

As they dragged her away, I felt the stain of her death settle into my soul, a heavy weight I would bear until the end of my days, and one that other women before me had borne. I felt Alaqai at my side, smelled her gentle scent of horses and hearth smoke, and smiled.

"We're the last ones left," she said. "My father, mother, and brothers, our husbands, Toregene, and Fatima . . . Only we remain."

I felt the spirits of the dead settle around us, yet their presence was comforting, reassuring even, as if they approved of this new empire ruled by my sons. I glanced at Möngke sitting on the golden Horse Throne and Kublai standing triumphant behind him, and linked my arm through Alaqai's.

"We, each in our own ways, safeguarded and nurtured this empire, you and your mother, Fatima and Toregene, and me." I gestured to my sons. "And now we leave it in capable hands."

She followed my gaze and rested her head on my shoulder. "That we do, Sorkhokhtani. And I have no doubt that in the coming days those capable hands are going to accomplish great things for my father's empire."

I smiled at that, hearing Genghis' laugh in my mind and knowing that somehow, she was right.

Epilogue

A man's spirit is housed in the trembling pennant of his Spirit Banner after his soul flees his body, but a woman's spirit is forever housed within her *ger*, sheltered by the felt walls beaten by her own hands.

On the plain of Khodoe Aral, eight white *gers* stand proudly against the green of the grasses. The lesser three off to the side each belonged to one of Genghis Khan's secondary wives: Yesui, Yesugen, and Gurbesu. Five more cluster together like hunchbacked old women, four faded and worn by the wind and rain of many years and the last as pristine as newly fallen snow with walls that still smell of freshly felted wool. If one listens closely enough, the whispers and laughter of the conversations once held inside can still be heard on the northern breeze.

These are no ordinary *ordus*, but the Eight White *Gers* of Genghis Khan, the sacred tents belonging to the wives and daughters of his empire. Their felt doors flutter as spirits brush them aside to peer onto the steppe, as their mortal bodies once looked for husbands or sons returned victorious from battle, or courtiers come from foreign lands to witness the might of this new empire.

One solitary woman stands in the pale green grasses, her gray hair plaited in a long braid down her back and a bulky square package clasped to her withered chest. Slowly, she circles each tent, a prayer rumbling in her throat.

She pauses before each *ger*, reaching out a gnarled hand spotted like a rotting alder leaf so she might touch the lone emblems belonging to each tent.

The charcoal remains of a hearth fire.

A sword inlaid with tigers of jade and gold.

A second tiger's snarling face, painted and carved into the door of a *ger*.

The delicate bloom of a poet narcissus.

In the center of the circle, the gray-haired woman places a package, untying the string that binds it and unfolding the stunning red silk wrapping.

It is a stack of manuscript pages, bound in blue leather and embossed with glittering gold. This is only one of several copies of the history of the Golden Family, but despite her sons' protests, she insisted upon carrying it here.

After all, its pages contain our story.

Finally, the Princess of the Hearth pauses outside the fifth *ger*, nondescript with its plain white felts and cedar door. Her sons had begged her to remain with them during her final days—the Great Khan had even ordered her to stay within his camp—but she'd torn down the plain white *ger* with her own trembling hands until finally the entire family had helped disassemble the wool panels and wooden supports. They had carried them here, to this desolate, windswept plain, and reassembled the tent in silence. Now, at her request, they embrace one last time, draw their last breaths of one another's spirits, and the sons mount their horses, the final words of parting lodging in their throats.

She watches them go and raises her hand in farewell when the broad-shouldered men all turn back for a final glance. She carried them in her womb, brought them squalling and slick with her own blood into this world, and as fierce as a tiger, spent every breath since then fighting for them. In one eloquent movement, the men bow to the stooped old woman standing on the horizon.

Then they turn and gallop away, leaving her alone on the steppe.

But she isn't alone.

She glances at the *gers* surrounding her in a circle and settles down cross-legged on the threshold of her tent to play a familiar melody on the ivory flute she keeps forever with her. *We have always been her family, and her spirit will join us for eternity.*

She has come home.

Cast of Characters

denotes a historical figure

Borijin Clan

*Temujin/Genghis Khan: The Khan of Khans

*Borte: Genghis' wife, mother of his sons

> ***Jochi:** Borte's firstborn son, likely son of Chilger the Athlete, claimed by Genghis

> ***Chaghatai:** Second son of Genghis and Borte

> ***Ogodei:** Third son of Genghis and Borte

> ***Alaqai:** Genghis and Borte's daughter

> ***Tolui:** Genghis and Borte's final son, Prince of the Hearth

*Hoelun: Genghis' mother

> ***Khasar:** Genghis' younger brother

*Temulun: Genghis' younger sister

*Yesui and Yesugen: Tatar sisters, secondary wives of Genghis

*Checheyigen: Yesui's daughter, mother of Oghul Ghaimish

Gurbesu: Borte's childhood friend, minor wife of Genghis

*Al-Altun: Daughter of Genghis Khan

*Toregene: Naiman noblewoman, Ogodei's wife

*Güyük: Ogodei and Toregene's son

*Sorkhokhtani: Kerait princess, Tolui's wife, Princess of the Hearth

*Möngke: Tolui and Sorkhokhtani's eldest son

*Kublai: Tolui and Sorkhokhtani's younger son

The Onggud

*Ala-Qush: Alaqai's first husband

Orbei: Ala-Qush's first wife

*Jingue: Ala-Qush's eldest son

Enebish: Ala-Qush's daughter

*Boyahoe: Ala-Qush's younger son

Others

*Jamuka: Genghis' blood brother, leader of the Jadarin clan

*Teb Tengeri: Shaman to Genghis Khan

*Mother Khogaghchin: Elderly servant of Hoelun

*Chilger the Athlete: member of the Merkid clan, Borte's kidnapper

*Shigi: Tatar captive, adopted younger brother of Genghis raised by Hoelun

*Fatima: Persian captive from Nishapur

*Batu Khan: Jochi's eldest son, leader of the Golden Horde

*Korguz: Uighur scribe to Ogodei

Author's Note

The Tiger Queens is an unabashed work of fiction that draws the majority of its characters and events from Paul Kahn's translation of *The Secret History of the Mongols*, an original text that most scholars believe was written by Shigi. This source chronicles the thirteenth-century Mongolian account of Genghis Khan's rise to power. I also relied heavily on Jack Weatherford's excellent scholarship in *Genghis Khan and the Making of the Modern World* and *The Secret History of the Mongol Queens: How the Daughters of Genghis Khan Rescued His Empire*. Most Western knowledge of ancient Mongolia focuses on Genghis' brutal conquest of Asia and Europe and then skips to Marco Polo's voyage to the court of Kublai Khan, but few people have heard about the women who safeguarded Genghis' empire. This novel, of course, is their story.

Borte is mentioned throughout *The Secret History of the Mongols*, including her early betrothal to Genghis, her kidnapping and resulting pregnancy with Jochi, and her decision to separate Genghis from Jamuka at the beginning of their feud. I took liberties with her role as a seer, for while modern Mongolia has female shamans, there is no mention of Borte fulfilling that role, although she did loathe Genghis' seer, Teb Tengeri. Also, while it is unlikely that Jamuka was ever in love with Borte, he did help Genghis retrieve her from the Merkid and scorned his own wife as a "babbling fool." Many clan leaders claimed to have sent their daughters to marry Genghis, but the historical texts typically record only four official wives: Borte, Yesui, Yesugen, and a young woman named Khulan, Genghis' favorite wife in his old age. However, a Naiman woman named Gurbesu is sometimes referred to as another of Genghis' wives, and it was her story I chose to include. Regardless of Genghis' number of official and unofficial wives, Borte remained his first wife, his "wise queen," and the mother of all his male heirs. And while it's unlikely that Borte was present at Genghis' deathbed, I couldn't resist the chance to allow her to usher her beloved warrior husband into the next life.

The historical record confirms that Genghis had at least six daughters but it remains tight-lipped about the identities of their mothers. In a story with a complicated character list, I chose to focus only on Alaqai and Al-Altun in order to highlight the differences between two of Genghis' daughters. One of his daughters (likely his youngest, although history failed to record her name) did order the destruction of Nishapur in revenge for her husband's death in battle, and Alaqai argued for mercy when the Onggud revolted against her, marrying first Ala-Qush, then Jingue, and finally Boyahoe. The details of Alaqai's death are lost to history, so I chose to have her survive long enough to see Sorkhokhtani's son installed as Khan.

History mentions Fatima, a Tajik or Persian captive from the campaign in the Middle East who went on to become Toregene's closest adviser. The siege of Nishapur is recorded in great detail, so it's possible that Fatima was taken as a slave during that battle and later became Toregene's "sharer of intimate confidences." While most scholars agree that Shigi was the author of *The Secret History of the Mongols*, it appears that the original text ended in 1228 CE, after Genghis' death, and information about Ogodei's reign was added at a later time, allowing me to imagine that perhaps someone else—Fatima, in this case—was a coauthor, or even wrote a concurrent history. The relationship between Shigi and Toregene is entirely a product of my imagination, but Shigi did serve as judge and historian during both Genghis' and Ogodei's reigns, and Toregene ruled as regent until Güyük came of age. Tragically, the end of Fatima's story is based in fact, and imagining her brutal demise at Güyük's hands was the most horrific part of this story to write. Toregene disappears from history shortly after refusing to allow Güyük to arrest Fatima, and Shigi died of unknown causes in 1250 CE, four years after Toregene. She may have died of natural causes, although at least one Muslim historian claims that Güyük was so villainous as to have his own mother assassinated.

Sorkhokhtani Beki is far from a household name, but Genghis' wily daughter-in-law deserves the accolade of being one of the most influential women in history. It was she who served as regent for Genghis' ancestral lands after Tolui's death and then maneuvered her sons in a power grab against Güyük and Oghul Ghaimish, finally organizing a ruthless purge of Güyük's supporters to ensure that Möngke, and later Kublai, would remain secure on their thrones.

While I tried to remain true to history, the scope and staggering cast of characters in this book forced me to take some liberties. For ease of reading, I severely condensed the timeline in the latter half of the book. So while the major events are in the correct order, they unfolded over the course of many more years or even decades. Several historical characters have been omitted from the story, including Borte's other daughters with Genghis, and Toregene and Sorkhokhtani's other sons. While Al-Altun was ruler of the Uighurs and one of Genghis' eldest daughters, some scholars believe that it was Genghis' youngest daughter, Tumelun, who ordered the destruction of Nishapur. I chose to combine both historical women into one daughter: Al-Altun. In addition, I combined Jochi's character with that of Jelme, one of Genghis' adopted brothers. It was Jelme who was present when Genghis was injured in the neck, and not Jochi.

This book is the result of much sweat and tears. (And not just my own!) My agent, Marlene Stringer, encouraged me to keep writing about women whom few people have ever heard about, and my editor, Ellen Edwards, made this novel much more than I ever could have achieved alone. Eileen Chetti did a phenomenal job copyediting for continuity. My fearless first readers—Renee Yancy, Jade Timms, and Stephanie Dray—read the terrifying first draft of this novel and listened to me sob over cyberspace when I swore that Genghis Khan and his women were going to conquer me. I'm indebted to Mariah McCoy for allowing me to live vicariously through her travels to Mongolia, and I never would have survived to write the last page without the moral support of Kristi Senden, Megan Williams, Claire Torbensen, Eugenia Merrifield, Cindy Davis, and Katie Hill. I promise to keep plying you all with cookies if you keep listening to me rant about obscure historical figures.

My family deserves a parade for their patience in putting up with me while I fought to weave the stories of these very different, very foreign women into one coherent novel. Thank you, Dad, Daine, and Hollie, for your enthusiastic support. Stephen, you deserve several very large statues for never giving up on me, and for keeping the freezer stocked with ice cream cake to fuel my late-night writing sessions.

Lastly, to Isabella . . . You're my little monkey, but you're already growing up to be as fierce as any tiger queen.

Further Reading on the Empire of Genghis Khan

Avery, Martha. *Women of Mongolia*. Seattle, WA: Asian Art and Archaeology, 1996.

Axworthy, Michael. *Empire of the Mind: A History of Iran*. New York: Basic Books, 2008.

Fitzhugh, William, et al. *Genghis Khan and the Mongol Empire*. Washington, DC: Smithsonian Institution, 2013.

Foltz, Richard. *Religions of the Silk Road*. New York: St. Martin's Press, 1999.

Khan, Paul, translator. *The Secret History of the Mongols: The Origin of Chingis Khan*. Boston: Cheng and Tsui Company, 1998.

Khayyám, Omar. *The Rubaiyat of Omar Khayyam*, translated by Edward Fitzgerald. 1889.

Maulana Jalalu-'D-Din Muhammed I Rumi. *Masnavi i Ma'Navi*, translated by E. H. Whinfield. 1898.

Polo, Marco. *The Travels*. New York: Penguin Classics, 1958.

Rossabi, Morris. *The Mongols: A Very Short Introduction*. New York: Oxford University Press, 2012.

Stewart, Stanley. *In the Empire of Genghis Khan*. Guilford, Connecticut: Lyons Press, 2000.

Waugh, Louisa. *Hearing Birds Fly: A Nomadic Year in Mongolia*. London: Abacus, 2003.

Weatherford, Jack. *Genghis Khan and the Making of the Modern World*. New York: Three Rivers Press, 2004.

Weatherford, Jack. *The Secret History of the Mongol Queens: How the Daughters of Genghis Khan Rescued His Empire.* New York: Broadway Paperbacks, 2010.

Whitfield, Susan. *Life Along the Silk Road.* Los Angeles: University of California Press, 1999.

William of Rubruck. *The Journey of William of Rubruck to the Eastern Part of the World, 1253–1255,* translated by W. W. Rockhill. 1900.

Photo by Katherine Schmeling Photography

Stephanie Thornton is a writer and history teacher who has been obsessed with infamous women from ancient history since she was twelve. She lives with her husband and daughter in Alaska, where she is at work on her next novel.

THE TIGER QUEENS

THE WOMEN OF GENGHIS KHAN

STEPHANIE THORNTON

A CONVERSATION WITH STEPHANIE THORNTON

Q. What a terrific novel! Am I correct in thinking that no one has ever before fictionalized the story of Genghis Khan's women? What made you want to tell their story?

A. While there are a number of novels about Genghis Khan, I'm not aware of any that focus solely on his women. I actually chanced upon both of Jack Weatherford's nonfiction books and was especially intrigued by *The Secret History of the Mongol Queens: How the Daughters of Genghis Khan Rescued His Empire.* We all know the name Genghis Khan, but few people know anything about his wives and daughters. It seemed to me that these women were begging to have their story told, and I was happy to oblige!

Q. What do you think distinguished the women of ancient Mongolia from women of other times and places?

A. There are a number of exceptionally accomplished women throughout ancient history—Pharaoh Hatshepsut, Empress Theodora, Queen Eleanor of Aquitaine, to name a few—but as a general rule, Mongol women had to be incredibly tough to survive not only the harsh environment of the steppes, but also the often brutal lives that involved raiding and, later, violent political intrigue. These women truly were the rulers of the hearth and home, raising the children, tending the animals, and performing the backbreaking labor of eking out a living on Mongolia's grasslands. Giovanni DiPlano Carpini, an envoy from Pope Innocent IV, claimed that Mongol women "carry quiver and bows . . . they drive carts and repair them, load camels, and are quick and vigorous in all their tasks." In addition, we have records of Genghis' wives occasionally accompanying him during his conquests and evidence of Mongolian women being present at various sieges, such as Genghis' youngest daughter, who ordered the slaughter at Nishapur.

Q. *It's interesting to me that* The Secret History of the Mongols, *a major source for your novel, is a historical text focusing almost solely on the exploits of Genghis, his sons, and his generals. Do we know how the manuscript survived, what language it was originally written in, and when it was first translated?*

A. Likely first written in the Uighur script, the family history is a mix of history, folklore, and poetry that was begun shortly after Genghis' death in 1227 CE. Only members of the royal family had access to the text, and certain sections of the manuscript were censored during antiquity, namely, the portions dealing with Genghis' daughters. Jack Weatherford recounts one section in which Genghis Khan states, "Let us reward our female offspring," yet the next section of the text has been removed. While Borte's role in Genghis' early life is faithfully chronicled, the manuscript remains mysteriously silent about the role of the Khan's daughters.

The earliest translations of *The Secret History of the Mongols* were written in Chinese, and the text was translated into modern Mongolian from 1915 to 1917, and finally published in English by Francis Woodman Cleaves in 1982. Interestingly, during World War II, the Soviets, Germans, and Japanese all sought translations of the then recently discovered text in order to glean military knowledge from the conquests of Genghis Khan, and during the Cold War, the Russians sought to suppress the manuscript to avoid promoting Mongolian patriotism.

Q. You make Genghis Khan a likable character, despite his violent conquest of vast stretches of territory and his responsibility for untold human slaughter. I've also heard that an astonishing number of people on the earth carry some of his DNA. If success is defined by biology, then that must make him one of the most successful men to have ever lived! You suggest that on the plus side, he ushered in the rule of law, record keeping, and methods of communication over vast distances, and later, his daughters built hospitals and schools. Ultimately, what legacy did the empire of Genghis Khan and his descendants leave behind?

A. One of the most enduring legacies of Genghis Khan might be the genetic link between the ancient Golden Family and the fact that approximately 8 percent of men in the regions of the former Mongol Empire (about 0.4 percent of the world's modern population) may be descended from the Great Khan and his male relatives through the star-cluster C3c sublineage, a result of their many marriages, rapes, and concubines, and the fact that the Mongols tended to decimate the male populations of those they conquered. However, Genghis Khan left the world more than just his DNA. While the Mongols didn't build great stone pyramids or massive cities, they successfully integrated a polyglot of world cultures and religions into one cohesive empire, the greatest empire seen throughout history. The Mongols were brilliant conquerors, but more than that, they were masters at assimilating the best from the cultures they conquered, and it was along Mongol roads that silks, spices, religions, and new technologies spread throughout Asia and into Europe. So, while Genghis Khan certainly earned the accolade of the world's greatest conqueror, he was also a master of propaganda and an effective administrator, and he encouraged the creation of the Jasagh law code. I'd say those accomplishments have more than earned him a place in history's hall of fame!

Q. Do we have a sense of what made Genghis Khan such a successful conqueror?

A. Genghis Khan's name was enough to make the Persians, Chinese, and Europeans quiver with fear, and for good reason. The Mongols were the finest horsemen in the world, brutal and fearless. Mongol children were taught to ride almost before they could walk, and the Mongol cavalry were fast and well armed, carrying bows, shields, lassos, daggers, axes, and swords. They carried a variety of arrows, including ones that whistled to distract the enemy before larger and more lethal versions sailed in. Genghis also favored the use of propaganda, stories that his soldiers had chisels for noses, could subsist off dew, and could ride the wind, while the Khan himself was molded from impenetrable copper. He also used his scholars' pens to spread word of inflated casualty lists to cities he planned to siege in the hope of easy surrenders. In addition, the Mongol army was supported by their women, and there are accounts of Mongol women carrying quivers and bows as well as remaining home to administer to the Mongol camps.

Q. You say in your author's note that Sorkhokhtani "deserves the accolade of one of the most influential women in history." Can you expand on that? Was she the one who ensured that Genghis Khan's empire would have a lasting legacy, and if so, how?

A. The rivalry between Sorkhokhtani and Oghul Ghaimish actually lasted three years, a contest that Sorkhokhtani won after waiting her entire life to seize power for her sons. While Genghis' sons were inept, Sorkhokhtani shaped all of her sons into capable men who followed their mother's example of being highly educated while also respecting Mongolian law and the wide range of faiths present in their empire. And it was Sorkhokhtani who conspired with Batu Khan and organized the *khurlatai* to have Möngke elected as Great Khan, effectively usurping power from Ogodei's inept side of the family. Historian Jack Weatherford even goes so far as to say that Sorkhokhtani stands second to only Genghis Khan, a statement I would agree with.

Q. The ancient Mongol culture of Genghis Khan seems so foreign to us today, so much a part of the vast grasslands of central Asia, and so incredibly violent. Given the climate's extremes of hot and cold, the limited natural resources, and the constant danger from marauding groups, it must have been an incredibly tough life. Can you comment on that?

A. Life in Mongolia, both ancient and modern, is a constant fight for survival against the elements. Even today, the winter slaughter is a key element in providing enough food for Mongols to survive the winter while also eliminating excess livestock that would have to be fed throughout the harshest months of the year. Of course, in Genghis' time the Five Snouts ate the grass and the people relied on those horses, sheep, goats, camels, cattle, and yaks for everything from food, to shelter, to the dung with which they lit their fires. The animals also provided transportation for their nomadic existence and for conquest. While subsisting on solely meat and dairy doesn't sound very healthy to those of us who are told to eat our fruits and vegetables every day, this diet allowed Mongol soldiers to travel vast distances while carrying their food with them via reserve horses. In fact, as the Mongols were known as Tatars in the West, the term "steak tartare" may have come from the Mongol practice of placing meat under their saddles to be tenderized and then eaten raw. In addition, their protein-heavy diet may have given them an edge fighting against sedentary peoples whose grain-based diets rotted their teeth, stunted their growth, and left them susceptible to diseases.

Q. By and large, you describe Genghis Khan's sons and grandsons as drunken louts. Do you have any sense of why they turned out so badly?

A. Genghis Khan was possibly the greatest conqueror the world has ever seen (only Alexander the Great can really match him), but he was a terrible father if one judges him on the way his sons turned out. Genghis' sons grew up in their father's very large shadow but likely feared him and were more intent on wrestling, racing horses, and drinking than on learning how to rule. I suspect Genghis was too busy conquering the world to worry about reining in his sons' excesses, a decision that would threaten to destroy his empire once he was gone.

Genghis' grandsons, on the other hand, were more of a mixed bag. Güyük was certainly cruel, ordering Fatima's brutal execution and possibly murdering his own mother, but Möngke made significant reforms within the empire and Kublai founded the Yuan dynasty, which was popularized in Marco Polo's famous travelogue.

Q. This is your third novel. Has your writing process changed since you began writing?

A. My writing process has always been to squeeze in a few hours of work after I'm done teaching and grading papers, and my daughter is asleep for the night. *The Tiger Queens* took me a year and a half to write and presented unique challenges due to its vast character list, its immense scope of time, and the staggering amount of land covered by the Mongolian Empire. While I always read historical texts from the era before I begin writing, and numerous secondary sources as I write, *The Tiger Queens* involved much more research, so I could write about not only Genghis' generation, but also his sons' and grandsons', as well as describe the cultures of the Mongols, Onggud, Uighurs, and Persians. There was so much more that I wanted to include; this book could have easily been two hundred pages longer!

*Q. Can you tell us something about your next novel? Will it be about an-
other forgotten woman of ancient history?*

A. My fourth novel focuses on the women of another great conqueror in
antiquity: Alexander the Great. After finishing *The Tiger Queens*, I
began searching for another forgotten woman in history and was thrilled
to discover the tangled web of intrigue woven by Alexander's mother,
sisters, and wives. While Genghis Khan is known for his brutality, Alexander's women could have given the Mongol conqueror a run for his
money!

QUESTIONS FOR DISCUSSION

1. What did you most enjoy about the novel? Did any one of the four female narrators appeal to you more than the others?

2. Genghis obviously cares for Borte, despite leaving her to be kidnapped and marrying several other women. How does their love change throughout the book?

3. Many of the women in this book—Borte, Alaqai, Toregene, and Sorkhokhtani—are mothers. Who is the best mother, and why?

4. Shigi and Boyahoe discover Fatima in an act that could be viewed as madness, painting calligraphy in blood around her husband's and father's bodies. What is the difference between her and Oghul Ghaimish, who falls so quickly into madness after enduring the rape of the Oirat girls?

5. By the end of the book, each of these women has endured unspeakable tragedies. What traits do they have that allow them to survive—and sometimes flourish—during times of such terrible violence?

6. Many of the women in the novel survive by using careful strategy in reacting to particularly dangerous situations. Compare how Toregene, Alaqai, and Sorkhokhtani react to the most dangerous situations they face.

7. Fatima makes a fateful decision to stay with the dying Toregene rather than escape to safety with Alaqai. Why do you think she makes this choice? Is she fully conscious of all that she is risking?

8. Discuss some of the ways in which the women in the novel—even the minor characters—support and honor one another. How do they betray one another?

9. What do you expect you'll remember about the novel long after you've finished reading it?

If you enjoyed Borte and the fearless, tenacious women of the Mongolian steppes, you won't want to miss Alexander the Great's women: cunning Roxana, witty Drypetis, and his pampered but strong-willed half sister Thessalonike.

Read on for an excerpt from Stephanie Thornton's exciting new novel,

THE CONQUEROR'S WIFE

THE WOMEN OF ALEXANDER THE GREAT

Available in print and e-book in November 2015 from New American Library.

---

336 BCE
PELLA, MACEDONIA

Thessalonike

It was a wedding feast to honor our newly made political alliances, a celebration that also saw the return of my golden brother to Pella's court.

Yet that splendid day would end with a funeral.

The morning began with a predawn banquet of honeyed apricots, flat *staititas* topped with sesame and goat cheese, and crusty loaves of olive bread meant to symbolize the fertility of the recently deflowered bride—my half sister Cleopatra of Macedon—and her dour bridegroom, Alexander Molossus of Epirus.

"You have honey on your cheek, Thessalonike." My father's youngest wife and current favorite, Eurydice, pursed her cinnabar-stained lips at me from across the women's table.

I rubbed my sleep-heavy eyes and licked away the sticky sweetness, earning stern glares from all my father's wives and a lopsided grin from my half brother Arrhidaeus.

"Like a frog, Nike," he said, clapping his fat hands before him. The son of a common Illyrian dancing girl, Arrhidaeus was twice my nine summers, but his mind remained that of a child's. Despite his towering height and broad shoulders, he was allowed to sit on the women's side of the hall, although I feared that was because none of the men would have him.

"Or a salamander." I laughed with him, letting my tongue flick between my teeth until Eurydice kicked my foot beneath the table. I scowled, wishing my pretty stepmother were still confined with her infant son to her chambers, where she couldn't nag me with her insistence on propriety.

The last apricot drizzled with honey beckoned to me, so I stuffed it into my mouth before Eurydice could swat my hand. In the afternoon there would be endless recitations of Homer's moth-eaten poems and prizes of gold bullion for the finest sculpture celebrating the marriage alliance between Epirus and Macedon, but I was hoping to sneak away for the wrestling and athletic games.

"Come," Eurydice said, standing and smoothing the elaborate pleats of her woolen *peplos*. "We shall continue our weaving until the men return from the arena. Then Philip has granted us permission to listen to the poets."

I stabbed my finger inside an olive, wishing I could do the same to my ears when it came time for the recitation. I dropped the pit on the ground, then winked at Arrhidaeus before I crushed the salty green flesh between my teeth. My half brother didn't notice, too busy digging with a tiny silver spoon into a pomegranate. Eurydice rose and was swept away in a wave of giggling women and a cloud of violet perfume. No one noticed—or perhaps cared—that I didn't follow. My father's youngest wife had pretensions of being a dutiful matron, but Eurydice was better suited to gossiping about the latest fashions or how much her recent treatment of foul-smelling cerussa had whitened her skin.

"Follow me," I whispered to Arrhidaeus, casting a furtive glance around the hall.

"Where?" he asked. His thick lips drooped into a frown as he gave up on the spoon and used his fingers to fish the last juicy red seeds from the pomegranate's husk.

"To the arena," I said, pulling him from the table even as he licked his scarlet-stained fingers. "I'd rather gouge my eyes out than spend the day weaving."

"No," he said, shaking his head. "Don't hurt your eyes."

"I won't, my joyful giant, at least not if you hurry."

My half brother grinned at my name for him. It was kinder than the other names my father's court used: walnut brain and half-wit. Several of the nobles' foulmouthed sons had felt the sting of my slingshot in response, so now they held their tongues when I was nearby.

I glanced at the hall's entrance, the wilted olive branch that announced the birth of Eurydice's son still over the door, and saw that my eldest half brother, Alexander, and his boyhood companion Hephaestion had arrived, fresh from the baths, if their damp hair and ruddy complexions were any indication. Their heads—one the color of a lion's mane in sunshine and the other with curls as dark as a crow's wing—were bent in deep conversation. Their claims on each other's affections were well-known throughout the palace, and they'd walked in each other's shadows since Alexander's recent return to Pella following his exile. Despite that, most of the women—and some of the men—now swiveled in the direction of my beautiful, scandalous brother, several holding chunks of olive bread suspended in midair as he and his friend passed.

Hephaestion's chiseled features softened as he stooped to whisper in my brother's ear before striding toward the feast-laden table on the men's side of the room. Alexander arranged himself stiffly on a wooden bench, his tawny hair parted in a severe line down the middle. His lips curved into a frown as he glanced at our father's empty dais. My brother had only recently been allowed to return to court, inspiring the continuing whispers that Eurydice's newly delivered infant son would supplant him as our father's heir.

Life had been simple until my father married Eurydice of Macedon, her belly already swollen with a boy-child, or so she had crowed to anyone who would listen. Perhaps it was a result of the wine or the summer's heat, but at their wedding ceremony Alexander's blood had almost been shed after Eurydice's father offered a public prayer to Zeus to grant my father a new, full-blooded heir. Alexander—born of Philip's Macedonian and Olympias' Epirean blood—leapt from his seat in a rage and threw his cup of wine at Eurydice's father, causing my father to draw his sword. There was a collective gasp of shock as Philip lunged forward, presumably to stab his own son, but instead slipped drunkenly on a puddle of wine and fell face-first to the ground. In the outrage that followed, Alexander and his mother had been forced to flee Pella, leaving me bereft of both a brother and the woman who had raised me after my own mother died giving me life.

Alexander had been ordered home for Cleopatra's wedding—although our father utterly ignored him now that he had his fully Macedonian son—but his mother, Olympias, remained in exile, abandoned in Epirus and left with only her devotions to Dionysus and her famed pet snake, and her hope of one day seeing Alexander on the throne, to keep her content. And that meant Eurydice remained in control of my father's household.

And in control of me, at least when she was paying attention.

We were almost to the doorway when a strong hand encircled my wrist. "Sneaking off again, Thessalonike?" Hephaestion's voice held an undercurrent of laughter. "Tell me you're not planning to climb trees again. I thought you'd have learned your lesson the last time."

Arrhidaeus' frown deepened. "No trees. Wasps hurt."

I raised up on tiptoes to pat his shoulder. "I know. It's not our fault the wasps built their nest in our favorite oak."

Or that I'd knocked the nest down while climbing to the tree's topmost branch, narrowly missing Arrhidaeus' head and releasing a swarm that attacked both of us. Arrhidaeus and I had spent the remainder of the day plastered in Eurydice's medicinal mud. Altogether, it was an experience I didn't care to repeat.

Hephaestion gave an exaggerated sigh and tossed a date into the air. "I suppose I'll have to return you to Eurydice," he said, popping the fruit into his mouth and chewing it thoughtfully. "I heard her mention an important tapestry, something about a design of Athena's defeat of Enceladus involving thousands of very complicated and extremely tiny knots."

I groaned and fell to my knees. "Please, no. I'd rather you killed me first."

"No, Nike," Arrhidaeus said with an emphatic shake of his head. "No killing."

"Is my sister threatening still another dramatic death?" Alexander asked as he stepped forward, his shadow falling on me. "What is it this time, Thessalonike? Impaled by Persian swords? Ripped apart by lions? Drowned by Scylla and Charbydis?"

"Nothing so glorious," I muttered. "Death by weaving."

Alexander, my golden half brother and avowed descendant of the half god Achilles, shared a grin with Hephaestion and then threw back his head in laughter, leaving me scowling and Arrhidaeus' brows knit together in consternation.

"Are you two going to release me or return me to my doom?" I asked, folding my arms in front of me.

Hephaestion tapped his chin. "She's a demanding little thing, isn't she?"

"Always has been," Alexander said. "When she isn't stuffing her face with figs or honey rolls."

I stuck my tongue out at him. Some people stuttered in Alexander's presence, fearing his mercurial temper and the aura of the gods that clung to him, but I'd spent the full nine years of my life in his mother's household and knew that the man before me had recently been a boy who drooled in his sleep and kept a tattered copy of Homer's *Song of Ilium* under his pillow, believing it would imbue him with the power of Achilles.

"If you're going to continue insulting me," I said, "then Arrhidaeus and I are leaving for the arena."

"I'm sure that will go over well," Hephaestion said, glancing heavenward. "Surely no one will notice Philip's daughter at the men's games."

I narrowed my eyes in speculation. "They won't care if I'm accompanied by my father's son and heir."

A dark cloud passed over Alexander's features. I'd forgotten for a moment the talk of Eurydice's son supplanting him, but the storm passed as Hephaestion threw his arm around Alexander's broad shoulders. "You," he said to my brother, "must accompany your father into the stadium, but perhaps Arrhidaeus and I can escort young Thessalonike."

Alexander didn't answer. He looked past us as to where my father was entering the hall, with every guest lifting a terracotta *skyphoi* of wine in his honor. Before my birth, the poets claimed that the birds sang of Philip's beauty, but now a livid pink scar ruined one side of his face, a battle wound from the siege of Methone that had also claimed his left eye. The damage only added to his imposing figure.

"If you do, go quickly." Alexander's own eyes—one the pale blue of a spring sky and the other a darker hue, like a coming storm—remained shut as he tugged my blond curls, identical to his own. "Your secrets are safe with me, little sister."

I shrieked with glee, then grabbed Arrhidaeus' and Hephaestion's hands and dragged them from the hall, my scarlet *himation* flapping behind me while Arrhidaeus' chortles of laughter chased us on through the palace courtyard with its potted quince trees and then the apricot and pomegranate orchards, beyond the town gates and the shuttered market—closed in preparation for the glorious spectacle awaiting us—and then to the arena, nestled into the base of Pella's tallest hill, its autumn grasses muted to a dull gold. Already crowds of men swathed in furs jostled for the best view of the naked wrestlers and javelin throwers, but we found seats near the front row. My eyes bulged to see my eldest and recently widowed half sister Cynnane seated close by, a lone woman among a sea of men, her crinkly curls somewhat tamed by a sheen of olive oil and her body dressed not in her customary short *chiton* but in a refined *peplos* that flowed all the way to her ankles. Women weren't allowed in the arena, but Cynnane wasn't a proper woman; she'd been instructed by her Illyrian mother in the ways of war and told of traditions passed down by the chieftains of their family for generations. Although being near Alexander never made me tongue-tied, words always failed me in Cynnane's presence.

I squatted behind Arrhidaeus, glad for the shield of his hulking shoulders. The meager autumn sun had scarcely climbed over the horizon when the music of lyres and horns proclaimed the arrival of the twelve gods of Olympus.

Priests dressed in white *chitons* strained under the weight of a sedan chair holding a life-size statue of Zeus with his marble beard of curls, his massive bare chest, and a mighty spear in his hand. The priests set down the sedan, and next came Hera, swathed in layers of billowing stone linen and crowned by the *polos* of the Great Goddess, followed by their siblings and children, the remainder of Olympus' pantheon. Behind the gods and goddesses of the sun and oceans, death and love, wisdom and war, came a thirteenth statue, bearing a striking likeness to the man of flesh and blood who entered the earthen floor of the arena. The spectators cheered wildly at the sight of my bearlike father, dressed in his customary greaves and boiled leather armor, his black beard trimmed to the sharpness of a spear-point. I shrank back as his good eye scanned the arena, my heart thudding in my chest.

And, like the gods that surrounded him, my father decided he need not rely on mortals for protection. He raised his arms beneath his white *himation*, dismissing his seven royal bodyguards, with their distinctive scarlet capes, long swords, and sun-motif shields. Next, my brother Alexander and Cleopatra's bridegroom entered the arena, two princes taking their places behind the battle-scarred warrior who had conquered Macedonia and united all the Peloponnese people under his rule.

My father strode toward the center of the arena, hiding well his limp from his battle-ruined shin. Three years ago, on his return from the Danube, laden with cattle, broodmares, and child slaves, he'd been attacked by the wild Triballians in Thrace and been wounded in the leg.

Now a single guard doubled back from where the others were exiting, a black-haired man in a scarlet cape whom I recognized as Pausanius, my favorite of my father's royal bodyguards. Pausanius had spent much of his time guarding Alexander's mother, Olympias, before her exile and had often slipped me salted almonds from his pocket. Now I thought that perhaps he was bringing some urgent message to Philip. I hoped it wasn't of another revolt in the provinces. He came close to my startled father and seemed to embrace him. Then silver flashed in his hand like one of Zeus' lightning bolts thrown to earth.

A dagger.

Philip of Macedon, my indomitable father, with a face ruined from battle and a body riddled with sword wounds, gave a mighty roar. Pausanius stumbled back, then ran across the open ground and through the doors of the stadium, the same entrance through which my father had just strode, ready to be enthroned as a god.

No one moved as crimson stained the ground. It wasn't until an ocean of red spread from the vulnerable spot in my father's cuirass and down his chest that the crowd began to scream and my mind made sense of what I'd seen.

My father had been stabbed and now his lifeblood lured Hades to drag his shade to the underworld.